HERE LIES DANIEL TATE

Also by Cristin Terrill

All Our Yesterdays

HERE LIES DANIEL TATE

CRISTIN TERRILL

SIMON & SCHUSTER BFYR
NEW YORK LONDON TORONTO SYDNEY NEW DELHI

SIMON & SCHUSTER BFYR
An imprint of Simon & Schuster Children's Publishing Division
1230 Avenue of the Americas, New York, New York 10020

Also available in a SIMON & SCHUSTER BFYR hardcover edition
Cover design by Chloë Foglia
Interior design by Hilary Zarycky
The text for this book was set in Granjon.
Manufactured in the United States of America
First SIMON & SCHUSTER BFYR paperback edition June 2018
4 6 8 10 9 7 5 3
The Library of Congress has cataloged the hardcover edition as follows:
Names: Terrill, Cristin.
Title: Here lies Daniel Tate / Cristin Terrill.
Description: New York : SSBYR, an imprint of Simon & Schuster, [2017] |
Summary: A young runaway is welcomed into the arms of an affluent family after he takes on the identity of the family's missing son, Daniel, only to slowly realize that the family knows more about Daniel's disappearance than they are letting on.
Identifiers: LCCN 2016014525 (print) | ISBN 9781481480765 (hardcover)
ISBN 9781481480789 (eBook)
Subjects: | CYAC: Runaways—Fiction. | Missing children—Fiction. | Impersonation—Fiction. | Families—Fiction. | Secrets—Fiction.
Classification: LCC PZ7.T27532 He 2017 (print) | LCC PZ7.T27532 (eBook)
DDC [Fic]—dc23
LC record available at https://lccn.loc.gov/2016014525
ISBN 9781481480772 (pbk)

HERE LIES DANIEL TATE

The first question everyone always asks is, *what's your name?*

I won't tell you, because I don't want to lie to you. I want to tell the truth for once; no fake names like the ones I used to give when people asked me. I had no choice back then. I was a born liar and, by the time everything began, I barely remembered my real name anyway. I left that boy dead and buried in a Saskatchewan town where the snow somehow turned gray the moment it hit the ground. I don't mean that metaphorically, like I just shed his name and history, although I did that, too. I mean I *killed* him.

I crept back into town one night, skirting the bright pools of light from streetlamps and avoiding the houses where I knew dogs barked. Old, stale snow crunched under my feet. Inside my coat pocket I fingered a glossy baseball card that was creased and fraying at the corners from too much handling. It wasn't a real baseball card, just a picture of me in my T-ball uniform with my name in block letters across the bottom. I was six in the picture, and already there was a gap in my smile, the tooth knocked loose by a closed fist. But I was still smiling.

When I reached my mother's house, I stood in the darkness below the trees outside and watched her through the window. She was sitting in her usual chair, flipping channels on the television. I hadn't seen her for a year, and I guess I expected to feel . . . something. But I didn't. There was only the familiar hole in my chest where the feeling should have been.

I dialed her number from memory. Snow fell and clung to my eyelashes, and I blinked the flakes away to watch her. After three rings, she rose from her chair and crossed to the ancient handset mounted on the wall.

"Hello?" she said, the word partially muffled by a cigarette.

"Mrs. Smith?" I said. Not *exactly* that, of course, since "Smith" isn't my name. "This is Officer Green of the Royal Mounted Police."

"Yeah?" she asked. Getting a call from the cops didn't faze her.

"It's about your son," I said. "I'm sorry to tell you there's been an accident."

I told her I was dead, hit by a speeding car as I crossed an icy road. I watched her close. She didn't move or speak for a long time.

Then she said:

"I don't have a son."

She hung up and went back to her chair, and that was it. I left, and I left the boy I'd been behind with her, dead and buried in the dingy gray snow.

But that's not where this story starts, not really. It began on another snowy night a few years later, with police lights bathing the world in red and blue.

I hunched against the cold at one of the few remaining pay phones on the east side of Vancouver. It was too fucking cold to be on the streets. I dialed 911 and counted along to the rings. After the seventh, someone answered.

"Nine-one-one. What's your emergency?"

"Hello?" I ground my voice down against the back of my throat, making it sound low and gravelly. "My wife and I just came across this kid, and there's . . . well, there's something wrong with him. He seems really out of it."

I heard the dispatcher suppress a yawn. Either bored or new to the night shift. "How old is he?"

"Like fifteen or sixteen," I said. I'd learned by then what a crucial part of the scam that was, and luckily I had enough of a baby face to pull it off. "I think maybe he's lost. Someone should come get him. It's freezing out here."

She asked for the address and told me they were sending a car. I sat down on the sidewalk in a protected alcove that had once been the doorway of a boarded up pharmacy. The cement was like ice through the fabric of my jeans, but I wouldn't be there long. I pulled my baseball cap down over my eyes, flipped up the hood of my sweatshirt, and waited.

The squad car pulled up with its siren off but its lights flashing, painting red and blue beams across the lacy curtain of falling snow. I burrowed deeper into my hoodie and bowed my head to hide my face under the brim of my cap.

"Hi there," one of the officers, the younger one, said as he climbed out of the cruiser. His voice was kind, but he kept his distance. Fresh out of the academy and still a little jumpy. "You okay?"

The older officer was less cautious and crouched down beside me. He had a ring on his left hand, maybe kids of his own around my age at home. "Hey, buddy, what's your name?"

I didn't speak. I didn't even look up.

"Come on, you've got to know who are you," the older officer pressed, his tone light and teasing. "Everyone knows who they are."

Not true.

"Okay," he said when I didn't respond. "How about you come with us? You've got to be half-frozen."

He reached for my arm, and I recoiled violently. It wasn't a hard reaction to fake. The officer held up his empty hands, while his partner's hand flew to the holster at his side.

"Hey, hey, it's okay," he said. He looked back at his partner, who was still poised to grab his gun if I turned out to be violent. "Jesus, Pearson. Relax, would you? We're not going to hurt you, son, I promise."

I gradually let them talk me up off the sidewalk and into the squad car. They tried to engage me in conversation as they took me back to their station, but I kept my head down and my mouth shut. I used to talk, tell some sob story, but I'd learned there was more power in silence.

They stuck me in a holding room with a vending machine sandwich and a cup of hot chocolate until they could figure out what to do with me. I would have preferred not to have involved the authorities—it was riskier this way—but Covenant House was full and it was cold. These guys were my best chance for a bed. It took about an hour for them to come back with a small white woman in jeans and a messy ponytail. I had moved to the corner of the room, sitting on the thin carpet with my knees pulled up to my chest. She crouched down at my eye level, but well out of my reach, so she'd obviously been doing this for a while. She told me her name was Alicia, in that low, soothing voice that people who work with troubled children or wild animals seem to be born with. She worked at a province-run care home, and she was going to take me there so I could get some sleep.

"Then, tomorrow morning," she said, "we'll work all this out."

The cops passed me off to her like I was a piece of lost luggage. Alicia sat beside me in the back of a squad car as a deputy drove us to Short Term 8. When we got there, Alicia's coworker Martin—a big black man with the widest, whitest smile I've ever seen—took over. He took me to a bathroom and waited outside while Alicia went to get me something to change into. I washed the dirt from my face, frowned at the pale stubble that was reappearing on my jawline, and rummaged through the cabinets to see what was inside. I found a half a tube of toothpaste and rubbed some across my teeth with a finger. Martin knocked on the door and handed me a T-shirt and pair of sweatpants that smelled like mothballs and laundry detergent. After I'd changed, he showed me to an empty bed in a room where two other boys were already sleeping.

"You need anything?" he asked. I noted the way he curled his shoulders in, trying to minimize his physical presence. He was that kid everyone assumed was a bully because of his size but would never hurt a fly. Made sense he'd ended up in this line of work.

I shook my head and climbed into the bed. The sheets were worn thin from a thousand washings, but they were cool and soft against my skin. A much better bed than the pavement or some shitty adult homeless shelter, and as long as I kept my mouth shut, I could probably keep it for a couple of weeks.

My eyes flew open. I'd been dreaming about a small, dark space, and then someone was standing above me, their hand on my arm. Before my eyes had even focused enough to make the person out, I had hit their arm away and scrambled back until I hit a wall.

"Whoa, sorry!" A skinny black boy stood beside my bed, rubbing his arm. He shoved his glasses farther up his nose with one knuckle. "I just wanted to tell you breakfast is ready."

I felt a little bad—I could tell from the sting in my hand how hard I'd hit him—but I couldn't apologize. And, anyway, he shouldn't have touched me while I was sleeping.

"Hey, what's your name, man?" the other kid in the room asked. He had a shaved head and an amateurish tattoo on the side of his neck that looked like it was made with a safety pin and ink in juvie. His eyes were full of evaluation as he looked me up and down, trying to get the size of me. I met his gaze coolly.

"You deaf or something?" he said.

"Hey, guys!" Alicia appeared in the doorway with my clothes, clean and folded, in her hands. "Head on to the dining room, okay? Martin made pancakes."

Both boys gave me wary looks before leaving the room. Alicia closed the door behind them and sat on the bed closest to me, knitting her fingers together in front of her.

"Hey," she said. "How you feeling this morning?"

I shrugged.

"Ready to talk?"

I shook my head.

"That's okay—you don't have to," she said. "But can you tell me your name, at least? We've got a lot of boys around here, so 'hey you' isn't very effective."

In response, I swallowed and looked down at the bedspread, worrying it between my fingers.

"Okay, no problem," she said, "but we've got to call you something. We picked you up at the Collingwood Police Station, so how about we call you Collin for now? That's a pretty good name."

I shrugged again.

"Okay, I'll take that as a yes." She smiled and went to put a hand on my shoulder but wisely reconsidered. Instead, she handed me my clothes. "Get dressed, and then we'll go get some breakfast. You can meet the other guys."

Alicia waited outside while I changed into my old jeans, tee, and hoodie, and then she showed me to the dining room at the other end of the building. The room was overflowing with boys and noise and the ambient heat of so many bodies packed in such a small space, and I could feel her watching me, waiting to see if I'd freak out. I probably should have faked it to keep up my traumatized act, go hide myself in the bedroom and refuse to come out, but dammit, I was hungry.

Alicia sat, and I sank into the empty seat beside her. She handed me a platter of pancakes, and I forked three onto my plate while I felt eyes around the table sliding in my direction.

"Guys, this is Collin," Alicia said. "He's going to be staying with us for a while. He's a little on the quiet side, so don't bug him, okay?"

The other boys, a dozen or so, reacted in a variety of ways. A couple said hi, a couple grunted, a couple didn't respond at all. After that everyone went back to their pancakes, and that was all it took for me to become one of them.

When I still wouldn't talk on my third day at Short Term 8—wouldn't tell the staff or police who I was or where I'd come from so they could return me there—they took me to a government psychologist. I pulled out all the stops for her. The night before the appointment I bit my nails until they bled, because I knew she would notice. I cowered in my chair when she talked to me and rocked back and forth ever so slightly when she started to push. She told them to give me time, that I would open up when I was ready. Just like I knew she would.

I figured she'd bought me at least a week.

"Jason! Tucker!" Martin called from the hallway. This is how we were awoken most mornings. The only thing my two roommates had in common was they hated getting out of bed. "I said, get up!"

Jason moaned, and Tucker rolled over, jamming his pillow over his head.

"What about Collin?" Jason said. He pushed himself into a sitting position and groped for his glasses on the bedside table. "Doesn't he have to get up?"

"Nope!"

"That's not fair!"

"I know. Life's a bitch." Martin appeared in the open doorway brandishing a water pistol. "Now wake up!"

He shot streams of water at both of the boys. Tucker told him to go fuck himself, and Jason sputtered and protested that he was already up.

"Don't make me get the hose," Martin said. "Be in the dining room in five. Collin, come down whenever you're ready."

"What the fuck makes him so special?" Tucker demanded,

but Martin was already gone. I smiled, rolled over, and went back to sleep.

I liked it at Short Term 8. Three square meals, a bed of my own, and enough noise from fourteen other boys to drown out the voices in my head. Besides Jason, who was a sweet kid who brought me Oreos whenever he raided the pantry behind the staff's back, and Tucker, who was an asshole, the other boys mostly ignored me. If you don't speak for long enough, people eventually stop seeing you as an oddity and start seeing you as a piece of furniture, which suited me just fine. I liked to blend in to the chaos they caused until I as good as disappeared. Sometimes Alicia or one of the day staff would remember I existed when the others gave them a break and would take me aside for a kind word and a reassuring hand on the shoulder, which was all I needed.

But I knew it couldn't last.

The cops got impatient first. They wanted to close the file on the kid they'd found in the snow and move on. They sent a couple of detectives over to talk to me. The day manager Diane had just arrived to take over from Alicia, and she took charge of getting boys out the door while Alicia sat beside me in the lounge. The detectives opposite us pulled out their notepads and pens, and I hung my head, keeping my eyes on the floor. One of them—the bigger one, whose buzzed haircut suggested a man who'd never quite let go of the military even years after rejoining civilian life—had been looking at me real close since the moment they'd arrived, and I didn't like it.

"We need you to tell us your name, son," the smaller one finally said after a reasonably polite preamble.

I started to rock back and forth in my chair, and I bit on the nail of my thumb. It was probably too late for my theatrics to do any good, but it wouldn't hurt to try.

"Did you run away?" the smaller detective asked. "Were you being hurt?"

I didn't say anything, and Alicia put a comforting hand on my knee.

"We can protect you," he continued, "but we've got to know who you are."

"Alicia." The big detective spoke for the first time. "If this boy is really so traumatized he can't answer a simple question, I don't think it's right for him to be staying here. He should be section sixteened."

Section sixteen. Every kid who's spent time in care or on the streets knows what that means: a psychiatric hold.

"Come on, Frank," Alicia said. "Dr. Nazadi said he just needs some time."

The detective turned to me. "Son, we need to know who you are. I want your name and where you're from, or we're going to have to take your prints and your picture and find out for ourselves."

"This isn't necessary, Frank," Alicia said.

"Isn't it?" he asked. "There aren't a hundred other kids who could use that bed?"

Alicia glanced at me from the corner of her eye, and the detective was looking at me with a hard glint in his.

It was over.

That night I waited for Short Term 8 to go dark and quiet before I climbed out of bed. I'd had a good run here, but this was the end of the line. No way was I going to let them stick me in a mental ward or put my prints into the system. The bed wasn't worth it.

I put on my warmest clothes, including the decent winter coat Martin had procured for me, and packed what little else I had in my backpack. I looked down at Jason for a second. I would miss him, I guessed, as much as I could miss anyone. I didn't bother looking at Tucker.

I crept through the quiet building in my socked feet, boots held in my hand. Martin and Alicia were the staff on duty this time of night, and they were predictable. Martin would be at the television in the common room watching whatever sport was on with the volume turned down low, and Alicia would be on the computer in the office. They were pretty much there just to make sure no one died or burned the place down.

I crossed through the dining room, running my fingers along the grain of the table in the spot where I usually sat as I walked past it. I peered around the door of the dining hall to get a look at the front office. As I'd guessed, Alicia was in there, catching up on celebrity gossip on the Internet. I'd have to get past the office to get to the front door, and the office walls were lined with windows.

I thought about trying to sneak past her. If I crouched down low enough, I could get under the windows. But that wouldn't get me past the open door unnoticed unless Alicia also happened to be in a mild, Kardashian–induced coma. I could go out an emergency exit, but that would set off the alarm, and the idea was to get out without anyone noticing I was gone until the morning. Anything that might wake Jason and Tucker or prompt Alicia and Martin to do a bed check was too risky.

Finally, I decided on the easiest option. I would wait. I felt like there were ants crawling under my skin every moment I was trapped in there, but I had all night. The important thing was to just disappear.

I sat down behind the door of the darkened dining hall. Neither Martin nor Alicia had any reason to come in here, and by cracking the door, I could see Alicia in the office. Eventually, she would get up to go to the bathroom or get herself another Diet Coke from the kitchen. I just had to be patient.

I'm not sure how long I waited. Maybe an hour. Finally, Alicia got up from her chair. I watched her walk down the hallway toward the staff restroom, and then scrambled to my feet and grabbed my boots. I had maybe a minute to get out before she came back. I stuck my head out into the hallway, checking both ways first. Alicia was gone, and the glow from the common room in the other direction meant Martin was almost certainly in front of the TV. I took a step into the hallway. My left foot had gone numb from being folded under me, and it came awake with painful pins and needles as I snuck toward the front entrance. There was an alarm panel beside the door, and I started to punch in the code I'd watched Alicia plug into it the first night they brought me here. I heard the distant sound of a toilet flushing. My finger slipped, and I hit the wrong button. The light on the panel flashed red.

"Shit," I whispered, and quickly reentered the correct code. The light turned green, and I heard a door opening. I yanked open the front door and slipped through it, pulling it nearly closed after me. I tried to slow my breathing as I stood on the outside, ears straining. Had Alicia gotten there in time to see the door closing behind me? Could she see the small gap I'd left so that she wouldn't hear the noise of the latch catching when the door closed? I waited, but nothing happened. Short Term 8 stayed quiet.

I carefully put on my boots and then, millimeter by millimeter, eased the door closed, the *snick* of the latch almost inaudible. Nothing. I was out.

I zipped up my new coat and started the walk to the bus station. I only had a little bit of cash that I'd gotten under the counter doing odd jobs my first few days in Vancouver, but it was enough to get me onto a bus and out of there. My feet crunched on the salted pavement, and soon I was downtown, where there were enough people for me to blend in with that I felt safe taking the hood off my head. I tried to remember how long I'd been doing this, moving from city to city, scamming my way into juvenile care homes by pretending to be younger than I was. I'd left home for good at sixteen. Sometime after that there'd been the petty robbery that went really, really wrong, and I'd gone from being a runaway to being someone on the run. The danger of being caught had long passed, but once you start running, it's hard to stop, so I hadn't stayed in any one place for long. Since I couldn't say exactly how long I'd been doing this; I'd lived so many lives that it was hard to keep track.

I arrived at the bus station, which was lit up even in the middle of the night with fluorescents that gave the place a queasy, yellow glow, and walked up to the ticket window.

"What . . ." I cleared the frog from my throat. I hadn't spoken for days. "What's the cheapest bus ticket you've got?"

The cashier raised a perfectly drawn on eyebrow at me. "You don't care where you're going?"

"Nope."

She gave me a couple of options, and I picked the $82 bus to Calgary that left in less than an hour. After she handed me back my change, I had enough money for a coffee and muffin now and a sandwich on the road later.

I was standing in line at the station McDonald's when I spotted him. Martin. He was hard to miss since he was a head taller than almost everyone else around.

I didn't feel much anymore, but I did still feel fear. Every animal feels fear. It was a nice change from the usual nothingness, actually. I dropped my head, slipped out of the line, and began to walk slowly in the opposite direction from Martin. There weren't enough people here in the middle of the night to disappear into the crowd, so I would have to be careful not to do anything to attract his attention. I headed toward the men's restroom I'd clocked earlier. He would check it, but if I hid in a stall, maybe he wouldn't find me.

How did he know I was gone? Maybe Jason or Tucker had woken up and reported me missing.

As I was headed to the men's room, a cop on a radio started to head toward it too. He went inside, and I changed directions, flipping my hood over my head. I strolled toward a side exit instead. I'd wait around the corner until a few minutes before my bus was scheduled to leave and then slip back inside.

"Collin!" a voice called.

I ran.

"Hey, Collin!"

The footsteps behind me were moving fast. I dashed toward the exit just as a woman with a huge rolling suitcase came through the door I was aiming for. She slowed me down for only a few seconds, but it was enough. Martin caught up to me, a helpful cop on his heels. I immediately dropped to the ground and wrapped my arms over my head, burying my face against my knees. When in doubt, play the traumatized child.

"Hey, it's okay, man," Martin said, kneeling beside me and putting a careful hand on my back. "I know you're scared, but everything's going to be okay. Come on, let's go home."

I went with Martin back to Short Term 8, and Alicia hugged me hard as soon as I came inside. They took me back to my room. Jason and Tucker were both awake, and I wondered which one of them had ratted me out. My money—not that I had much left—was on Jason. Tucker was a dick, but he also wouldn't care if I ended up dead in a ditch somewhere. He rolled his eyes at me and turned over in bed when I came in, while Jason handed me a mini Snickers from the candy stash he kept hidden in his dresser. I was pissed at him, but I was also hungry, so I took it.

I bit into the candy bar as I walked to the bathroom down the hall. I could hear faint voices coming from the kitchen and crept closer toward them. They were probably talking about me, and I wanted to know what they were saying.

The kitchen had double swinging doors, and I pressed my eye up to the gap between them. Alicia was making tea.

"The cops must have scared the hell out of him," she was saying as she poured milk into two mugs and handed one to Martin. "Threatening to section him like that. If he understood what they meant, it's no wonder he ran."

"Yeah, but they'll take him away for sure now," Martin said.

Alicia sighed. "Poor kid."

I wasn't going to any fucking mental ward.

Locked up. Walls and darkness closing in on me, suffocating me, the close air stale from my breath . . .

Never again.

I would do whatever it took to prevent that, whatever they wanted.

"I have to tell you something," I said the next morning.

Forks hit plates and silence descended on the dining table, like something out of the movies.

Alicia recovered first. "Sure, Collin. Why don't you come to the office, and we'll—"

"My name's Daniel," I said. "Daniel Tate."

The name meant nothing to Alicia. She hadn't grown up in Southern California, where my name had made headlines.

Daniel Tate, son of the food packaging heiress. Daniel Tate, American prince. Daniel Tate, the boy who disappeared.

Did you believe me when I said I was some no-name runaway from the Canadian backwoods? You shouldn't have. I *told* you I was a liar. That boy was just one of my many fictions. I invented him because he was tough enough to survive when I wasn't, and because even his terrible life was better than the truth.

It was sunny the day it happened. I was walking beside my bike, because the chain had come off and I didn't know how to fix it. I was taking it home to my father, because he would know. Dad knew everything.

A white van turned the corner and pulled up beside me. I was too naive to be scared. The door slid open, and hands emerged from the shadows. Some grabbed me, dragging me into the darkness and muffling my shouts. Others pulled my bike in behind me, erasing any trace I'd ever been there. That was it. Ten seconds and I was gone, with no one having seen a thing. A kidnapping can happen that quickly and that invisibly, even on a sunny street in a safe neighborhood.

They tried to make me forget who I was, and for a long time, they succeeded. I conjured dozens of different lives for myself as they moved me from dark room to dark room, passing me off from stranger to stranger. When it hurt, I would close my eyes and become someone else. I was a superhero captured by his evil nemesis. A king in hiding. An outlaw from a small, snowy town who was running from the cops. Anyone but Daniel Tate.

"I got away," I told Alicia. "One day they accidentally left my door unlocked, and I ran for it. I didn't know where I was, or even what year it was."

Alicia's eyes swam with tears, but she didn't let them fall. "Why didn't you tell anyone?"

"There's so much I don't remember," I said. "For a long time I didn't even know who I was. And . . ."

"And what?" she pressed gently.

"They're powerful." My hands clenched into fists in my lap.

"More powerful than the police. If they find me, they'll take me back."

She put a hand over mine. "That's not going to happen," she said with the blithe confidence of someone who had no idea what she was dealing with.

"You don't understand," I said. "You don't know who these people are, who they *know*. If I'm in some government hospital or mental institution, they'll find me. They'll get me out and I'll disappear again and I'll never get away a second time."

"No one's taking you anywhere," she said fiercely. "We'll go to the police—"

"No!" I said. "You can't tell them who I am!"

"We have to," she said, "but then you'll be safe. Daniel, you'll get to go *home*."

Alicia took me back to the Collingwood Police Station, and soon we were entering the office of the detective who'd threatened to have me committed, Detective Barson. When we came in, he pushed aside a half-eaten sandwich and asked what we needed.

I told him I was Daniel Tate, that I'd been kidnapped from Hidden Hills, California, six years ago. He looked at me with total incomprehension, and I couldn't blame him. I knew it sounded crazy.

"What did you say the name was again?" he said as he woke up his computer.

"Daniel Tate."

He entered my name into a search engine, and the first hit was the Center for Missing and Exploited Children. Barson clicked the link, and up came a missing poster with the same information I'd just given him. My name, age, and the place I'd gone missing. Beside that was a picture. Dirty blond hair that was a few shades lighter than my hair now, hazel eyes, freckles across the nose, and a pointy chin. Barson looked back and forth between me and the picture.

"You sure this is you?" he said. "You said you don't remember much."

"I remember who I am." *Motherfucker*, I added silently.

"It doesn't look that much like you."

"Come on, Frank," Alicia said. "He's ten years old in that picture. You know how much kids change between ten and sixteen."

Barson thought about that, the frown lines on his face deepening. "Why didn't you come forward before?"

Alicia's patience abruptly ran out, and she threw up her hands. "The boy was imprisoned and traumatized! It's a miracle he's been able to come forward now!"

"Now, hang on there, Alicia. These questions aren't unreasonable." Barson studied me for another moment and then angled his computer screen so I couldn't see it. "What's your date of birth?"

I saw a brief flash of a blue birthday cake and foil balloons glinting in the sun. "November. The sixteenth."

"Year?"

"Two thousand."

Barson, his jaw clenched, stood. "Wait here a minute," he said, and walked out of the office.

I turned to Alicia. "He doesn't believe me." My voice came out shaky.

"He will," she said. "It's just a lot to take in at once."

The minute stretched into two and then ten. Barson stuck his head back inside the office.

"Do you remember your address?" he asked. "Phone number?"

I shook my head. "I-I remember I lived in Hidden Hills."

"But you don't remember what street?"

Alicia put a hand on my shoulder. "Don't worry, Daniel. No one could possibly expect you to remember something like that after all this time and everything you've been through."

Barson just grunted and disappeared again. An hour passed and he still hadn't come back. One of the officers brought us a couple of turkey sandwiches and sodas and told us Barson was talking to the chief. I grabbed a legal pad off the corner of Barson's desk and started to sketch.

Alicia looked over my shoulder at the picture I was drawing of Tucker, scowling and holding up his middle finger.

She laughed. "That's good. Can you do Martin?"

I worked on a drawing of Martin flipping pancakes and wearing a flowery apron while Alicia called Diane and filled her in. Alicia had just worked her full night shift, but it didn't look like she was planning to go anywhere.

"I'm sorry," I said. "You must be tired."

"Hush," she replied.

When Barson still wasn't back a half an hour later and I'd gone through a half a dozen sheets of the legal pad, I couldn't sit still anymore. I began to pace his office. It was exactly four steps wide. I thought about that bus to Calgary. How I might be on it now if I had spotted Martin a minute sooner or just walked a little faster.

"What if they're coming to get me right now?" I said. I couldn't contain the words anymore. Everywhere I looked, I saw hands reaching out of the darkness to grab me. "What if they take me back there and—"

"No one's going to take you, Daniel," Alicia said. She tried to take my hand, to stop me pacing, but I threw her off.

"You don't know that!"

That's when the door opened. I jumped away from it, but it was just Barson, followed by another man. Barson stood against the wall while the other man took his seat behind the desk, and I sat down too.

"Daniel, I'm Chief Constable Harold Warner," he said. "I'm sorry you've had to wait."

"That's okay," I said shakily.

"As I'm sure you can imagine, there's been a lot happening since Detective Barson informed me of your situation," he said, "but if you're ready, I have your brother on the phone."

I felt like I'd hit the ground after a long fall. All the air rushed out of my lungs. "What?"

"I've spent the last half an hour on the phone with the Malibu PD, confirming your story," he said. "They put me in touch with Patrick McConnell. He's your half brother, right?"

I nodded.

"Well, he's on the phone now," Warner said. "Do you want to talk to him?"

"Oh, Daniel," Alicia said softly.

My throat was too dry for me to speak, but they were both staring at me, so I just nodded again. Warner said something to me as he picked up the phone on Barson's desk and hit a button, but all I could hear was the rushing of blood in my ears and my mind repeating *Patrick, Patrick, Patrick*. I had just slivers of memory from my past life—even added together they only showed how much was missing—but lots of those pieces were of my big brother. Patrick teaching me to swing a baseball bat. Helping me with my math homework. Letting me stay up late to watch scary movies with him when our parents were out for the night.

Warner handed me the phone, and I immediately dropped it. Alicia grabbed it for me and squeezed my shoulder. "It's okay," she said.

I nodded and lifted the phone to my ear.

"Danny?" a voice said. "Danny, is that you?"

"Patrick?" I choked.

Alicia stood and gestured to Barson. He followed her reluctantly from the office, and Warner left after them, leaving me alone.

"Are you . . ." Patrick hesitated. "Are you really my brother?"

I nodded, even though he couldn't see it. "It's me, Patrick."

"They said you're in *Vancouver*?"

"They brought me here," I said. "I was with them for so long, b-but I got away . . ."

"Oh my God. Danny." Patrick started to cry. "It really is you."

I started to cry too. "I want to come home."

"Don't worry," he said. "We're coming to get you."

Alicia drove me back to the police station the next day. My half siblings Patrick and Alexis—my mom's kids from her first marriage—had gotten on a plane that morning and were coming to get me. At least that's what everyone kept saying. I knew they were really coming to *see* me. To see if I was who I said I was and not some sociopathic con artist posing as their brother. That was the only reason it could be them coming and not my mother, because some part of them was afraid I was a fake.

It hurt, but I didn't exactly blame them. I probably wouldn't believe me either.

But what if they didn't?

I chewed on my nails as we drove to the police station.

"Nervous?" Alicia asked.

I nodded.

"Everything's going to be okay, Daniel," she said. "It's going to be great."

I rubbed my thumb over the back of my hand and nodded. "Yeah."

Chief Constable Warner was waiting for us when we arrived. He took Alicia and me into an interview room, the same one they'd put me in the night they picked me up off the street. It seemed smaller than I remembered, and grubbier. Suddenly, I saw everything in hyperfocus, from the coffee stains on the carpet to the chipping paint around the doorjamb. *This is where I'll see Patrick and Alexis again*, I thought. Surrounded by these paint chips and stains.

I looked down at my clothes, taken from the pile of second-hand stuff Short Term 8 kept in a closet. I pulled at the slightly too short sleeves of the sweater. What would they think when they saw me like this? The drip-drop of panic I'd felt all day turned into a steady stream pooling inside of me, filling up that empty space that usually gaped in my chest.

The door opened, and I jumped, but it was only Warner.

"They just called," he said. "They're in the cab. Should be here in about ten."

I paced. This room was wider than Barson's office, almost six steps across. I counted them over and over as I walked from one wall to the other. When I was a kid, I saw a tiger in a cage at the zoo who did this exact thing, pacing back and forth in front of the viewing window, danger coiled in the muscles that rippled under her coat. I wondered if she did it because she was scared too.

"Daniel," Alicia said cautiously. "How you doing? Can I get you something?"

"I can't do this," I said. "I can't do this, Alicia. I have to get out of here."

"Hey, it's going to be okay," she said in her most soothing voice. "I promise."

"You can't!" I snapped. "You don't know it's going to be okay. You don't know anything!"

Then the door opened. And the world started to move real slow.

Warner came in first. Behind him I could see just a corner of a person, an impression of neatly brushed brown hair. Then he stepped out from behind Warner and became whole. Patrick. Broader in the shoulders than I remembered but with a thinner face. Tall and handsome and solid except for the sharpness of his patrician nose. He was dressed in an impeccable gray suit, something I was not expecting. I guess I wasn't the only one who'd changed in the last six years.

Behind him, holding on to his hand, was Alexis. As insubstantial as Patrick was solid, blonde and delicate, a dandelion of a person. Patrick had always been like a god to me—gigantic—and he still seemed that way, but Alexis seemed to have gotten smaller.

They stood just inside the doorway, staring at me. I stared back at them. My joints and nerves and blood vessels were all quaking, and I was sure I would shake apart at any moment. They looked at each other, something complex passing between them in their eyes and expressions, and then back at me.

Patrick was the first to move, just a small step taken toward me.

"My God," he whispered. "It's really you, isn't it?"

I nodded dumbly.

He huffed like the air had been pushed out of his lungs, and then he was rushing toward me, grabbing me in a tight hug, filling my nose with the smell of expensive wool and aftershave. His shoulders were shaking as he laughed or cried or both. He believed me, and I felt like a little boy again in his arms.

But it didn't lessen my fear. If anything, it made it worse. Disappointment after hope can be lethal, and behind Patrick's back, Alexis was still just standing there. Staring at me. Her eyes looking as scared as I felt.

Patrick pulled away from me and turned to our sister. He reached a hand out to her.

"It's okay," he said. "It's Danny."

Her eyes were filled with tears, and she shook her head, just a little.

"Don't be scared," Patrick said firmly. "Come hug your brother."

She looked back and forth between me and Patrick, and then she took a step closer to us.

"Danny?" she said softly.

I nodded, and she reached out slowly, touching the tips of her fingers to my cheek. Like she was afraid her hand might pass right through me.

"I can't believe it," she said. She started to cry and wrapped her arms around my neck, holding me with more strength than I would have thought her capable of.

"Hi, Alexis," I whispered.

Patrick laughed. "Why so formal, little brother?"

I swallowed. Warner nodded at Alicia, and the two of them slipped silently out of the interview room, leaving the three of us alone. Alexis let go of me.

Time passed in a blur of tears and laughter and talk. I couldn't stop staring at them, drinking in the way they looked at me. Patrick asked what had happened to me, where I'd been for the last six years. Warner had told them what I'd told him, but he still had so many questions. Alexis just looked at me and silently swiped at tears that escaped her eyes while Patrick asked me question after question.

But my answers wouldn't come. My throat locked up around them, holding them inside of me. Patrick told me it was okay, that they weren't going to push me to talk about things I wasn't ready to. Now was the time for happy things.

"The constable said you don't remember much," Patrick said. "About us or your life."

I nodded. "I guess . . . I guess it was just easier that way. To forget who I'd been."

He glanced at Alexis and squeezed her hand. "We understand." Then he smiled in a wobbly way. "It's so strange to hear you speaking with a Canadian accent."

"Oh." I hadn't thought about that. "I guess . . . the people who had me . . ."

"You don't have to talk about it now," he said.

"Thanks," I said. I tried to make the vowel rounder, more like the way Patrick would say it.

"Lex, where's your phone?" he asked.

Alexis—*Lex*—dug into her purse and pulled out her cell phone. She seemed to understand exactly what Patrick was asking, because she opened up the pictures she had saved there, and the three of us bent over the screen.

"That's Mia," Lex said when she brought up a picture of a brunette little girl in pigtails and a yellow dress. "Can you believe how big she's gotten? She was practically a baby when . . ."

She couldn't finish the sentence. Patrick reached behind me to lay a hand on her back.

"She looks just like your dad, huh?" he said. He swiped the photo of Mia aside, and one of a pale, slim boy with glasses and a hint of a smirk around his lips replaced it. "And there's Nicholas. He started visiting colleges a few months ago, and he swears he's not going to pick any school within a thousand miles of California."

I smiled. "Sounds like Nicholas."

Lex looked up at me and then back down at her phone, swiping through photos until she found one of Mom, who was like a perfect blend of Patrick and herself. Tall and solid like Patrick. Blonde and beautiful—even if that beauty was fading around the edges—like Lex. In the picture, Mom was standing beside Mia as she blew out candles on a birthday cake. She was smiling, but the expression didn't reach her eyes, which were focused somewhere in the distance.

"How is she?" I asked.

"She's . . ." Patrick cleared his throat. "She'll be happy to see you."

They showed me dozens more pictures. My dad, our house, our old golden retriever Honey, my best friend Andrew, who Lex told me had moved to Arizona with his family a few years ago. Neighbors and cousins and playmates whose names I couldn't tell them. I feigned some recognition for their benefit, but I doubt it was convincing. It was like looking at pictures of another person's life.

But it was a life I wanted.

"Don't worry," Lex said. "We'll help you remember."

The door to the interview room opened, and Warner stuck his head in. "How are we doing in here?"

Patrick stood. "When can we take our brother home?"

"Well, now, that's a bit of a tricky question," Warner said. "He can't just stroll over the border. He has no passport or identification."

Lex dug into her purse and came out with a folder that she handed to the constable. "His birth certificate and social security card."

"That takes care of the identification part," Patrick said.

Warner looked at the documents inside the folder, faint frown lines appearing between his eyebrows. "Well. I'm sure this will help, but . . ."

"What?" Patrick asked.

Warner's eyes flicked over to me and back again. "Maybe we should speak out in the hallway, Mr. McConnell?"

Patrick followed Warner outside, while Lex stayed with me. Even with the door closed, we could hear their muffled voices, but not well enough to make out any of their words. I didn't have to hear to know, though. Daniel Tate's birth certificate only proved that he had been born, not that I was him.

"Don't worry," Lex told me. "Patrick will get this all straightened out."

She sounded sure. How could she sound so sure?

"Yeah?" I said.

"He's very persuasive. And *very* stubborn." Her eyes shifted to the door. "He always gets what he wants."

The voices in the hall were getting louder. I could make out words now.

"Absolutely not!" Patrick said.

Warner was calmer and therefore harder to hear. ". . . simple test . . . verify . . ."

My nails dug into the flesh of my palms.

". . . not doing a DNA test! That boy has been terribly abused, and we won't subject him . . . don't want him to think we have any doubts . . ."

I looked at Lex. Her eyes dropped from mine, but she wrapped an arm around my shoulders, her cashmere sweater warm and soft where it rested against the bare skin of my neck. I could feel her trembling. The door suddenly opened, and Patrick came back into the interview room.

"This *is* my brother, Constable," he was saying. "Do you think there's any chance my sister and I wouldn't be able to tell?"

"It's not that I don't believe you," Warner said, "but if you'd just let us confirm—"

"We're not waiting weeks for a test to come back and tell us what we already know," Patrick said. "My brother is coming home with us as soon as possible."

"I'm not an expert, but I'm sure the authorities will require some kind of proof besides your word before they allow him across the border," Warner said.

"We'll see about that. I've already called the embassy, and they're sending someone over. In the meantime, you're not to touch him." Patrick's voice was steely. "He's a minor, and I have power of attorney from our mother, making me his legal guardian, and I forbid it. We'll see what the embassy has to say."

The official from the embassy arrived with surprising—or maybe not so surprising—swiftness. She introduced herself as Sheila Brindell. Although her suit couldn't have cost half of what Patrick's did, she had the aura and graying hair of someone with authority. She wore no wedding ring but did have a small heart pendant around her neck. Only children buy women jewelry with hearts on them, so my guess was she was a career bureaucrat who'd been too consumed with climbing the professional ladder to bother dating and now smiled wistfully at babies in strollers and doted on her nieces and nephews to make up for it. Hard on the outside with a gushy, sentimental center. She sat down opposite Patrick, Lex, and me while Warner observed from a chair in the corner.

"I'm sure you'll understand this is a highly unusual situation, Mr. McConnell," she said, clicking the top of her pen subconsciously.

"I think you'll find that no one understands that better than we do," Patrick said. "We appreciate you accommodating us on such short notice."

"Yes, of course," she said. "The consul asked me to handle this *personally* and to ensure that everything was settled as quickly as possible."

Patrick just smiled coolly. There was something happening here that I didn't understand, some unspoken transaction taking place between this woman and my brother.

"However, before we can issue Daniel an expedited passport, I need to ask him some questions," Ms. Brindell continued. "I need assurance that he is who you claim."

"Of course," Patrick said.

"In the absence of a DNA test . . ."

Lex tensed beside me.

". . . this interview will have to serve," she said. "Daniel, can you tell me your middle name?"

"Wait," Patrick said. "My brother has severe memory loss from the trauma—"

"It's okay," I said. I knew the answer. "My middle name is Arthur."

She nodded. "And your date of birth?"

"November sixteenth, 2000."

"Can you tell me the names of your family?" she asked. "Just immediate family will do."

My throat was dry, so with the very tips of my fingers I grabbed the bottle of water a deputy had brought me earlier, taking a long swig before I answered. "My parents are Jessica and Robert Tate. Patrick and Alexis McConnell are my half brother and sister. My older brother is Nicholas, and my little sister is Mia." I could see that Ms. Brindell was trying to keep her face neutral, so I added, "They're the best family in world."

She looked down briefly at the table top and then exchanged another meaningful glance with Patrick. Then she opened her briefcase and pulled a stack of paper from it. She handed the stack to me, and I found it was photographs printed on regular office paper.

"Can you identify the people you just named for me, Daniel?"

I started to leaf through the photos. "Here's Nicholas," I said, pulling out what looked like a school portrait and sliding the picture toward her. I flipped past a couple of pictures of people I didn't recognize, looking for Mia or my parents, when my eyes caught another familiar face mixed in with the strangers. My pulse quickened. I pulled out the picture: a teenage girl with round cheeks and spiky hair, posing with a snowboard. I never would have recognized her if Lex hadn't shown me her picture just a couple of hours earlier.

"This is my cousin. Her name is . . . Ravenna." It was lucky for me she had such a stupid name; it made it easy for me to remember. "After the town in Italy where she was born."

Ms. Brindell raised an eyebrow and then, slowly, smiled. It had been a test. She wanted to see if I could pick out people from my past I wasn't explicitly told to look for. I looked at the photographs more closely as I went through the rest, picking out the faces I recognized from Lex's phone.

"This is my grandmother. She died when I was young. This looks like my best friend Andrew." I could feel Lex and Patrick exchanging glances over my head, but none of us said a word. I flipped past a photograph of Mia on a swing set without comment and eventually reached the final picture, where a blonde woman and dark-haired man in formalwear danced at some kind of party. "This is my mom and dad."

"You didn't recognize your sister, Mia," Ms. Brindell said.

I blinked. "She was only a baby the last time I saw her."

She just nodded. I handed her the stack of pictures. Beside me, Patrick gasped and grabbed my wrist, and I jumped.

"My God," he said, examining the small, dark patch of skin on the back of my hand, halfway between my thumb and forefinger. I could feel his hand shaking, and he looked from the spot up to me with wide eyes. "Jesus Christ."

I frowned. Why was he—

"Mr. McConnell?"

Patrick dragged his gaze away from mine to look at Ms. Brindell. "You want proof?" he said shakily. "Check your file. Danny was born with this birthmark."

Ms. Brindell looked at the spot on my hand and then down at the papers in front of her. Lex leaned forward to look too, and one of her hands flew to her mouth.

"You're right. *Café au lait spot above left thumb*," Ms. Brindell read from the report. She looked up at us and smiled. "I'm satisfied."

"So . . . you'll approve an expedited passport?" Lex asked breathlessly.

Ms. Brindell began to pack up her things. "We'll get the paperwork started immediately. You can go home tomorrow, Daniel."

Go home, go home, go home. The phrase thumped in my ears like a heartbeat as I packed my meager belongings.

The next morning, with my stiff new passport stuck in the pocket of my coat, I said good-bye to Alicia in front of the American Embassy. She hugged me and whispered in my ear.

"Good luck, Danny."

Patrick beckoned from the town car he'd hired to take us to the airport. In that moment all I wanted was to go back to Short Term 8 with Alicia, to disappear again into the crowd there. I was right on the verge of getting everything I'd always wanted, but if I didn't know they would catch me before I got five blocks, I would have run like hell.

Instead, I got into the car and watched Alicia wave to me until she was out of sight.

We sat in first class. The flight attendant brought Patrick and Lex glasses of champagne, which Lex quickly downed, and gave me a couple of warm cookies before we'd even taken off. The week before I'd been sleeping in a bus shelter and subsisting on bags of chips and candy bars pilfered from convenience stores.

I should have been happy. I shouldn't have been struggling to swallow around the cookie that felt dry and tasteless in my mouth, but maybe happiness wasn't something I was capable of anymore. Even if I was, I didn't think I'd have been able to feel it over the fear pounding through my veins, like a tide that only came in, rising higher and higher inside of me until I could barely breathe.

They were going to be waiting at the airport when we arrived. The Tates. They would look at me and this would all be over, and it scared the hell out of me.

Because, of course, I wasn't Daniel Tate.

I know I said I was going to tell you the truth. But I lied. It's just what I do. Frankly, you have no one to blame but yourself if you believed me for even a second.

Everything from this point on is true, though. I swear. Not even I could make up what happened next.

I was screwed. Somehow I had fooled Patrick and Lex, but I wouldn't fool the whole family. I couldn't.

Lex caught my hand as I brought it to my mouth to bite at a stubby fingernail.

"Don't be nervous," she said, although she looked as uneasy as I felt. She lowered my hand back to my lap and squeezed my fingers. "Everyone's going to be so happy to see you."

"Who's going to be there?" I asked.

"Just Mom and the kids. We didn't want to overwhelm you."

I nodded. Just Jessica, Daniel's mother, and his siblings Nicholas and Mia. I'd found out from Patrick and Lex yesterday that Daniel's father had been in prison for the past two years for tax evasion and embezzlement, and Mia had been too young when Daniel disappeared to even remember him, so that just left two people for me to worry about. It might as well have been a hundred, because I couldn't imagine a mother looking into the eyes of a stranger and believing for a second that he was her son. No matter how badly she wanted him to be.

The flight attendant noticed my soda was almost gone and brought me another, along with a third flavorless cookie. This was my first trip on an airplane, and I tried to imagine how different the second one would be, when they'd be deporting me back to Canada and jail time after I was exposed.

This wasn't what was supposed to happen.

Lex leaned over the armrest and pressed a kiss to my temple. She smelled of fancy shampoo and lavender laundry detergent, and all I could think of was how desperate and *stupid* she must be to swallow whole the ridiculous lies I'd told her. As she looked at me, her eyes started to shine. Ever since I'd met her, she'd been wide-eyed or trembling or crying, sometimes all three together. I should have felt sorry for her, or guilty for what I was doing, but I wasn't capable of it.

"We're together again, and that's all that matters," she said. "Everything's going to be okay now."

I walked up the jet bridge like a man must walk up to a scaffold. Dragging my feet, eyes on the ground, slipping once again into the traumatized child routine I'd used to fool people so many times in the past. I pulled my baseball cap down low over my eyes like I always did, and I'd shaved carefully that morning, even though what little blond stubble I had was barely visible. Usually these two things were effective at hiding my true age from disinterested cops, but I couldn't hope this would slow down the Tate family for long. Maybe, if I was lucky, the act would last long enough for me to get away from them and disappear, something I'd been trying unsuccessfully to do ever since this thing started.

Patrick put an arm around my shoulder as we walked, both to reassure me and to move me along. He didn't *seem* stupid. Maybe, despite all I knew about deception, I had underestimated people's ability to fool themselves when it suited them.

The blast of cold air from the AC as we stepped from the gangway into the airport was shocking. Outside the floor-to-ceiling windows, the sky was a bright expanse of uninterrupted blue, and the sun made the tarmac shimmer like water. In Vancouver the gutters were still full of slushy brown snow. I had emerged from that plane into a different world.

Want to know how it happened?

I came up with the plan the night Martin caught me at the bus station. There was no way I was going to let myself be sectioned, but I'd blown most of my money on a bus ticket I'd never get to use and was being watched like a hawk by the staff at Short Term 8, who had also changed the code on the security system. I needed a scam that would occupy the cops for a while and give me the time I needed to figure a way out of there so I could run my traumatized-teen-found-by-a-tourist scheme in another city.

Things were never supposed to go this far.

Martin returned me to my bed at about one in the morning that night. I lay there thinking, figuring out my next move. Every half hour, Alicia cracked open the door to my room to make sure I was still there, and I feigned sleep. Five minutes after her 4:00 a.m. check, when I was sure she'd be back in the office,

I slipped out of bed and retrieved my remaining cash from the hidden pocket in my backpack. I had one ten, one five, and a bit of change. Not much, but it should be enough.

I crept out of my room and into the room next door. It was a double occupied by two boys: Marcos, a twelve-year-old who was bigger than most linebackers and talked almost as little as I did, and Aaron, a scrawny kid who was prone to outbursts and mild kleptomania. I shook Aaron's shoulder to wake him. He blinked up at me in confusion.

"Want ten dollars?" I said.

"What do you want?" he answered.

"I want you to scream."

He eyed me warily. "Show me the money."

I pulled the ten out of my pocket and let him see it.

"What are you going to do?" he said.

"None of your business."

He sat up. "Fifteen."

I clenched my jaw. That would leave me with next to nothing, but I didn't have time to waste negotiating with this little asshole.

I handed over the fifteen dollars and told Aaron what I wanted him to do, and then I returned to my room. A couple of minutes later, Aaron started to scream. Tucker muttered a curse but didn't open his eyes, and Jason just rolled over and covered his head with a pillow. When you grow up in care, you learn to sleep through a lot of shit. Seconds later, footsteps came pounding down the hallway, Martin's heavy ones and Alicia's lighter ones. When something set Aaron off, he would not only scream at the top of his lungs but punch and kick. It took two people, one holding on to each arm, to restrain him until he had calmed down. And during the night shift there *were* only two people on duty.

As soon as I heard Martin and Alicia enter Aaron's room, I got out of bed again. I only had as much time as Aaron's lungs would hold out, so I moved quickly. I went straight for the office but found the door closed. I was hoping Alicia would leave it open, but no such luck. The door locked automatically whenever it was closed, so I needed to find a way in. I inspected the doorknob. It was just a standard lock, which seemed generous and not a little naive given the type of kids who occupied Short Term 8. I could crack it easy.

I crossed the hallway to the recreation room and rummaged through a box of art supplies. A handful of paper clips and safety pins floated around at the bottom. I grabbed a long silver paper clip and straightened it as I returned to the locked office. Aaron was still going strong.

It took me a minute or two of fiddling and changing the bend in the paper clip, but eventually I got the office door open. I slipped behind the ancient desktop and jiggled the mouse to wake it up. Alicia had a game of solitaire going; she must have been *really* bored. I minimized the window and opened a web browser.

After a few minutes of searching, I found Daniel Arthur Tate on the website for the U.S.'s Center for Missing and Exploited Children. I felt pretty clever, coming up with the idea to pose as a missing American child. They wouldn't section a poor abducted kid, and the amount of red tape that would need to be untangled in an international kidnapping should give me enough time to get my hands on some cash and get out of Vancouver. Daniel seemed like a perfect cover. He looked vaguely like me and would be about the age I'd been posing as, which was several years younger than my actual age. He'd been missing for long enough that the old pictures of him wouldn't immediately give me away as a fake.

Because I was on borrowed time, I printed his missing poster and the first article I found about his disappearance to read later. Normally, I planned my scams better than this, but I didn't know how long Aaron could occupy Martin and Alicia. I folded up the printed papers and stuck them in the waistband of my pajamas, cleared the browser history, pulled Solitaire back up, and put the computer to sleep. Then I closed the office door and crept back to my room. Once I was safely back in bed, I banged on the wall with my fist. It was the signal I'd prearranged with Aaron. Over the next few minutes he pretended to calm down, and everything inside Short Term 8 returned to normal.

I read the missing poster and printed article in the dim glow of the blue safety light outside my window, memorizing the details so that I'd have some basic information to back up my claim. If there were any questions I couldn't answer, I would just claim trauma related amnesia. I stared at Daniel Tate's face, imagining who he was, imagining myself becoming him. I constructed a story about where I'd been for those missing six years, and I felt Daniel start to take shape inside of me.

It had seemed like a good plan. There was no way for me to know what I was getting myself into.

Things weren't supposed to get this far. I kept saying that to myself, like it would make some kind of difference, as I walked with Patrick and Lex toward baggage claim. The racing of my heart had become physically painful. Black fuzz was beginning to encroach on the edges of my vision. We'd see them at any moment.

We got on the escalators and began to descend toward the baggage carousels, and suddenly we were engulfed in pops of light. They came from the dozen photographers waiting below. I stared at them dumbly, my comprehension lagging a moment behind events.

Were we standing near someone famous?

"Oh my God," Lex said. She pulled me behind her, shielding me with her body.

"Sons of bitches!" Patrick said. "How did they know we were here?"

Wait.

"Patrick, don't—" Lex said, grabbing for him, but he was already storming down the escalator, taking the steps two at a time.

The flashes continued to go off, and now people were calling Danny's name. *Fuck.* They were here for me. The press knew—and *cared*—that Daniel Tate had been found. I was furious at myself for not considering this possibility. I had always been so unimportant that it had never occurred to me that Daniel Tate wouldn't be, but the Tates were rich, and people paid attention to what happened to rich people.

This was incredibly bad.

Patrick dove into the clump of paparazzi, who split and re-formed around him like a school of fish around a shark. He was red faced and spitting legalese, and he shoved the man closest to him. Hard. I only noticed the security guards who had been struggling with the photographers when one of them grabbed Patrick by the arm to restrain him.

"Patrick!" Lex cried.

A pair of cops rushed to our sides, and my panic doubled. Patrick had told me I wouldn't have to talk to the cops right away, that he'd take care of things. I'd been counting on that time to get away before the authorities here in the States busted me.

"This way, ma'am," one of them said.

And then suddenly we were moving, pushed along by the tide of people. Lex called for Patrick again, and he shoved his way through the crowd to her side, braiding his fingers into hers. The cops took us to a door that required a security card to enter. One opened the door and went in, while the second stayed outside to close it after us. As quickly as the circus had started, we found ourselves alone in a quiet hallway.

Lex's hands were on me, checking to see that I was still in one piece.

"Are you okay?" she said. "I'm so sorry, Danny. I had no idea . . ."

I was shaking. What a terrible, catastrophic mistake I'd made coming here.

"Don't worry," Lex said to me. "We'll be home soon. You'll be safe there."

I don't know what made her think that. Danny hadn't been safe there.

"If you'll just follow me," the remaining cops said. "Your family is waiting down here, and we've arranged for you to exit via a side door."

"Thank you, Officer," Patrick said.

I'd barely had time to catch my breath after realizing the cops were just an escort and not here to question me before we were standing in front of the door that separated me from the rest of the Tates. I caught a glimpse of them through the small panel of glass above the knob and had only a fraction of a second to size them up. A fading beauty queen, a sharp slip of a boy, and a pigtailed girl. Then the cop was opening the door.

They jumped to their feet when the door opened. I could see how nervous they were. At least I wasn't the only one. For a moment everyone was silent and still, just staring. I kept my head down, hiding my face beneath the brim of my hat. I waited for someone to see through me, to start shouting.

Mia was the first to speak.

"Danny!" She ran to me, limping from the cumbersome brace on one of her legs. She flung her little arms around my waist, and I jumped. Lex gently pried her off me.

"Easy, honey," she said. "Let's give Danny a little space, okay?"

She nodded. Unlike anyone else, her face was shining with pure excitement. It was weird. She hadn't even known Daniel, could never truly have missed him.

I looked at Nicholas next, eyeing him from underneath the brim of my cap. He was looking me up and down and not bothering to hide it. Nicholas was my first real test.

"Look who it is, Nicholas," Patrick said.

A creeping, stuttering smile started across the boy's lips.

"Danny?" he said. He wanted to believe it.

I nodded. "Hi." My instinct was to call him "Nicky," and usually my best lies came from trusting my instincts. But I'd already gotten things wrong when I'd called Lex by her full name, which I soon noticed Patrick never did. Better to err on the side of caution and not arouse any more suspicions, however small.

Nicholas shook his head, like he was responding to some internal voice, and then stepped forward to embrace me. His hug was oddly sharp, just like him, all angles and bones.

Two down.

I risked a brief glance at Jessica. This is where the wheels would come off this thing. No mother—not even the woman who'd given birth to me—could look into the eyes of a stranger and see her own son—I was sure of it. Jessica was staring at me, her lips pinched into two thin lines with uneven lipstick drawn over them. I waited for her to open them and scream.

"Mom." Patrick reached out to her. There was a gray tinge to her skin underneath her blush. "It's okay. It's Danny."

She turned her shoulders ever so slightly toward the door, like she was on the brink of running. The air-conditioning was raising gooseflesh on my arms as I waited to see what she would do. She kept her eyes on me, and I remembered how someone from my dead-and-buried life once taught me you're supposed to maintain eye contact with a mountain lion to stop it from attacking you.

"Mom," Patrick said more firmly. "Come hug Danny."

Jessica took a hesitant step toward me, and I forced myself not to back away. Two fat tears built in her eyes and rolled down her cheeks as she stared at me silently.

"My son," she finally said. She reached out to hug me. Her grasp on me was weak, but she held me close enough that I could smell the cigarette smoke beneath her perfume.

I was stunned. Could she really believe I was Daniel? Or was she just bowing to the excitement of the moment and the pressure from Patrick?

"Let's go home," Lex said.

We went out an employee entrance and climbed into a hired car for the trip to the Tate house. It was almost an hour's drive up the coast from LAX to Hidden Hills, California. From the news story I'd read about Daniel's disappearance, I knew the Tate family had money, but nothing had prepared me for Hidden Hills. The entire town was cloistered behind a gate, where a guard in a crisp uniform spoke to Jessica before waving the car through. This is what Lex had meant about us being safe here; no press would ever be able to enter the town. Once inside, it was all rolling green hills and elegant mansions bathed in sunshine and hidden from the world. My coat was bundled in a ball at my feet; I'd realized as soon as I'd stepped out of the airport and into the perfect twenty-four-degree weather that I wouldn't need it here. I would have thrown the ratty thing away if I wasn't sure they'd be shipping me back to Canada any second now, when the adrenaline wore off and they realized I was a fake.

We drove deeper into the community, and the houses got farther apart and farther from the road. At the top of a winding hill the car pulled up to a scrolled wrought iron gate where the driver punched in a code to open it. We drove into a tree lined lane where the sunlight turned soft as it filtered down through the green leaves and the white and purple blooms of the flowering trees. Then the foliage opened up, and I was looking at a mansion of pale yellow stone and endless windows poised on the hillside, red mountains distant on the horizon.

I struggled to swallow, my throat suddenly tight. What the

hell had I done? Without even meaning to, I had stumbled into the biggest con of my life.

"Home sweet home," Patrick said as the car stopped in the circular driveway, complete with fountain, in front of the house. "Does it look familiar?"

"A little," I said.

The driver unloaded our bags and left. I felt everyone watching me as we walked up to the house. I didn't know what they expected me to do, so I didn't know how to act. All I could do was try to focus on keeping up the con. Don't look too scared. Don't look too shocked.

Patrick opened the door and ushered me inside. "Welcome home, Danny."

"Thanks," I breathed. Maybe it was just my imagination, but my voice seemed to echo in the cavernous foyer, reverberating off marble and crystal and glass.

We all stood together inside the door. The Tates just staring at me.

Lex was the one who finally spoke. "You're probably tired, huh, Danny? Do you want to rest for a little while?"

"Yeah," I said. "That would be good."

No one moved. It took me a second to realize, with horror, why. They were waiting for me to leave, to go to my bedroom. *Danny's* bedroom. If I walked in the wrong direction, I risked giving myself away, but if I kept just standing there like an idiot . . .

Lex raised the handle of her rolling suitcase. "Come on," she said. "I need to drop off my stuff too."

Saved by Lex again. She might not be bright, but she was helpful.

I followed her up the curving staircase. At the landing she turned right. The hallway was lined on one side with oversized windows that overlooked the velvety lawn below and the mountains in the distance. I counted the doors as we walked. She stopped in front of the fourth.

"Here you go," she said. "Come back down whenever you're ready, okay?"

She walked back in the direction we'd come, and I slowly opened the door to Danny's bedroom.

Like everything else I'd seen of the house so far, the room was pristine. The kind of museum clean that made me simultaneously nervous to touch anything and tempted to wreck it all. It was obvious that no one but the maid the Tates certainly employed had been in here for a long time. The room felt faded and stale, like it belonged to a world that didn't exist anymore. It was an interior decorator's vision of a little boy's dream room, with navy blue walls and framed vintage baseball posters and tasteful furniture. A bulletin board over the small desk held photos from fishing and beach trips, flyers for Little League tryouts, and ticket stubs from sporting events. Something inside of me started to come apart as I looked at these objects. I opened the middle drawer of the dresser and found little-boy clothes inside, the creases in the fabric permanent from going undisturbed for so long.

This wasn't a bedroom. It was a tomb. A mausoleum for a body they'd never found.

I fled into the hallway and started opening doors until I found a bathroom. I locked the door behind me and stared at myself in the mirror. What was I doing here? What the *fuck* was I doing here?

Maybe you won't believe me, but I honestly never meant to take Daniel Tate's life. He was just supposed to buy me time and breathing room so I could get away from Short Term 8. I had no idea how quickly things would start to move once I became him.

I picked Daniel because he was the first missing boy I'd come across who was the right age and look. It was probably the worst choice I could have made, because, as I soon realized, the Tates weren't a normal family. I'd been counting on many days or weeks of bureaucratic red tape to give me the chance to make my escape, but then Patrick McConnell had swooped in. He and Lex had gotten on a plane the next morning. They'd greased the skids at the American Embassy with their money and their connections to get me a passport within hours, after only a cursory examination of my claims. Even Alicia had commented on it.

"I've never seen anything like this move so fast," she told me as we drove back to Short Term 8 for my last night there. "Detective Barson said there was a lot of pressure coming from the Americans to get this sorted out quickly. You're lucky, you know, that your family is so powerful and loves you so much."

That was me. Mr. Lucky.

It all moved too fast, and I couldn't put the brakes on it without exposing myself as the fraud I was. So I'd been forced to play along, and now I was in California with a family that was somehow buying my bullshit, and when they caught me, I was screwed. I wasn't sure exactly what laws I'd broken, but the power the Tates had wielded in getting me out of Canada would no doubt be brought to bear in a serious fucking way on the con artist who'd impersonated their missing son.

I ran my fingers back and forth over the fake birthmark on the back of my hand as I considered what to do next. I'd only had the thing for a few days, but already it had become a nervous habit. The birthmark had been mentioned on Daniel's missing poster, so the night before Patrick and Lex came to Vancouver to see me, I'd given one to myself. Inspired by Tucker's juvie tattoo, I'd swiped a brown marker and a safety pin from the box of art supplies in the rec room and spent an hour in a bathroom stall pricking the ink into my skin and most of the night holding an ice pack I'd swiped from the first aid kit that hung on the wall in the kitchen against it to curb the redness and swelling. It looked surprisingly convincing if you didn't look too closely, which so far no one, not even Patrick, had.

I would never pull this off.

I had only one choice, which was to do what I'd always

intended. Run. Before the Tates' emotional high wore off and they realized I was a fake. Sure, now I would be in a strange country where I was out of my element, but at least it was warm here. I didn't have a penny to my name, and there would be people looking for me, but I'd been through worse.

I returned to Daniel's bedroom and rummaged through my backpack. I pulled out the baseball card I kept in the hidden pouch inside of it and put it in my pocket. It was the only thing in the bag worth keeping, so I would be ready anytime.

First chance I got, I would go.

I thought about leaving right then but quickly dismissed the idea. I was inside a giant gated community, basically a fancy prison. We were a couple of kilometers from the nearest entrance, and the odds were the Tates would notice I was gone before I could even reach one. My Daniel act had been convincing enough so far; it would hold up for at least a few more hours, maybe days. Part of me wanted to just lock myself in this room until it was late enough to sneak away, but that would seem too suspicious. So I took a deep breath and went in search of the family. Once I reached the foyer, I followed the voices toward the back of the house. By habit, I paused and peered around a corner when I got close, to get an idea what was going on in the room before I entered. I could see a sliver of Patrick leaning against a kitchen counter.

"—have to be patient," he was saying. "He's not the way

you remember him. His personality is different, and a lot of his memories are gone. He barely even remembers us. The doctor said we shouldn't push him to remember or to talk about what happened to him until he's ready. We just need to treat him normally, okay?"

"Why doesn't he remember us?" Mia's little voice asked.

"That's hard to explain, sweetie," Lex said. "Bad things happened to him while he was gone, and his brain sort of . . . protected him. By hiding his memories away."

"What happened to Danny?" Mia asked.

There was the scrape of a chair, and then Patrick said, "Mom, wait—"

"I'm not listening to this—"

Jessica turned the corner, moving fast. She slammed into me and recoiled, horror on her face.

She knew. I was suddenly sure.

But she didn't start to scream or accuse. "I'm sorry," she said. "I'm . . . I'm sorry."

She fled upstairs with Patrick on her heels and Lex on Patrick's.

"Mom!" Patrick yelled after her. *"Mom!"*

"I've got it," Lex said, and she followed Jessica up the stairs, taking them two at a time.

Patrick turned to me, his annoyed expression changing into one of concern when he saw my face. I must have looked as ready to bolt as I felt. "Hey, you okay?"

Somewhere above us, a door slammed closed. Back in the kitchen, the phone started to ring.

"I . . ." Shove down the panic. Play the part. "She's not happy I'm back," I said, hopefully with enough pathos in my voice to tug at his heartstrings and keep him from noticing I wasn't his brother.

"No, no," he said, looking more stricken than I could have hoped for. "It's not that, Danny. It's just . . ." The phone was still ringing. Patrick glanced back into the kitchen, where Nicholas and Mia were still sitting. "Nicholas, can you get that, please?" He put a hand on my shoulder and guided me into a sitting room down the hall. He lowered himself onto a sofa that looked like it hadn't actually been sat on in years, and I sat beside him. "Look, there are things you have to understand about Mom. She's not the mother you remember. It started with my dad's suicide, but you were so young, you might not remember."

I tried not to show my surprise. I didn't know Lex and Patrick's father had killed himself. I didn't even know he was dead.

"They'd been divorced for years, but they were still close, so it hit her hard," he continued. "Then less than a year later you disappeared, and she just went to pieces. Barely got out of bed for months. Eventually she went to rehab and things got better for a while, but then your dad went to prison and they divorced and things got bad again."

I nodded along and filed each fact away. Patrick was saving me a lot of research.

"I don't want to upset you by telling you these things," he continued, "but I need you to understand why she's reacting this way. Any kind of change, even something good, is hard for her. And now that you're back, she's having to deal with all of her old grief and guilt. It's overwhelming for her."

Bad news for Jessica, but good news for me. Maybe she didn't suspect me after all, and if she did, her instability would work in my favor. It looked like Patrick and Lex were the ones actually in charge in this family, and they both believed me.

"She'll come around," Patrick said. "She just needs a little time and some space. We all just need to leave her be until she gets her head around things. Got it?"

"Got it," I said. That suited me just fine.

Someone cleared their throat. Patrick and I turned to find Nicholas standing in the doorway. Neither of us had heard him approach.

"Who was on the phone?" Patrick asked.

Nicholas's eyes flicked over to me once and then back to Patrick. Instead of replying he asked, "Is Mom upstairs?"

Patrick nodded. "Lex is talking to her."

Nicholas snorted. "Great. She'll never come out."

Patrick gave him a look.

"I'll take care of it," he said, and headed toward the stairs. Over his shoulder, he added, "Mia's starving, by the way, and there's nothing in the house."

Having been replaced by Nicholas, Lex took over dinner and ordered from a local restaurant that delivered an obscene amount of food an hour later. Patrick made a face at her as he handed the delivery driver a couple of crisp hundreds from his billfold, but she just shrugged.

"We don't know what Danny will like," she said.

Despite Nicholas's spending twenty minutes talking to her through her door, Jessica wouldn't come out of her room, which was a little worrying. I just figured a mother would *want* to eat dinner with the son she hadn't seen in six years, but apparently Patrick was right and it was too much for her. Or she suspected I wasn't her son.

But as long as her belief held for a couple more hours, it wouldn't matter either way because I'd be gone.

The rest of us sat down at the elegantly carved dining table that probably cost more than the house I grew up in and ate dinner from plastic containers, with filigreed silver flatware. It was one of the more uncomfortable meals of my life, which is saying something. Mia was the only one unaffected by the undercurrent of tension in the room. She chattered happily, telling me all about her teacher and her best friend, her horseback riding lessons, the puppy she desperately wanted. Trying to fill me in on the bulk of a life that Danny had missed all in one meal.

"I wanted to quit riding because my friend Daisy got thrown and broke her arm, but Mom said I can get a horse of my own when I'm twelve if I keep taking lessons, because that's how old she was when Granddad got *her* a horse . . ."

"Gran and Granddad are in Europe right now," Lex said, "otherwise they would be here to welcome you back."

"That's okay," I said. The fewer relatives around, the better.

"It'll take us some time to get you on the visitors' list to see your dad," Patrick added, "but he knows you're home, so I'm sure he'll call soon."

When Mia finally ran out of things to say, silence descended on the table. I could practically see Patrick, Lex, and Nicholas struggling to think of a topic of conversation that wouldn't reference something I couldn't remember or the ordeal I'd been through.

"How's the sea bass?" Lex finally asked. She'd already asked me a dozen questions about the food, what I liked to eat, could she pass me the salt or get me anything else. Food was a safe topic.

I looked down at the container I was eating from. I hadn't even known the thing I was eating *was* sea bass.

"It's good," I said.

"Good," she said, giving me a weak smile.

I glanced at the grandfather clock on the wall. It was almost late enough for me to plead exhaustion and go to bed. The phone rang, and Patrick jumped up and went to the other room to answer it. He came back a moment later.

"Who was it?" Mia asked.

"No one," he said, at the same time Lex asked, "Who wants dessert?"

When dinner was over, Patrick announced that he'd better

leave for his own home in L.A. Since he'd missed the last couple of days at the office, he needed to go in early the next morning to start catching up. He hugged Lex and Mia and then turned to me. He reached for me, hesitated, then laughed at himself and reached for me again. His embrace was quick and stiff. "We're so glad you're home, Danny," he said.

"Me too," I said, very aware of all the eyes in the room watching us.

He let me go. "I'll be back tomorrow night. We should catch up."

"Sure," I said. I didn't intend to still be here tomorrow night.

"I'll walk you out," Lex said to her brother. As she and Patrick left the room, she said over her shoulder, "Nicky, Mia, will you?"

They nodded and immediately started to clean up, collecting food containers and paper napkins for the trash and silverware for the dishwasher. I guess I got out of cleaning duty on account of having been kidnapped, which left me hovering awkwardly, unsure what to do with myself. For a while I stood in front of one of the floor-to-ceiling windows in the dining room, pretending to care about the view of the darkened lawn and mountains in the distance. Then I decided to go find Lex and tell her I was going to bed.

I walked through a darkened corridor toward the foyer. Lex and Patrick were standing in the doorway, their profiles illuminated by the lights in the fountain outside as they spoke quietly to each other. I stopped in the shadows and watched them. Although

I couldn't hear them, the way they looked at each other indicated an intense conversation. Lex shook her head, and I could tell from her pinched lips that she was crying again. Patrick put his hands on her shoulders and said something that made her take a deep breath and nod. They exchanged a few more words before Lex turned to go, but Patrick caught her by the wrist and pulled her back to him. He cocked his head to one side as he asked her something. She looked at him for a long moment before nodding again and gently removing his hand from her wrist. He kissed her cheek and left, and after she'd closed the door behind him, she leaned against it for a long time. The air felt charged and uneasy, so I slipped away without saying anything to her.

I returned to Danny's untouched bedroom and locked the door behind me. I didn't know what to do. I needed something to occupy me until the time I could sneak out, but, truthfully, I was having trouble keeping my eyes open. I'd barely slept the night before, and maintaining the Danny act was draining. The exhaustion had seeped into me, burrowing all the way to my bones. I noticed an alarm clock on the bedside table and grabbed it. I could let myself get a few hours of sleep before I snuck away, I told myself. It would probably be even better. When you're tired, you make mistakes. I set the alarm for three and turned the sound down as far as it would go. I didn't want to risk waking anyone else, and I was a light sleeper anyway.

I had nothing of my own to change into for bed, and I

wouldn't have worn Danny's eerie, mummified clothes even if they weren't child sized. I was about to shuck my jeans and shirt to sleep in my boxers when there was a knock on the door. I opened it to find Nicholas standing in the hallway.

"I thought you'd need these," he said, holding out a T-shirt and a pair of sweatpants. "Doubt you still fit into whatever's in the dresser."

I took the clothes. "Thanks."

Nicholas kept looking at me. It was the first time he'd made eye contact with me for more than a second or two, and other than that first hug at the airport, it was the closest he'd been to me. A fine crease started between his eyebrows.

"No problem," he said. "Uh . . . do you need anything else? I'm sure Lex will—"

"What about me?" Lex asked cheerfully as she appeared in the hallway behind Nicholas. She looked like a different person from the fragile girl who had leaned against the door like she couldn't stand on her own when Patrick left. Her smile was loose and her eyes warm and sleepy. I would have said she was tipsy, but I was pretty sure she'd only had the one glass of wine with dinner. "Oh, good, you lent him some clothes," she said. "Danny, I was thinking that tomorrow we'd go shopping and get you the essentials you're missing. Sound good? In the meantime here's a spare toothbrush and some toothpaste." She pressed the toiletries into my hand. "Is there anything else you need tonight?"

Maybe a less creepy room to sleep in—there must have

been at least a couple of guest rooms in a house this size—but I couldn't exactly ask for that. Besides, I wasn't going to be in it much longer. "No, I'm fine."

"Okay, well, my room's the fifth one past the stairs if you think of anything," she said. Nicholas had drifted away at some point, so it was just the two of us. "Don't worry about waking me, okay? I won't mind."

I nodded. "Thanks, Lex."

"You're welcome." She looked at me and smiled, and then . . . something changed. I don't know exactly how to describe it. It was like the texture of our eye contact became different somehow. It felt like she was really *seeing* me instead of just looking at me. It made my breath hitch painfully in my chest.

She reached out and hugged me, and this time her arms were solid around me instead of weak and trembling.

"I missed you, Danny," she said softly, the words warm against my neck. "I'm so happy you're safe now."

I lay in bed unable to sleep. The sheets were too crisp, the house too silent. I stared up at the ceiling, where I could just make out the outline of plastic star stickers that had long ago lost their glow.

I couldn't stop thinking. First, I decided to stay the night. I told myself it was because it made more sense to run tomorrow night, after Lex had bought me some new clothes and other supplies. The truth, which I think I knew even then, was that I had felt . . . *something* when she looked at me and told me she was happy I was there. That I was safe. I'd believed her, and I hadn't wanted to give that up so quickly.

And would it really be so bad to stay? For good? The Tates had eaten up my story, and in a way, I was doing them a favor. Danny was long gone, probably dead, and definitely never coming back. Me being here made them happy. And as for me, somehow I had stumbled into the con of a lifetime. A scam with the biggest risks I'd ever taken on but also the biggest rewards. If I could become Danny Tate, I could have a real life here, a better one than the little boy in Saskatchewan had even been able to *dream* of. Did I really want to just walk away from that? Wasn't it stupid to go back to living on the streets and group homes when there was a perfectly good bed in a perfectly good mansion filled with a perfectly loving family right here?

Finally, I couldn't lie there any longer, playing scenarios in my head, preparing lies. It was late; the rest of the family had to be asleep. I climbed out of the bed. If I wasn't leaving tonight, I needed to learn the layout of the house. The Tates were less likely to get suspicious of me if I seemed at home here.

I padded on bare feet to the end of the hallway and started there. The farthest room was an office, lined with built-in bookcases and dominated by a massive desk. The next room was the bathroom I'd hidden in earlier, then a linen closet, then Danny's room. Nicholas's room, I knew, was next to mine. I was surprised to see the light on underneath the door and walked past extra carefully. Mia's room was next, a night-light plugged into the outlet beside her door. There was one final room on this side of the stairs, a guest room that had probably belonged to a nanny once. Jessica didn't strike me as the type to change diapers in the middle of the night.

I reached the stairs and ascended to the third floor, where I discovered just one set of locked double doors. The entire level must have been the master suite. I went back down to the second floor and turned left to explore the rooms in the wing on the other side of the stairs. I found two guest rooms, another bathroom, a bedroom I judged to be Patrick's old room from the band posters on the wall, and then Lex's room. A light was on inside. It seemed everyone was having trouble sleeping tonight.

I spent another twenty minutes exploring the first floor and the basement, walking from room to room until I had a good handle on the layout. I checked the alarm panel by the front door—it wasn't activated—and then ventured out of the French doors and onto the back patio. It was overhung with a wooden lattice crawling with ivy and some kind of white flowers, and beyond that was a pool that glowed in the dark like a chlorine moon. I dipped a foot in the water. It felt good, just warm enough in the cool night air. It must have been heated.

I looked back at the house. It was dark; Nicholas and Lex must have finally gone to sleep. Fuck it, I thought. I might only be rich for this one night, so I might as well enjoy the perks while I could. I stripped down to my boxers and slipped into the pool, the shallow end, since I didn't swim too well. The world went silent beneath the surface of the water. I kicked and twisted and spun and surfaced laughing. Then I floated there, weightless, looking up at the starry sky above me.

When I finally returned to Danny's room, I fell straight to sleep.

At some point in the night, I woke. I opened my eyes and blinked at the dark figure standing in the doorway. At first all my eyes could pick out was the silhouette against the glow from the hall. Forgetting where I was, I thought that it must be Jason, returning from a raid of the pantry at Short Term 8.

But then I remembered.

"Nicholas?" I murmured.

He silently turned and walked away, closing the door behind him, and the chill that raced up my spine had nothing to do with the aggressive California air-conditioning.

When I woke the next morning, I wasn't sure it had really happened. The memory felt fuzzy around the edges and hollow in the middle, like a dream.

What was definitely real was the weight in the bed beside me. I scrambled back and threw aside the comforter. Underneath I found Mia curled up, the tip of her thumb lying between her lips. I took a couple of deep breaths to calm the pounding of my heart and then nudged her.

"Hey," I said. She was lucky I hadn't hit her when she tried to climb into bed next to me. I must have been exhausted to have slept through it.

She frowned and blinked as she woke. "Morning," she said blearily.

"How long have you been here?" I asked.

She shrugged and sat up.

"*Why* are you here?" I asked.

"I used to come and sleep in here sometimes," she said, "when you were gone. Lex caught me once and got mad. Don't tell her, okay? She wanted me to stay in her room with her, but she kicks in her sleep."

I swallowed. "Why did she want you to sleep with her?"

"She said she didn't want me to bother you by accident if I got up in the middle of the night," she said. "Sometimes I wake up at night, and Magda used to help me go back to sleep, but she went home to Ukraine a few days ago."

"Magda was your nanny?" I asked.

She nodded. "Lex said I could only sleep in my room if I stayed inside and kept the door locked so I wouldn't bother anyone. I don't want her to know I broke my promise."

"I won't tell," I said. Was Lex worried her damaged, potentially destructive little brother might do something to Mia? It was a reasonable thought, but one that seemed at odds with the way she'd been treating me.

"Thanks, Danny," Mia said. "Did you sleep good?"

"I . . . not really," I said. I wasn't sure how I was supposed to talk to a kid this young. She was like a little alien creature to me.

"It's always weird being in a new bed," she said. "That's why I bring my pillow with me anytime we go on a trip, so the bed isn't *totally* new."

I smiled. "That's pretty smart."

"Well, tonight your bed won't be new anymore," she said, "so hopefully, you'll sleep better." She climbed awkwardly out of the bed. I wondered again about the brace on her leg. It had pins that went into her skin. Had she gotten hurt, or was it some kind of disability she'd been born with? If the problem with her leg was something Danny had known about, it would be suspicious if I asked, but if Danny hadn't known, it would be suspicious if I didn't.

"I better go back to my room before Lex wakes up," she said, and then she leaned toward me and wrapped her thin little arms around my neck, squeezing me with so much passion I could hardly breathe.

"I really missed you, Danny," she said. And she sounded like she meant it, even though she couldn't possibly remember the brother who'd disappeared when she was just a toddler.

I raised a hand to her back and gave it a couple of awkward pats. "Missed you, too."

Mia returned to her room, and I brushed my teeth and changed into my one set of clean clothes before heading downstairs. Nicholas was in the kitchen, his wet hair looking almost black and dampening the collar of his shirt. He was pouring glasses of orange juice, and there was already a plate of toast on the table in the breakfast nook.

"Morning," he said when I walked in.

I tried to smile like I thought I should. "Morning."

"How'd you sleep?" he asked.

I looked at him closely. The question sounded almost too innocent coming from him, like he was daring me to ask why I had woken in the middle of the night to find him standing over my bed like some creepy fucking wraith.

But it was possible I was being paranoid.

"Fine," I said.

"Great," he replied, turning back to the fruit he was cutting. "Have a seat. Breakfast is almost ready."

As I took a seat at the table, Mia came bounding in and sat across from me. I sipped my orange juice while she slathered a piece of toast with raspberry jam. Nicholas had a cordless phone on the counter beside him, and when it began to ring, he hit a button and it went silent.

"So what's on the agenda today, Mimi?" he said.

"I don't know. I was supposed to go to Eleanor's house," Mia said, "but Magda was going to take me."

"I can take you," Nicholas said. "What are you two going to do?"

"Work on our play," she said around a mouthful of toast.

"You have a play?" I asked while I wondered why Magda had left with such apparent abruptness.

Mia nodded and licked some stray jam off her finger. "We've been working on it for a long time. It's about a mermaid with magical powers. I play the mermaid, because I want to be an actress someday."

"Acting's pretty cool," I said. "Getting to pretend to be another person."

"Yeah, I'm really good at it. Eleanor does the costumes."

"Does she want to be a fashion designer?" I asked. It turned out the kid was actually pretty easy to talk to.

"Not really," she said. "She's just not a very good actress, and she needed something to do."

I started to laugh but stopped when Nicholas approached us, balancing several plates in his arms. He set a raisin bagel with cream cheese and honey down in front of Mia and a bowl of cornflakes with freshly cut strawberries in front of me.

"I decided to make everyone their favorite for breakfast today," he said with a smile, "in honor of Danny being home."

"Thanks, Nicky!" Mia said, pushing aside her toast in favor of the bagel. "What about Mom's?"

Nicholas sat down beside her with his plate of scrambled eggs and took the uneaten half of Mia's raspberry toast. "I don't think she'll be down for a while. Eat up, before it gets cold."

Something seemed different about him. I frowned as I tried to put my finger on it, and he noticed.

"Something wrong?" he asked.

I shook my head. Behind him Lex walked into the kitchen,

rubbing her head and making straight for the coffee maker.

"Morning, guys," she mumbled.

"Morning," we all replied.

I raised a spoonful of cereal to my mouth, and suddenly Lex was sprinting across the kitchen and knocking it from my hand.

"Danny!" she snapped. "Don't touch that! Who gave him strawberries?"

"I did," Nicholas said.

"He's allergic!" she said. "What were you thinking?"

Nicholas looked at her and then me with wide eyes. "I'm so sorry, Danny. I completely forgot."

The air was thick with tension. Nicholas stared at me and I stared back, and in my peripheral vision I saw Lex clench her hands into fists.

Then she sighed, and the room seemed to exhale with her. "Well, there's no harm done," she said. "I'll make you something else to eat, Danny. What would you like?"

She took the bowl of cereal away, pouring it down the drain, while I looked at Nicholas, who just stared back at me. Did he suspect?

"Did you forget too?" he asked.

I nodded slowly and started my eyes watering. I'd always been able to make myself cry whenever I wanted. It was a useful trick.

"I guess . . . ," I said. "It's been so long since I've had fresh fruit that . . ."

Nicholas's stony expression wavered.

"Oh, honey . . . ," Lex said.

"I'm sorry." I got up from the table. "I'm sorry, I've got to . . ."

I fled the kitchen. Behind me, I heard Lex going off on Nicholas and him apologizing, and I smiled.

I was holed up in Danny's bedroom for maybe ten minutes before a soft rap on the door signaled that Lex had come to find me.

I curled into the most pathetic ball I could manage on top of the bed. "Come in."

"Hey," she said softly as she inched the door open. "You okay?"

"I guess," I said. I sat up and rubbed my eyes. "I'm sorry. I'm sorry I freaked out. I just want to be normal, you know? But I can't, and it makes me so mad sometimes . . ."

"Hey, hey." She sat down beside me and put a hand on my shoulder. "You didn't do anything wrong."

"I upset everyone."

She rubbed my shoulder. "No, you didn't. We're all just . . . feeling this out. It's going to take a little time, and there are going to be some bumps. But don't you ever blame yourself, you got it?"

I swallowed and nodded.

"You know you can talk to me anytime, about anything, right?" she said. "I don't want to push, but I'm always here."

"I know," I said.

She smiled and nudged my leg. "And don't let Nicholas get

to you, okay? I love him to death, but he's an idiot sometimes."

I cracked a smile.

"Aww, there's my baby brother!" she said, ruffling my hair. "Come on, how about we go do some shopping? It'll be fun."

We climbed into Lex's car and headed into town to buy me the essentials I was missing. It turned out my definition of "essential" was pretty different from hers. For hours we went from store to store, buying clothes and toiletries and shoes and a cell phone and a laptop, everything charged to the shiny platinum credit card Lex produced from her wallet. If I liked something, she bought two of it and never looked at a single price tag. It shouldn't have surprised me after seeing the house or climbing into Lex's tricked out BMW, but there was something almost magical about how she could trade a swipe of plastic for anything she wanted.

"We'll go to the bank on Monday and get you your own card," she said as we ate a late lunch. "We all have one for the family account. For emergencies."

I guess our definition of "emergency" was different too. For me it was not having any money for a bus ticket out of town when I needed to disappear. For her it was seeing some shiny thing in a store window that she wanted.

I preferred her definition.

"I've always loved this color on you," Lex said as she brushed the sleeve of the new blue button-down I was wearing. I looked down at the shirt. I had always understood the lack of money; growing up poor etched it into your bones. But in the clothes Lex had pushed into my arms to try on, in this fine cotton shirt, I was getting a glimpse of what life was like with money. It was easy to sit up straight and take up space when everything that touched your skin was clean and soft and expensive. "Makes your eyes look almost green."

The glow in her face as she smiled at me was so full of warmth and affection that I felt something move inside my chest. The lurch of a dormant heart trying to wake up.

"I'll be right back," I said, and headed for the restroom. Somehow I kept finding myself hiding in bathrooms. I washed my hands and then stared in the mirror until my face stopped being something I recognized and morphed into nothing but a collection of shapes and shadows. I blinked at the shapes and took deep breaths until they became a face again.

When I returned to the table, Lex was throwing back a pill with the glass of wine she'd ordered with lunch. When she spotted me, she gave a little shrug.

"Headache," she said, stuffing the bottle back into her bag. "Are you ready to go?"

I nodded, and with another swipe of her magical plastic, lunch was paid for, and we left the restaurant.

"So," she said as we climbed back into her car, "I think you have everything you need now, right? I gotta say, I much prefer shopping to class."

"Is that where you'd usually be?" I asked.

"Yep! I'm the loser who's still in college at twenty-four."

Her smile was bitter around the edges. "I haven't exactly been a model student."

"I guess that's my fault, huh?" I said, angling an air-conditioning vent away from me.

"Please," she said. "That was *all* me. But I've been getting it together, and I should graduate next semester. And I've got my own place now, out in Century City. It's a dump, but at least it's mine."

"Oh," I said. "I thought you lived—"

She shook her head. "No, I'm just crashing in my old room for a while. Patrick and I thought it would be better for everyone if I was around while you got settled in."

I was suddenly nervous. What constituted "settling in"? If Lex left, I'd be stuck practically alone in that house with Jessica and Nicholas, the two members of the family I was on the least stable ground with.

That is, if I decided to stay.

"How long will that be?" I asked.

She glanced over at me and smiled. "Don't worry, you're not getting rid of me for a good long time. We even let Mia's nanny go, since I'm going to be around for a while."

Slowly, I smiled back.

On our way back to Hidden Hills, Lex stopped at a Starbucks. The backseat of her car, which was otherwise pretty neat, was littered with discarded coffee cups, and as she parked, she tossed the empty one in her cup holder back onto the pile.

I followed her inside, surprised again at the gust of cold air that hit me as I stepped in. I guess Southern California had to manufacture its own winter. Lex joined the line, drawing her phone out of her bag and immediately typing out a message. I was amazed at how quickly her thumbs moved. I'd never had a smartphone before, just a shitty pay-as-you-go flip phone that quit going pretty quickly since I quit paying.

With Lex occupied, I looked around the coffee shop. This was one thing that wasn't different from my old life at all. Starbucks was Starbucks whether you were a homeless guy in Canada or a rich teenager in California. It was strangely comforting. And also irritating. Like it was trying to remind me who I really was.

I looked at the array of pastries in the case by the register and then at the customers in the seating area. An old Hispanic man with a paper, probably a widower just trying to fill his day. A bored white woman in yoga pants and expensive sunglasses—a reluctant stay-at-home mom—who talked on the phone while her toddler dismantled a muffin. An Asian girl a little younger than me working at a laptop in one of the leather chairs against the wall, her legs folded underneath her in a way that looked extremely uncomfortable. I watched her a little longer than the others, trying to figure out her deal, like I automatically did with everyone, so of course she looked up and caught me. I immediately looked away.

"Do you want anything, Danny?" Lex asked.

I shook my head, and Lex gave her order and handed over

her credit card. I flipped through the CDs at the cash register while Lex waited for her receipt, but I found my gaze drifting to the girl in the chair again.

For the second time she looked up and caught me. *Dammit.* I turned my head away. But when my eyes slid back to her a third time, she was still looking at me.

She crossed her eyes.

I laughed.

It took me a second to realize that's what the sound had been. My mouth snapped shut. The girl was grinning.

"What's funny?" Lex asked as the barista handed her a latte.

"Nothing," I said.

I looked back as we left the coffee shop, but the girl was concentrating on her laptop again.

Patrick came over for dinner that night. Jessica wasn't in the house. No one but Mia seemed worried or curious about her absence, and she still wasn't home when Lex convinced Patrick to stay the night, and everyone headed to bed. If I'd thought becoming Danny Tate would mean getting a more loving and attentive mother than the one I'd grown up with, I would have been disappointed, but I was relieved. I could play Lex like a fiddle, but Jessica made me uneasy. I didn't get her, and I wasn't good with mothers.

I didn't go to sleep when everyone else did. Instead, I sat on the floor of Danny's room with everything Lex had bought me that morning spread out in front of me. It was all I needed to make a decent attempt at getting away from here. Clothes, including a new coat that would be warm enough even in Vancouver, and several good pairs of shoes to choose from. A laptop and a smartphone that would get me a nice chunk of cash at any pawn shop. The passport with Danny Tate's name on it next to my picture. If I moved fast enough, flying back to Canada before the Tates realized I was gone and raised the alarm, I could use it to get across the border if I wanted.

I had everything I needed to go.

But, after more than an hour of staring at the supplies in front of me, I got up and started to put them away. Clothes hung in the closet, laptop plugged in on the desk, new toothbrush dropped into the cup by the sink in Danny's bathroom. I was going to stay. If I was honest with myself, I had made the decision the night before as I floated in the pool and looked up at the sky. I was going to see the con through, take this chance to have a real life.

I was going to become Danny Tate.

I had a million rationales. Staying was actually, weirdly, the safer choice. Right now they believed I was Danny, with the possible exception of Nicholas. If I ran, they would all know I wasn't. The power and wealth of the Tates had cut through government bureaucracy like a hot knife through butter to get me out of Canada, and that the same influence would be brought to bear on finding me and putting me in prison for impersonating their son. For years I'd relied on my ability to read people, and

I was confident that if they started to suspect me, I would see it coming. There would be time for me to get away if I needed to. And in the meantime I'd live like a king.

Because I'm just as good at lying to myself as lying to other people, I even believed those were my real reasons.

I wasn't sleepy, so I decided to go through the house again while everyone was asleep. I walked the upstairs halls, quizzing myself on what lay in the room behind each door, and then moved downstairs. I went through each cabinet and drawer in the kitchen, learning where the Tates kept the forks and cookie sheets and what kind of cereal they ate. I was in the fancy living room—the one no one ever seemed to use—going through the drawers in a side table when headlights swept across the windows.

Jessica was home.

Seconds later I jumped at a sudden loud noise from outside. A plastic *crunch-pop* and the yelp of a car horn.

Shit. As quickly as I could on silent feet, I headed for the stairs. But I was too late. I heard a door open and close and the pounding of footsteps above my head, and I ducked back into the living room as Lex and Patrick came running down the stairs together.

"Son of a bitch," Patrick was saying as he headed for the front door.

"She's got to stop this or . . ." Lex's reply was swallowed up by the night as she followed Patrick out of the house. I followed silently behind them, and, hidden by the shadows of the open doorway, looked out over the driveway. Jessica had driven her SUV up onto the lawn and into a concrete pillar that held a large planter overflowing with flowers. The front end of the vehicle was crumpled and steaming.

"Mom?" Patrick called.

Jessica wobbled out of the SUV.

"I'm fine," she said.

"You're not fine!" he snapped. She was obviously wasted.

"Jesus, Mom," Lex said. "You could have killed yourself!"

Patrick stepped toward his mother, taking her arm as she stumbled. She tottered on sharp heels that sank into the grass, and tried to push him away.

"What's going on?"

I spun. Nicholas was standing behind me. He was even stealthier than I was.

"I . . ." I didn't have a lie prepared for this. "I'm not . . ."

He looked past me through the open door and sighed. "Great."

"I won't . . . ," Jessica was saying as Patrick maneuvered her back toward the house, and Lex climbed into the wrecked car to kill the engine. "I won't go back."

"You should get upstairs," Nicholas said to me. Then he stepped outside to help Patrick with their mother. She was crying now, mumbling words I couldn't make out.

I watched, transfixed, seeing ghosts of my own superimposed onto Jessica's beauty queen face.

Then I heard her say it.

"He's not my son," she said, the words slurred but unmistakable.

My heart dropped like an anchor to the sea floor. This was it.

"Mom!" Patrick barked. "Stop it!"

"He's not my son!" Jessica said to Lex.

Before the last word had died on the warm April air, the crack of Patrick's hand meeting her face replaced it. Jessica reeled backward. He hadn't hit her that hard—I could tell—but she took the blow like it was a fatal one and crumpled to the lawn. Lex screamed at Patrick, slamming her hands against his chest, and knelt beside their mother, who was now moaning on the grass. Nicholas turned and looked right at me.

"You shut your mouth," Patrick said as he towered over his fallen mother.

Jessica looked up at him, then at Nicholas. She followed his gaze to me, standing in the doorway, and Lex and Patrick turned to look at me too. For a moment everything was frozen and silent, me staring at Jessica, them staring at me.

Jessica looked down at the ground, her nails digging into the grass as she struggled to stand.

"You're not my son," she said again, but when she raised her head, it wasn't me she was looking at. She was looking at Patrick. Lex grabbed her arm and tried to help her up, but Jessica pushed her away. "You're not my daughter. None of you are my children! A mother's children wouldn't treat her this way!"

A painful shudder of relief went through me.

"None of you are my children!" she sobbed.

Patrick looked down at her as she struggled. His body cast a shadow over her face, obscuring her expression.

"Don't you ever say that again," he said. Then he turned and walked back into the house, brushing past me on his way, leaving me cold in his wake.

"Nicky," Lex said after he was gone, waving Nicholas over. The two of them managed to get their arms under Jessica's and helped her to her feet.

"Everything's okay, Danny," Lex said brightly, sounding for all the world like she believed it. "Go on back to bed."

I returned to my room, closed the door behind me, and blocked the air-conditioning vent with a pile of books so I could try to get warm again.

From my bed I listened as Lex and Nicholas moved Jessica upstairs, and the water somewhere above me began to run. I was finally beginning to drift off, maybe an hour later, when there was a light knock at my door. It was so quiet I thought I had imagined it until the door opened a sliver, and I could see the glint of Mia's night-light off Lex's corn silk hair.

"You asleep?" she whispered.

"No."

"Can I come in?"

I nodded, and she stepped inside, closing the door behind her so that we were in the dark together. She sat on the edge of the bed while I propped myself up on the pillows.

"I'm sorry you saw that," she said in a low voice.

"It's okay," I said.

"No, it's not." She put a hand on my knee, though I could barely feel the touch through the thick comforter. "I hope she didn't scare you with all that talk. She doesn't mean it; it's just what she says when she's been drinking. *You aren't my kids, this isn't my home, this isn't my life*. She's . . . she's a very unhappy woman sometimes."

I thought of my mother—the real one—and I nodded.

"I think she's been a little overwhelmed by everything," Lex continued with a commendable flair for understatement. "But she'll be okay. We'll make sure of it. You don't have to worry."

I tried to remember the fear I used to feel as a little boy when my mother disappeared for days at a time. Tried to let that scabbed over old feeling show on my face when I nodded.

"And Patrick." Lex shifted, uncomfortable. "He's not . . . I mean, I want you to know that he's not . . . a violent person. He would never hurt any of us, so you don't have to be afraid of him. Okay?"

I frowned, because it never would have occurred to me to be afraid of Patrick, as long as he didn't find out who I really was. Then all bets were off, violent person or no.

"I get it," I said. "He was just protecting me."

"Yes." She seized my words like a struggling swimmer grabs a life ring. "Yes, exactly. He's not a bad person."

"Of course not," I said, bemused.

"Good." She smiled and reached out to touch my face. At the last moment, though, she changed her mind. I don't know if it was something I did or something that changed in her thoughts, but she ended up just tracing the air beside my cheek. Air molecules moving against my skin instead of hers.

She drew back her hand and stood, looking down at me. "Good night, Danny," she said, and left.

After Lex left, I got out of bed and went to the desk against the window, where I'd left my new laptop. I could tell I wouldn't be able to sleep, and now was a good time to do something I'd been wanting to do for days.

I opened the browser and did an Internet search for *Daniel Tate*.

The top result came from the Center for Missing and Exploited Children, the place I'd first discovered Daniel. The second result was the news article from two days after his disappearance that I'd printed off that same night and read after sneaking back to bed. Nothing to learn there.

The third result was an AP story about my return, complete with a photograph taken at the airport, which thankfully showed little more than the brim of my hat and part of my jawline. "Missing child Daniel Tate, subject of the recent *LA Magazine* article that revived public interest in his case, has been reunited with his family . . ."

I typed in a new search.

Daniel Tate LA Magazine

Up came the article—"Two Thousand Days Later: The Disappearance of Daniel Tate"—a detailed examination of the case on the sixth anniversary of the last day Danny was seen. It was published just over three weeks ago.

The door to my room cracked open, and I slammed the laptop shut.

"Danny?" Mia poked her head into my room.

"Hey," I whispered. "You okay?"

"I'm thirsty," she said.

"Isn't there a cup in your bathroom?"

"I don't like that water," she said. "Magda used to leave me a glass of water from the kitchen, but Lex forgot. Will you come downstairs with me? It's dark."

What I wanted to do was retroactively remember to lock my bedroom door, but then I thought about being a little kid creeping alone through the darkness, not sure what dangers were lurking there, and what a difference having a hand to hold would have made to me. Suddenly, I saw the gap-toothed boy in the T-ball uniform standing in front of me instead of Mia, and I smiled at him.

"Sure," I said. "Let's go."

The next day, and the next and the next, all passed the same way. Breakfast, shower, fine new clothes on my back that felt too nice for a day of just hanging around the house. I'd watch the others go off to school while I stayed behind with Lex hovering over me all day. I kept waiting for my interview with the police to come, bracing for it every morning when I came downstairs for breakfast, but whatever Patrick was saying or doing to put them off was obviously working. That left me with nothing to do but kill time with Lex. We spent hours together watching TV on the couch in the non-fancy living room. She filled me in on her favorite soaps—Harrison was secretly in love with Savannah, Lucinda was cheating on Jack with Mateo, Clark had been the one to sabotage the breaks on Sabine's car—and I began to understand why she still hadn't graduated college. I couldn't totally blame her though. The soaps were weirdly addictive, and I liked watching them with her, the two of us passing back and forth a bowl of popcorn that Lex had added extra melted butter to.

I read the article in *LA Magazine* about Danny's disappearance. It was like a bad pulp novel, the story of senseless tragedy fracturing the glamorous, idyllic façade of Hidden Hills. It was heavy on details like what kind of shoes Jessica had worn for the press conference and light on facts, but judging by the hundreds of comments people had left on it, it had struck a chord. No wonder the paps had shown up to the airport.

I had two phone calls with Robert Tate from the minimum security prison upstate where he was due to spend the next eighteen months. He cried for most of the first one. We were actually able to talk during the second, and he swallowed my story as easily as everyone else had. I promised I would visit soon.

I barely saw Jessica. She rarely left her room, and when she did, it was just to get into her rental and drive away. I had no idea where she went, and no one else seemed to either. Weirder, none of them seemed to care.

One morning after everyone else had left, Lex went down to the basement and came back with the family photo albums and a handful of home videos.

"I don't want to push you," she said, "but I thought these might help you start to remember more. Want to have a look?"

I nodded. The amnesia act would deflect suspicion for only so long; I needed to start learning this stuff if I was going to make everyone believe I was truly Danny.

Lex flipped through the book, naming everyone and narrating the events the pictures captured. Every now and then she'd look at me and say, "Ring any bells?" or "Do you recognize this?" I would say something noncommittal, and she never pushed. It was exactly what I needed. The more cousins' names I could commit to memory, the more birthday parties I witnessed via Sharpie-labeled DVDs, the more I could start to become Daniel Tate. Lex made me a crunchy peanut butter and jelly sandwich for lunch, and I ate it happily, even though I didn't care for peanut butter. This had been Danny's favorite, and now it would be mine. To tell a good lie, part of you has to believe it's true. With each piece of his past and each day spent under this roof, with this family, I could feel Danny growing inside of me. He was the parasite and I was just the host. Eventually, he would take over until I was only the skin he wore.

It was all I'd ever wanted. To finally bury the boy from Saskatchewan who had mattered to no one and become something else. Something better.

But it was a slow process, and the days were long in that house. I wasn't used to my every movement being watched, to having to weigh every word and action so carefully. When I was in care, all I had to do was keep my mouth shut and everyone ignored me. It was a totally different story here. Lex never left me alone during the day, Mia clung to me when she got home from school, and I feared making even the smallest misstep in front of Nicholas, who was standoffish, if not downright suspicious of me.

"Adam Sherman messaged me on Facebook to ask about you," he said one day at lunch. "I can give you his e-mail if you want to talk to him."

I blinked. "You mean Andrew?" Andrew Sherman, I'd learned from Patrick and Lex, had been Danny's best friend and had moved away several years ago.

"Oh, right," he said vaguely. "Want his e-mail?"

It could have been an honest mistake, but I wouldn't have put money on it. At least if it *was* a test, I'd passed.

The only time I had to myself was when I went to bed, which

I did increasingly early just so I could escape the eyes for a little while. I wasn't made for this. I was used to being invisible, and I'd never realized before how much freedom there was in that.

On my twelfth day at the Tates', I finally snapped. Lex had been following me from room to room all morning, never more than five feet away from me, asking every ten minutes if there was anything she could get or do for me. Nicholas looked up at me from his computer every time I moved or breathed. But the last straw was Mia. I usually didn't mind being around her as much because there was no chance of her doubting me, but she'd developed a habit of climbing up next to me anytime I sat down, her overly warm, sticky hands clinging to me like she was trying to absorb every lost moment with Danny through her skin. It was stifling. Like the walls were closing in on me, the big bright rooms of the Tate mansion getting smaller and darker around me, trapping me in a tiny room, a closet, a coffin.

I disentangled myself from her and got up, intending to go to the bathroom in the hallway to catch my breath. But my feet just kept walking, taking me out the front door, down the driveway, and onto the street. I walked and walked in a kind of frenzy, sweat beading on my forehead and stinging my eyes. My muscles burned from following the swells of the hills, but I could breathe. The walls I'd felt pressing in on me had fallen away. No one was looking at me. No one was expecting anything of me.

At the gate, a security guard asked me if I was Daniel Tate, that my sister had called down and asked them to look out for me. I said no and kept walking.

What I learned pretty quickly was that people in California don't walk. I wanted to disappear, but instead, everyone was staring at me from their cars.

Why is he walking?

What's wrong with him?

My God, is that person walking?? I HAVE NEVER SEEN SUCH A THING.

I needed to get off the street.

I crossed a heavily trafficked road and found myself in some kind of outdoor mall. At the far end I spotted a movie theater. Perfect. A place where I could sit in the dark for a couple of hours and not be looked at. With a swipe of my new magical plastic, I bought a ticket for the movie starting the soonest and hoped it would be something dumb and loud enough to drown out the voices in my head for a while.

I got in the concession line to buy a Coke, and that's when I saw her. At first she was just a curtain of black hair two people ahead of me, but when she turned her head and I saw her profile, I recognized her as the girl from Starbucks.

I'm not sure why I suddenly felt so exposed. Like she might recognize me and ruin my escape, which was ridiculous. Normal people don't recognize someone they saw for five seconds in a coffee shop two weeks before, and even if she did, what did it matter? There was no reason for her presence to make me nervous.

I watched her order a popcorn, soda, and a box of candy. Holding all three was awkward; she had the drink in one hand, the popcorn in another, and the candy gripped in the crook of her elbow. I had pegged her as a shy loner, the type who would go to coffee shops and movies by herself, but then she said something to the cashier that made him laugh out loud, and I had to rethink my assumptions, which was rare.

She moved off to an area near the concession line where there were straws, napkins, and self-serve butter, and I watched her, trying to figure out her deal, while the cashier got my Coke. She had finished up by the time I had my soda, and she stepped toward the ticket taker just in front of me, attempting to get the ticket out of her pocket with all the snacks in her arms. I was so busy watching her struggle that I didn't see the ripped piece of carpeting in front of me. I tripped and crashed into her from behind. Her popcorn went flying and her box of Sno-Caps hit the floor and somersaulted to a stop under the ticket taker's stool.

"Jesus, sorry," I said. Way to stay invisible. There weren't many people in the theater lobby, but they were all staring at us.

The girl burst out laughing. Not the reaction I'd been expecting.

"At least I held on to the drink!" she said.

"I'm sorry," I said. "Let me buy you another popcorn."

She smiled. "Thanks."

We returned to the concession stand, where the kid behind the counter offered to replace her popcorn for free. While he was scooping a new bag, she looked at me, and I looked down at the ground. She was wearing brown sandals and radioactive green polish on her toenails.

I was being weird; I could feel it. I didn't want to be weird anymore. I summoned the new Danny persona I was creating, one that was friendly and confident and cool, and lifted my chin.

"So, what movie are you seeing?" I asked.

"Oh, *The College Try*?" she said. "It looks pretty silly, but I just wanted to get out of the house and eat some popcorn. What about you?"

"Same," I said. My ticket was actually for some action movie sequel. I'm not sure why I lied, other than it being my first instinct in most situations. The cashier handed her the fresh bag of popcorn, and we walked back toward the ticket taker.

"We may be the only people in there," she said. "Anyway, thanks for the popcorn."

"I hope it's everything you wanted it to be," I said.

She nodded and walked ahead of me. There was a smattering of other people in the theater, and the trailers had started. She took a seat in the center of a row in the middle. I sat a couple of rows behind her and off to the left. I found myself watching her almost as much as the movie. She had a loud laugh, and I tried laughing whenever she did.

It felt kind of nice.

After the movie was over, I started walking back toward the Tates' and formulating a plan for getting out of that house on the regular so I wouldn't lose my mind. The same guard was posted at the Hidden Hills' gate. When I showed him the credit card with Danny's name on it as identification so he'd let me inside the closely guarded community, he frowned at me.

"You said you weren't Daniel Tate," he said.

I shrugged. "I lied."

It was getting dark by the time I arrived back at the house. At *home*, I reminded myself. Jessica's car was absent from its usual spot in the circular driveway. Lex's car was inside the open garage. No sign of Patrick's or Nicholas's.

I stepped into the house, glad for the blast of cold air against my hot cheeks.

"Hello?" Lex called from the direction of the kitchen. "Danny?"

"It's me," I said.

Lex ran into the foyer, her pink flats tapping against the marble, and gathered me up in her arms. I shrank, but she just held on to me harder.

"Oh, thank God," she said. "Are you okay?"

She pulled away and looked at my face, her eyes moving up and down my body, as if checking me for injuries.

"I'm fine," I said.

She raised her cell phone to her ear.

"He's here," she said. "Yeah . . . I know . . . Thanks."

She stuck the phone back in her pocket, hugged me again, and then punched me hard in the arm.

"Ow!" I said.

"Daniel Arthur Tate, don't you *ever* do that to us again!" she said, and burst into tears.

"I . . . I'm sorry," I said, bewildered by the emotional whiplash I'd just witnessed.

Lex swiped the tears from her cheeks. "You just can't leave here without telling anyone, okay? You just can't."

Then I got it. It was so obvious in retrospect. Of course she would freak out when her poor kidnapped brother disappeared for a few hours. It was something I would have realized if I'd spent even a second thinking about my decision to get the hell out of the house earlier that day, but I hadn't. I'd wanted a break, so I'd taken it. I wasn't used to my actions impacting other people.

"Where's your phone?" she said. "I called you about a hundred times."

I pulled the phone out of my back pocket. It wasn't even on. Had she called the cops? Was that who had been on the phone? The last thing I needed was the authorities on my case when I was still trying to solidify my relationship with the Tates.

This was bad, and it needed a big save. I bit my lower lip and conjured up tears in my eyes. "I'm sorry, Lex. I didn't mean to scare you. Oh shit, I'm so sorry!"

"Danny—"

"I think I just got overwhelmed," I said, aiming for a rushing stream of words that would disorient and disarm. "I'm not used to all of this, and all of a sudden I couldn't breathe, and then the next thing I knew I was walking down the street . . ."

She was just staring at me. I increased the tears and started to breathe more heavily, like I was struggling for air.

"I-I looked up and I didn't know where I was," I said. "I was so scared, and confused, and I . . . I . . ."

She sighed and closed for eyes for a moment, like she was steeling herself for something, and then she gave me a hug. "It's okay, Danny. It's all going to be okay. We were just so worried, you know? Patrick and Nicholas have been driving around the neighborhood for an hour. I was about to call the police."

The tension between my shoulders eased. She hadn't called the cops yet. "I won't let it happen again. I promise."

"Damn right you won't," she said with a gentle smile, "because I'm not letting you out of my sight."

Great.

"You hungry?" she asked. "I can make you a sandwich."

I wasn't hungry, but I nodded anyway. Lex liked to take care of me.

As I sat at the kitchen island while Lex made me another peanut butter and jelly sandwich, I thought for a moment about Danny Tate. The real one. A boy who left this house and never came back. It might sound weird, but since that first night when I saw his still-folded clothes in the dresser upstairs, I hadn't thought much about him outside of my own situation, as a person who existed independent of me. I wondered what had happened to him. He was almost certainly dead and probably had been since the day he went missing. If I were a normal person, I would have felt guilty for what I was doing, taking his identity, fooling his family. Ask anyone and they would tell you I was a monster.

But when Lex smiled at me as she slid the sandwich and a glass of milk toward me—like I was still the little boy she'd once known—I wondered why I should feel guilty for making her so happy.

"I'm telling you, he should be in therapy," Nicholas said in a low voice that wasn't quite a whisper. "At the *least*."

I froze in the hallway on my way down for breakfast the next morning. They were talking about me.

"We've discussed this. We don't think he's ready for that," Patrick replied. After Lex called him and told him I was home safe, he'd decided to spend the night. He'd spent most of the evening teaching me to play backgammon on a set inlaid with ivory and onyx in the basement's recreation room. Lex disappeared during that time, and I got the feeling he was watching me so she could take a break.

"Are you kidding?" Nicholas said. "You can't just keep him cooped up in the house. He'll lose it again. He needs—"

"He's *fine*," Lex said.

"He's not! How could he be, after what he's been through?" Nicholas said. "He needs help. What the hell is wrong with you two?"

There was nothing but silence for a moment. I waited, tense, to see how Patrick and Lex would respond. I'd been waiting for the Tates to send me to therapy ever since I'd arrived almost two weeks ago and had been dreading it just as long. I'd worked over my share of mental health professionals, but it was risky, and I had no idea what a real kidnapped child would act like. I was fucked up, but nowhere near the level the real Danny Tate, abducted and abused for years, would have been.

"When he's ready for help, we'll get it for him," Patrick said. "He's not ready to talk about what he went through yet."

"They told us not to push him," Lex added. "He just needs some time to settle in first. Readjust."

"You're both crazy," Nicholas said. "What does Mom say? And what about the cops? Why are you hiding him here?"

"We're not hiding him; we're giving him time to get his feet back under him," Patrick said.

"And Morales is all right with that?" Nicholas said, sounding dubious.

"I've taken care of it, okay?" Patrick said. "If it makes you feel better, I'll ask him again about therapy. After all, Danny knows better than we do what he's ready for and what he needs. Then will you lay off, Nicky?"

"Maybe."

A chair moved. I took several quick steps backward, so it would look like I was only just entering the hallway when Patrick stepped out of the kitchen.

"Hey, D!" he said. "How'd you sleep?"

"Fine," I said.

"Want to play some more backgammon after breakfast?" he asked.

"Sure."

Lex made me a bagel and poured me a glass of orange juice, and then I followed Patrick downstairs to the backgammon table. As he set the pieces, he asked me if I wanted to watch a baseball game with him that night and told me about the two teams that would be playing. He advised me on backgammon strategy and told me a story about a disastrous family vacation where the car my dad had rented caught on fire, and by the time we'd played a few games, I'd forgotten all about the conversation upstairs.

It didn't take much longer for Nicholas to come home one day and say something else I'd been waiting for.

"Everyone's asking me when Danny's coming back to school," he said.

"Danny's not ready for that yet," Lex said immediately.

She'd been true to her word since my little walkabout the week before: She'd barely let me out of her sight except to bathe and sleep, and I was only guessing about the second one. I'd decided on the walk home from the movie theater that Danny needed to go back to school, where I could escape Lex's constant surveillance and catch my breath. I didn't want to live inside the walls of this house forever. It was a big house, but it felt smaller every day, and if I was going to be Danny Tate, I needed to *be Danny Tate*. Start living a real life again.

"Actually," I said, "I think I am."

Nicholas stared at me. "Really?"

"Yeah," I said. I'd been planting seeds that week, asking Nicholas questions about school and making sure Lex saw me reading books on history and science I'd found on a bookshelf in Robert's library. I'd spent late night hours looking at the website for Calabasas High and the Facebook pages of my future classmates to prepare. For a while, I knew, I would be an object of intense curiosity, which would be hard. But it would pass, and then I'd be able to disappear into the press of bodies and noise just the way I always had. "I should be getting back to normal things, don't you think?"

"Danny, honey, are you sure?" Lex said. "You've only just gotten home. There's no need to rush this."

"I don't even know if they'd let you come back," Nicholas said. "You've been out of school for a long time."

"I know," I said. "I'm really far behind, and most things won't make sense to me, but I just want to *be* there. I need to start acting like a regular person again or I'm going to go crazy."

"I don't know . . . ," Lex said.

I could see she wasn't moved, so I reached for her hand. "I want to get on with my life, and . . . I want you to get on with yours, too. You shouldn't have to spend all day here keeping an eye on me. We've both missed enough already."

She frowned at me, but I could see her starting to waver.

"Please?" I said. "I need this."

She sighed. I had her. "I'll talk to Patrick about it."

Patrick was harder to convince than Lex had been. When he came over that night, I cornered him alone in the kitchen after dinner to talk about it. Lex had already tried and gotten nowhere, but I was determined. He was a stone wall of prevarication and denial. All of my talk of being ready to reenter society and longing for normality had no effect on him the way it had on her.

"Danny, no," he said. "I just don't think it's a good idea. Not yet."

I took a hard look at him. He was clever and ambitious, working long hours for a prestigious firm in L.A. He'd been spending a lot of time with the family since I'd arrived, but that didn't seem to be the norm. He was barely on speaking terms with his mother and didn't seem particularly close with Nicholas or Mia, either. Sentimentality worked with Lex, but it wasn't the right tack to take with Patrick. He'd require a different strategy.

I took a step closer to him and lowered my voice. "Please, Patrick. I have to get out of this house."

He looked up at me, and I felt a little rush down my spine. This was going to work.

"I'm so happy to be home—you can't even imagine how happy—but being cooped up here all day?" I continued. "It's starting to make this place feel like just another prison, and I can't handle that."

His expression shifted, softening ever so slightly.

"That's why I ran off the other day," I said. "I feel too isolated here. Too trapped. Please help me."

And that's how I got Patrick.

"He wants to go back to school," I heard Lex say. Her voice drifted down the stairs from the door to Jessica's room to where I stood in the shadows on the second floor landing.

"So?"

"So I need you to go enroll him," Lex said. "I'm not *actually* his parent, you know."

There was nothing but silence for a long moment. Then the door slammed closed.

A week and a half later, I started school at Calabasas High. I'd been surprised to learn that Nicholas went to a public school, but then this wasn't your typical public school. If my own research and the fact that Nicholas went there hadn't clued me in to that, the percentage of luxury cars in the parking lot would have.

But what *really* shocked me? Jessica was the one who was taking me to enroll.

I'd come downstairs that morning expecting to find Lex, full of worried looks and questions about whether I really wanted to do this, ready to take me to Calabasas High School. What I found was exactly that . . . plus Jessica in full makeup and hair and a fine silk blouse, the rich white lady's equivalent of armor. She even looked sober.

While Lex, Mia, and I ate breakfast, Jessica turned to me with a weak smile and said, "How did you sleep?"

I swallowed a dry mouthful of toast. "Fine, thanks."

"Are you nervous about today?"

"A little," I said.

"You know, you don't have to go," Lex said. "We could put it off another week or call it off entirely if you're not comfortable—"

"I'll be okay," I said.

"He's fine, Alexis. Nerves are normal." Jessica turned to me. "I'm sure it will go well."

Lex's lips thinned, and she turned back to her breakfast. Jessica sipped her coffee. It was one of the longest conversations we'd ever had.

Mia leaned across the table and handed me a penny.

"I found it on the playground yesterday," she said. "It's for good luck on your first day."

Eleanor's mom came to take Mia to school, and Lex called upstairs for Nicholas. When he came down, all four of us left for Calabasas High. I had quite the entourage, walking into the front office of the school with Lex and Jessica on either side of me and Nicholas trailing behind. I was pretty sure he'd been instructed to stay with me, to make sure I was okay and to call Lex if I got in over my head. My own personal, if somewhat reluctant, guard dog. And Lex, no doubt, was there to keep an eye on Jessica.

The office secretaries looked up when a bell chimed above Jessica's head as we entered. I could tell from their wide eyes that they knew exactly who we were.

"Good morning," Jessica said. "I'm Jessica Calvin Tate. I believe my daughter spoke with one of you on the phone about my son?"

I looked at Jessica in surprise. She was different. Straight backed and clear eyed, speaking in a steady voice above her customary murmur. Her armor was surprisingly effective.

"Oh, uh, yes," said one of the secretaries. She was pear-shaped and overdressed, a housewife who'd had to get her first job after losing her husband, and she didn't quite meet Lex's gaze. She turned to the other woman, who was sitting behind a desk and staring openly at me. "Could you get Dr. Singh, please?"

The bell chimed as a kid walked into the office. "Mrs. Day, I have a note from my mom—" He stopped when he looked up and saw me. "You know what—I'll come back."

He hastily retreated from the office, and Nicholas, who was slumped in a chair against the back wall, snorted under his breath. I was suddenly worried. It had been weeks since the photographers at the airport, and I'd just assumed interest in Danny Tate had ebbed, but maybe the protected enclave of Hidden Hills had kept me from realizing how big a deal this all was.

I took a breath and swallowed down my nerves. I could handle a little scrutiny. First you're an oddity and then you're furniture. Teenagers are too self-absorbed to care about another person for very long.

The secretary gave Jessica some paperwork she needed to sign, and while she was reading it over, a person I took to be Dr. Singh emerged from a hallway that branched off from the administrative area behind the counter. She was an Indian woman in her fifties or sixties who wore a sharp gray suit that matched her gray hair and sharp eyes. She looked at me without hesitating or staring when she introduced herself as the school's head guidance counselor.

"Mrs. Tate, Daniel, please follow me, and we'll get you squared away," she said.

She led Jessica and me back to her office while Lex and Nicholas waited in the outer office. As we walked, I put my hands in my pockets and felt Mia's lucky penny. I pinched it between my fingers.

Dr. Singh closed the door to her small office behind us, and we sat down across the large desk that dominated the room.

"So, Daniel," Dr. Singh said, knitting her fingers on top of a folder of paperwork, "this is a big step for you."

"I guess so," I said.

She just looked at me for a long moment before nodding and going on. "And, Mrs. Tate, it's good to meet you. I've spoken at length with your son and daughter about how best to help Daniel reintegrate to the school environment, and Principal Clemmons and I have discussed the situation with his teachers. What I want to be absolutely sure you understand, Daniel, is that we're here to support you. We know this might not be the easiest transition, so we just want to keep the lines of dialogue open, okay?"

I just wanted to get the hell out of that room. It was small and airless, and I could tell Singh wasn't stupid. The less time I spent with her, the better. "Yeah, okay."

She slid a piece of paper across the desk toward me. "This is the schedule we've drawn up for you. I've put you in ninth-grade classes for your academic subjects, just as a starting place. No one expects you to do any work yet. Just listen and focus on settling in. Nicholas isn't taking any electives this semester, so the only class of his I was able to put you in was the school's mandatory health class, but you do share a lunch period. If at any time you feel like you want to alter this schedule in any way, that's no problem. Nicholas will be walking with you to your classes until you get your bearings, and if it ever becomes too overwhelming, you're of course welcome to call your mother"—Dr. Singh looked up at Jessica—"or your sister to come and pick you up. There's no need to jump straight into the deep end."

"I think I'll be okay," I said.

"That's a great attitude," Dr. Singh said. "I'd also like you to come meet with me regularly so I can see how you're getting on. For the next few weeks, I'd like you to come here instead of going to your homeroom class. After that, if things are going well, we can meet perhaps just once a week."

"No," I said. I couldn't spend that kind of time with Singh.

She'd be too hard to play, I could tell. If I acted too normal, she'd get suspicious, but if I played my traumatized victim routine, she'd make the Tates put me into therapy or something else that would get me caught. I had to stay away from her. I turned to Jessica. "Please. I just want to be treated normally."

"Daniel—"

"Doctor," Jessica interrupted, "I support my son's decision. We've discussed this step extensively at home, and it's very important to Danny that he returns to a regular routine. No special treatment that will single him out."

"I really can't recommend that, Mrs. Tate," Singh said. "These are special circumstances, and Daniel will need—"

Jessica didn't blink. "I'm afraid I have to insist."

I stared. Who knew this steely woman existed inside Jessica's dissolute shell?

Dr. Singh opened her mouth to argue, but Jessica stared her down, and, with obvious effort, the doctor nodded instead. "Okay, we can see how things go. We'll adjust if it becomes necessary. And, Daniel, I want you to know you can always feel free to come and speak to me if you want. Understood?"

"Understood," I said.

The paperwork was done, and we left the office. Lex gave me a tight, nervy hug and asked if I was sure I wanted to do this.

"We can just go home," she said. "Cane is supposed to propose to Brooke today."

I smiled. "I'm okay. Really."

She sighed. "Okay, then. Call me if you change your mind. I'll come right back and get you."

She fussed over me. Straightened the collar of my shirt and smoothed my hair. I flinched, and she pulled back.

Jessica just stood there.

"Thanks," I said. And then, because Lex looked so anxious, I added, "I'll be fine." I immediately wondered why I felt the need to comfort her.

"Mom?" Lex said. "Is there anything you want to say to Danny?"

Jessica looked up at me, and already the confident creature I'd seen in the office was fading.

"Good luck," she said softly. "We should go, Alexis."

Lex squeezed my hand one last time, and the two of them left, disappearing into the flare of sunlight through the front door of the building.

My first class was English. Nicholas walked me to the other side of the school, and I wondered what Lex had said to him to make him agree to this guard dog duty. He looked like he'd rather be anywhere else.

We arrived a few minutes before the bell, and Nicholas introduced me to the teacher, Mr. Vaughn. He was one of those young guys you could tell was dying to be the Cool Teacher, his tweed jacket with the leather elbow patches tossed over his desk chair and his long hair almost brushing his collar. He'd rolled up his shirtsleeves just enough to show the edge of a tattoo on his forearm so his students would see he was hip, and he probably genuinely believed he could change their lives through the power of Shakespeare.

He shook my hand and showed me to an empty desk in the back row of the classroom. Nicholas told me he'd be back to walk me to my next class and disappeared. I sat down at the desk, and Mr. Vaughn perched on the edge of it.

"I don't want you to worry, Danny," he said. "You do prefer 'Danny,' right?"

"Yeah."

"It's all going to be cool, okay?" he said. "You just hang back here and watch for a while, and we'll ease you back in. If you get overwhelmed and need to leave, that's cool too."

"Cool," I said. What an idiot.

The bell rang soon after, and kids started trickling in. I kept my eyes down on the copy of *Jane Eyre* that Mr. Vaughn had given me and felt each pair of eyes on me like an unwanted touch against my skin. Maybe they knew who I was—had known Danny, even—or maybe I was just the new kid. Either way, I reminded myself, it would pass.

When the bell rang at the end of the period, I nonchalantly fled the stares in the room and the thumbs-up from Mr. Vaughn. As promised, Nicholas was already waiting for me in the hallway.

"You okay?" he asked.

I nodded and hitched my bag up higher on my shoulder.

A girl with a cloud of dark curls passed me. "Welcome home, Danny," she said. A massive dude in a letter jacket clapped a hand on my shoulder as he followed her and said, "Glad to have you back, man."

My smile felt more like a grimace. "Thanks." I turned to Nicholas. "Do you think *everyone* knows who I am?"

"Pretty much," he said. "The principal made an announcement yesterday and went to all your classes to warn everyone to act normal."

"Perfect." This may have been the stupidest idea I'd ever had. I could feel the eyes on me now like insects scuttling across my skin, and it was way worse than I had braced myself for. I just wanted to disappear, and I knew I could. Lex would swoop in and take me away from here in an instant if I called her, and she would never make me come back.

But.

But if I wanted to take advantage of this opportunity I'd stumbled into—to have a real life as Danny Tate, the kind I'd never been able to have as myself—I had to push through. I could do that. All I had to do was stop being me and start being him, the Danny I had pieced together from photo albums and family stories and my own imagination. The Danny who was cool and confident and rode just a little bit above everything.

"You okay?" Nicholas asked.

I took a breath, raised my chin, and put on my Danny mask. "Yeah, fine. Wherc to?"

I ignored the looks and the whispers I felt following me as Nicholas led me down the hall, and they didn't seem to itch as much. My next two classes were the same as the first. A quick talk with the teacher before class where they spoke to me in a low, comforting voice, like I was a rabbit who might spook. Watching quietly from a back seat, pretending not to notice the surreptitious glances and outright stares directed my way. A few words of encouragement from braver classmates and Nicholas waiting to shuffle me to the next classroom.

"Okay." Nicholas was looking down at my schedule when I came out of biology. Good thing no one actually expected me to do any work, because I hadn't understood a word of that class. "Next you've got beginners' art with Ms. Scofield."

Hey, something I might actually be able to do. I'd always liked to draw.

Nicholas silently led me toward the art class, which was on the opposite end of the school. He didn't look at me or speak to me as we walked, which made it pretty much the same as any other time I spent with Nicholas. I'd made no kind of connection with him yet, and it made him one of the most dangerous people to my goal of becoming Danny Tate for good.

"Sorry you have to lead me everywhere," I said. "But at least you're getting out of class early each period, right?"

He tried to smile but didn't quite succeed. "Yeah, I guess."

I looked down at my shoes and tried to project the air of vulnerability and guilt that worked so well with Lex. "I'm sorry, you know. For all the trouble I'm causing you."

He sighed and actually looked me in the eye for a moment. "It's no trouble. Don't apologize."

I lifted one corner of my mouth. "You're a really good big brother."

I'd always wanted a big brother.

He didn't know how to react to that. A half a dozen different expressions passed over his face before it settled into a smile. A small one, but it looked real.

"Thanks," he said softly. Then cleared his throat. "Here it is. I'll meet you back here before lunch."

He walked off quickly, and I watched him go. Maybe we were finally making progress.

Ms. Scofield treated me the same way the other teachers had. She showed me to an easel close to her desk and explained that the class was working on still life drawing. At the front of the room was a stool with a bowl of plastic fruit placed on it. The other easels, arranged in a half circle around the stool, had half-started drawings on them.

"Just do your best," she said.

I picked up a piece of charcoal from the easel and started sketching the outline of a peach. It was nice in the midst of this giant act to do something that actually felt natural. I used to have a notebook that I carried around with me and sketched in whenever I had a chance. Other than my baseball card, it was the one possession I gave a damn about. Someone swiped it from me at a group home in Edmonton.

With the drawing to focus on, it was easier to tune out the wide-eyed looks and muted whispers of the students entering the room. But when the girl from the movies came in, the part of my brain that never stopped monitoring what was going on around me noticed, and I looked up. She didn't see me, and I turned back at the bowl of fruit and tried to concentrate on my drawing. But I did note her last name when Ms. Scofield called the roll: Himura.

The class got to work, and Ms. Scofield weaved among the easels, offering critique and guidance. The girl from the movies sat opposite the semicircle from me, so every time I looked from my easel to the bowl, she was there behind it. A flash of dark and shine as she pushed her hair back from her neck. Her bright pink sweater like the sway of a matador's cape as she leaned over for a better view of the bowl. It was impossible for me not to keep glancing at her. But that was one of those normal things I never did that Danny could, right? Notice a girl?

She looked up and caught me watching her. She raised a couple of fingers in greeting before returning to her drawing.

She remembered me. People didn't usually do that. I'd spent years learning how to perfectly blend in to my surroundings and be forgotten, but she remembered.

After class Nicholas was waiting to escort me to lunch. California kids don't eat lunch inside a big cafeteria like we did when

I was in school in Canada. The weather is so perpetually perfect that students at Calabasas eat outside at tables spread across a grassy courtyard. Nicholas and I bought slices of pizza and sodas, and I followed him to a table that was obviously his regular spot. His shoulders seemed even tighter than usual, and I wondered if it was all the people looking at us. Looking at *me*.

"So," he said after a minute of silence. "How was class?"

"Good, I guess," I said. "How was yours?"

"Fine."

We went back to silently picking at our food. Maybe I wasn't making as much progress with him as I thought. Not for the first time, I wondered if it was *me* he was reacting to this way or if it was Danny. In all the home movies and pictures I'd looked at with Lex, Nicholas seemed to always stand a little apart from the rest of the family. Danny gravitated more toward his much older half siblings than the brother who was just a year older than he was. Maybe he and Nicholas had never gotten along. Maybe Nicholas was still dealing with his guilt over that.

I scanned the tables for the movie girl. Instead, my eye caught Dr. Singh standing under an awning, her arms crossed over her chest as she watched me. She smiled, nodding her head across the distance between us, and I smiled back to show her how fine I was and how much she didn't need to speak with me. She turned away to talk to a teacher standing near her. When I spotted the girl from the movies, she was sitting at a table by herself near the east wing of the school. I wondered where her friends were, if she had any. She was reading a book and picking French fries off the tray in front of her, managing not to look lonely even though she was alone. A pretty impressive trick it had taken me years to master.

A movement in my peripheral vision caught my attention, and I turned. A giant blond kid with a smile as wide as his broad shoulders was sneaking up on Nicholas from behind. When our eyes met, he grinned and held a finger to his lips. Nicholas took a swig from his soda bottle as the other boy jumped forward, jamming his fingers into Nicholas's ribs. He cackled as Nicholas went into a full body spasm.

"You asshole!" Nicholas said, slapping his hands away.

"Sorry!" the other boy said with no sincerity whatsoever. He sat down beside Nicholas and laid his fingers against his neck, drawing him in for a brief kiss on the lips. "I couldn't resist. It's your fault for being so ticklish."

"I nearly choked to death," Nicholas said, and I couldn't tell if he was amused or annoyed. "At least wait until I'm not drinking next time, you dick."

"Hey, you must be Danny," the other boy said, unfazed. He held out a hand to me. "I'm Asher."

"My boyfriend," Nicholas added.

Keen observer of human nature that I am, I'd gathered that much. I shook Asher's hand reluctantly, half-afraid he'd crush mine. "Nice to meet you."

"Nice to meet you, too," he said. "Nicky won't introduce me to any of his family. He's ashamed of me."

"It's not *you* I'm ashamed of," Nicholas said.

"Nice talk in front of your brother," Asher said, kneading Nicholas's tight shoulder with one hand. They were an odd pair. Nicholas was dark and thin, with delicate features that were dominated by his black-rimmed glasses. A complicated sort of handsome that matched his personality. He was the negative image of Asher, who was light and tan and built like a truck with a quick, ready smile.

Nicholas glanced at me. "No offense, Danny. But I don't always get along with the family."

Asher said, "Well, just a few months now and—" Nicholas shot him a look. "Uh, I mean, how's your first day back been, Danny?"

Well. That was interesting. I filed it away for later.

"It's been okay," I said.

"Must be pretty intense," Asher continued. "Especially since you don't remember anything, right?"

Nicholas stood abruptly. "I'm going to get an ice cream. Anyone want anything?"

Asher and I both shook our heads, and Nicholas walked back toward the building.

"Don't mind him," Asher said when he was gone. "He's been moodier than usual lately. I don't think he's figured out how to deal with all of this yet, but he's really happy you're home."

"He hides it pretty well," I said.

"No kidding," Asher said. "But, honestly, he cried like a baby when you were found. You know Nicky. The more that's going on, the quieter and snippier he gets."

"Then he must be *overjoyed* that I'm back."

Asher laughed. "It's a compliment, trust me." He glanced around us and said, "Dude, *everyone* is staring at you. How weird is that?"

I rubbed a hand across my forehead. "Pretty weird."

"Do you want them to stop?" he asked.

"That would be great, but—"

Asher stood up. He was well over six feet tall and almost half as wide. So when he bellowed, "Mind your own fucking business!" people took notice. All the heads that had been swiveled in our direction snapped back around instantly.

It was effective, if less subtle than I might have hoped.

"Um, thanks," I said.

He smiled. "You bet."

Lex was all over me when I got home. She ushered me into the kitchen where, to my surprise, Patrick was waiting, drinking a cup of coffee.

"So how did it go?" she asked. "Was it overwhelming? I knew it was too soon for this."

"Let him get a word out, Lexi," Patrick said.

"It was fine," I said. Patrick moved his briefcase off the stool beside him and I sat down. Lex started to clean. "I mostly just sat there and listened."

"How did people treat you?" she asked.

"A lot of stares, but no one really—"

"They were staring at you?" She threw the decorative dish towel she was trying to use to wipe down the kitchen counter into the sink. "You're not going back."

"It's okay," I said. "It'll be okay."

But Lex was shaking her head. "No. No. I don't like this."

"Lex—" Patrick started.

"No, Patrick! It's too much! I can't do this!"

Patrick stood and caught her hands as she tried to bat him away. "Look, he's fine! You're overreacting."

Lex got her hands free and shoved him. "Don't tell me how to react! You have no idea—"

"Lex!"

Her mouth snapped closed, and then, to my astonishment, she started to cry. Granted, Lex cried at almost everything, but this seemed particularly irrational. Did she really feel so protective of me now that the mere mention of some teenagers looking at me could unravel her like this?

She crumpled against Patrick's chest, hiding her face there, and he turned to me as he put his arms around her. "Give us a minute, would you?"

Gladly. I vacated the room, and a half an hour later Patrick came to find me. I was with Mia at her art table in the rec room, sketching a picture of an elephant for her in purple crayon while she colored in a world map for a school assignment.

"Can you give him really big ears?" Mia asked. "Like Dumbo, but even bigger?"

"You bet," I said, tracing the outline of a giant ear. From the corner of my eye, I saw Patrick enter. When I looked up, he beckoned to me. "I'll be right back."

"Hey," Patrick said in a low voice. "I just wanted to make sure you're all right after what just happened upstairs."

"I'm fine," I said. "Is Lex okay?"

He nodded. "Yeah, yeah, she's just . . . It's hard for her, you know. She wishes she could shield you from everything, and this is an emotional time for everyone. Mostly she's just embarrassed that she melted down like that."

"She doesn't need to be," I said. It was sweet, really. A little unhinged, but sweet.

"Well, she's gone up to her room to get some rest," he said. "She probably won't be back down tonight, so I'm going to stay over. She'll be good as new tomorrow."

I nodded. It was only five in the afternoon, but spending most of the day in one's bedroom must have seemed normal to Lex, given the fact that her mother practically lived in hers. Patrick squeezed my shoulder on his way out, and I returned to Mia and the elephant.

When I next saw Lex, the following morning at breakfast, she was back to her old self. Smiling and a little overbearing and pretending the previous day hadn't even happened.

"Scrambled eggs?" she asked when I walked into the kitchen.

"Sure," I said, and she turned back to the pan she was already stirring. The truth was I didn't care much for breakfast—my stomach didn't usually wake up until several hours after the rest of me did—but if I didn't eat something, she would fuss. And, well, it was nice to be taken care of.

On instinct I hugged her, wrapping my arms around her waist from behind. She froze. She'd hugged me several times, but this was the first time I'd ever hugged her. I didn't even know why I'd done it and was about to pull away when her hand came to rest over my arm.

"Thanks," I said. I let her go, pulling my arms back, her hand lingering on my skin as I did.

She cleared her throat. "You're welcome," she said without turning around.

I sat down at the breakfast table feeling bewildered with myself and trying to stamp out the warm, queasy sensation deep in the pit of my stomach.

Nicholas's phone rang as he was driving us to school. The car's touchscreen read "Asher." Nicholas hit the button that hung up the phone.

"What?" he said when he saw me looking at him. "I'm going to see him in like an hour."

The phone immediately began to ring again. Asher. Nicholas frowned and pressed a different button.

"Hey, don't hang up on me." Asher's voice crackled through the car. "This is important."

"What is it?" Nicholas asked.

"I just got a text from Vanessa Reyes, you know, the cheerleader who's been going out with Ben Peznick for a hot minute so now she thinks she's queen of the social universe?"

"Okay?" Nicholas said.

"There's—am I on speaker?" Asher asked.

"Yeah."

"Well take me off, would you?"

Nicholas grabbed his cell phone out of the cup holder in the center console, pressed a few buttons, and lifted it to his ear. "Okay, so? . . . Shit. Was there— . . . Okay. Okay, see you in a little bit."

"What is it?" I asked as Nicholas hung up the phone. It had to be about me.

"Someone took a video of you yesterday during lunch and put it on YouTube," he said. "Apparently it's spreading everywhere and people are talking. You may get some extra stares today."

Great.

"I can take you home if you want," he said.

I shook my head. So the whole school would know who I was now. That wasn't so different from yesterday, when only *most* of them had known.

"It's okay," I said.

"You sure?"

I nodded.

What neither of us had anticipated was the half a dozen news vans parked outside the school.

"Jesus Christ," Nicholas said, pulling off the road to idle on the shoulder across the street so we could survey the scene.

"What are they doing here?" I asked. I didn't have to fake the wild edge to my voice. I was already counting the number of people who would be able to recognize a photo or video of me, who could testify that I sure as shit wasn't some California kid named Daniel Tate. It wasn't many, but I could see this life slipping away from me before my eyes, could feel the cold bite of the handcuffs around my wrists.

Nicholas shrugged. "We were getting a lot of calls from the press, interview requests and stuff. It started with this stupid article that came out last month, but then it went crazy when you came back. Lex finally canceled the landline at the house, but if they've gotten wind you're back at school because of that YouTube thing . . ."

"Dammit," I said. "Why didn't Lex or Patrick tell me this was going on?"

"They were trying to protect you."

"Well that's just great," I said. "*Now* what?"

"I should take you home. That's what Lex would want."

I wanted to say yes. I wanted him to take me back to Hidden Hills, where I'd be invisible and safe, wrapped up in its guarded gates.

But then that would be my life. Locked in that house. Like the closet in the bedroom I'd grown up in, where I'd spent so many hours hiding in the dark, hands jammed over my ears, trying to escape whatever was going on outside. I couldn't do that again. I wouldn't.

"No," I said. "I'm going in."

Getting inside wasn't a problem. There was a separate parking lot and entrance for students that was well away from the main entrance where the reporters were camped out. Nicholas and I waited in the car until Asher came out to meet us, and I walked into the school flanked by Asher's bulk and Nicholas's lethal glare. Heads turned, whispers were exchanged behind hands, but no one approached. The stares still made me itch, but at least the expression in many of the eyes was now one of sympathy instead of naked curiosity. In the movies, people always say they don't want to be pitied when something bad happens to them, but I'm here to tell you that's bullshit. Pity can be very nice. It feels a lot like concern or even affection. I could live with pity.

But it didn't last. When first period began, Principal Clemmons came on over the loudspeaker to address what the whole school was already buzzing about.

"One of our students has had their privacy breached in an inexcusable fashion," he said. "Until further notice all students will turn over their cell phones and other devices to their first-period teacher to be collected again after the final bell. CHS is a place for learning, not the distractions of texting and social media."

Mr. Vaughn had a box ready to go. He walked up and down the rows of seats, collecting phones and tablets. I stared down at my desk. I could feel people looking at me, knowing this was because of me, resenting me for it. The silent indignation became audible grumbles when I tried to hand Vaughn my phone and he told me to keep it.

"Cool it, guys," Vaughn said. "Let's talk *Jane Eyre.*"

Reporters showed up every day for the rest of the week. A couple even tried to get inside. But the school stepped up security, and they lost interest. None of them got my picture and the original video of me put up on YouTube was distant and blurry, so I thought I was safe.

Finding the press camped outside of Calabasas High had been a harsh but necessary wake-up call. I'd gotten too comfortable. Whatever Patrick was doing to keep me from having to go and tell my stories to the cops wouldn't last forever, and I needed to be ready. I started to go over the story in my head whenever I had a quiet moment, embellishing and fine-tuning it based on what I was learning, trying to prepare myself.

It was ~~sunny~~ overcast the day it happened. I was walking beside my bike, because the chain had come off and I didn't know how to fix it. I was taking it home to my ~~father~~ big brother because he would know. ~~Dad~~ Patrick knew everything.

A white van turned the corner and pulled up beside me. I was too naive to be scared. The door slid open and hands emerged from the darkness. Ten seconds and I was gone, with no one having seen a thing. A kidnapping can happen that quickly and that invisibly, even on a ~~sunny~~ cloudy street in a ~~safe~~ gated neighborhood.

Hopefully, I would be ready.

On Tuesday someone came to the door of my art class with a note for me. Everyone stared at me while I read it. It was from Nicholas; he was going to be late to lunch. Luckily, I'd been living on the streets on my own for years, so I was pretty confident in my ability to make it to the cafeteria without his assistance. I was less sure, though, of what I'd do when I got there.

After class I headed toward the cafeteria and spotted Dr. Singh at the other end of the hallway, headed right for me.

"Danny," she said with a nod as she passed me. I was relieved that she hadn't wanted to talk to me, but then I turned and watched her enter Ms. Scofield's classroom.

She was checking up on me.

Dammit.

People were not forgetting about me as quickly as I'd thought they would. I guess I should have said good-bye to that naive hope when I got everyone's phones confiscated for the foreseeable future. Now Singh was asking my teachers about me, and everywhere I went the looks and whispers and abruptly halted conversations followed. I was not blending in, and that was the one thing I'd always been able to do, the one ability I'd depended on more than any other.

I bought a sandwich *and* a piece of pizza because dammit I could and hurried outside. The table Nicholas and I usually sat at was empty; I had hoped Asher would be there already. I noticed the movie girl at her usual table, eating alone once more. I wondered again how in the hell she managed to look like she didn't care—if it was for real or just a front so convincing even I couldn't see through it. I could feel eyes lingering on me already and imagined how much worse it would get if I sat at my usual table eating by myself, and suddenly I was bombarded with memories of all the meals I'd ever eaten alone, sitting on the floor with a microwave dinner watching *Frosty the Snowman* as a kid or scarfing a package of chips and a candy bar on a bus stop bench. I kept walking past the empty table, out of the courtyard, and around the side of one of the buildings. I sat down with my back against the bricks and looked out over the empty athletic fields.

I instantly felt better. And worse at the same time. The whole point of being Danny Tate was the chance for a new life, a *real* one, not just a repeat of my shitty old one.

Something had to change.

The next day I told Nicholas I didn't need him to escort me to my classes anymore. I could tell he hated it, and it was only drawing more attention to me. He agreed.

I beat him and Asher to lunch again, and this time I walked up to the table where the movie girl was sitting alone. I'd been thinking about this all morning. This was how I was going to change things.

"Mind if I sit?" I asked when she looked up from her book. I was new Danny. Cool, collected, above it.

"Oh sure, if you can find some space," she said, gesturing to the empty table. "I'm Ren."

"Danny."

"Yeah," she said with a half smile. "I'd picked up on that."

"Right."

We were silent for a long time. Maybe this was a terrible mistake.

"So, if you don't mind my asking," she finally said, "why are you sitting with me?"

It was a good question. This was how I was going to change things, but why had I picked her? She always sat alone, which made her a low risk target, and I'd talked to her once before, but it was more than that. Most people I could figure out with one look, but she was hard to read. She was either an actor like me, or she was something else entirely that I didn't understand. She was interesting to me.

I lifted one shoulder in a weak shrug. "My brother's not here yet. I thought we could keep each other company."

She smiled, but I couldn't tell if it was from gratitude or amusement or embarrassment.

"Okay," she said, folding down the page in her book and setting it aside. "How do you like Scofield's class?"

"It's okay," I said. "You?"

"I hate it. I'm hopeless at drawing," she said. "I never would have signed up, but it was one of the only classes with any space left when I transferred."

"When was that?" I asked.

"Last month," she said. "Hence my wild popularity. I probably could have scored a seat at one of the lower-tier tables by now, but I'd rather let the people come to me."

"How's that working out so far?"

"Not bad. I mean, I *did* just reel in the school's biggest celebrity." I grimaced, and she smiled. "Sorry, maybe that wasn't funny."

"It's okay," I said. "It was kind of funny."

She leaned toward me. "Seriously, how surreal is your life right now?"

There was warmth and sympathy in the question but not the least bit of hesitation. I'd picked well; she might be the one person at Calabasas who didn't have any previous connection to Danny and didn't seem fazed by my notoriety.

But, at the same time, she was completely focused on me. I had the sudden strange feeling that she was seeing *me* and not the cloud of Danny Tate around me. Her gaze was so direct that the feel of her felty brown eyes on mine was almost disconcerting.

"I . . . uh." I cleared my throat. "It's pretty surreal. I'm like this *thing* now—"

"Instead of a real person?"

I blinked. "Yeah."

She saw my surprise and explained, "The way people talk about you. It's like you're a character on TV or something to them. It's freaky."

"What do they say about me?" I asked.

She shook her head. "You don't want to know that."

"Actually, I kind of do," I said. It had become clear to me since I'd gotten here just how many of these kids had known Danny. This might not be the tiny community I came from where everyone went to school together their entire lives, but it was almost as insular. If they weren't buying my act, I needed to know it.

"Well, okay, but it's not very nice," she said. I nodded at her to continue. "The general conversation is that you were kidnapped as a little kid and, like, brainwashed and sold into slavery or something until you staged a daring, Jason Bourne–esque escape. And now you're this delicate creature who might snap at any moment and either kill us all or turn feral and start living in a hut in the woods somewhere like the Unabomber. Just bullshit like that."

But no mention of me being an impostor. I had to believe that a girl who would compare me to the Unabomber ten seconds after meeting me wouldn't be too tactful to leave that part out if people were saying it.

"That's actually pretty accurate," I said. "Except for the hut in the woods part."

"Oh. Well." She made this face that was part horrified, part comical. "Shit."

I laughed, and it surprised me. I wasn't often surprised.

"I was ten when it happened," I said. I told myself I needed to test run this story on someone low risk as part of my effort to get ready for my police interview, but I think I just wanted to keep talking to her. Keep trying to home in on what made her tick. "It was right around this time of year, and I was out riding my bike. My mom told me not to because it looked like it was going to rain, but I did anyway."

The faintest lines of a frown started to form between her eyebrows.

"I was walking beside my bike, because the chain had come off, and I didn't know how to fix it. I was taking it home to my big brother, because he would know. I was worried that it would start raining before he could get the chain back on, and then my mom wouldn't let me ride over to my friend Andrew's house like I was supposed to." The lies tumbled from my lips, gaining life and detail as the story unfurled in my mind. Like a real memory. A couple of kids at the next table over were looking now. But instead of making me shrink, their gazes sent a strange shiver through me. It wasn't me they were looking at, I realized. It was Danny Tate. They could stare all they wanted, and as long as I was him on the outside, I would be safe and invisible on the inside.

"I was jogging up this steep hill near my house, and it took everything I had just to keep my legs moving. I guess that's why

I didn't notice the van pulling up beside me," I continued. "Plus, what little kid around here worries about strange vans?"

Ren had noticed the eavesdropping table too.

"This is a bad idea," she said.

But I couldn't stop the momentum of the story. The next table was openly listening now, and it gave me this feeling I couldn't identify but wanted more of.

"I vaguely remember the van stopping beside me and hearing the door slide open," I said. "And then there were arms around me, hauling me inside. I tried to scream but they covered my mouth. It was dark in the back of the van, so all I really knew was that there were three other men back there with me. I could only make out the shapes of them, not what they looked like. They spoke to each other in a language I didn't recognize. They barely even looked at me after they had me tied up and gagged. Like I wasn't even there."

The group gathering around me had started to draw attention, and my audience was growing. A dozen students, then twenty, and then twenty-five hung on my every word as I spun the story of Danny Tate's abduction. The race to the border along with another boy who was taken the day after I was, the two of us smuggled into Canada in the hidden compartment of an eighteen-wheeler along with three other children. Ren's frown grew deeper and deeper, and I couldn't tell if it was because of the increasing darkness of the story or the growing crowd of listeners.

Then I realized what was happening.

All my life I'd tried to be invisible, and that gave the power to everyone else. To notice me stripped away my one protection. But they couldn't take anything from me if I was giving it away willingly. The power had shifted into my hands. *That's* what the crackle of electricity I felt along my spine was. The power to make them look and listen on my own terms.

For the first time in my life it felt good to have so many eyes on me. These kids weren't looking for ways to tear me down. Their eyes were full of sympathy and fascination, and that felt almost like admiration. Or even affection. Everyone leaned in, wanting to get closer to me. That's all they'd wanted since I'd arrived here, stealing glances and surreptitious pictures. To be close to me. I understood that now, and it made me feel invincible.

"What the hell?" The sound of Nicholas's voice was like cold water down my back. He pushed his way through the crowd to my side. "Danny, come on."

Nicholas grabbed my wrist and yanked me up from the table, hauling me back toward the school building. I still felt everyone watching me.

"You people are sick," I heard Asher say behind us. "Disperse!"

"What the hell are you doing?" Nicholas asked after he'd pulled me inside the building.

"I . . . they asked me what happened," I said. "I thought I should try to get to know some people, you know. Make friends."

"They're not friends, Danny, they're rubberneckers," he said. "They just want to gawk at the tragedy. That's all you are to them."

I could feel the rage and hurt radiating off him but didn't share it. What did it matter if they were only interested in my story? They wanted it, and I wanted to give it to them.

But I couldn't risk alienating Nicholas, not when I was already on such shaky ground with him. I scrubbed a hand through my hair, and when I spoke, I made sure that my voice came out sounding small and weak.

"I'm sorry," I said. "I wasn't thinking. I just wanted . . . I wanted them to like me and . . ."

He sighed, but it wasn't the soft sound the word implies. It was a hard one, like he was trying to expel all of his anger on that exhalation.

"It's okay. You didn't do anything wrong." He turned and looked out over the courtyard. "You know what, fuck this place. Let's get out of here."

Nicholas took me to a diner a few kilometers from the school, and we ordered burgers and milk shakes.

"Why did you want to go back to school so bad?" he asked. "You had a free pass to stay out of that place."

This was a prime bonding opportunity, and I was going to make the most of it by pulling out all my tricks. I shrugged and curled my shoulders in toward myself until I looked like Nicholas and tried to summon his sharp, cynical attitude. "It's better than staying home all day."

One corner of his mouth tugged up. "Lex driving you crazy?"

I smiled too. "A little."

"She means well, but—"

"But she's a pain in the ass sometimes, yeah," I said. "Anyway, no one expects me to do anything at school but show up, so it's not exactly taxing."

Nicholas snorted. "Like being a football player. Asher says as long as he puts in an appearance, no one cares what he does. That place is such a joke. It doesn't bother you though?" he asked. "Having everybody whisper and stare?"

"A little," I said, "but I've survived worse."

"Fuck," he said, dropping a French fry loaded with ketchup back to the plate. "Right. Sorry."

"It's okay," I said. "You don't have to be so careful around me, you know. I won't break. Is that why you've been avoiding me?"

"I haven't."

I gave him a look. "Nicky. Come on."

A flicker of . . . something . . . went through his expression. Was it doubt? If he did suspect I wasn't his brother, he was either biding his time until he could prove it or had convinced himself he was being paranoid. That must make him feel pretty guilty, the distrust in his gut when his brain and everyone around him was telling him Danny was back.

I could use that.

"It's hard for me to feel like I'm entirely home," I said, "because . . . I still miss you. Even though we're in the same house, it feels like we're still so far apart."

Nicholas looked down at the table and sighed long and slow. "Okay," he said. "Maybe I have been avoiding you a little. But it's probably just because I avoid the family in general these days."

"And?" I said, daring him to say he didn't believe in me after that.

"*And* . . . I don't always know how to act around you," he said. He folded his hands in front of him on the table. "It's weird. Things are different. *You're* different."

No shit.

I bit back my smile and folded my hands the same way he had. "You're different too."

"Well, I can't argue with that."

"Maybe we can just . . . get to know each other as the people we are now," I said.

He nodded, and this time when he looked at me, he actually *looked* at me. "Yeah. That sounds good."

"Good," I said. *Very* good. Now whenever Nicholas felt unsure about me, he would remember this conversation and feel so bad, he'd argue himself out of any doubts. "It's nice to be able to talk to you again."

His brow crinkled. "Yeah?"

"Yeah," I said. "I missed you so much."

He looked out the window suddenly, not because there was anything to look at out there, but because he didn't want to look at me. "Really?"

"Of course," I said. There was a softness around his mouth that made me think, crazy as it seemed, that he was on the verge of tears. He'd never seemed happy I was back, and I suddenly wanted that so badly. I wanted him to tell me he was happy to have me there. "You're not just my brother, Nicholas. I know we didn't always get along as kids, but deep down, you were my best friend."

His eyebrows twitched closer together, so briefly that most people wouldn't have noticed. My stomach dropped. He looked down at his watch and said, "We'd better go."

He slid out of the booth without looking at me and headed for the exit.

The next day at school an office assistant came to take me out of second period. It was the class I shared with Nicholas, and he and I exchanged a look as I followed the girl from Mrs. Whelan's health class. She took me to the front office and told me to have a seat.

"Dr. Singh will be with you in just a minute," she said.

Talking to Singh was the last thing I wanted to do, but I couldn't create a scene by arguing. It might look suspicious. Instead, I pulled the phone from my back pocket and dashed off a quick text to Lex.

"Put the phone away, please, Mr. Tate," the secretary said. "You shouldn't even have that."

I made a face but slipped the phone into my bag.

I waited there for at least ten minutes before Dr. Singh emerged from her office, still chatting with another student. She sent the girl on her way and waved me over.

"Come on back, Danny," she said.

I followed her back to her office, where she sat down behind the desk and gestured for me to sit in one of the chairs across from her. I did, and she studied me silently, waiting for me to speak first.

She'd be waiting a long time.

"So, it seems you left school early yesterday," she finally said. "I just wanted to check in with you and see how you're doing."

"I'm fine," I said.

"I'm told there was some kind of incident at lunch. Would you mind explaining what happened?" she asked.

"It was nothing," I said. "Someone asked me about the day I was taken, and a couple of kids started listening. My brother didn't like it."

"That doesn't sound like nothing," she said. "What did you tell those other students?"

"Does my mother know you're talking to me?" I asked. "She told me I wouldn't have to be questioned."

"I'm sorry if you feel like I'm interrogating you, Danny." Singh leaned back in her chair. Her sharp eyes belied her relaxed posture. The look she gave me cut straight through to my bones. "I'm just trying to make sure you're readjusting to school life. That's my job."

"I've got to get back to class," I said.

"I've already spoken to Mrs. Whelan," she said. "You've been excused from the whole period for the day."

My pulse picked up. I'd known from the moment I laid eyes on this woman that she wasn't as easy as my usual mark. And now I was stuck in this room with her, which seemed to be getting smaller with each passing second, for another half an hour.

"Do you think you could tell me what you were talking about with the other students during your lunch period yesterday?" she asked.

She was a psychologist; she would expect me to exhibit more signs of trauma than I usually bothered with. I looked back at the door to the office and then down at the ground, tucking my hands between my thighs and the seat of the chair.

"I'd like to call my sister," I said softly.

"Of course," Dr. Singh said, "but first, can we talk for a minute? We don't need to talk about anything you're not ready to. I just want to make sure you're adjusting to being back at school all right. How about you tell me how that's going?"

"It's okay," I said.

"How are your classes?"

"Fine." I bit my lip. "I like my art class."

"Are you getting along with the other students?"

"I guess," I said. "Most of them just ignore me."

"Is that why you told them that story at lunch yesterday?" she asked. "You didn't want them to ignore you anymore?"

"Danny?" A muffled voice spoke in the hallway. Someone said, "Excuse me!" in a sharp tone, and then the door to Dr. Singh's office was opening. Lex stood behind it like an avenging angel, beautiful and terrifying.

"What the hell are you doing?" she said to Dr. Singh.

"Ms. McConnell, come in," Dr. Singh said, rising from her chair. "I was just—"

"You're not supposed to be talking to my brother," Lex said. She pulled me up from my chair and away from Dr. Singh. Her hands were shaking. "He's been abused and traumatized and the last thing he needs is to be questioned about it by—"

"I'm sorry you're upset, Ms. McConnell," Dr. Singh said with perfect calmness, "but I'm just trying to do my job, which is to ensure that Danny is reintegrating into the school environment. I assure you, that's the only subject we were discussing."

"Our mother was very clear on this subject," Lex said. "Danny just wants to be treated normally—"

"And he skipped school yesterday," Singh said. "This is only what I'd do with any other student who'd done the same thing."

Lex's shoulders started to slump. She was ill suited to conflict under the best conditions, and now her righteous anger was wilting under Dr. Singh's patient onslaught of logic.

"I have to be allowed to do my job, Ms. McConnell," Dr. Singh continued. "Don't you agree?"

"Well, yes," Lex said, "but—"

"Please, Ms. McConnell." Dr. Singh stepped toward us, and although she was several inches shorter than Lex, she seemed to tower over her. "Have a seat, and we'll speak privately for a moment. Danny, how about you go wait in the outer office with Mrs. Day?"

I shot Lex a look, and she nodded. "I'll be there in a minute, Danny."

I wanted to protest, but I didn't know how without looking suspicious, and then Dr. Singh was closing the door on me and it was too late. What were they going to talk about? Mrs. Day was waiting for me at the end of the hallway, and I wondered how much she'd overheard. I started to walk toward her before I noticed the restroom across from Dr. Singh's office.

"I've got to pee," I said.

Mrs. Day frowned but nodded. I stood inside the restroom, door cracked, waiting. Less than a minute later I heard the *ding* that signaled someone entering the outer office, a person Mrs. Day would have to go deal with. I left the restroom, crossed the hall, and pressed my ear against the door of Dr. Singh's office. The odds of me getting caught were high, but I had to know what was being said in there.

". . . know this is hard to hear," Dr. Singh was saying in a low tone, "but I'm very concerned about Danny. He's not acting the way I would expect someone who's been through what he has to be acting. I cannot overstate how important I think it is that Danny be seeing someone—a mental health professional—regularly. Daily."

"I think he's doing pretty well, considering," Lex said.

"He's doing *extremely* well. That's what concerns me. I see signs of trauma, but nothing like what I'd expect from someone in his position," she said. "Either he's expending a tremendous amount of energy to repress his feelings, which will only cause him more problems down the line, or . . ."

The silence in the office was deafening.

"What are you trying to say?" Lex asked.

"I know it's not my place," Dr. Singh said, "but I feel I would be remiss if I didn't . . ."

"What?"

The counselor's voice dropped even further, until I could barely make out the words.

"Are you absolutely *sure* that boy is your brother?"

Fuck.

"Danny."

I jumped back from the door and found the secretary looking at me sternly. Stomach churning, I went to the outer office and took a seat, letting her watch me over her paperwork until Lex returned. Only the watery feeling in my legs kept me from running.

Are you sure that boy is your brother?

Was she?

For the first time, I really thought about prison, as a reality and not just an abstract threat. The thought of being locked up filled me with horror, but maybe it wouldn't be so bad. After all, it wasn't that different from a lot of the care homes I'd jumped through hoops to have the pleasure of staying in, and I'd always held my own against the delinquents and criminals who populated them. There had been entire years of my life where three square meals a day and a roof over my head, even if I was behind bars, would have been welcome. Some part of me had always suspected that's where I'd end up eventually, if I was lucky. So maybe being caught wouldn't be that bad.

Except being caught meant the Tates finding out I was a fake, and I was surprised to discover that that thought bothered me the most. I couldn't stop picturing it. Mia would cry. Patrick would punch me. Nicholas would hate me forever, and Lex would never recover. I didn't . . . I didn't want that for them. They didn't deserve it.

Lex emerged from the hallway. I stood, my pulse pounding hot in my head, waiting for her to look at me in horror or scream or something. But she didn't. She hardly looked at me at all, and maybe that was worse.

"Come on," she said to me. She'd only talked with Singh, but it looked like she'd been knocked around. Her face was pale and clammy and her hair was mussed. She struggled to get the strap of her purse back over her shoulder. "We're going."

I followed Lex out of the school and toward her car, scrutinizing her every movement for some clue of what she was thinking. She didn't say anything, just dug into her purse and popped a couple of mints into her mouth from the tin she always carried. We climbed into the car, where the air was as stifling as the silence. Lex let go of a big sigh and melted back into her seat, eyes closed, and stayed that way for a long time. I sat tensely beside her, waiting for her to do . . . something.

Then, with no warning, she sat up, cranked the AC, put on her sunglasses, and said, "What a bitch. Want some ice cream?"

Lex didn't say another word about what had happened. I had to assume that meant she hadn't taken Singh's concerns to heart. She took me for that ice cream, and we drove back to Hidden Hills with the windows down and the radio cranked up, arriving home in time to watch Sabine shoot her twin sister for poisoning her husband. Lex wasn't much of an actress; she wore every feeling right on her sleeve. If Dr. Singh had ignited doubts about me inside of her, I felt sure I would have seen it.

But when Patrick came over after work that night—which was unusual for him, since he usually spent weeknights in L.A.—she immediately said to him:

"Will you take a look at my car? It's making that weird knocking sound again."

"Sure," he said, and followed her out to the garage.

I hadn't noticed any knocking sound.

The back of my neck got hot. They were talking about me; they had to be. Had Lex fooled me? Was she telling Patrick right now that she wasn't sure I was Danny? I turned and saw that Nicholas had also watched them go. Our eyes met briefly, and he looked back down at his laptop. He hadn't asked me why I'd left school early. Either he didn't care or he'd heard from someone else.

Mia flung herself into the seat beside Nicholas and hung her head on his shoulder. "I'm *bored*. Will you play with me?"

"I've got to finish this paper," he said, carefully edging his shoulder out from under her cheek.

"I'll play with you," I said. I couldn't just sit there staring at the door to the garage, driving myself crazy wondering what was happening behind it. And I felt bad for the kid; she was so often overlooked by the rest of them.

Mia's eyes lit up. "Really?"

I smiled. It took only the smallest thing to make her happy. "Sure. Want to go swimming?"

"Yeah!" she said. "I'm going to go put on my suit!"

"Mia, Mom doesn't want you . . ." Nicholas sighed and let the sentence drift away as Mia bolted from the room. "Mom hates it when she swims in the brace. The hinges tear up the towels, and she tracks water everywhere."

"Well, Mom's not here," I said. Jessica's car was already gone when we left for school this morning, and she still hadn't come home.

It was cruel to let a kid grow up with a swimming pool in their backyard they weren't allowed to use, and if the cops were going to show up and haul me away from here any minute, I could think of worse things to do with my remaining time than swimming with Mia.

She changed into a ruffly purple swimsuit, and I put on the trunks that had been part of the haul Lex got for me when I first arrived. After glimpsing my bare chest in the mirror in Danny's bathroom, scarred and maybe a little too developed for a sixteen-year-old, I also pulled on a T-shirt.

Nicholas stopped me on my way out to the pool.

"You've got to keep a really close eye on her, okay?" he said.

"I will," I said.

"Seriously," he said. "She doesn't swim very well."

"Got it," I said. I didn't swim too well either, but the pool wasn't that deep.

Mia ran across the patio and leapt into the pool with a screech. She came up spluttering, and I immediately jumped in after her, catching her under the arms and making a motorboat sound as I pulled her to the shallower water, where she could stand on her toes. My eyes burned from hitting the water with them still open.

"You okay?" I asked.

She nodded and wrapped her wet arms around my neck. "Can we play Washing Machine?"

"We can if you teach me how."

Mia taught me Washing Machine and Sharks and Minnows and obliterated me in a half a dozen underwater handstand contests. She graciously promised she'd help me get better, for which I thanked her. I stayed within an arm's length of her, because whenever she struggled, her braced right leg lagging behind the left one, she reached out for me. She was trusting that I'd be there, and the idea of her reaching for help and not finding any made me sick to my stomach. Each time her little hands closed around me, I felt this warm, tight feeling in my throat that I didn't want to look at too closely.

I looked back toward the house. The light in the garage was still on, and, just like he had been for most of the past hour, Nicholas was still standing in a window, watching us.

It was starting to get dark by the time Mia's fingers got pruney enough for her to decide it was time to get out of the pool. I'd been covered in gooseflesh for a while but hadn't had the heart to bail on her.

I ran into Patrick at the foot of the stairs as I was headed up to my room to change. The light in the garage had gone out only a few minutes earlier.

"Hey, if that school counselor bothers you again," he said, "you call me, okay? What she did today was unacceptable."

"Okay," I said, instantly relieved. That's what they'd been talking about. How Singh had overstepped her bounds, not how I was a con artist posing as their brother.

"I don't think she'll cause problems again though," he added. He must have laid some lawyerly smack down already, or would be soon. "You have plans this weekend?"

I shook my head.

"Want to go to the Dodgers game with me? The firm has a box."

"Yeah, sure," I said. It seemed like a very brotherly thing, going to a baseball game together. I thought of Danny's room with his baseball posters and the signed ball in the plastic case. Danny loved baseball. I loved baseball. "That would be great."

"Don't tell Lex," Patrick said, leaning close to me, "but I was thinking I might also give you a driving lesson. What do you think?"

"Yeah," I said. Finally, something I wouldn't have to pretend about. I couldn't drive worth a damn. "Can we take the Jag?"

Patrick laughed. "Sure. But only because your dad won't be out for another year."

"Cool," I said. Being rich was *fun*.

"Okay, go change," Patrick said. "You must be freezing."

I remembered that I was. I headed up the stairs, but stopped on the landing when I heard raised voices to my left. My first thought was Jessica; she was the only Tate I'd ever heard yell. But the voices were coming from Lex's room.

". . . like some stupid child," Nicholas said as backed out of the room.

"Then grow the fuck up, Nicky!" Lex replied from inside.

"Bitch!" Nicholas turned to stalk away but froze when he saw me.

"And don't you—" Lex appeared in the doorway and stopped in her tracks. The scowl instantly disappeared from her expression, and her voice was soft and sweet when she said, "Hey, Danny. Are you hungry?"

Nicholas gave her a look that was part incredulity, part disgust, and then he brushed past me on his way to his own bedroom. The *click* of the lock was audible in the silent hallway.

The next day at lunch I sat with Ren again. We talked about art class and *A Life of Love*, Lex's favorite soap, which Ren also happened to be a fan of. Nicholas watched me from his table across the courtyard, and Dr. Singh watched me from a window. Neither tried to speak to me.

This is when the old me would have run.

The new me was starting to have too much to lose.

"Want to come over to my house later?" Ren asked when the bell rang at the end of our lunch period.

I blinked. "Why?"

I'd blurted the word out without thinking and was afraid she might be offended, but Ren just laughed.

"Sorry, did you have other plans?" she asked. Although the mockery was gentle, it was still mockery. Pretty ballsy when you're talking to a poor, delicate kidnapping victim. "Plus, I don't totally hate your company."

"I, uh . . ." I swallowed.

"It's cool. You don't have to if you don't want. Or I could make up a good reason if that helps? Like how I'm really terrible at art, and I'm afraid our stupid class is going to sink my GPA if I can't learn how to make a bowl of fruit vaguely resemble a bowl of fruit. Actually, that's not even made up. That's totally true."

Ren was not scary. Ren could not expose me. But she made me nervous anyway, in an odd way I couldn't explain.

When I didn't answer, she waved a hand. "You're obviously not into it. No worries."

"Yeah, okay," I said quickly. "I'll come."

This was the whole point of becoming Danny Tate, wasn't it? To have the friends and family and opportunities I could never have as myself? Surely that list was supposed to include a pretty girl.

When the final bell rang at the end of the day, Nicholas wasn't waiting for me at the doors to the student parking lot like usual. He'd barely spoken to me since the day before, but it was hard to believe he'd just leave me to find my own way home. If nothing else, he had to know Lex would kill him for it. He had history last period, so I checked with his teacher, who was packing up to leave when I poked my head into the classroom.

"He was called to the guidance office," she said. "Check there."

My stomach dropped. "Okay. Thanks."

I walked quickly toward the front office. Dr. Singh wasn't allowed to speak to me, so she was going to interview my relatives instead? She wouldn't dare say the same thing to Nicholas about my real identity that she'd said to Lex, would she? I walked faster. This was bad. I'd deeply pissed Nicholas off during that lunch at the diner when I'd said that stupid thing about him being my best friend, and he'd never been completely sure about me in the first place, so there was no telling what he might say to Singh.

I reached the front office just as Nicholas emerged with Dr. Singh. The woman nodded to me—"Danny"—and disappeared back inside the office.

"Ready?" Nicholas said as if nothing had happened.

"What were you talking to her for?" I asked.

"Nothing."

"It wasn't nothing," I said. I'd decided earlier that day that I was going to try harder with Nicholas, be extra nice to him and win him back to my side, but I couldn't stop the heat rising in my voice. "You've been there since the middle of last period. Did she ask about me?"

"Not everything's about you," he said. "Are you ready to go home?"

"I just want to know what you were doing in there." I knew I was losing it but I couldn't stop. "You know how upset Lex was—"

"Look, this isn't really any of your business," he said. "It has nothing to do with you."

"Just tell me what the fuck she said!" I burst.

For one stunned moment Nicholas just stared at me.

"No," he finally said, slowly. "I don't think I will. Now, let's go, okay?"

I took a deep breath. Shoved everything back down inside.

Acting out right now would only make things worse. I shook my head. "I don't need a ride."

"What? Don't be stupid."

"I'm going to a classmate's house," I said.

"Who, that girl you sat with at lunch?" he asked.

"Yeah." He was looking at me with such confusion that I added, "She needs some help with an assignment."

He laughed. "You're helping someone with homework? You just started school again. *You're* not even doing homework yet."

I didn't understand why he hated me so much. So Danny and Nicholas hadn't gotten along great as kids, but I was still his loving brother, miraculously returned to him. Shouldn't that have made up for any childhood issues he had with me?

Unless the real problem was that he suspected I wasn't his brother at all.

"It's an art assignment," I said. "I'm good at art. Besides, she's new here too."

Nicholas looked at me closely. "Danny, you're not *new* here."

I swallowed. "You know what I mean. Anyway, tell Lex I'll be home in a couple of hours." I started to walk toward the library, where Ren and I had arranged to meet.

"You haven't talked to her about this yet?" Nicholas called after me. "She's not going to like it—"

"Just tell her, okay?" I said as I turned the corner and Nicholas disappeared from view. I would start being extra nice to him tomorrow.

A few minutes later I was climbing into Ren's car. I surreptitiously scoped it out; any place where a person spent a lot of time could tell you a surprising amount about them if you knew how to look. Like Nicholas's BMW: It was gray and pristine and he always kept it cold. Ren's car was chaos. It was messy but not dirty, a blue Mercedes convertible from the '70s or '80s that had the right hood ornament to fit into the student parking lot but whose sharp, boxy lines refused to conform. It smelled of old leather and the cucumber hand lotion that lay on the passenger's seat along with some crumpled papers, a half-empty water bottle, a phone charger, a candy bar wrapper, and a tube of lip gloss. Ren scooped all of this up without apology and tossed it into the backseat with the other teenage detritus that littered the leather seats. Some aggressive, upbeat girl rock blared from the speaker when she turned the car on, and she turned the music down but not off as she drove us to her house in Calabasas. I filed every detail away to analyze later, because despite a couple of days of careful study, I still hadn't figured Ren out.

Her home was an ultramodern place of glass and steel that wasn't quite as big or grand as the Tate house, but that was grading it against a brutal curve. It still would have held a dozen copies of the house I grew up in. She parked her car in the driveway and led me in through a side door that connected to the kitchen. She grabbed a couple of sodas from the fridge and handed me one.

"When did you move here?" I asked.

"Six weeks ago," she said. "It's my aunt and uncle's place. My parents are working on this skyscraper in Dubai for the next year, so I'm staying here until they get back."

"You didn't want to go with them?" I asked.

She screwed up her face. "Hell no. I mean, I love my parents, but no way was I going to change my entire life to be with them. Transferring schools junior year is bad enough. My aunt and uncle are cool. They're not around a lot, and they basically let me do whatever I want."

"Hey, cuz!"

Ren and I both jumped and turned to look at the guy who had come into the kitchen behind us. He was maybe four or five years older than me and wearing a wrinkled shirt and battered flip-flops that went well with his shaggy hair and vacant expression. Naturally, he reeked of pot.

Ren sighed. "This is my cousin, Kai."

Kai nodded at me. "Hey."

"This is Danny," Ren said.

Kai looked at me blankly, and then his expression slowly—painfully slowly—shifted into realization.

"Oh," he said. "Shit."

Ren punched him in the arm. "God, Kai!"

"It's okay," I said. "That's the usual reaction."

"Cool," Kai said. "So, hey, how's your sister doing? She still hot?"

I blinked. Ren looked like she was considering punching him somewhere other than the arm.

"You know my sister?" I asked.

"Sexy Lexi? Hell yeah!" he said. "We were pretty tight in high school. Me and Patrick, too. He used to get me the best weed."

I wasn't sure how to respond to that. I didn't know what to say about Patrick procuring him drugs, and I definitely wasn't going to confirm that Lex was, indeed, *still hot*. So I just said: "Cool."

"Yeah, dude," Kai said. He opened the refrigerator and started to gather food in his arms: turkey and cheese slices, a gallon of orange juice, anything he could lay his hands on.

"You're not supposed to raid the big house fridge, *dude*," Ren said.

"Yeah, whatever," Kai said. "So Lex is good? I always worried about her. I tried to look out for her when I could, but she was—oh, but hey, don't worry! I never hooked up with her or anything. Not that I would have minded, because *damn* was she—"

"Jesus, Kai," Ren said. "That's his *sister*!"

Kai started to giggle. "Oh, right! Sorry! That's some seriously ironic shit." He opened the door to the pantry and added a box of cookies to the haul in his arms. "I gotta go."

He drifted out of the kitchen, and Ren shook her head after him.

"How tragic is that?" she said. She turned to me. "Want to go upstairs?"

"Sure," I said and followed her into the hallway.

"I know he's family and all," she said as we climbed to the second story, "but he's an idiot. Like his parents won't noticc the fridge is empty when they get home. I'm always telling him, just take a little at a time. It's all about plausible deniability!"

I smiled. She would make a decent scammer.

"He lives here?" I asked.

"*Technically*, he lives in the pool house," she said. "He's supposed to pay rent and buy his own groceries and everything, but as you can see, not so much. He pretty much just gets high and plays video games all day."

Most of the kids I had gone to school with in my past life were probably living similar existences, albeit in less grand locations. I probably would be too if things had been different. "Not a bad life," I said.

"Could be worse, I guess," she said as she opened the door to her bedroom.

I hadn't been in many girls' bedrooms. I was suddenly very aware of that fact as I stepped inside. I was interested in what other clues I could gather here about Ren, but I instantly saw that this room wouldn't be much help. Even if she hadn't told me earlier than this was her aunt and uncle's house, I would have been able to tell from a glance that this was actually a guest room. It had that sterile, unlived-in feeling that Danny's room had, and it was decorated in somber creams and navies while its occupant was currently wearing yellow and electric blue. But scattered over the top of this sedate and antiseptic base was evidence of the same Ren who drove that chaotic Mercedes. Colorful clothing thrown over the backs of chairs, books piled up on a dresser since there was no bookcase, the bottle of that green nail polish on the bedside table. Artifacts of a girl in motion. One who didn't much care what people thought. A confident girl who didn't mind showing her room to a near-stranger, even when it was kind of a mess. There was more evidence of Ren imprinted on this room that wasn't really hers than I'd ever leave on the room that wasn't really mine back in the Tate house.

She pushed the clothes off the back of the desk chair so I could sit there and then lowered herself cross-legged onto the bed.

"So," she said. "How's it going?"

"Okay," I said.

And then I just stared at her with no idea what to say next, while she just smiled at me. This should have been easy. She was the one person I didn't have to be careful around, who I could just be myself with, because she'd never known Danny Tate. But being around her turned me into this empty, blank person. Someone dull and mute and fumbling. Was it just nerves? Was this what normal people felt when talking to a pretty girl they actually liked and didn't just want something from?

"Should we make fun of Kai some more?" she finally said. "That's endless fodder for conversation. Like, lately he's been making these halfhearted attempts at becoming a professional surfer, which I'm sure you find *shocking*—"

"Sorry," I said. "I know I'm not easy to talk to."

"It's not just you," she said. "My mouth has no filter, which has always been a problem for me, and I don't want to say something stupid to you, so I'm really overthinking things over here."

"It's okay," I said. "I'm not as fragile as people think."

She cocked her head at me. "You do seem weirdly well-adjusted, considering."

I kind of nodded, kind of shrugged. Why had I come here? I couldn't talk to this girl, not like this, without a crowd to perform for. I often chose not to talk to people, but it wasn't because I *couldn't*. I could always summon the right personality for any situation; it was what had gotten me this far. Why couldn't I talk to her?

Then I realized.

I couldn't talk to Ren because I didn't know who she wanted me to be. She didn't seem to want me to be anyone but whoever I was, and I wasn't anyone, not really. I'd spent a lifetime becoming a mirror that just reflected back the person others wanted to see, but she didn't want anything. So I was nothing.

"Sorry," I said with rising panic. This was stupid. She was just a girl, I shouldn't be this scared, but I suddenly felt like I was treading into something dangerous. "I just . . . maybe I should go . . ."

"You're not going to help me with my drawing?" She reached into her school bag and fished out her sketch pad. "Look, it's seriously messed up, and I can't figure out how to fix it. Any ideas?"

She stood and laid the drawing out on the desk where I

was sitting, and we both looked at it. It was recognizably a bowl of fruit, but only just. Like someone had passed the drawing through a fun house mirror.

"Oh," I said. This drawing I understood. This I knew how to fix. The hot, frantic rushing of blood in my veins started to slow. "Yeah. It's the proportions. See this apple?"

"Yeah."

"It's too small. See how thin it is compared to the orange?"

"But that's because it's farther away," she said. "I was trying to show perspective."

"You've got the right idea," I said, "but you've taken it too far. Do you have any scratch paper?"

She found some blank paper and a couple of pencils and pulled an armchair up to the desk beside me. I quickly sketched a copy of her drawing but with the fruit in better proportion to each other.

"See?" I said.

She leaned over my paper. I could smell her shampoo as her hair fell over her shoulder, a sharp, sweet smell like nothing that existed in nature, and tried to focus on the drawing instead. "Yeah, but how do you do that?"

I'd never had to explain this before, and I struggled. "You just . . . look at the lines of whatever's in front of you and then copy them," I said.

She laughed. "No kidding, but how do you make sure it's right? I can't translate what I see onto the paper just by looking."

"You've got to . . ." I looked around the room and spotted a vase containing a small, tasteful arrangement of flowers on her bedside table. "Hand me that, would you?"

She grabbed the vase, and I put it on the far end of the desk.

"Okay, so let's start with the lily on the far left," I said. "For me, at least, I can't look at the whole thing at once. There's too much going on to deal with. So, I break it down. Just look at that one outside petal. Got it?"

Ren frowned in the direction of the flower. "Yeah."

"Now break it down further," I said. "Just look at the very tip of the petal."

"Okay."

"Now look just at the line where the tip of the petal meets the air. Don't look at the whole petal. Just that line."

Together, working line by line, petal by petal, we drew the flower.

"This is hard," she said as we worked. "How do you concentrate on such a small piece?"

I shrugged. "Practice, I guess. Use your hands if you have to."

"Huh?"

"Like . . ." I turned to her and put my hands on either side of her eyes like blinders.

She looked right at me, her eyes closer than I expected them to be. I was suddenly very aware of the places where the skin of my fingers met the skin of her face.

A thought pushed itself to the front of my mind. *You could kiss her.* That was something people did, normal people.

I dropped my hands and turned back to my drawing.

"I'm going to feel really silly doing this in class," she said, peering at the vase with her hands cupped around her eyes. "Have you always liked to draw?"

"Yeah, I guess." I smoothed out a line with the side of my thumb. All I was thinking about was that line, my entire attention focused on it.

"What do you like about it?" she asked. "Maybe it's just because I'm bad at it, but I don't get the appeal."

I shrugged. "I always liked to study things and see how they worked. With drawing I could use that to actually create something."

"That's kind of profound," she said as she erased a line she wasn't happy with.

I snorted. "I guess. I've always liked drawing people the best. I used to draw my mom when she—"

I stopped.

"Yikes," Ren said. "Did we wade into painful territory?"

"No, I . . . it's okay." I hadn't been thinking Jessica, of course. I'd been thinking about my mother. How I used to sit on the floor and stare at her as she sat in her chair, chain-smoking and arguing with the TV, studying each line and curve of her face. Like understanding the shapes could help me understand *her* and why she hated me so much. I had a whole notebook full of drawings of her face, which she'd found and thrown out, yelling at me for wasting paper.

I didn't mean to tell Ren that. I never told anyone anything true about me. It was rule number one, and for good reason.

"I'd better go," I said.

"You sure?"

"Yeah," I said. "My sister's going to be pissed."

Her eyes narrowed a little bit as she looked at me. I couldn't decipher the expression. It could have been confusion or disappointment or annoyance or a dozen other things. For someone who seemed like such an open book, sometimes I couldn't read her at all.

"Okay," she said. "I'll take you home."

Lex *was* pissed.

"I don't know what you were thinking," she said as she ushered me into the kitchen. "You couldn't have even called me first? Who was that?"

"Just a girl I go to school with," I said. "She's new."

Lex looked down at the floor, and when she looked up at me again she was wearing a faint smile. "Well . . . I'm glad you're making friends."

But I wasn't sure I'd be able to talk to Ren again. I was still shaken from what had happened, the way I'd slipped out of Danny's skin and into my own without even realizing it. I couldn't let that happen again, ever. I felt the precariousness of my position here in a way I hadn't before, not even the night I thought Jessica had seen through me.

I went to find Nicholas. I *had* to fix whatever had gone wrong between us, and I had to do it now. Making sure he believed I was really his brother was the only thing I could think of that would make me feel safe again.

I searched the house but found no sign of him. I knew he had to be here, though, because his car was in the garage, and, as I'd learned, people in California don't walk anywhere.

"Hey," I said when I found Mia in the rec room, watching a movie about a talking horse. "Have you seen Nicholas?"

She shook her head. "Sometimes he likes to hide in one of the chairs out by the pool though. Don't tell him I told you."

"I won't. Thanks."

I stepped out onto the back patio and scanned the pool area for Nicholas. I wasn't sure how he could hide in one of the lounge chairs until I noticed that one on the far side of the pool was angled away from the house so that only the back was visible. Then, in the faint glow from the underwater lights, I saw a blue trail of smoke rising from the chair. Either it was on fire, or I'd found him.

I walked out to the chair, and Nicholas looked up at me.

"Shit," he said.

"To be fair, it's not the best hiding place ever," I said.

He took a drag off the cigarette between his fingers. "No one's ever found me here before."

"They must not look very hard," I said. True to my word, as I occasionally was, I didn't give up Mia.

He didn't respond to that, just blew a lungful of smoke toward the stars.

"Mind if I sit?" I asked.

He didn't look at me. "Whatever."

I sank into the cool grass beside the lounge chair. Nicholas went back to smoking and contemplating the sky.

"Sorry I was a jerk this afternoon," I said.

"It's okay," he said. "I'm actually surprised you didn't go off on me sooner."

"Yeah, I guess I've been a little more stressed out about going back to school than I realized."

He laughed quietly to himself, some private joke I didn't understand. I ignored it and moved forward with my extra nice strategy.

"I know this has probably been a lot harder on you than anyone's realized," I said. "I feel bad, you know. Everyone's worried about me, but this happened to all of us. I just want you to know that I'm sorry for disrupting your life again, and I really appreciate everything you've done for me. I know it hasn't been easy for you, but you've been great anyway."

Nicholas looked at me, and I could see in his eyes that there was a war going on inside of him. "I haven't been great, and you don't have to apologize," he said softly.

"But I want to," I said. "I want to be as good a brother to you as you've been to me. I don't want there to be anything bad between us. Not anymore. Not ever again. I'm sorry, for everything."

I'd rerun our conversation in the diner a dozen times in my mind. It was clear to me that I'd gone too far in trying to bond with him when I said that thing about him being my best friend. The divide between Nicholas and Danny must have been wider than what I'd assumed from the childish squabbles and distance I'd seen in home movies. This was my attempt to undo that damage, but in a vague enough way not to cause more problems if I was wrong.

As I sat there, waiting for his response, I realized my problem with Nicholas was similar to the one I was having with Ren. I couldn't get a handle on how he'd seen Danny, so I never knew what act to put on for him. If I could just figure that out, I was sure I could put his suspicions to rest once and for all.

Nicholas's Adam's apple bobbed as he swallowed. He was taking a long time to speak, and I was growing increasingly tense. He scrubbed his free hand through his hair and sighed.

"That sounds pretty good," he said.

"So we can try to put the past behind us? Start over?"

He nodded. "Yeah. We can try."

I smiled and lay back in the grass. Nicholas handed me a cushion from the lounge chair to prop under my head, and we looked up at the stars in reasonably comfortable silence.

"So, did Lex freak?" he asked after a minute.

"Totally. I think she would keep me on an actual leash if she could."

One corner of his mouth turned up. "Like a little kid in the mall."

"Exactly."

"Who's the girl?"

"Her name's Ren," I said. "She's in my art class."

He took another drag off his cigarette. "She's kind of cute."

"It's not like that," I said. "Really. It's not."

"Methinks the lady doth protest too much."

"I was just helping her with an art assignment," I said, but then I remembered the way she looked at me when I put my hands on her face, the warmth of her skin.

"Sure," Nicholas said. "Okay."

We sat there together while he finished his cigarette and started a second. I asked about his classes, and he asked about mine. He told me about a trip to Barcelona he and Asher were planning for the summer. It wasn't exactly groundbreaking, but it was still the longest conversation we'd ever had. The night was cool and quiet around us, and even the sharp smell of the smoke seemed oddly pleasant in its familiarity.

"We'd better get inside," Nicholas finally said. "I've got like four hours of homework to do."

"I don't have any," I said, "but Lex will buy that leash if I'm out of her sight too long."

He smiled, and we stood. He put his cigarette out on the bottom of his shoe and stuck the two butts into the pack, which he shoved in his pocket.

"I didn't know you smoked," I said.

"I don't, usually. Just every once in a while. The family would flip out if they knew." He looked up at me with something fragile in his expression. "Don't tell anyone, okay? I'll owe you one."

"Don't worry about it," I said. "I can keep a secret."

"*Please*, Danny."

"What, you don't trust me?"

Nicholas's expression hardened. "Come on. That's not funny."

My skin went cold. I was missing something. Something important.

"Nicky, wait," I said, trying to catch his arm as he stalked away from me. I only managed to brush his sleeve, but he still turned back to look at me. He stared at me like I was a total stranger, and I just stood there as he backed away from me and then disappeared into the house.

That night I got out of bed after everyone else had gone to sleep. It had been my worst day since I came here, from letting some of the old me slip through the cracks when talking to Ren to making another misstep I didn't understand with Nicholas, and there was only one solution I could think of. I needed to learn more—a *lot* more—about Danny Tate.

There was a reason I hadn't bothered with this before: It hadn't mattered. I could see what most of the Tates wanted from me. Lex wanted a little boy to take care of. Patrick wanted someone to teach things to. Mia wanted a playmate. All I needed to do was be those things for them and they'd be happy.

But unless I could figure out what Nicholas expected me to be, I would keep screwing up with him. That wasn't a risk I could take.

After everyone else went to bed, I snuck down to the basement rec room, to the projector and movie screen where Mia had been watching her horse film earlier. Lex had already shown me several home movies to try to jog my memory, but I'd spent most of that time concentrating on the rest of the family, learning everything I could about *them* so I would understand who they wanted me to be, who'd they'd seen Danny as. This was the first time I was going to watch for Danny alone, to try to understand who he'd actually been.

The home movies were kept in a cabinet against the wall. I grabbed one labeled CHRISTMAS 2008/KLOSTERS 2009 and put it in the DVD player. I sank into the giant leather sofa across from the screen to watch and turned the volume down low even though the nearest human was two stories away.

The video started with a blur and the focusing of the lens, and then it showed the formal living room upstairs with a giant Christmas tree decorated all in gold and silver in the corner. Underneath was a pile of presents that spilled out from under the tree and across the floor, the room overflowing with ribbon and bows and sparkly paper. Jessica sat in an armchair in her pajamas and a silk robe, massively pregnant, with Nicholas cross-legged at her feet.

"Smile, Mom!" Patrick said from behind the camera.

She grinned and waved, a much different woman from the one I (barely) knew. Nicholas made a funny face at the camera, and Jessica mussed his hair.

It was like a Christmas card, a snapshot of a perfect family. My heart gave a painful lurch inside my chest even though I knew just how little the snapshot captured the full story of the Tates.

The camera swung to the right, and there was Danny. This was shot in 2008, so he was eight years old. In a couple of years he'd be gone. He was sitting by the edge of the present pile, towheaded and dressed in the same matching pajama set Nicholas was wearing, only his were blue instead of green. He had ripped the wrapping paper off the corner of a box and was snooping at what was beneath.

"No peeking, Danny!" said a voice from somewhere off camera. It sounded like Lex.

"Hey, that's mine!" Nicholas cried.

"I was just looking!" Danny said. "Don't be such a baby."

Danny's father entered the room, carrying a tray filled with steaming mugs. I hadn't met Robert Tate in person yet, only spoken to him on the phone. No one seemed to be in any hurry to take me to the state penitentiary in Lompoc where he was doing his time, which was just fine by me.

The family drank hot chocolate and started to open the massive pile of presents. Nicholas carefully peeled the tape and paper off his boxes and examined each gift closely, while Danny tore into his in his frenzy to get to the gift beneath. He took one look at the remote controlled car Jessica had given him before putting it aside in favor of the mystery of the next wrapped box. Pretty typical kid behavior, which was only remarkable in how different it was from Nicholas's. Patrick had Lex sit beside him and unwrap his gifts so he could keep filming, which took a while since Lex kept coming and going from the room. Robert gave Jessica a diamond bracelet he said he'd seen her eyeing in a store window in New York the month before. She stumbled over her thank-you, and when he leaned in to kiss her, she turned her head toward one of the speaking children, and his lips hit her cheek.

It was all here. Everything there was to know about these people, if I could just watch closely enough.

I closed my eyes for a moment and imagined myself in Danny's place, felt the crinkle of the wrapping paper under my hands, the sweet aftertaste of the hot chocolate on my tongue, the warmth in my body that came from being loved and belonging. I could almost believe it was a real memory.

I watched the entire video of Christmas/Klosters—which turned out to be some fancy ski resort—and another of the grandparents' wedding anniversary. Mostly, the videos reinforced what I'd already learned about Danny. He was extroverted, funny, and high-spirited, with a tendency to be inconsiderate of others. He worshipped Patrick, but he and Nicholas fought frequently, which had to explain some of Nicholas's ambivalence to me, although it did seem a bit extreme for him to be holding a grudge against his kidnapped brother over some childhood scraps.

But then, half-asleep and almost ready to throw in the towel for the night, I noticed something I hadn't before. I couldn't believe it had escaped my attention for so long.

In one way, if no other, Danny was a lot like me. He was a watcher.

I was well into the anniversary video before I caught it, because he was surprisingly subtle, but when I ran back the DVD, I saw things I'd missed the first time through. Danny eavesdropping on a conversation between his parents, pretending to fill up his drink while Jessica and Robert had a low conversation just a couple of feet away. Peering around Lex's shoulder to read what she was texting. Even peeking at Nicholas's present. I'd assumed that Danny's thoughtlessness was the product of a childlike obliviousness to his surroundings, but now I was thinking that very little escaped Danny's attention.

For the first time I felt a real kinship with him.

By the end of the anniversary video I could barely keep my eyes open anymore. The rest of my research would have to wait for another night. I shut down the DVD player and replaced the DVDs I'd removed. On my way back to my room I stopped in the kitchen. It had been many hours since dinner, and my stomach was rumbling. I grabbed a bottle of water from the fridge and was rummaging in the pantry for a snack when I heard the front door open. I froze as the beeps of someone entering the security code into the alarm panel echoed off the marble floors of the foyer and into the kitchen. I was stuck with no way to get back upstairs.

I heard the soft tapping of shoes in the hallway, and then, before I could decide what to do, Jessica was standing in front of me.

She startled when she saw me, and I could tell from the quickness of her reaction that she was actually sober. She reached automatically for the light switch but then dropped her hand without flipping it.

"What are you doing down here?" she asked.

"I was thirsty," I said.

"Oh," she said.

Silence.

"I guess I'll go back to bed now," I said.

"How is school?" she asked, the words coming out in a rush.

"Um, it's okay," I said.

She nodded. "That's good."

"Yeah."

She twisted the two rings she wore on her right hand, spinning them around and around. "I'm sorry I haven't been around much lately. I haven't been feeling well."

Rampant alcoholism will do that to you.

"That's okay," I said. "I hope you feel better soon."

"Thanks," she said.

This was bizarre. I had to get away.

"I'm going to go back to bed," I said.

"Okay," she said.

To get to the stairs I had to pass her. Her hands clenched into fists as I got closer to her, like she was afraid they would reach out to me of their own accord.

"Good night, Mom," I said over my shoulder as I walked away.

She didn't turn look at me. "Good night."

After those first few days in the Tate house, I'd rarely thought about Jessica. Except for the day she resurfaced to enroll me in school, she was such a nonentity that I sometimes forgot she even existed. Aside from Mia, who sometimes asked where she was, no one ever talked about her.

Maybe because of the mother I'd had, it didn't strike me as particularly strange at the time.

I still can't believe how blind I was.

"She hates me," I told Lex the next morning. "She won't even look at me."

"I told you, Danny, she's sick," Lex said. She was scrambling eggs while I was keeping watch over the toaster. It was Saturday morning and we had the house to ourselves. Patrick was at work, Mia was at Eleanor's house, and Nicholas had gone hiking with Asher, which I assumed was a lie, because I couldn't imagine Nicholas hiking. He had been pointedly ignoring me since whatever happened out at the pool, and he'd even snapped something I couldn't make out at Lex this morning on his way out the door.

"She keeps all of us at arm's length, not just you," Lex continued. "And I think . . . Honestly? I think she's a little scared of you."

The toast popped out of the toaster, and I jumped. "What? Why?"

She shrugged. "If she lets herself believe you're really back, you could disappear again. I know it sounds stupid, but I think she's just trying to protect herself. Because she loves you so much."

"Is that Nicholas's excuse too?" I asked.

Lex's back was turned to me, but I saw her freeze. "What do you mean?"

"He just seems mad at me all the time," I said.

She turned and scooped some eggs from the skillet onto my plate, a tight smile on her face. "Well, there's always been tension between you two, and he's not great with change. I'm sure he just needs a little more time to adjust to all of this."

"Maybe," I said.

"Don't worry about Mom and Nicky," she said. "It'll be okay."

That night at dinner Jessica and Nicholas both showed up. I wondered what threats and/or bribes Lex had handed out to make this happen.

Mia was updating us on the progress of *The Magical Mermaid*, and Jessica was well into her second glass of chardonnay when she suddenly looked up at me and said, "How was your day, Danny?"

Everyone fell silent.

"I . . . fine," I said.

She nodded, her eyes barely meeting mine. "That's good. Are you enjoying your classes?"

"I like my art class."

Nicholas abruptly stood, his chair scraping against the wooden floor, and walked out of the room.

Patrick dropped his fork and grabbed his drinking glass. His face was full of thunder.

"I need more soda," he said. "Does anyone else want more soda?"

We all shook our heads, and he went after Nicholas in the direction of the kitchen.

"So, Mia," Lex said as though nothing out of the ordinary was happening. "What happens after the mermaid battles the Octopus King?"

Even Mia, who was usually too young to pick up on the tension in a room, was shaken. She struggled to pick up where she'd left off, and I could see the tears starting to well in her eyes. I felt a powerful rush of heat—like anger, but different—wash over me. Like no one had ever done for me, I reached out and took her hand.

"Hey," I said, squeezing her fingers. "It's okay. Remember, the mermaid had frozen four of the Octopus King's tentacles with her magic powers, but the other four were still free, and he was trying to catch her with them? What did she do next?"

Mia gave me a tremulous smile. "She swam around and around in circles until his tentacles got all tangled up."

"That was pretty smart of her," I said, and Mia nodded.

In the other room, we heard the muffled sounds of Nicholas and Patrick arguing and then the slamming of the front door. Patrick came back a minute later with his knuckles white from how hard he was gripping his full glass of soda.

"Pass the green beans," he said as he sat.

I didn't know what to do. The harder I tried to make things work with Nicholas, the worse I made it all. I couldn't tell if he didn't believe me or just didn't like me, but either way he was the thorn in my side, the one thing ruining my perfect scam. At any moment he could convince Lex and Patrick I was a fraud or go to the cops, and there was nothing I could do but wait for it to happen and try to be ready if it did. I kept a packed bag in my closet at home and in my locker at school, and I moved my baseball card—the only truly incriminating item I owned—out of the house and into my locker, where I stuck it in the pages of book. I figured it would be safer there, where it was locked up, than in my room at home, where Nicholas or Lex could easily find it. I had to be extra careful now. Somehow I had gotten everything

I'd ever wanted, but whenever I looked at Nicholas, I felt it all slipping away from me.

Luckily, I didn't have to feel that very often, because Nicholas did everything he could to avoid me. He still had to drive me to and from school, but he ignored me at home and no longer sat beside me in the one class we shared. I sat with Ren at lunch, and he sat with his back to us, while Asher gave me the occasional awkward wave across the courtyard.

"Hi, Danny!" a cheerleader whose name I didn't know said to me as I walked toward my regular lunch table. The guy with her put out his fist for me to bump as I passed. This was what school was for me now. Ever since that day I'd told a group of students about my abduction and realized the power in choosing to be seen on my own terms, I'd gone from infamous to just famous. Stares and whispers had become waves and fist bumps. Everyone wanted to be my friend, to laugh at my jokes and invite me places after school, and they all acted like it had always been this way. Their transparency would have been gross if it wasn't so fun.

Ren definitely thought it was gross, but she still let me sit with her at lunch. The day after I'd fled her house like some kind of freak and vowed I'd stay away from her, I found myself watching her across the room during art class again, and whenever her eyes met mine, she smiled. It did something to me. It made me not care that I didn't know how to act for her, because it wasn't about *me* anymore. It was about her. All I wanted from her was to get to know her, if she'd let me, and when I approached her at lunch that day, she called my name and moved her bag aside so that I could sit down next to her. I'd sat with her every day since, and she put up with the circus that followed me now. I think she was even amused by the more desperate bids for my attention.

"What's that blonde's name? Taylor?" she said as we walked to the science wing after lunch together.

"I think so, yeah."

"You mean you don't remember her from when you two were *OMG-best-friends* in the second grade?" she said, imitating Taylor's vocal fry and hair toss. "She totally let you cheat off her math homework *all the time*!"

I laughed.

"How does it not drive you crazy?" she asked.

I shrugged. "I kind of like it. I've never been popular before."

We stopped in the hallway near her biology class. There were still a couple of minutes until the bell, so I leaned against the wall and she leaned up next to me.

"Don't take offense at this," she said, "but you know they're all fakes, right? Leeches. They only want to be around you because of the reflected fame."

"I know," I said, "but they still *want* to be around me."

"You can do better than that," she said.

I looked up, and when my eyes met hers, something felt *different* about it. I couldn't put my finger on it. Her eyes were the same as always, pretty but not particularly special. Yet the texture of the gaze felt new and strange. It gave me a weird, hollow kind of feeling in my belly. Was this what normal people felt? Did she feel it too? It drove me crazy that I couldn't tell.

"You think?" I said, leaning closer to her. I didn't even mean to; my body just did it.

She nodded. "I do."

"Interesting."

"Listen." This time she was the one who inched closer to me. "I know we haven't been hanging out that long, but I want to make sure you know I'm not another Taylor."

"I do," I said.

She gave me a mysterious little smile. "Good."

"Yeah?"

"Yeah. I'm hoping that means I'll get to see the guy behind the act sometime."

My chest hitched. "What act?"

She gave me a look. "Please. You do a good job of faking with the fakers, but I see right through you. You'd better get moving; the bell's going to ring any second."

But I didn't move. I was thinking about her seeing through me and how she actually *wanted* to and how, maybe, I wanted to let her. Comfortable home, loving family, adoring girlfriend. Everything a person could ever want, right?

"Earth to Danny!" she said.

I shook myself from my thoughts. "Sorry."

She squinted at me. "No teachers ever write up the miracle boy for being tardy, do they?"

"You've got it," I said.

"You're shameless and I kind of love it," she said. "Now get out of here."

"Hey, you want—" I took a breath. "Want to do something? After school?"

She smiled. "Yeah, okay."

I nodded, and we went our separate ways.

At the end of the day I met Nicholas at the glass doors to the student parking lot to tell him I didn't need a ride, but he forestalled me.

"Lex just texted," he said, already more words than he'd spoken to me all week. "She wants us to come straight home."

"Oh," I said, and there was my old friend Disappointment. "Okay."

I texted Ren on the way home, said a family thing had come up. She texted me back a picture of a man sticking out his tongue. When Nicholas and I arrived home, I went to look for Lex. She was in the kitchen, making a snack for Mia.

"What's going on?" I asked.

"Not sure," she said. "Patrick's on his way over."

My hands suddenly felt cold. If Patrick was leaving work in the middle of the day, something was wrong.

"Sit down, Danny. I'll make you something to eat while we

wait," Lex said. She handed Mia a plate of apple slices with a spoonful of peanut butter.

Nicholas sat down beside Mia, and I frowned at him. On the rare afternoons he didn't spend at Asher's, he usually went straight to his room.

"I'll take an apple too," he said. Apparently, he'd decided to wait with us.

Lex had the line between her eyebrows that indicated annoyance but dutifully started to cut up another apple for him. I sat down on the other side of Mia. She was knocking her heel against the chair leg in an erratic pattern that mirrored the beat of my heart, and we waited.

Patrick walked through the front door only a few minutes later. His face was flushed, probably from driving here with the top of his convertible down. His eyes sought out Lex first, and something wordless passed between them.

"What's going on?" I asked.

"It's no big deal," Patrick said, which meant that it was. "We knew this was coming. The FBI needs you to come in for an interview."

Lex closed her eyes. Nicholas looked over at me. My stomach dropped.

"I put them off for as long as I could, Danny," Patrick continued, "but they won't let me delay them anymore. I told them that you're in no state to discuss what happened yet, but they're insisting. They want you to come in on Thursday."

"It's okay," I said, shoving down the sudden surge of fear that went through me. I could handle this. "I'm ready."

"No! You shouldn't have to do this. Not yet," Lex said. She looked at Patrick with the big eyes that had probably gotten her her way more times than not. "Isn't there anything else you can do?"

"I've done everything I could to get us this much time," Patrick said.

"Why can't we just say no?" she pressed.

"You remember Agent Morales. She won't let anything go, and I don't think we really want to piss off the FBI."

"Why not?" Mia asked.

"You'd think you'd *want* to talk to them," Nicholas said. "You know. Help them catch the people who did this to you."

Fuckfuckfuck.

Lex shook her head. "It's not—"

"Don't you want that?" Nicholas said. "Danny?"

"Why don't you want to piss off the FBI?" Mia asked.

"Don't say 'piss,'" Nicholas told her.

"Of course," I said. "It's okay, Patrick. I want to go."

"No!" Lex said again.

"Lexi, he's got to," Patrick said. "I'll call in sick tomorrow. Danny, you stay home with me and we'll prepare for your interview."

"What's to prepare?" Nicholas said. He picked up his plate and dropped it in the sink on his way out of the kitchen.

It wasn't until much later that I realized no one had answered Mia's question.

That night, after everyone had gone to bed, I went back down to the basement to watch more home movies. There were still a couple I hadn't gotten to, and I had to learn as much as I could about Danny and his family before the FBI interview. I had scammed my fair share of law enforcement officials before, and it never used to make me nervous, but the stakes were a lot higher now. If I couldn't be Danny Tate for them, I'd be trading this mansion for a jail cell.

I found a DVD labeled BARBADOS 2009/AS YOU LIKE IT 2010. After that, the volume of home movies dropped off considerably. Danny had disappeared in the spring of 2010, so I was betting these were the last videos taken of him.

The first half of the DVD was yet another family vacation to a beautiful and exotic location. This time it was New Year's in the Caribbean, the family surrounded by white sand beaches and glassy turquoise water the likes of which I'd only ever seen as backgrounds on computer desktops.

But this wasn't the same family I'd watched skiing in the Swiss Alps. Robert Tate's voice sounded strained as he narrated behind the lens of the camera. Jessica was noticeably distant and was often filmed with a cocktail in her hand. Danny and Nicholas fought constantly, and Lex had dark smudges under her eyes and was shockingly thin in her bikini. Mia wasn't present, probably left at home with some nanny, and neither was Patrick, whose absence wasn't commented upon. I could explain some of these things. Jessica's first husband—Lex and Patrick's father, Ben McConnell—had recently committed suicide, which explained Lex's appearance. Robert Tate was probably already getting himself into the financial trouble that the SEC would nail him for in a few years' time. Mia had been born with a congenital defect of her right leg that had probably been very stressful for her parents. It was not a good time for the Tate family, and things were about to get a lot worse.

I was surprised at how sorry I felt for them.

The second event on the DVD started here at the house. Robert had Nicholas, who was wearing a suit and had his hair slicked back, explain to the camera that they were going to see Lex perform in the school play. The camera panned to Danny, who was sitting on the floor playing blocks with Mia. It was the first time I'd seen a video of Mia when she was little, and I felt myself smile. She had wispy brown curls and incredibly fat cheeks and she shrieked with laughter when Danny knocked over her block tower.

I felt a sudden, sick lurch of jealousy deep in the pit of my stomach.

I wished that were me.

I didn't know if I was capable of love, but if I was, then Mia was the person I was closest to loving. I liked who I was when she was the one looking at me. I wanted her to be *my* sister. I wanted to be her brother, and not just because Danny came from a family that lived in a mansion and vacationed in Barbados. Not because he'd never gone to bed hungry or been slapped around or been told he was worthless, but because—

"Danny?"

My head snapped up as Patrick—clad in pajama bottoms, his hair rumpled—walked into the rec room.

"Hey," I said, reaching for the remote and pausing the video. How was I going to explain this? It must look suspicious as hell, especially given the timing.

"Couldn't sleep?" he asked, sitting down beside me.

I shook my head. "Did I wake you?"

"No, I was just getting a snack and I heard the TV." He looked at the screen. "Which video is this?"

He didn't seem to think it was odd that I was watching old home movies in the middle of the night—maybe because he was too sleepy to think too much about it—so my heartbeat started to return to normal.

"Um, Lex's play," I said.

"Oh, right." He smiled, took the remote from me, and started the video again. The screen switched from the parking lot of Calabasas High to a darkened auditorium where the only thing visible was a red curtain illuminated by footlights. Patrick fast-forwarded. "She wasn't in the first scene. Do you remember any of this?"

"Not really," I said.

He hit play when the scenery changed. Lex was standing on stage in a white dress, her hair curled around her face, softening the sharpness of her chin and cheekbones. She was still alarmingly thin, so fragile-looking it was hard to believe she could even stand, but when she smiled, it looked real. Her voice was clear and bright when she recited her lines, romping and laughing and flirting her way across the stage, a confident and sassy creature who was entirely unlike the Lex I knew.

"She was good," I said.

He made a noncommittal sound.

"Did she ever try to pursue it?" I asked.

He shrugged. "When she was younger. She made a couple of commercials."

So she gave up. I wondered if that was because of Danny. Losing her father and her brother in quick succession must have been devastating for such a sensitive girl. God, how I envied Danny, being loved like that, *missed* like that. The air conditioner blowing cool air across my skin suddenly felt like the biting wind of a snowstorm many years before, and I shivered. No one was missing the person I had been.

"Hey," Patrick said softly. "You okay?"

A lump rose in my throat. I didn't want this all to be taken away from me. Not just because it meant I'd end up back on the street or in a group home or in prison. Not just because this life was easy or because it meant never having to be myself again. But because, improbable as it seemed, I'd actually started to give a shit about these people, and I felt like they gave a shit about me, too. I didn't want to lose that.

I bit my lip hard.

"Danny?"

Patrick put a warm hand on my shoulder, and I couldn't hold it together anymore.

"I'm scared," I said softly.

He put his arms around me, hugging me tight, and I unwound a little further.

"I know," he said. He rubbed his hand up and down across my back. My brother. "I know."

Patrick and I sat at the dining room table for most of the next day, going over my story for the FBI. He said he didn't want there to be any surprises. That it would be easier for me if I knew what to expect and that the clearer my story was, the more likely it was that the FBI would be able to catch the people who'd done this to me.

"I was walking beside my bike, because the chain had come off, and I didn't know how to fix it," I said. "I was taking it home to my brother Patrick, because he would know. A white van—"

"I'm going to stop you there, Danny," Patrick said. "This sounds really similar to when you first told Lex and me what happened. I'm sure you've gone over those events in your head a million times and that's why, but the FBI is going to ask you to tell your story more than once. I worry they might start going down the wrong track if you sound at all rehearsed."

"Right," I said, heart jumping into my throat. *Dammit.* How had I not thought of that? "I, uh, I guess I use the same words because it's easier, you know? I don't have to think about . . . what they did to me . . . as much."

"I totally get it," he hastened to reassure me.

Patrick and I continued to work through my story, and I made an effort to switch up the way I told it from the way I'd rehearsed it in my head. Patrick offered comments and asked questions along the way, and though I was sure it wasn't his intention, he helped me flesh out the story, find and plug the holes in it.

Jessica emerged from her room sometime before midday. I saw her walk past the dining room on her way to the kitchen while Patrick and I were going over how the men who kidnapped me smuggled me and the others kids across the Canadian border. As the lies grew inside of me, they became more and more real to me. This always happened whenever I spoke a lie out loud; it gained its own life and energy. I began to feel like I was breathing in the stale air of the hidden compartment in the eighteen-wheeler, listening to the muffled whimpers of the other children packed in there with me as I tried to free my hands of their bindings and my mouth of its duct tape gag.

But some part of me was still in the dining room, monitoring Patrick's reactions, and that part of me noticed when Jessica appeared in the dining room doorway with a bottle of the fancy French water the Tates bought by the case. She hovered there, clutching the bottle instead of opening it. Patrick's eyes flickered over to her once, then twice, as if he didn't really believe she was there. Which was understandable.

"Sorry, Danny," he said, stopping me. "Do you need something, Mom?"

She shook her head. "I'm fine."

He frowned. "Well then, maybe you should . . ."

Jessica just stood there, unmoving, and Patrick finally turned back to me.

"Okay, Danny," he said. "Then what happened?"

"We drove for a long time," I said. "It was hard to tell inside the compartment, but I think it was at least a day."

"They kept you in there the whole time?" Patrick asked. "What about food or water?"

I shook my head. "They didn't give us any food. Didn't even take our gags off. I got so nauseous from fear and hunger and the bumping in the compartment that I threw up, but I had to just swallow it back down again."

Jessica abruptly turned and walked out of the room. A moment later, we heard the front door close behind her.

"I didn't want her to hear any of this," Patrick said. "It's too hard for her. She thinks it's her fault."

"What? Why?" I asked. I'd researched Danny's disappearance. There had been surprisingly little news coverage outside of the immediate area—the effect of the Hidden Hills bubble, I'd guessed, although it seemed pretty strange—but the story was clear. It had just been one of those freak things, the kind of random tragedy that fueled suburban nightmares and the Lifetime original movies Lex liked to watch.

Patrick shrugged. "For not being a better mother. For drinking too much and letting you ride your bike in the neighborhood. For not noticing you were gone sooner. Anything and everything a person could blame themselves for."

"It wasn't her fault," I said.

He looked down at his watch, twisting it around his wrist so that he could check the time. "No. It wasn't."

When he didn't look back up, I said, "Patrick?"

He said, "What happened next?"

We spent the rest of the day going over my story. Whatever Patrick felt at what he heard, much of which I'd never told him before, he hid it behind his lawyer's mask. It was a good mask. Almost as good as mine.

Lex was less adept at hiding her feelings. Although she avoided the dining room, she was agitated all day, constantly keeping herself busy and snapping at everyone over tiny things. When we were set to leave the next morning, she was pale and her hands were visibly trembling.

"It's so unfair you have to go through this," she said as she forced me to take another pancake from the mountain she'd made before I came down to breakfast. "Being interrogated, like you're some kind of criminal."

"They just want my help," I said. I was more anxious than I'd ever been in my life, but I was Zen compared to her.

"Danny's right," Patrick said. "Maybe you should stay here. You don't look too good."

"No way," she said. "I'm going."

Patrick gave her a look, and they engaged in the kind of wordless conversation I'd seen pass between them a hundred times. Whatever was said, Lex came out the victor.

Out in the foyer, the front door opened.

"Mom?" Lex called.

Jessica appeared in the kitchen. She was wearing shapeless clothing and no makeup, which made her look like a ghost of herself.

"Why aren't you ready?" Lex asked. "We're leaving soon."

"I'm not going," Jessica said in a voice so subdued it sounded like she barely had the energy to get the words out. "You don't need me there, do you, Patrick?"

Patrick turned his head toward her, but not enough to actually look at her. "No. The power of attorney you signed is still in effect, so we're good."

"Mom," Lex said. "I really think Danny could use your support—"

Jessica suddenly came alive, like she'd grabbed a live wire.

"I won't play this game with you, Alexis!" she snapped.

Lex looked stricken, like she'd been slapped. Patrick jumped to his feet.

"That's fine, Mom," he said. "We're okay. How about you go on upstairs?"

Jessica walked away, and Lex turned to the sink and started vigorously washing the dishes inside. I looked at Patrick.

"Want another pancake?" he asked.

Ten minutes later the three of us were walking out to Patrick's car. On the way we passed Jessica's rental, which was parked haphazardly in the driveway as usual. It was covered with a thin film of orange dust up to the windows, and I wondered where she'd been.

My interview was set to take place at the FBI's Los Angeles field office. The building seemed to loom over me, taller than the buildings I was used to, and I wondered if it had been designed to be intimidating. My pulse kicked up, and I tried to tell myself that it was just a bigger version of the Collingwood Police Station. I'd been scamming cops for years now. Nothing to it.

As we walked inside, Patrick filled the air between us with last minute reminders and assurances.

"Just tell the same story you told me," he said, "and if you start to feel uncomfortable, let me know and we'll put a stop to it."

"It's going to be fine," I said.

"Of course it is," he said. "Morales will try to put you on the defensive, make you feel like you've done something wrong. Don't let that fluster you. It's just her strategy for getting the most information."

"I hate that bitch," Lex said.

I'd done my research on Agent Morales, the FBI's lead investigator on the case from the beginning. She never gave anything but the most perfunctory statements to the press, so it was hard to judge her personality, but she was always insistent that the investigation was active and ongoing, even years after the fact. She'd been interviewed in the wake of the *LA Magazine* article—which mentioned rumors of tension between her and the Tates, including one that they'd tried to have her removed from the case—and had intimated that there was a recent development in the investigation, although she'd declined to elaborate. Was that true or just something to cover her ass since she still hadn't solved the case six years later? It made my feet itch to run thinking that the FBI might have some mystery piece of evidence I couldn't be prepared for.

When Agent Morales came to meet us in the waiting room, I was surprised by her appearance. The picture I'd built in my head was of an older woman with a severe haircut and ill-fitting clothes. In reality, she was young, maybe thirty-five, and pretty. She had curly, dark hair that she wore in a half ponytail and full, pink lips with a shine of gloss on them, just like Lex. But she had a slightly masculine way of walking, probably the result of time spent in the military, and an air of seriousness that was more what I expected from a Fed.

"Mr. McConnell," she said, shaking Patrick's hand. There was something in her expression I couldn't quite read, a tightening at the corner of her eyes so subtle it was hardly noticeable. She nodded at Lex. "Ms. McConnell. Thank you for coming in."

Lex's smile was more like bared teeth. "It seems we didn't have much of a choice."

Morales stood with her hands clasped lightly behind her back. Definitely a military background.

"And you must be Danny," she said. "It's good to meet you after all these years."

She reached out to shake my hand as well, but I shied a little closer to Lex. I'd let the traumatized routine lapse in the past few weeks, and I needed to bring it back now. Danny wouldn't be eager to touch strangers after what he'd been through, and this bit of acting now would reinforce my story later.

Morales withdrew her hand. "How about we head back?"

She led us into the building, past cubicles and offices, like any insurance or accounting company in the world. As we walked, Patrick exchanged a small nod with a young man bent over a computer screen behind Morales's back. I curled my hands into the sleeves of my hoodie. This was part of the traumatized act too, with the added bonus that it would keep me from accidentally touching anything.

"There's no need to be nervous, Danny," she said with that overly gentle tone that people use with small children or the mentally disabled. "We just want to hear your story to help us as we look for the people who did this to you, okay?"

"Okay."

"Here's the interview room we'll be using," she said as we approached an office with closed blinds over the windows. Interview room, not interrogation room. She opened the door to reveal someone already inside, a man with a weak chin and premature bald spot that contrasted oddly with the thick arms and chest visible under his button-down. A bullied loser who'd decided to get tough and go into the FBI so he could finally be the one in control. He was fiddling with an electronic recorder. "This is my partner, Timothy Lynch. I don't think you've met before."

Lynch shook everyone's hand and offered us coffee and soda, which we declined. Everyone was smiling, and I wasn't sure if the undercurrent of tension in the room was real or just the product of my own nerves.

"Okay," Morales said, clapping her hands together. "We'll make you two comfortable outside while we have a chat with Danny."

Any pretense of friendliness evaporated.

"Are you fucking kidding me?" Lex said.

Patrick gave her a warning touch on the wrist. "I'll be staying with my brother, Agent."

"Mr. McConnell, there's no reason—"

"Excuse me," Patrick interrupted, "but I'm Danny's lawyer and his legal guardian, so how about we cut through the bullshit?"

Morales's smile was tight but not displeased. "You're right.

Mr. McConnell, of course you may stay. Miss McConnell, we'll make you comfortable in the waiting room."

"I'm not going anywhere," Lex said.

"I'm afraid I have to insist."

"No!"

"Lexi." Patrick caught Lex's fingers in his own and drew her to the corner of the room, where they exchanged a few low words. Whatever he said subdued her. She drew her hand out of his, kissed my head, and walked out of the office.

The rest of us sat down at the table—Patrick and me on one side, Morales and Lynch on the other—and Lynch started the recording. He began with a few simple, establishing questions to ease me into the interview. My name, age, that sort of thing. At first I was surprised he was the one questioning me, since it was obvious Morales was the one in charge here, but I quickly understood. Morales wanted him to ask the questions so she could focus on watching. She was leaned back in her chair in a way that was designed to look relaxed, but her eyes betrayed her. They saw everything, moving back and forth between Patrick and me as I answered Agent Lynch's questions, and I wondered what she saw.

"So if you're ready, Danny," Lynch said, "I'd like to move on to the day you were abducted."

I took a deep breath and looked at Patrick. He nodded and squeezed my shoulder. Morales watched us.

"I'm ready," I said.

"Great," Lynch said. "Just tell us what you remember. Take your time."

I swallowed once, then twice, then cleared my throat. I added a small waver to my voice when I said, "I was out riding my bike . . ."

I started the story I'd worked on with Patrick the day before, making sure to switch up my language as I went. I told them about the white van that came out of nowhere, the hidden compartment in the eighteen-wheeler, the tense ride over the border into Canada. Everyone was silent as I spoke. The lies started to gain momentum as they tumbled out of my mouth, and I found myself leaning in toward the recorder. As soon as I noticed, I slowly drew back and curled my shoulders in on myself instead.

"We drove for a long time," I said. "Every once in a while, they'd stop the truck in some empty place and drag us out to let us pee or give us something to drink. Then they'd shove us back inside, and we'd start to drive again."

"Any idea how long this lasted?" Lynch asked.

"I'm not sure," I said. "Maybe two or three days."

I sank into the lie. Never enough to lose sight of my surroundings, keeping an eye on Lynch's and Morales's reactions so I could adjust if necessary, but enough that I saw the lies superimposed over the present, like film that's been double exposed. A dark road lit only by the headlights of the truck, which made my eyes—so used to the darkness of the hidden compartment now—contract painfully as someone with rough hands and a bandanna over the lower half of their face pushed me toward the trees so I could piss. Barely able to stand because my legs were so weak beneath me from fear, hunger, and lack of use. The stench inside the compartment as I was shoved back in, not even resisting anymore, knowing that it was pointless to fight. One glimpse into the eyes of the terrified girl with the freckles and strawberry blonde hair whose body warmth would be my only comfort once we started driving again before the door clanged close and took all the light away.

Lynch was blinking a lot. Patrick was rigid beside me. Morales was watching Patrick.

It began to feel like the driving would never end. Like the rest of the world had disappeared, and there was nothing and no one outside of this truck and this road. We never stopped during the day, so the day had ceased to exist too. I began to think the whole world was dark.

Then we stopped again, and something felt different. I don't know why, but we all felt it. I could tell by the way the other little bodies in the compartment tensed, the way they started to breathe differently. There were voices outside, muffled through the layers of metal separating us, but definitely raised. My heart started to pound wildly. I was convinced it was the police, that someone was about to save us. But when the doors opened again, it was one of the same bandanna men, the one with the scar through his right eyebrow. And that was it, the moment that I realized that hope was more dangerous to me than anything else.

Lynch had his head turned now, looking at the wall. I had upset him. He recovered quickly and put on his brave boy face, but my story had gotten to him. Morales wasn't similarly moved. Her expression hadn't changed the entire time I'd been speaking.

The man with the bandanna blindfolded me again before hauling me out of the truck. I felt warmth on my face and realized it was sunlight just as he led me back into shadows. My feet were on a solid surface; I was inside a building. We went down a flight of stairs, and it grew colder around me. The smell of moisture and moldering surrounded me, like rotting leaves, brown decaying things. I imagined the walls dripping with fetid water, moss creeping across the floor, slime oozing up between the cracks. He put me in a small room, more like a cell, with no window, no light, nothing but a thin foam mattress on the floor, a blanket balled up on top of it, and a bucket in the corner. He locked me in there, and he didn't come back. I curled up on the mattress, pulled the blanket over my head to hide my face, and prayed to God with all the words I could barely remember from infrequent visits to Sunday school to wake up back at home in my own bed, with my own family.

Patrick shifted beside me. I turned to glance at him, realizing that between visualizing my lies and keeping an eye on Lynch and Morales, I hadn't been paying him any attention. He was staring down at the surface of the table, blinking his eyes rapidly. I felt a sudden, sick twist of guilt in my gut. I hadn't even considered what it would be like for him to hear these things.

We'd gone over the story a hundred times yesterday, but I'd been embroidering it as I went along, and each new detail must have been like another blow to him.

"Are you all right, Mr. McConnell?" Agent Lynch asked.

"Perhaps you'd like to step outside for a moment," Morales added.

Patrick shook his head and took a sip from the glass of water Agent Lynch poured for him. "I'm fine. We can continue."

"Are you sure?" Morales asked. "It's no problem—"

Patrick's expression was carved from marble. "I'm fine."

"Okay," Morales said at length. "Danny, whenever you're ready."

I stuck to the story. No more embellishments. I told them how they left me alone in that room for many days, the door occasionally opening to admit some food or water or to take the bucket for emptying. Sometimes a man would come in and ask me my name. When I said, "Danny," he would hit me. What did I say my name was again? he would ask. "Danny," I would say. Defiant. Lower lip wobbling but chin raised. Then I would be beaten and left with no food for days. This happened again and again until every inch of my skin had been broken and reknitted a half a dozen times. After the third beating I stopped telling him my name. After the twentieth I genuinely didn't remember it anymore.

Once they had broken me, well. That's when things really began.

Morales leaned forward in her chair, clasping her hands together on the table in front of her.

"One day the man who always came to ask my name showed up with another guy," I said. "He was different. Cleaner. He seemed like someone important. He asked my name, and I told him I didn't know what it was, which was true. He told me they were going to call me 'J' from then on. We all had names like that, just letters of the alphabet. He asked where I was from, and I told him I was from that room. I could barely remember anything else. I think . . . I think it was probably too painful for me to remember, you know? So I just forgot. It was easier for me to think I'd been born there in that room and never known anything different. I remember the man smiled at that."

Agent Lynch glanced over at Morales. She gave a nod so small that it seemed to come more from her eyes than anything.

"We'll come back to that man, Danny," Lynch said. "For now, just tell us what happened next if you can. Unless you need a break first?"

I shook my head. "I'd rather just get through this," I said, and it was true. Telling the lies, making myself believe them as much as possible so I would sound convincing to the people listening, took its toll.

"Of course. Go on."

"They took me out of my room and gave me a shower," I said. "It was only the second or third one I'd gotten since I'd been there. They dressed me in new clothes and then the clean man put me in a car and drove me somewhere. He didn't bother blindfolding me or trying to tie me up or anything. I guess he knew I wouldn't run." I faked a crack in my voice, but it wasn't hard. All good lies contained some truth, and I knew what it was like to be young and scared and feel beyond saving. "He took me to another house in the middle of nowhere. There were other children there too. That's where we lived when we weren't . . . being used somewhere else."

My stomach started to feel unsettled as I continued the story. What they told me I'd have to do. What they did to me when I refused. How bad it got before I finally agreed, and how much worse it got after that.

"This one guy, he was always smoking. If I made him mad, he would burn me." I pulled down the neck of my shirt, showing them a circular cigarette burn just under my collarbone. Might as well put my real scars and the healed breaks any X-ray would detect to use. "They broke my ribs a couple of times. My arm, too."

"Did they take you to the hospital or a doctor?" Lynch asked.

I shook my head and rubbed my arm where the phantom pain of bones grinding together still lived. "No, they just made me a splint. Couldn't risk anything else."

The more truth I wove into my lies, the more the constructed memories blurred with my real ones. The dark room where I slept on a mattress on the floor was no longer in some human trafficker's safe house but in a trailer home in Saskatchewan, the screaming voice suddenly a familiar one, the close walls those of the closet where I tried to hide. The metallic tang of fear in the back of my throat as I heard footsteps in the hallway at night was as vivid now as it had been then, and soon tears I had never cried for myself were building up in my throat for my invented Danny Tate, so thick it was hard to breathe.

Patrick reached out and slowly, carefully touched my shoulder. That did it. I broke down. "Crying" is too delicate a word for what it was. Patrick put his arm around me, but I flinched away violently, because I wasn't in that room anymore, with the man who'd been nothing but the perfect big brother to me. I was back there, in the dark and the cold with *her* and with *them*.

"Danny," Patrick said. "It's okay. You're okay."

I looked up at him, remembering where I was. Patrick looked bewildered and worried, and I let him squeeze my shoulder.

"Okay?" he said.

I took a deep breath and nodded. I was safe now. I was okay. And that very rare, very real display of emotion surely wouldn't have hurt my cause here.

"I know this can't be easy for you, Danny," Morales said. "We really appreciate your bravery in telling us all of this. Take a minute if you need to."

I shook my head and swiped at my eyes. "I just want to get this over with. I just want you to stop them."

Morales nodded at Lynch, who asked, "Can you tell us how you got away?"

"They accidentally left a door unlocked," I said. "I made a run for it."

"How long ago was that?"

"About a year."

"Why did you never seek anyone out?" Morales said, asking her first question of the day. "Go to the police?"

"You make that sound like an accusation, Agent," Patrick said. "My brother is the victim in all of this. He's not here to defend his actions."

"I did go to the police," I said. "That's why I'm here now."

"I'm sorry. I didn't mean to sound accusatory," Morales said. "I'm just wondering why you didn't reach out for help in the year before you arrived at the juvenile facility in Vancouver."

"I was scared," I said, thinking about that first time I ran away and the look on my mother's face when she had to come get me and take me back. "To me, the men who had taken me were like gods. All powerful. I was sure if I told anyone who I was, they'd find me and take me back."

"Even the police?" she asked.

"Especially the police. I'd been abused for years, and the police had never done anything about it," I said. I tasted bile at the back of my throat and tried to swallow it down. "They never found us kids and saved us the way I thought they would for so long. Never investigated any of the houses where we were kept or any of the men who did this to us. I thought the only way that could be was if the police were a part of it."

Morales sighed, and her eyes were a little softer when she looked at me. "I'm sorry we never found you, Danny."

"Me too," I said.

"So what changed when you got to Short Term 8?" she asked. "Why did you decide to come forward then?"

"I started to remember who I was." I looked at Patrick. "I started to remember my family."

Patrick met my eyes for a half a second before looking down at his watch abruptly. "I think that's enough for today."

Morales frowned. "Actually, I still have some—"

Patrick stood. "He's told you everything you need to know about his kidnapping and imprisonment. Nothing else is relevant to finding the people who did this to him. Are we free to go?"

Morales stood as well, buttoning her jacket. "Mr. McConnell, if you could just—"

"Agent, we've been very cooperative," he said, "and we've also been here for hours. My brother's still in a delicate state, and I can see that he's exhausted. I don't want to overtax him."

"I think Danny's been clear that he wants to do everything he can to help." Morales turned her sharp eyes on me. "Right, Danny?"

"Thank you, agents," Patrick said, without waiting for my answer. "Come on, Danny. Let's go."

I got up and followed Patrick from the room. I was holding up and would have been happy to stay if it meant getting this part of the process over with, but I suspected Patrick needed a break more than I did. His face looked drawn and clammy, and the least I could do was let him use me as an out.

Lex tossed aside a magazine and jumped to her feet when we entered the lobby. "Finally! How did it go? Are you okay, Danny?"

"I'm fine," I said. "Tired."

"It was fine," Patrick said. "Let's get out of here."

I glanced back at the building as we reached the car. Morales was standing just outside the door watching us, and the sight of her gave me a cold feeling in the pit of my stomach I couldn't explain.

Lex climbed into the backseat with me and wrapped her arms around me while Patrick drove home. I gave in and leaned against her. It was starting to hit me now. I had expected the nerves and fatigue from so many hours of thinking through every word I said, but the grief that had bubbled up from inside of me had caught me off guard, and Lex was surprisingly solid for such a wispy, dandelion person. Maybe she treated me like a little kid, but at this moment it felt nice to be held, surrounded by her softness and the smell of the lavender hand lotion she kept in her purse. Made me understand why normal people sought this out.

"Was it awful?" she asked. "I can't imagine how awful it must have been."

"It . . . it was okay," I said.

"He did great," Patrick said, glancing at us in the rearview mirror.

"Well, we're not going to make you do that again. Right, Patrick?" she said. "They got everything they need, right?"

"We'll see," he said. "I doubt it."

"It's just going to have to be enough." Lex leaned her cheek against the top of my head. "They're not making you relive all of that again. It's all over now."

And I realized, slowly, that she was right. The cold, lonely boy I'd once been was gone. I had a home now, people who loved me. People I was starting to love back, as impossible as that seemed. Maybe I didn't deserve it, but Danny Tate did, and I was him now.

I wondered if this was what happiness felt like.

A few hours later I was lying in the sun out by the pool, watching Patrick try to teach Mia how to do the front crawl. Lex was sitting in the lounge chair next to mine working on her second glass of wine. My phone buzzed in my pocket. It had taken a while to get used to, but I actually kept it turned on and with me now.

"Who's that?" Lex asked as I pulled the phone out to check it.

It was a text from Ren. *You okay? Didn't see you around today.*

"Just that girl from school," I said.

I'm fine, I texted back. *Had things to do. Be back tomorrow.*

Good, because the leeches were very disappointed at your absence and lunch is boooring without you.

I smiled.

"I think Danny's got a *girl-friend*," Lex crooned.

"Shut up," I said.

"Ooh, he does!"

"Is she cute?" Patrick asked.

"I'm not talking to either of you," I said.

"*Danny and his girlfriend, sitting in a tree . . .*," Mia sang.

"Not you too!" I said while Patrick and Lex laughed.

Doing anything right now? Ren asked.

Not really, I said.

Want to come over?

I thought of a dozen things simultaneously. Ren's eyes on mine and her laugh and the feel of her skin against my hands and the pleasant queasiness I felt when I was talking to her.

"Hey, Patrick, can you drive me somewhere?" I asked.

"What, now?" he said. "She must be really cute."

"Wouldn't you rather stay home tonight?" Lex asked. "Take it easy?"

"Actually, I think I'd rather do something normal for a little while," I said.

Lex's lips were pinched together. "I don't think—"

"It's fine," Patrick interrupted. "Whatever you want, Danny. Just let me go change."

A few minutes later Patrick and I were getting into his car.

"We should get you enrolled in a driver's ed course this summer so you can get your license," he said. "Technically, Nicholas isn't allowed to drive with another minor, so the sooner we can get you your own car, the better."

I smiled, imagining myself in my own car, the smell of new leather and music blasting from the speakers. A convertible like Patrick's so I could have the sun on my shoulders, but black or maybe red.

It wasn't until we were nearly to Ren's house in Calabasas that I realized I hadn't considered how useful a car would be to me if I needed to run. How far I could get in it, how much I could sell it for. It gave me a strange twinge in my stomach, because not that long ago it would have been the *first* thing I thought of.

But things were different now, and I knew it.

I wasn't going to leave. Not ever.

I stayed at Ren's house for a couple of hours. I met her aunt and uncle, who were nice and kept offering me things to drink, and then we watched a movie in her media room. Kai, baked out of his mind, came in when it was almost over and announced that he needed some marshmallows immediately, but there weren't any in the house and his license was suspended for another week. Ren told him that was too damn bad, but after a few minutes of negotiations, we took Kai to the store and ended up sitting with him at the fire pit in the Himuras' backyard roasting marshmallows. Kai wandered off, but Ren and I kept sitting there in the dim glow, talking about nothing in particular.

"How can you eat that?" I asked as Ren pulled a blackened marshmallow out of the fire.

"This is how I like them," she said, pulling the sticky thing apart with her fingers. "Don't judge."

"I would never."

"Good, because I think accepting someone's personal weirdnesses is the foundation for all good relationships," she said. "I believe in unconditional love, you know?"

Unconditional. It was a nice thought, if it really existed. Maybe it could.

"Now what are you thinking when you make that face?" she asked.

I smiled and looked down at the fire.

"Mystery man," she said with a sigh. "It's okay. Someday you'll tell me."

It was nice, all of this. And it was *mine* now. Home, family, pretty girl. Everything a person could ever want.

I didn't know it then, but it was probably the happiest night of my life.

Ren drove me home, and after I'd watched her headlights disappear around the curve in the driveway, I went inside, following the voices back to the kitchen. Mia was eating grapes from the stem at the kitchen island, Patrick was working at his laptop at the breakfast table, and Lex was wiping down the spotlessly clean counters. They didn't notice me immediately, and I spent a moment just looking at them. Drinking them in. Loving them.

For a second I wondered where the real Danny was, if he

would understand that it was better for us all, including them, that I was here.

Mia spotted me. "Danny!" She hopped off her stool and flung herself at me. I caught her and spun her in circles until she shrieked.

"Careful!" Lex said.

"Are you going to pass out?" I asked when I lowered Mia back to her feet.

She grinned and swayed drunkenly. "Maybe."

"Then my work here is done."

"Time for bed, Mimi," Lex said. "Go brush your teeth and get changed. I'll be up to adjust your brace in a minute."

Mia kissed us all and headed upstairs. Patrick looked at Lex. Lex swiped at more invisible crumbs.

"What is it?" I said.

"The FBI called," Patrick said. "They want to schedule another interview."

I felt a hot flush pass over me. "So soon?"

He nodded.

"Why?" I asked. "I told them everything."

The FBI didn't buy my story. They wanted to prove I was a liar. I felt suddenly nauseous, the sickly sweet aftertaste of marshmallow sugar in my mouth turning my stomach. Lex was scouring a plate, even though she was standing right beside the dishwasher.

"I don't want you to worry about this, okay?" Patrick said.

"I'm sure it's no big deal, just a routine follow-up. I know it's going to suck having to go through it all again, but you did great today and you can do it again. After this you'll be done for a while. I'll make sure of it."

I took a deep breath. I was sure Patrick was right. I still felt uneasy about Morales, but there had been no concrete signals that they didn't believe me—hell, Lynch had practically wept—so this was probably just routine.

It was just that now I felt like I had things to lose.

"Do you want something to eat?" Lex asked. "I can make you something."

"I'm okay," I said. "I think . . . I think I'm just going to go to bed. I'm wiped."

She nodded. "Whatever you need. We're here."

Despite my exhaustion, sleep wouldn't come. I lay in bed, staring at the faded stars on the ceiling, buried deep under the covers to stay warm in the air-conditioning. I eventually got up to block the air vent and open a window to let the balmy night air in, but it didn't help. The cold had settled into my bones.

My stomach rumbled. I hadn't eaten anything for dinner but marshmallows, and there was an ache inside of me that was something like hunger but different. It was a lack. A *want*. One too complex for me to label. I threw off the covers and got up. I would wake up Lex and ask her to make me something to eat after all. She'd told me to wake her if I ever needed anything, and she was always trying to feed me. Take care of me. It would help.

I walked toward her bedroom and was a little surprised to see a dim light showing through the crack at the bottom of her door. It looked like I wouldn't be waking her after all. I raised my hand to knock when I heard her voice, hushed but agitated.

"How are you so calm about this?" she said. I could tell from the way her voice moved that she was pacing the room. I dropped my hand and moved my ear closer to the door.

"Freaking out about it isn't going to help anything." Patrick was inside as well. "It's probably nothing."

"I *hate* this," she said. "We never should have done this. We never should have brought him here!"

I frowned. What was she—

"Maybe you're right, but it's too late to second-guess things," Patrick said. "He's here now, and we just have to make it work. We have so far."

"God, what were we *thinking*?"

"We had no choice and you know it. She was getting too close. It's all going to be okay."

"You don't know that!"

"I'll *make* it okay if I have to," he said. "Come here."

Lex made a soft sound, and the room went silent.

Or maybe I just couldn't hear them anymore over the rushing of blood in my ears. Tiny black dots had taken over my vision, and I was nothing but a silent, blind, breathless gasp in the dark.

They were talking about me.

I backed away from the door, numb and plodding, almost tripping over myself in my effort to get away.

We never should have brought him here.

How could she say that about me? Her own brother?

She couldn't.

She knew. They both did.

Lex and Patrick knew I wasn't Danny.

When I came back to myself, I was . . . well, I didn't know where I was. I was in my pajamas, barefoot, sitting on the grass of someone else's lawn. I must have run from the house. I had no idea how far I'd gone or how much time had passed, and I didn't care.

Because Lex and Patrick knew.

They knew I wasn't their brother.

No. *No, no, no*. I pressed my fists against my forehead like I could jam the word into my brain and force myself to believe it. I didn't know what they knew. The snippet of conversation I'd overheard could be anything. I tried to remember every word. Lex was freaking out, Patrick was telling her it would be okay . . .

We never should have brought him here.

I could hear her saying that in my head, and I dug my fingers into the grass. I tried to think of anyone else, no matter how far-fetched, that she could have been talking about, but there was no one. I couldn't explain it away.

It was suddenly so obvious. Pieces that had never quite fit

before began sliding into place. All this time I thought they'd been fooling themselves, willfully missing the clues because they wanted to believe so badly, but it was just the opposite. *I* was the one who had been deluded.

They had instantly accepted me—a stranger with a Canadian accent living thousands of kilometers away who was several years older than their brother—without any kind of proof that I was Danny. They had refused to let my DNA be tested. They had never once questioned the fact that I couldn't remember my life before my kidnapping and had never pressed me for information about what had happened to me.

I was such an idiot.

I thought back to our first meeting at the Collingwood Police Station, trying to remember the exact look in their eyes when they saw me, the exact words that were said. Lex should have pursued acting the way she'd dreamed, because she was good. The way she'd smiled at me when . . .

"Oh my God," I whispered as another piece slotted into place.

That time we spent alone together, when Lex and Patrick showed me pictures of the family on her phone—they hadn't been trying to bond with me or reassure me about my loving family waiting at home. They were prepping me for the test they *knew* the immigration official Patrick had contacted would give me. They were making sure I would pass.

Then there was the way Lex had watched me so closely in my first weeks here. Not because she was worried about me, but because I was a stranger she couldn't trust. Lex telling Mia to lock her door at night. Patrick not blinking when he discovered me studying video of the real Danny and coaching me on how to get through my FBI interview without sounding rehearsed. The signs kept piling up in my head.

My stomach roiled, and I lay back in the grass, the dew cool through my thin T-shirt. Every outburst or whispered conversation I had overlooked or explained away suddenly made sense. And every affectionate look and touch and encouraging word had been a lie.

Who else knew what I really was? Mia couldn't, and I held tightly to that fact, one little piece of stillness in a world that was suddenly spinning around me. She was too young for such a complex deception or to recognize that I wasn't the brother she'd never really known.

Nicholas had been openly suspicious of and even hostile toward me, which was harder to parse. Was he angry because he *knew* I wasn't his brother, or because he suspected I wasn't even when everyone else told him I was?

I had fewer doubts about Jessica. She had to know. I'd always doubted a mother would mistake a stranger for her own child, but I had assumed her alcoholism and disconnection from the family kept her from seeing through my deception. But now that disconnection seemed less selfish—and, frankly, convenient for me—and more sinister. Maybe she wasn't just a self-involved alcoholic who never should have had children. Maybe she had a very big secret to hide, and the only way she could do it was to hide herself. If I hadn't been so determined to believe I'd found a home here, I would have realized what was really going on the night she crashed her car and started screaming that I wasn't her son. But I'd wanted to believe so badly that I'd swallowed every half-baked excuse I'd been given.

This family, this home that I thought was becoming mine, it was all lies. Nothing here had ever been real.

I'd never felt as alone as I did in that moment. Not when I was a little boy hiding in the back of a closet from the raging monster outside or when I was hungry and cold and spending the night walking empty streets so I wouldn't freeze. It was one thing not to be loved, but it was another thing entirely to believe that people loved you and then learn all at once that they didn't. It crushed the air from my lungs.

I lay there, struggling to breathe, for a long time. I searched all of my memories, looking for more clues I had missed and any hint that there'd been something real. Goose bumps rose on my skin, but I didn't sit up, didn't try to warm myself.

I was dimly aware of a thought trying to make its way through all the noise in my head, like a snake through tall grass. It had a long way to travel, but eventually it reached me.

Why?

The question was soft at first, but persistent.

Why?

Why would they lie? Why would they accept a boy they

knew to be an impostor into their home and family? Why play such a risky game?

Because they had to, Patrick had said.

There was only one reason, and I tried to push it away. To focus only on my own tragedy, my own anger that they'd played me at the game I'd thought I invented, the death of my own hopes. But I couldn't escape it. My skin had been covered in goose bumps from the cold only moments ago, but now it flushed hot, my forehead prickling with sweat, the heat building in my gut until I rolled over and vomited bile from my empty stomach onto the neighbor's lush lawn.

There was only one reason the Tates would let me pretend to be Danny when they knew I wasn't. Only one reason they would *have* to.

Because my presence hid their crime.

Because one of them had killed him.

Fuck this. Fuck them and all of this. I was gone.

I stood up on wobbly legs and headed in the direction I thought the house was. I would've taken off right then except I didn't have any shoes. I had to go back into the Tate house one last time, but then I would disappear for good.

It took me fifteen minutes to figure out where I was and make my way back. Patrick's car was still in the driveway, and the lights were off in all the windows, so he must have been spending the night. I slipped in through the front door and then stood in the foyer, listening for sounds of movement anywhere, but the house was silent and still. I took the stairs up to the second floor two at a time. I opened the door to my bedroom—Danny's bedroom—and saw it fresh. This was a dead boy's room. I had always known Danny was probably dead, but I suddenly *felt* it. The chill wasn't just from the air-conditioning. Danny Tate—the boy who'd stuck those stars to the ceiling, who had loved baseball and the color blue—was dead, and one of the people under this roof had killed him.

I dug my old backpack out of the corner of the closet. It was already packed with some spare clothes. I grabbed the laptop Lex had bought me, the stash of cash I'd been collecting bit by bit for weeks just in case, and the credit card with Danny's name on it. I would make one last cash withdrawal tonight and then toss it.

I looked around the room. There was nothing of my own to take with me. The one possession that was really mine—the baseball card with the smiling boy—was in my locker at school where I'd hidden it. I'd always wanted to get rid of that boy, and now that I had to leave him behind, I felt a pang that was akin to a knife in the belly. But there was nothing I could do for him now.

I walked out of the room and out of the house. I paused only once, outside of Mia's door. I pressed my palm against it. She was my one consolation in all of this, the one memory that wouldn't feel poisonous when I was gone.

Then I left the Tate house, and I didn't let myself look back.

Once I was outside of Hidden Hills, I caught a bus to Calabasas and walked a couple of kilometers to Ren's house. By the time I got there, the moon was so high in the sky that it cast no shadows.

I'm not entirely sure why I felt like I had to go there. I'd never said good-byes before when it was time for me to leave a place. Leaving was what I knew best, and I knew it was best to do it clean.

But Ren made me feel messy.

I stood outside the gate that protected her aunt and uncle's house and watched her windows as I called her. After the seventh ring, she picked up.

"Hello?" she mumbled.

"I'm sorry to wake you," I said.

"That's okay. What's up?"

"I'm outside."

"O-kay," she said. "That's a little creepy."

"I need to talk to you," I said. "Can you come down? It's important."

She sounded awake now. "You all right?"

"I'll explain everything," I said, which was a lie. I wouldn't explain anything. I didn't want to disappear with her hating me. There'd be plenty of time for that later.

"I'll be right down," she said.

A couple of minutes later the gate slid open and Ren stepped out wearing a robe tied over ice cream cone pajamas. Her hair was up in a loose ponytail, and she was wearing glasses and a bewildered expression, but still she was incredibly pretty to me in that moment. People are always their most beautiful when you know you're never going to see them again.

"What's going on?" she said.

"I just . . . wanted to see you," I said. Which, weirdly, was the truth. She'd never cared that I was Danny Tate, so our relationship was one of the only things I had that hadn't just been tainted forever. Maybe that's why I'd needed to come here.

She looked at the backpack slung over my shoulder. "What's going on? Are you going somewhere?"

"No," I said.

"How about you come inside?" she said. "It seems like you're wigging out a little—which is cool, we've all been there—but I think you should call your sister."

"No," I said.

"Then, I can call her and—"

"No!"

She started at the sharpness of my tone, and then she was looking at me in that way that so many people did but that she never had. Like I wasn't quite human. Like I was an animal or a thing, something fundamentally different from her. It was the last thing I needed, and she might as well have punched me. I sank down onto the curb and buried my head in my hands. After a moment, she sat down beside me. We were both silent.

"You said you wanted to get to know the real me," I finally said. "Did you mean it?"

"Yeah," she said softly, and when I looked up at her, that look in her eyes was gone, and I was a real person again.

"It's hard for me," I said. "To be honest with people."

"Makes sense," she said. It was true, too, just not for the reasons she thought. It wasn't because I was some traumatized kidnapping victim, but because I had learned to be a con artist at the feet of my mother and the parade of losers she brought into our house. Saying just what I had to to keep someone from raising their voice or raising their hand. Being whatever they wanted me to be in that moment. Increasingly, saying and being nothing at all, because nothing made them happy. Ren bumped my knee with hers. "But hey, no rush. We've got time."

Except we didn't.

"I had—" I swallowed and tried again. "There was . . . this bat."

She cocked her head at me in confusion.

"When I was in Canada," I said. "I'd never had any pets, and I didn't really have any friends or even a stuffed animal, but there was a hole in the screen over the window in the room where I slept, and there was a little silver-winged bat that would crawl in and sleep between the window and the screen during the day. And I . . ."

"What?" she asked.

"God, I don't even know why I'm telling you this story. It's stupid."

"It isn't."

"Well, I . . . I sort of made that bat my friend," I said. "I called him Grey Wing because of this comic book I once read, and I'd make myself wake up before the sun every morning so that I could wait for him to come back after hunting all night. Sometimes I felt like . . . as long as he came back, I could keep going, you know?"

She nodded.

"I was so scared that someday he wouldn't, so I waited," I said. The words had taken control now, and I watched as though outside of myself as I told her this story. This ridiculous but entirely true story. Something that was completely me and no one else and which I had never told another soul. I wasn't even sure why I'd started, except that I wanted to tell her something true before I was gone from here and she discovered how much of me had been lies. "I would talk to him. I'd ask him how his night had been and imagine the story he was telling me in response about flying through the night, hunting moths, hiding from owls. Then I'd tell him about my day. I'd tell him everything that was bothering me, things I never told anyone else. That bat . . . he knew me better than anyone else in my life ever has. Maybe better than anyone ever will."

"What happened to him?" she asked.

I tried to shrug. "One morning he didn't come back."

"Danny . . . ," she said.

I couldn't stand the sound of that name in her mouth. Not after the truth. I stood up.

“I have to go,” I said.

She got up too. “Are you sure? Want me to drive you home?”

I shook my head. “I’ll be okay.”

She frowned. “Okay.”

I looked at her for a second, thinking about what I should say, what I should do, what someone other than me would say or do right now.

And then I thought, fuck it. I was already gone. No reason not to do exactly what I wanted.

I pulled her to me and kissed her. My bottom two fingers curled into the top of her pajama bottoms, which were cool and fuzzy-soft, and my top two fingers curled into her flesh, which was sleep-warm and smooth. She was startled, but she didn’t pull away, and, slowly, she raised one hand to touch my jaw with her fingertips.

I’d never kissed anyone like that before.

She pushed me back, not entirely, just enough for me to see the worry in her eyes.

“What’s wrong?” she asked.

“I don’t want to go,” I said.

“Then don’t,” she said. “You’re really freaking me out here.”

“I’m sorry,” I said, backing away from her. “I have to leave.”

“Danny, wait,” she said.

But I couldn’t say any of the things I wanted to, and I couldn’t stand to hear her call me that name again. I started to walk away.

"I'm sorry," I said over my shoulder, and then I turned a corner and she was gone.

That should have been the end of it. I should have disappeared after that. But I didn't. If I had, I wouldn't be here telling you this story, would I?

I called a cab to take me to the airport. With the stack of cash I'd been building up over the weeks, I bought a ticket to Toronto on the first flight in the morning and then sat in a chair under a flickering fluorescent light to wait.

For a long time I just stared blankly out of a window, watching lights coming and going outside. Then, slowly, the numbness started to ebb. I began to think. The question got louder and louder in my head until I couldn't ignore it anymore.

Did I really need to leave?

Did anything have to change just because I knew the truth now?

As fucked up as it was, the Tates and I had the perfect symbiotic relationship. They needed me to deflect suspicion away from them, and I needed them to live something resembling a real life. If I left, it meant living on the run again, alone and on edge. If I stayed, knowing what I knew now, I'd actually be *more* secure than before. Lex and Patrick knew I wasn't Danny, which meant I no longer had to fear exposing myself. I would not only have a roof over my head, and a damn nice one at that, but I would have a new kind of freedom. And I'd have Mia, and Ren, which was already a lot more than I'd ever had before.

Over the loudspeaker, a voice announced that my flight to Toronto was starting its preboarding.

As much of a sham as continuing to live as Danny Tate would be, if I was honest with myself, which I sometimes was, it was still better than any of the alternatives. The Tates and I would all be better off if we kept living with our lies.

I stood, looking down at my ticket. To my left, the line was forming to board the plane. To my right, the airport exit. I took a deep breath, then another, and then I threw my ticket into the trash, walked out of the terminal, and caught a cab back to Hidden Hills.

Slipping under the covers of Danny's bed after sneaking back into the house as the sun rose made me feel like some kind of grave robber, and it was hard to sleep.

But when I woke up, I smelled pancakes and Lex smiled at me when I entered the kitchen and handed me a plate and it didn't feel that different.

Nicholas drove me to school as usual, and as usual we didn't speak. We went our separate ways as soon as we were inside. Him toward the library, where I knew he met Asher before classes. Me to Mrs. Deckard's classroom, where Ren had French first period.

She arrived a minute or two before the bell was due to ring. I saw her footsteps slow down as she spotted me waiting for her at the other end of the hall, but there was also a tentative kind of smile on her face.

"Hey," I said when she reached me.

"Hey, you're here," she replied. "I thought maybe I wouldn't see you today."

We hugged the wall, staying out of the traffic of kids heading toward their first class.

"Yeah, I was being crazy last night," I said. "Things just kind of . . . got to me, all at once, and I lost it a little bit. I'm sorry."

"Are you feeling better now?" she asked.

I nodded, even though it wasn't entirely true.

She frowned. "Are you getting help, Danny? I think you need to be talking to someone. Someone qualified, I mean."

I kept my face perfectly still even though it felt like my heart was now somewhere in the vicinity of my stomach. I'd scared her. She thought I was crazy. She didn't want me talking to her anymore.

"I . . . yeah, maybe you're right," I said.

"What you've been through, it's too much for anyone to go through alone," she said. "I want to be here for you, but last night . . . You know you can always talk to me, but . . ."

You scared me. I can't handle this. I don't want this.

"I get it," I said, backing away from her.

She caught the bottom of my shirt between her fingers and pulled me closer, lowering her voice. "Wait. I like you and I think you like me, too. But . . ." She sighed. "I just don't think you're ready—"

The bell rang above us.

"I've got to get to class," I said, pulling away from her. I didn't need to hear the rest. I'd heard it enough times from enough people to get the gist.

I don't want you.

She tried to grab my wrist. "Danny—"

"See you later," I said, and joined the flow of students in the hallway.

Normally, that's when I would have disappeared. Become another face in the crowd, one so unremarkable that it just melted away.

But now I was Danny Tate, and the crowd parted around me like the Red Sea before Moses, faces turning toward me, people saying my name, offering me fist bumps and invitations and all the attention I'd soaked up just one day before. Now that I knew Danny had died at the hands of one of the people who was supposed to love him the most, that he was probably nothing more than bones now, it all felt suddenly gross and ghoulish. I spotted a restroom up ahead and ducked into it, closing a stall door behind me and locking it. I sat cross-legged on top of the toilet seat and held my head in my hands, taking deep breaths.

I ignored the squeak of the door opening until a voice said, "Danny?"

Fuck.

There was a knock at the stall door. "Hey, man, it's just me. Asher."

I reluctantly stood and unlocked the stall. "Hi."

The door to the restroom started to open.

"Out of order, try the next one!" Asher said, pushing a wide-eyed freshman back into the hall. He closed the door behind the kid and jammed the stop into the crack at the bottom of the door so no one else could enter. Then he turned to me. "You didn't hear me saying your name in the hall just now?"

"No, sorry," I said.

"I guess a lot of people were trying to talk to you all at once," he said with a knowing look.

"Did you want something?" I asked. Asher had barely spoken to me since Nicholas started giving me the silent treatment, so I didn't see why he'd bother now unless he was here on some mission from his boyfriend, which I had less than zero interest in.

"You don't look so hot, man," he said. "Are you feeling okay? Do you want me to get Nicholas?"

I laughed. "Nicholas doesn't give a shit if I'm feeling okay."

"I know it may seem that way, but you're wrong," he said. "He's really struggling right now, but that doesn't mean he doesn't—"

Whatever Asher was selling, I wasn't buying.

"Look, thanks for the concern, but I'm fine," I said. "I should get going."

I kicked the stop out from under the door and got out of there.

Just a few minutes into second period, an office assistant came to get me out of class. She told me to bring my stuff. I glanced over at Nicholas. His frown of confusion was the same as mine.

When I approached the office, I spotted Lex waiting for me in the hall. My steps slowed. In the early morning bustle of getting everyone ready for work and school, I'd managed to avoid saying much to her and Patrick. I wasn't sure how to now that I knew the truth.

When she looked up from her phone and saw me, she beckoned me toward her.

"Come on," she said. "We're leaving."

She hooked her arm into mine and led me outside. I was caught.

"Why?" I asked. The bright glare of the sun hurt my eyes. She was acting normal, but I knew now how little that meant, and my mind jumped to worst-case scenarios. The FBI wanted to see me again right then. Lex and Patrick were tired of this game and had decided to turn me over. They knew I knew and were going to make me disappear the same way Danny had.

"You tell me," she said as she slid into the driver's seat of her car, which she'd left idling by the curb.

If I started running, now, how far could I get before she caught me?

The passenger's window came rolling down, and Lex peered at me from behind the steering wheel.

"What are you doing?" she said. "Get in the car."

If I did get away, how far could I get?

"Danny!" She laughed. "Get in the car!"

It's not like I had a real choice. I opened the passenger's door and climbed inside. Lex started to drive.

"Nicholas's mystery boyfriend called me," she said as we pulled out of the CHS parking lot. "Seems like a nice kid. He said it looked like you could use a personal day."

I was relieved, and annoyed. "I told him I was fine."

"Well then I sprang you for nothing," she said with a shrug. "But at least you can keep me company today. It gets so boring when you guys are all at school. We'll have fun."

"Okay," I said. I'd have to figure out how to be around Lex at some point anyway, and at least this way I wouldn't have to figure out where to sit at lunch today.

She turned and smiled at me, and it turned out that Lex was ten times the liar I was, because if I didn't know better, I would have sworn it was real.

She took me to lunch, where we talked about my school and Mia's upcoming surgery to have her brace removed and a hundred little mundanities. Truthfully, once I relaxed a little, it wasn't that different from before. We were both still lying. The only difference was I now knew it, just like she always had. Well, that and the sour, queasy feeling I got in my gut whenever she gave me one of her loving smiles or asked with apparent interest how I was doing, not because she actually gave a shit about me, but because it was her job to manage the impostor and make sure nothing went wrong with the scheme. I couldn't believe what an idiot I was for not seeing it before. Me, of all people.

We returned home to find Jessica's car—the now repaired SUV she'd crashed the night I should have realized the truth—parked in the driveway, that mysterious orange dust lining the treads of the tires. We didn't see her, though, and Lex and I ended up in the rec room, sprawled out on the couch, watching her soaps on the big screen.

"Wait, Savannah is with Gage now?" I asked as the two characters kissed passionately.

Lex nodded and popped back a couple of chocolate covered coffee beans from the package she'd grabbed from the kitchen on our way down. Then she passed it to me. "Yeah, his girlfriend—"

"Cordelia?"

"Right. She died in the same plane crash that killed Savannah's fiancé, so they bonded."

"Cordelia's dead?" I asked around a mouthful of coffee beans. "I liked her!"

"Well, they *think* she's dead," Lex said, "but no way they'd kill off such a big character. I'm guessing she's still alive."

After the next commercial break the camera zoomed in on Cordelia waking up in the home of the strange mountain man who'd saved her from the wreckage of the plane crash. I laughed, and Lex whooped and turned to me for a high five.

For a second I'd forgotten. And when I remembered, it stung all over again.

It must have shown on my face, because she said, "Hey, you okay?"

"Yeah, I just . . ." I swallowed. "This is nice."

"Oh, sweetie," she said. She scooted over until we were right beside each other and wrapped me up in her arms. I let her hold me. Part of me hated her, but it still felt nice. It still, somehow, made me feel better, even though I knew it was a lie.

It *had* to be a lie. Lex was just that good an actress. I couldn't let myself start to believe that maybe she'd really come to care about me outside of the con, the way I'd really started to care about her.

That would be incredibly stupid.

"Lex," I said.

"Hmm?" I felt her response more than heard it, the hum of her voice against me.

"Can we watch one of the home movies?" I asked. "From before everything got so messed up?"

I wanted to see her again with Danny. Maybe it was different from the way she was with me. Maybe it would show me that some of whatever this was between us was real.

She pulled away and looked at me. "Yeah. Sure, we can do that."

"Thanks," I said.

She got up and went to the credenza where the DVDs were

kept. She read the labels on the spines before grabbing one and putting it into the player, then sat down beside me again as the movie started. The date at the bottom of the screen said it was 2009. On the screen Robert Tate was filming his wife, who had baby Mia, dressed in a pink bathing suit with little blue dolphins printed on it, held in her arms. Jessica kept trying to hide her face from the camera, telling Robert to go film the kids. Instead, he zoomed in close, until her face—ocean blue eyes, her cheeks pink from the sun, an American sweetheart face—took up the entire frame. Jessica batted him away, and Mia started to cry. Jessica gave Robert an exasperated look, and retreated to the cabin of the boat with the baby.

Robert turned the camera on himself and made a grimace. An I'm-in-trouble face. Then he turned the camera toward the kids who were swimming off the back of the boat.

"Oh, I remember this. It was the Fourth of July," Lex said. "It was so hot it felt like we would die if we got out of the water for even a second."

Danny climbed back onto the boat. He ran, dripping, up the stairs to the wheelhouse and climbed over the barrier until he was standing on a tiny perch, only his grip on a metal railing holding him there. A teenaged Lex yelled at him to be careful. He grinned and let go, cannonballing into the water below. My eyes went back and forth between the video and Lex as she watched it.

"You never had any fear," Lex said with a sad smile.

The picture suddenly grew dark, cutting from the kids

horsing around in the water to the family huddled together under blankets after the sun had gone down.

"Remember the fireworks?" she asked.

"No," I said.

"Oh, Danny." She put a hand on my leg. "I'm sorry."

On the screen the fireworks began. Robert panned between the colors and the family. Jessica had her arms around Nicholas, Lex and Patrick were smooshed together under one big blanket, and Danny was lying on the deck, looking straight up at the sky.

"Stay still," I heard Jessica say while Robert was filming the fireworks above.

Nicholas said, "Danny pinched me—"

"I did not," Danny said. "Don't be such a girl."

"Shut up!"

"Boys!" Robert barked.

Lex grabbed the remote. "You know I love your dad, but he was obsessed with that camera. Who wants to watch a video of fireworks?"

She fast-forwarded until the picture changed from the darkness of the fireworks to another sunny day on a beach somewhere. Nicholas was the one filming this time. First, he captured Robert, Patrick, and Danny throwing a football back and forth, then panned to Jessica talking on her cell phone farther down the beach, then Lex holding Mia in her lap while she stuck her chubby little hands into the sand.

It was easy to forget how young Lex had been when Danny

disappeared, just seventeen. Younger than I was and only a year older than Danny would be now. She was such a good sister, singing Mia a little song as they played in the sand together back then and taking care of all of us now.

But she might be a killer.

That was the only reason I was here. Because a crime couldn't be investigated, its perpetrator put in prison, if the crime had never happened. Someone in this family had killed Danny and was using me to make it all disappear.

Lex and Patrick were my only ironclad suspects, because they were the only ones I *knew* were aware I wasn't really Danny. But at this moment it was impossible to imagine Lex had anything to do with Danny's death, even knowing what a gifted actress she was. She'd obviously had her troubles—I thought of how sickly thin she'd looked in the last home movie I watched and the vague allusions she'd made to problems that kept her from finishing college on time—but her love for her siblings was palpable. She was Mother Lex, the one who'd stepped into the vacuum Jessica had left when she retreated behind her bedroom door, who made us all breakfast every morning and adjusted Mia's brace four times a day and was comforting me now, when she didn't have to, even though she knew I was a liar. I couldn't believe she could hurt Danny.

I *could* believe her love for her family would make her play along in order to protect someone else.

I watched the rest of the video closely, taking in every detail I could and turning my eyes as often as I could to Lex to see if there were any clues I could glean from her face as she watched her old family on the screen. I didn't know what exactly I was looking for, since it was unlikely that one of the Tates, in the midst of frolicking on an exotic beach or attending some family function, would threaten to kill Danny while the camera was rolling. But if there's one thing I've learned, it's that people are bad at keeping secrets, and eventually everything shows. You can learn all there is to know by watching someone hard enough, long enough.

Slowly, as we watched the movie, it dawned on me what I was doing.

I was investigating Danny Tate's death.

For weeks I'd been living in Danny's skin. Sleeping in his bed, sitting in his chair at the table, answering to his name. I had mingled his pain with my own in that FBI interrogation room, and I had smothered myself so that he could live inside of me. I was Danny Tate, and he was me. I felt a strange loyalty to him, maybe even an affection for him, and I couldn't let what had really happened to him stay buried. When someone hurts a child, that person should pay. I was a liar and a con artist and probably a terrible person, but I still believed that.

I would find out the truth, because Danny deserved it. And because Mia, who was the only person I *knew* to be innocent in all of this, deserved it. I could get them that justice.

. . . or, because I was a terrible person, I could use the truth for myself, as leverage whenever I needed to.

I hadn't decided yet.

That weekend I made a password protected folder on my laptop to hold all of my research on Danny's disappearance. When I was supposed to be sleeping, I spent hours scouring the Internet, adding to it. There was a lot less information online than I'd hoped to find. A photogenic young white boy had gone missing from one of America's safest and wealthiest communities. The story was a cable news producer's dream. It should have been *everywhere*, but it had barely made a blip on the radar.

It seemed the rarefied nature of Hidden Hills, the very exclusivity that made Danny's kidnapping such a shocking story, also helped keep it from becoming a widely known one. The gates around Hidden Hills slammed shut after Danny disappeared, the community withdrawing to protect its people and its way of life. The Tate family did the same thing. Other than one televised appeal given by Robert with the rest of the family in the background and the occasional comment from the family's spokesperson and lawyer, the Tates never spoke publicly about Danny. When I'd first found out about this, I'd chalked it up to a weird rich people thing I couldn't understand. Like seeking out publicity in the midst of their personal tragedy would seem common and crass to them. But it made more sense once I realized someone in the family had something to hide.

There was still some information to be found now that I was really digging, though. The basics were well documented in the recent *LA Magazine* article and elsewhere. Jessica had called the police at eight in the evening on a Saturday to report Danny missing. The last time he'd been seen was at breakfast that morning, when he'd told the family he was going to ride his bike to his friend Andrew's house. When Jessica got home at six and Danny still wasn't back, she and the kids—Robert was out of town on business—called Danny's friends and drove around the neighborhood looking for him. When she got ahold of Andrew's parents and learned that Danny had never been to their house that day, Jessica phoned the police.

The cops immediately issued an AMBER Alert. A house-to-house search was conducted in Hidden Hills, and the security tapes and logs from the community's gates were examined. Nothing suspicious was found. It was like Danny had disappeared into thin air. More likely, of course, was that he had left the community in the trunk of a car or the back of one of the dozens of authorized work vans that had passed through the gates that day.

The press that *was* following the case—mostly the local paper and news stations—was focused on the idea of an outside threat. Hidden Hills was home to wealthy CEOs and movie stars; what better place to scoop up a kid who could be ransomed for millions?

But from the start law enforcement seemed to have a different view. Judging by the number of times he was reportedly brought in for questioning, it was clear to me who the FBI's main suspect was.

Patrick.

Patrick found me out by the pool, where I was keeping an eye on Mia as she swam.

"Hey," he said as he sat down in the lounge chair next to mine.

"Patrick!" Mia said. "Look how fast I am!"

She dog-paddled with little grace but great enthusiasm across the shallow end of the pool. Ever since the weather had turned warmer, she'd been practically living in the water, only emerging for school and meals, her fingers permanently puckered.

"That's great, Mia," Patrick said with a wide, white toothed smile. For a second I imagined him with blood spattered across his face, and I had to shake my head to lose the image. His smile was gone when he turned to me. "I need to talk to you."

"Sure," I said. I had a handful of quarters that I'd been throwing one at a time for Mia to dive for. I grabbed them all and chucked them into the pool at once. Mia shrieked and dove. "What's up?"

"It's the FBI," Patrick said. "I've put them off as long as I can. We need to go in again tomorrow."

I swallowed. "Okay. At least I had a little time off, right?"

He put his hand on my shoulder, and I wondered why the FBI had suspected him. Was it just demographics, the fact that most killers are young men, and Patrick was the only one who fit the bill? Or was there some evidence against him I didn't know about?

"I'm sorry, D," he said, "but after this we'll both be done with them."

Mia swam up to the edge of the pool closest to us and dropped another quarter onto the small, wet pile on the concrete. "I'm rich!" she said.

Lex was not pleased.

"No way!" she said, slamming the cabinet door shut after pulling out a stack of plates for the takeout she'd ordered for dinner. "He's not doing it!"

"Lexi, you knew this was coming," Patrick said.

"It's too much to ask of him," she said, tearing up. I knew now that she was only scared for herself and whomever she was protecting, but for a moment it felt like it was me she was protecting again. "He's only been home a few months. He needs time to heal, not all this constant questioning."

"I wish there was something I could do, but—"

"Well try harder!" Lex snapped.

She fled the room, throwing off Patrick's hand when he tried to catch her, and didn't come out of her room for the rest of the night.

Patrick and I went back to the L.A. field office alone. Lex pulled a Jessica and disappeared after spending the night locked in her room. Maybe if I spent more time locked in *my* room, any suspicions Morales might have that I wasn't really a Tate would be laid to rest.

Morales greeted us coolly when we met in the lobby. I understood now why just the sight of her made Patrick and Lex so tense and angry. Her cool professionalism, brisk walk, and smartly pressed slacks felt like a slap in the face when she was trying so hard to ruin my life. It made me want to shake her until she was as much of a mess as the rest of us.

"How's school, Danny?" Morales asked as she walked us back into the office.

"Fine," I said.

"Are you catching up okay?"

I could feel Patrick's eyes on me. I just shrugged. "It's a lot to catch up on."

"Well, I'm sure you'll get there," she said.

She took the two of us back to the same interview room we'd used last time. Lynch came in a minute later with a laptop under one arm and a couple of bottles of water cradled in the other. He put the water on the table in front of us while he got the laptop up and running. Neither Patrick nor I took one.

Morales and Lynch showed me dozens and dozens of mug shots, asking if anyone looked familiar. I told them no a hundred times, that I had been blindfolded for most of my abduction, but pointed out a couple of men who I said looked a little like the men who'd held me captive over the years. I picked them out of the sea of faces at random. Hopefully that would keep them busy for a little while.

"Thank you, Danny. This is helpful," Morales said. "Now my colleague Margaret Hamilton is going to come in here and talk to you. I'd like you to tell her your story, and Mr. McConnell, while that's happening, I'd like to speak with you privately, if you don't mind."

Patrick's hands curled into loose fists on the table. "Actually, I do. I wasn't aware *I* was here to be questioned. I came as Danny's lawyer, and I need to be present during his questioning."

"It's not questioning, Mr. McConnell," Morales said. "Danny's not in trouble. We just want to see if there's any other information he may have that can help us catch whoever did this to him."

"Regardless, I won't—"

"It's okay," I interjected.

"No, Danny, it isn't," Patrick said.

"Really, it is," I said. Hopefully, cooperating with Morales would earn me some goodwill, and I could lie just as easily—if not more so—without Patrick hovering over my shoulder.

Plus, there was a chance that being questioned by Morales would knock Patrick enough off-balance that I might be able to learn something from him.

"I'll be fine," I told Patrick when he continued to protest. "Let's just get this over with."

Patrick's jaw strained against his skin, but he had to know

that if he continued to argue, he risked making himself look more suspicious to a woman who already had her doubts about him. He looked at me and I looked right back at him, and something like honesty passed between us. I wasn't his traumatized kid brother; I was a practiced con artist, and he knew it. I could handle this, and he knew that, too.

"Fine," he said. "But if you start to feel uncomfortable, you tell them you want to see me, and you don't say another word until I get here, got it?"

I nodded, and Patrick left the room with Morales while Margaret Hamilton came in and took Morales's vacated chair. She was older than Morales and not as put together—wavy blonde hair that was graying at the roots, like she hadn't had time to dye it in a while, a suit with a button coming undone, glasses instead of contact lenses—and she was wearing a wedding ring and another band with three small stones, the kind husbands bought for their wives to represent their children.

I wasn't worried.

Agent Hamilton settled herself in the interview room and offered me a soda. I said no thanks. No playing fast and loose with my DNA inside the FBI field office.

"Good choice," the agent said. "I always tell my kids that stuff will rot your teeth right out of your head."

She was trying to make an emotional connection with me, to put me at ease. It was such a transparent tactic that I felt compelled to use one of my own.

"It tastes too sweet to me," I said with a shy little shrug. "I guess I'm just . . . not used to it."

The smile melted off her face, and I knew I had her.

Agent Hamilton had me tell her my entire story again. The abduction, the weeks of torture, the places they took me and the things they made me do with the men there. She tried hard to maintain her professionalism, but I saw the sheen in her eyes when I told her some particularly gruesome detail, and it spurred me on. Most of my story was pre-scripted with Patrick, but I also made up a few flourishes as I went along, because all great artists follow their intuition sometimes. I focused on things that I thought would really get to someone like her, like how I would comfort myself at night by quietly humming the tune of a lullaby my mother used to sing to me long after I forgot the words. She actually teared up when I said that.

It took more than an hour for Hamilton to finish with me, and then I was passed off to another agent. It was clear to me now what they were doing—testing to see if my story would change at all as I told it over and over again. They were probably doing the same thing with Patrick, making sure our stories aligned with each other's as well.

Agent Willis took me to his office for our interview. He was in his sixties, a gruff and grizzled man who walked with a limp I was willing to bet was the result of an injury on the job, either with the FBI or in the military. I took a quick look at the two framed photos on his desk that were angled enough for me to glimpse them. A staged family photo with a couple of kids and a couple of grandkids, and three men in camouflage in a deer stand. Vulnerable and emotional wouldn't work with Willis the way it had with Hamilton. It would make him uncomfortable, and he'd start looking for holes in my story as a way to keep his distance from it. So with Willis I went tough. Danny Tate was defiant in the face of what had been done to him, angry and ashamed of his victimization.

When Willis asked, "What can we do for you, Danny?" I looked him in the eye and said, "You can find those bastards and kill them." And Willis nodded.

When Willis was done with me, he clapped his hand on my shoulder and said I was a damn brave kid and those sons of bitches wouldn't get away with this. Then he passed me on to the next person.

Interviewer number three introduced himself to me as Sean Graves, and I knew even before he told me—from the way he shook my hand and the soothing tone of his voice as he asked me to call him Sean—that he was a psychologist.

This one was going to be a little bit trickier.

Sean took me to a different kind of room, one with a leather couch and armchair and a ficus that needed dusting.

"So, Danny—do you mind if I call you Danny?" he said.

"Everyone does," I said.

His grin was sharp around the edges. "That's not what I asked."

Shit.

"Danny's fine," I said.

"Okay then, that's what I'll call you," he said. "First, I just want to make it clear that I'm not here in any law enforcement capacity. The agents just wanted me to talk to you and see how you're doing."

"You're not FBI?" I asked.

"I'm a consultant," he said. "Do you want to tell me a little bit about how things have been since you returned home?"

Sean was hard for me to nail down. He was a young guy, probably early thirties. He wore no wedding ring. His suit was nicer than the ones worn by most of the agents—the result of not being on a federal salary—but it wasn't particularly nice either. His expression was pleasant but bland, and it never wavered. It was a mask as unmoving as the plastic ones kids wore at Halloween and only slightly more lifelike. He was smart and observant, but beyond that he was a cipher. Without knowing who he was, I didn't know who I needed to be for him, and that made me uneasy.

"Things have been okay," I said. Without knowing what role to play, I decided not to play one. Something told me Sean would see through theatrics anyway. "It's been hard, but it's good to be with my family."

Sean just nodded. "How has it been hard?"

"Well, it's a lot of adjustment," I said. "Even normal things, you know, seem new to me."

"What about your relationships with your family members?" he asked.

I thought of Mia throwing herself into my arms, trusting completely that I would catch her. Nicholas watching me across a crowded courtyard. Lex trying to get me to take second helpings of food and ruffling my hair as she passed my chair. Jessica haltingly asking me about school and Patrick laughing at my terrible attempts to shift gears in the Jag when he took me to drive in an abandoned parking lot. They were the best family I'd ever had, and it was all total, total bullshit.

"They're good," I said. "Everyone's been so supportive, and—"

"I'm going to stop you right there, Danny," Sean said. "Let's try that answer again, but this time, tell me what you really feel instead of what you feel like you should."

Shit shit shit.

This guy was good. I had no choice but to be as honest as possible if I wanted to get out of this interview without arousing any more suspicion than I already had.

"I . . . it's hard," I said. "They *are* supportive, but I know I'm not the same boy I was when I was little. It's like . . . it's almost like we're strangers sometimes."

"That does sound difficult," Sean said.

"It is . . . ," I said.

"But?" he prodded. "It sounded like there was something else you wanted to say there."

I swallowed around the sudden, very real lump in my throat.

"But . . . I love them. And I want them to love me, not wish I was the boy who disappeared six years ago. I want them to know the me I am now."

"You've changed," Sean said.

"Yeah." I rubbed a hand across my forehead. "Yeah, I have."

It was the best damn performance of my life, because for once I was telling the truth.

Morales came to collect me from my meeting with Dr. Sean. She told me they were done. Patrick was waiting for me in the lobby, and we could go. She escorted me back to the front of the building.

"I'm sorry we had to bring you in again," Morales said. "I know it can't be easy for you to relive."

"I would have thought that was the point," I said.

She looked taken aback, which was pretty satisfying. "Excuse me?"

"Well, the reason you brought me back is you wanted to see how I'd respond to the stress, right?" I asked. "If my story would change at all?"

She smiled slowly. "Well, you never know what pressures or different approaches might cause a breakthrough, and that's all we're after here."

"I understand," I said.

"I thought you would," she said. "You're a very clever young man. Very perceptive."

Morales opened the door to the lobby for me. Patrick was waiting.

"I had to be," I said, and Patrick and I left.

Patrick drove me home. When I asked him on the way what Morales questioned him about, he dodged.

"Just the usual stuff," he said. "You hungry?"

I said no, and Patrick dropped me off at home. He said he had an early deposition in the morning that he had to get ready for and I should give everyone his love. His headlights were gone before I'd even gotten to the front door.

Once I was alone, I took a deep breath and allowed myself to smile. I'd done it. Morales might be suspicious, but I'd gone through four FBI interviews and they had nothing on me. Maybe now I was out of the woods with them, and that meant I was as safe here as I could ever be.

I went inside the house and found Nicholas and Mia in the den, him on his laptop and her watching a movie. I sat down next to Mia, who put a pillow in my lap and laid her head down.

"Where is everyone?" I asked.

"Out," Nicholas said without looking up from his screen.

"Where?" It wasn't strange for Jessica to be gone, but it was weird for Lex not to be here. I would have thought she'd be waiting at the door for me, probably with food in her arms.

Nicholas shrugged. He obviously didn't find it as strange

as I did. He closed his laptop and left the room.

For the next couple of hours I hung out with Mia, serving as her human pillow while she finished her movie and then playing game after game of Spit, her new obsession.

"I'm hungry," she finally said, and I checked the clock on the cable box. It was after seven, and still neither Jessica nor Lex was home.

"Me too," I said. "Let's see what there is to eat."

We went to the refrigerator and peered inside.

"Oh," I said. "Nothing."

"Can we order a pizza?" Mia asked.

"Yeah, sure," I said. "Go ask Nicholas what he wants."

Mia ran upstairs and came back with Nicholas in tow.

"Lex isn't home yet?" he asked when he came into the kitchen.

I shook my head. "I'm going to call her."

While Nicholas called to order two large pizzas—"And mozzarella sticks!" Mia said—I dialed Lex's number. It went to voice mail, so I tried texting her. *Where are you? Everything okay?*

A half an hour later, the gate buzzer went off.

"I'll get it," I said. Mia followed me into the foyer, singing, "Mozzarella sticks, mozzarella sticks!"

I hit the button that would automatically open the gate, and opened the front door to wait for the pizza guy to drive up. But he was already there, climbing out of his car. Behind him Jessica was pulling up.

"Evening," the delivery guy said.

"Hey, how's it going?" I said, but I wasn't really paying attention. I was watching Jessica climb out of her car. She seemed more or less sober, which was good. Her windshield was coated in dust. She didn't wobble on her high heels as she walked up behind the delivery guy and swept into the house.

"Want some pizza, Mom?" I asked her retreating form.

"Or some mozzarella sticks?" Mia added.

Jessica didn't say anything, just disappeared up the stairs. I was probably imagining it, but I swear I could hear the click of the lock as she hid herself behind the door to her bedroom.

"She never wants to eat with us anymore," Mia said.

I signed the delivery guy's receipt while Mia took the boxes he handed her. "Did she use to?" I asked. "Before I got back?"

Mia shrugged. "I usually ate with Magda, but sometimes Mom would eat too. More than she does now."

So Jessica *was* avoiding me. Mia and I took the pizza to the kitchen, where Nicholas was setting cold sodas and a roll of paper towels on the kitchen table.

"Mom's home," Mia said as we came in.

"She went upstairs," I added. "She . . . wasn't hungry."

Nicholas smiled grimly. "Of course not."

"Why doesn't she eat with us anymore?" Mia asked.

Nicholas's eyes flickered up to me and then away again. "I don't know, Mimi. I guess she's just tired."

The three of us ate and cleaned up and watched another movie and Mia went to bed, and still Lex wasn't home. I sent her another text and left another voice mail. Nicholas called Patrick, but he didn't answer either, which was not unusual if he was working like he said he would be. He often turned off his phone whenever he went to the law library.

"This is weird," Nicholas said. "Something's wrong."

If he was worried enough to be voluntarily speaking to me in more than monosyllables, it had to be.

"What should we do?" I asked.

Nicholas fished his keys out of his school bag. "I'm going to find her."

"I'm coming with."

He shook his head. "Someone's got to stay here with Mia."

"Mom's upstairs," I said.

"Whatever," he said, and didn't protest when I followed him to the garage and climbed into the passenger's seat of his car.

"Where do you think she is?" I said as we left the gates of Hidden Hills behind.

"Her house," Nicholas said. "Maybe one of her friends'. I have no idea. Try calling again."

I called for the fourth time, and this time it went straight to voice mail without any rings. "Her phone is off," I said.

Nicholas drove to Lex's house, which I had never seen before. It was a small Craftsman in Century City on a street full of small, pretty houses. From the light of the streetlamp, I could see that Lex's place had an air of neglect that none of the other homes had. The lawn had patches of dead, brown grass, and the paint was beginning to peel. Maybe it was because Lex wasn't here very often, or maybe it didn't occur to her to take care of a place that was already so much less grand than the home she had come from. Her car was parked at the curb, but Nicholas didn't seem relieved, so I didn't feel relieved either.

Nicholas knocked on the front door, but at the same time he tried the knob and found it unlocked. Without waiting for Lex to answer, he walked inside and I followed him.

"Lex?" he called. I spotted a switch on the wall and flipped on the lights. The place was a wreck. Unopened mail was piled up by the door. Clothes were strewn across the floor. Empty bottles lined the countertops. It was hard to reconcile this place with the Lex who was always cleaning at home.

"Lex?" Nicholas called again. There was no answer, and he started walking through rooms. I followed behind.

"Goddammit," he said when he reached an open doorway. I came up behind him and saw Lex in her bedroom, passed out on top of the covers, a bottle of wine on the nightstand.

It looked to me like she'd just had a little too much to drink and fallen asleep—not exactly an emergency—but Nicholas rushed to her side and began to shake her.

"Lex, wake up!"

She roused slightly and moaned, but she didn't open her eyes. Nicholas bent over her and lifted one of her eyelids with his fingers. The eye underneath was shockingly blue, her pinprick sized pupil almost swallowed up completely. I knew that look.

My heart seized in my chest.

"Fuck," Nicholas said. He knew it too. "Go into her bathroom. Grab any pill bottles you find in the medicine cabinet and then come back here."

The bathroom was next door, and behind the mirror I found a half a dozen prescription bottles. I grabbed all of them with unsteady hands and shoved them into the pockets of my jeans. There was no way to know which she had taken. In the next room I could hear Nicholas saying Lex's name, trying to get her up.

When I came back in, he had her sitting up, all of her weight flopped forward on his shoulders.

"I can't get her up," he said.

"We'll carry her," I said.

Together we got Lex to her feet. She wasn't totally unconscious, but she wasn't exactly awake, either, and she did little more than hang limply between us as we carried her out to the car. I sat in the back with her as Nicholas got into the driver's seat.

"Should we call an ambulance?" I said.

He shook his head and gunned the car to life. "This will be faster. Tell me if she stops breathing."

I shook Lex whenever she started to drift off. "Stay awake!"

In the front seat Nicholas honked at a slow moving car in front of us and cursed when we hit a red light.

"Look at me, Lex," I said, slapping her cheek just hard enough to focus her. "Keep your fucking eyes open!"

When we reached the emergency room, Nicholas ran inside and came back out with an orderly and a nurse with a wheelchair, who took Lex away. I gave the medications I'd found in her bathroom to another nurse and told them we didn't know what she'd taken. Then Nicholas and I went to the waiting room and took seats in the plastic chairs against the wall. He called Jessica and told her what had happened, while I called Patrick and left him another voice mail. After we'd both hung up, we just sat there in silence for a long time as the last of the adrenaline burned out of our systems.

"This isn't the first time, you know," he finally said. Unnecessary, since his response to the situation was clearly one of familiarity. "Probably no one's told you this yet, but Lex and pills go way back."

"Yeah?" I said.

He nodded, staring off into the middle distance. "I guess it started around the time her dad died. But things got really bad after . . ."

"After me," I said. "I really ruined everything, didn't I?"

"Not *you*," he said. "The animals who took you."

We were both silent for a minute. I kept seeing Lex's eyes, unfocused and unseeing. I felt shaky and hollow. What would I do if she died? What would any of us do?

"She OD'd in college," Nicholas continued after a long pause. "Patrick found her half-dead, and she was unconscious for two days. She went to rehab and relapsed a couple of times, but she's been sober for almost two years now. At least we thought she was."

Why now? The question hung in the air between us like the antiseptic smell of rubbing alcohol, thick and sharp. Patrick and I had spent the entire day being questioned by the FBI, and Lex had thrown back a fistful of pills with a half a bottle of wine. I wondered if the connection was as clear to Nicholas as it was to me.

The numb, impassive look on his face was starting to crumble. His lips thinned into two straight lines and his brow furrowed as he tried to hold it in, but he couldn't. He rested his face in his hands and started to cry.

"Hey . . ." I leaned closer to him. "Hey, it's okay . . ."

"It's just first Mom went off the deep end, then Dad got put away, and Patrick became this total stranger," he said, his voice muffled, "so if something happens to Lex . . ."

"She's going to be okay." I didn't know what to do. Should I hug him? I wasn't good with things like this.

"This fucking family," he said. "Who's going to look out for Mia? I'm going to be trapped here with these fucking people just as I was about to get out."

I finally put a hand on his back. He tensed beneath the touch at first, but slowly I felt his muscles begin to relax.

"It's going to be okay. Lex will be fine." She *had* to be. "And so will Mia and so will all of us."

Slowly, then all at once, Nicholas turned and put his arms

around me. His hands fisted into the back of my shirt.

"We'll get through this," I said, finding the words I wished someone had said to me once. "You're not alone, okay?"

"Thanks, Danny," he said, and it sounded so strange that I wondered if it was the first time he'd ever called me by name.

I swiped Nicholas's phone when he went to the restroom to wash his face and texted Asher, asking him to come. He arrived less than an hour later, so he must have redlined it. He rushed right up to us, pulled Nicholas out of his chair, and threw his arms around him.

"Oh my God, hon, how is she?" he said. "How are you?"

Nicholas's initial look of bewilderment changed to one that looked like a mixture of pain and relief.

"They told us she's stable, but that's all we know," he said. "How are you here?"

"Danny texted me when you didn't, you big idiot," Asher said, still holding him tight.

Nicholas turned his head to look at me. After a moment he nodded his head in a way I thought meant 'thank you.'

Together, the three of us waited. Asher got us snacks from the vending machine and chided Nicholas until he ate. I tried Patrick's cell again. We watched the news on the television in the waiting room with no interest.

Patrick arrived—breathless and panicked, explaining that he'd been in the library—just as a doctor came to tell us they were ready to discharge Lex. After a couple of hours of oxygen and charcoal, she was safe to go home to rest. When a nurse brought her out, she took one look at us and started to cry.

"I'm so sorry," she said, the words practically unintelligible, as Patrick wrapped her up in his arms, nearly swallowing up her tiny frame.

She tried to reach for Nicholas, but he shied away from her, and she just cried harder. Patrick kept an arm around her waist and steered her toward the door, saying he'd meet us at home. Asher stood awkwardly against a wall, keeping his distance, until they were gone. Then he kissed Nicholas and said he would call him in the morning and left as well.

Nicholas and I drove back to the house in silence. Patrick took Lex up to bed, and we all went to sleep.

The next morning Lex made French toast and smiled and asked Mia about her homework, and it was like it had never happened.

Lex's overdose brought home for me again how good this family could be at keeping secrets and how little I actually knew about them. It was time to move on from what had happened the day Danny disappeared to the suspects. Maybe it was just the effect of sitting in that waiting room not knowing if Lex was going to live or die, but I felt like something bad was coming, nipping at my heels. Like time was running out.

When everyone else was occupied, I made my way to Robert's

office, just down the hall from Danny's bedroom. There was a filing cabinet in the closet that I had spotted when I'd first arrived and was familiarizing myself with the house. I'd tried to open it but found it locked. Maybe some of the Tate family secrets were kept inside.

When I got to the office, I closed the door behind myself and began to look for a key to the cabinet. If I couldn't find one, I'd probably be able to jimmy the thing open with a screwdriver or a crowbar, but I didn't want to leave evidence of what I'd done if I could avoid it. Besides, most people didn't go to great lengths to hide the keys for these kinds of things.

I sat in the leather chair behind the desk and began to go through the drawers one by one. You'd be surprised how many people leave the keys to a filing cabinet in their top drawer. Robert Tate wasn't quite that dumb, though. I searched every drawer and the cabinets behind the desk thoroughly, but all I found were dusty office supplies and, to my surprise, a distinctive kind of triangular case that could only hold a small handgun. Another item added to my list of reasons to consider Robert a suspect.

I got up and peered out of the window into the backyard. Lex was in the pool with Mia while Patrick worked on his laptop in one of the lounge chairs. Nicholas was out of the house, and Jessica was upstairs. I had all the time in the world.

I took another look at the filing cabinet. Could Robert Tate be one of the rare people who took home office security seriously? When he lived in a gated house in a gated community? The pistol seemed to suggest so, and this was a big house. He could have hidden the key anywhere. I shined my phone's flashlight down at one of the middle cabinets, trying to get a look at the gap between the drawer and the cabinet itself, to gauge what kind of tool I would need to get into it.

That's when I noticed the scratches.

The hardwood floor was scratched, extending about a half an inch from the front corners of the filing cabinet. Not deep scratches, but the diffuse pattern of many smaller ones.

I smiled, grabbed onto the cabinet, and tipped it forward. It scraped against the floor as I did it. Holding the cabinet with one hand, I brushed the other along the back that had been pressed to the wall until I found the key taped there.

Not bad, Robert. But not good enough.

Inside the cabinets I found the usual things. Tax returns, financial statements, lots of business and legal stuff I couldn't decipher. I kept looking until I found what I was after. In the bottom drawer there was a file on each family member.

Mia's was the first. It had her birth certificate and social security card, correspondence with the private Montessori school she attended for preschool, and a couple of crayon drawings she must have made for her daddy. Behind it was a second file labeled MIA—MEDICAL that had hospital bills, insurance statements, and other documents related to Mia's limb length discrepancy. Nothing out of the ordinary, not that I was expecting to find anything there. If there was anyone I knew to be completely innocent, it was Mia.

Next was Danny's file. In most ways it was similar to Mia's, except instead of an accompanying file of medical information, there was an accompanying file labeled DANIEL—DISAPPEARANCE. It looked like Robert had made note of every interaction the family had with the local police and later the Feds when the FBI took over. I pulled the thick file out of the cabinet to go through it more carefully later.

Then came Nicholas. His file was the thinnest so far. Birth certificate, some school records, a hospital record from when he broke his wrist in 2009, and a story written in wavering pencil. I pulled it from the file and read it. It was about a knight who saved a poor dragon from a cruel princess.

Nicholas was eleven when Danny disappeared. It was difficult to fathom *any* eleven-year-old—let alone quiet, controlled Nicholas—killing someone, but his relationship with Danny had been a troubled one, and he was the only member of the family who seemed angry that I was around. Maybe one day all of the anger that Nicholas had been bottling up over his brother's taunting and petty bullying finally exploded. If Lex and Patrick, and probably Jessica, were going to engage in such a risky and emotionally difficult deception, it had to be to protect someone they really cared about and didn't want to see punished for Danny's death. Who could fit that description better than Nicholas? Still waters run deep, and no one's face was more still than that serious, secretive boy. Maybe he didn't seem capable of killing someone, but then, lots of killers don't.

Next was Lex's file, and it had an addendum as well: ALEXIS—ADDICTION.

Nicholas wasn't kidding. It was bad.

It had started in high school. There'd been some trouble her freshman and sophomore years—a suspension for fighting in school and an incident where she was a passenger in a car where the driver was caught smoking weed—but things had escalated sharply around the time Ben McConnell killed himself. She was arrested a handful of times for possession and hospitalized twice. Robert pulled some major strings to keep her from being expelled from school. She was hospitalized a third time after Danny disappeared in what appeared to doctors to be a suicide attempt instead of an accidental overdose. She dropped out of school to do six months at an inpatient rehab facility. The next couple of years were a cycle of relapse, chaos, and more stints in rehab. She'd been released from Promises Malibu almost two years ago, and the file ended there. To an objective observer it would seem like nothing more than a troubled, privileged girl struggling with the tragic death of her father. And maybe that's what it was.

Or maybe not.

I got up and looked out the window again, just to make sure everyone was still in the backyard. Lex was spinning Mia around in the water. It was hard for me to imagine her hurting anyone, let alone one of the siblings she doted on like a mother. But I had to remind myself that a few weeks ago it would have been hard for me to imagine that Lex was pretending to think I was her brother. She was a gifted actress covering for someone, and maybe that person was herself.

I tried to envision how it could have happened. Lex, high on prescription pills, behind the wheel even though her license had been suspended. Too out of her mind to react in time when Danny darted in front of the car on his bicycle. Maybe she panicked and hid the body rather than owning up to what she did. Maybe that's what she and Patrick were covering up. There was nothing they could do for Danny, but at least they could keep Lex out of jail. The shock of what she'd done made her try to get sober, and the pressure of the FBI sniffing around again made her crack. It was possible.

I moved on to the next file, Patrick's.

It was empty. I guess Patrick also knew where the key to the filing cabinet was hidden. Or maybe, being a lawyer, Patrick simply wanted to take possession of his own records, and Robert had given them to him. It wasn't necessarily suspicious.

But then again, there was no one Lex would go to more lengths to protect than her brother. They were closer than any siblings I'd ever known, probably because of the shared trauma of their father's suicide, and Patrick, as an up-and-coming young lawyer brimming with ambition, had a lot to lose if the truth of Danny's death ever came out. Agent Morales had had Patrick in her sights for years; there had to be a reason for it.

Jessica's file contained her various forms of identification, the marriage license between her and Robert, a ream of financial information, paperwork from two car crashes and two DUI arrests, and the records of her stints in rehab. Why did Jessica drink so much? Was she just the cliché of the rich, alcoholic housewife, or were there more specific demons she was trying to drown? If I had killed my youngest son, I'd want to live in a world of blurred oblivion too. Or if I was already loaded, it might make it easier for me to lose my temper with a high-spirited boy who liked to push buttons and accidentally take things too far.

Robert's file was the last one in the back of the cabinet. There wasn't much to it, just his birth certificate and some insurance documentation. Either the filer didn't feel the need to keep a file on himself, or, more likely, most of it had been taken as evidence when he was indicted. I barely knew Robert Tate. We'd spoken on the phone a half a dozen times, but no one had mentioned the possibility of me going to visit him in prison after my first night here. Maybe *because* I knew him the least, he was at the top of my suspect list. It was preferable to imagine that a stranger and not one of these people I'd come to care about was responsible for killing Danny. Robert had already proved himself capable of criminal activity—although financial malfeasance was a far cry from killing someone—and his alibi the day Danny disappeared was thin. He'd been driving home from a business meeting in Palo Alto, so his movements for much of the day couldn't be accounted for. And it wasn't impossible to formulate a motive for him. The money all came from Jessica's side; her family, the Calvins, owned a food packaging empire. Robert's roots were much humbler, and when Danny disappeared, his business was in trouble. He was already dodging his taxes and embezzling from investors to keep it afloat, and the SEC was closing in. Maybe he'd planned to stage Danny's kidnapping as a way to extract money from the Calvins to solve his financial troubles and stave off an indictment, but then something went terribly wrong and Danny died.

I liked this theory, but I had no real evidence for it, and it contained two major flaws: I had a hard time imagining Lex and Patrick going through with this charade in order to protect a stepfather who was already in prison, and it was hard for me to believe that any man who would save his children's drawings and stories in his filing cabinet could have purposefully endangered one of them.

But no matter how many excuses I made, how much evidence I found for why someone wasn't capable of this, there was one truth I kept circling back to. Someone in this family *had* killed Danny. I was wrong about one of them. And I was no closer to figuring out who.

I was back to eating lunch at school with Nicholas and Asher. Our shared experience with Lex had thawed some of the ice between Nicholas and myself, and I'd been doing my best to avoid Ren ever since she'd given me the brush-off. She often came over to my easel to chat for a minute or two before art class and said hi whenever she passed me in the halls, but I just couldn't deal with her and the conflicting ways she made me feel right now on top of everything else. It was better for me to keep my distance.

Our eyes met across the courtyard, and she gave me a smile that made my stomach do a weird sort of flip. I'd been watching her without realizing it.

"Who is that woman?" Asher asked, interrupting Nicholas as he complained about his history teacher. "She keeps staring at us."

Nicholas and I turned to look. I'm not sure what I was expecting, but it sure as hell wasn't Agent Morales casually chatting with Dr. Singh under the awning of the science wing.

Despite the sunshine my skin went cold.

"Oh shit," Nicholas said. "Lex is going to lose her mind."

"Why?" Asher asked. "Who is it?"

"The FBI," Nicholas said, already standing up. He marched toward the two women, and I hurried after him.

"Can I help you?" he demanded as he reached Agent Morales.

"Nicholas," she said. "It's good to see you again—"

"What are you doing here?" he said. "I hope you don't think you're going to talk to my brother."

"Nicholas, please—" Dr. Singh said.

"*You're* not supposed to be talking to him either," he said. "Danny, go back to the table."

Under any other circumstances I would have felt relieved or even touched that Nicholas was defending me. But I was too occupied with trying to figure out what Morales was doing here.

I stared at her, trying to get some clue from her expression, and she just looked coolly back at me.

"You're absolutely right, Nicholas," Morales said, barely glancing away from me. "It was inappropriate for me to come here. I just wanted to check that you were okay, Danny, and to thank you again for being so helpful the other day. I know it must have been difficult."

"No problem," I said.

"Well, I'll be going now," Morales said. "I'm sorry to have disturbed your lunch."

Morales and Dr. Singh headed back into the building, leaving Nicholas confused and me shaken. I had the distinct feeling a shot had just been fired across my bow.

Before I left school that day, I removed my baseball card from the book in my locker where I'd hidden it. I'd thought it would be safer here than at home, but obviously I was wrong. I'd need to find a better hiding place for the boy in the picture.

I was in Danny's room going over my research again when everything changed.

Lex was out picking up dinner and Jessica was gone, but I kept the bedroom door locked just in case Nicholas or Mia decided to stroll in while I was going through my documents. I was taking pictures of everyone's medical records from the files in Robert's office and e-mailing them to myself so I could return them to the filing cabinet before anyone discovered they were missing. I didn't know what might end up being useful, so I was collecting all the information I could get my hands on. A question was starting to form in the back of my head when Mia suddenly screamed.

"Danny!" Her voice was piercing, slicing through the walls and distance that separated us. "Nicky! Somebody!"

All my thoughts fled. I was out of my room and stumbling down the stairs in an instant. I found Mia standing half inside the door to the patio.

"Danny, help!" she cried.

"What is it?" I looked her over as I ran to her side, and she didn't appear to be bleeding or broken.

"There's a mouse in the pool!" she said.

My relief was palpable, like suddenly finding the ground under your feet after missing a step. "Jesus, I thought you were being chased by an ax murderer or something."

But her eyes were filled with giant tears. "He's drowning!"

"It's okay. We'll help him," I said. Anything to take that look of fear out of her eyes.

She took me by the hand and led me out to the swimming pool, where, sure enough, a little field mouse had fallen in somehow. He was trying to climb out, but the tiled walls of the pool were vertical and slick. He started to swim toward the center of the pool, his head barely above water.

"Run and get the skimmer," I said.

"I couldn't find it!" Mia was frantic. She knelt down by the side of the pool and said, "Keep swimming, mousy! We'll save you!" For a moment I thought of the bat who used to sleep in my window.

"We need something to scoop him up with," I said, looking around.

"Danny!" she screeched.

I turned to look. The mouse had disappeared under the water.

"Danny, he's dying!"

Without thinking I jumped in, caught the mouse between my hands, and lifted him up onto the warm concrete lip of the pool. Mia knelt beside him, crying and urging him in her tear-thick voice to wake up. I pulled myself out of the pool and poked the little guy. Slowly he roused, shook himself, and darted into the grass.

Mia threw her arms around me, and I patted her back.

"There, he's okay now," I said. "You saved him, Mimi."

"Thanks, Danny," she said as she pulled away. I wiped the tears off her cheeks. She was all wet from hugging me. "What if he comes back and falls in again?"

"I don't think he'll ever come near this pool again," I said, "but we'll put the cover on just in case, okay?"

She smiled. "Okay."

I turned on the switch to roll out the automatic cover, while Mia watched carefully to make sure no field mice took a last second dive before the pool was sealed up.

"Come on," I said. "We'd better change."

Mia fetched me a towel from one of the downstairs bathrooms

and ran upstairs to get out of her wet clothes. I dried off as best as I could in my soaking jeans and tee before stepping inside. I took the stairs two at a time, gooseflesh prickling on my arms as the air-conditioning hit me, stepped into my bedroom, and felt my heart stop beating.

Nicholas was sitting on the floor, surrounded by Robert's notes, with my laptop open in front of him. He looked up at me with eyes that were like gasoline meeting a spark.

In retrospect, I'm surprised it took that long for everything to fall apart.

"What the fuck is this?" he asked.

"What are you doing in here?" I said.

"I was going to Dad's office to get some printer paper, and your door was open and I saw all of this," he said, gesturing to the stack of papers spread across the floor. "Not that I really feel like I have to answer your questions right now when you should be explaining just what the fuck you're doing with all of this."

I closed the door behind me and began scooping up the papers on the floor, stuffing them back into the file. Nicholas grabbed for them too.

"Stop it!" he said. "What *is* this?"

"I'm just . . ." I swallowed. "I just thought maybe it would help me remember, you know? There's so much about my life from before that's still a total blank to me, so I did some research—"

Nicholas jumped to his feet. "Bullshit."

"It's true!" I stepped toward him. "I wanted to understand what was happening here while I was gone, because no one will talk to me about it—"

"Stop it!" He pushed me back so violently that I hit the door with a dull thud. "You're lying!"

We both stood there, silent, staring at each other.

"You're a liar," he said slowly. "And you're not my brother."

"Nicholas—"

"I knew it," he was saying, more to himself than to me. "I knew it from the moment I saw you, but everyone else—I tried *so hard* to believe it, but you're not him. You're not Daniel."

The fight went out of me. He knew. Part of him had always known. And I knew there was nothing I could say now that would make him forget that.

"No," I said. "I'm not."

Nicholas pushed past me and out of the bedroom. He stalked down the hallway and stairs, and I ran after him.

"Nicholas, wait!" I said as he opened the front door and began to run down the driveway.

"You come any closer, and I will kill you!" he shouted over his shoulder. "I will *kill* you!"

I caught him at the end of the driveway.

"Let me explain," I said.

He didn't let me explain. He punched me.

I automatically dodged the blow, so his fist only clipped the side of my head. He cried out in fury and lunged at me, falling on top of me as I tumbled to the ground. We rolled around on the grass as he tried to hit me and I tried to protect myself. I was bigger but he was angrier, and after several minutes of wrestling and scrabbling, he got in a solid punch to my jaw. My vision went momentarily black and fuzzy, and he collapsed beside me, cradling his hand. For a long moment the only sound was our heaving breaths.

Well, at least there was one thing I was now certain of. Nicholas hadn't been in on Lex and Patrick's plan.

"Who are you?" Nicholas finally said softly.

"Nobody," I said.

"Did you hurt my brother?"

"No," I said. "I'd never heard of your brother until this started."

"Why did you do this?"

I sat up, fingering my jaw. My knee was scraped and bleeding.

"I didn't mean to," I said. "It just sort of . . . got out of my control."

"Bullshit." Nicholas sat up too and straightened his glasses and shirt. The neckline was stretched from where I must have grabbed him. "You don't *accidentally* impersonate a missing kid, you sick fuck."

"I didn't think it would go this far. But I . . ."

"What? You *what*?"

"I liked your family, okay?" The words burst out of me. "I never had anything likc this."

His face turned like he'd just encountered a foul smell, and he rose to his feet. "Oh God, spare me your pathetic sob story. I'm going to make sure you rot in jail for what you've done to my family."

Every part of me ached or stung. "What about what your family has done to me?"

Nicholas stepped toward me, his hands clenching into fists. "What, house you? Feed you?"

He needed to know the truth. Whether he hit me again or called the cops, he needed to know.

"You don't *really* think they believe I'm Danny, do you?" I said.

For a moment he just stared at me.

"Of course they do," he finally said. But his voice was wobbly.

"Mia does. Maybe your mother, although I doubt it," I said. "But Lex and Patrick? Come on."

Nicholas shook his head. "No way. Why would they pretend?"

"You're one of the smartest people I know, Nicholas," I said. "You must have figured it out. Subconsciously at least."

"Shut up!" he said.

"They're pretending because I'm a convenient cover."

"Shut up!"

"Because no one will investigate Danny's death while I'm here."

Like a puppet with its strings cut, Nicholas collapsed back onto the grass.

We sat there under one of the crepe myrtles that lined the driveway for a long time, the crushed petals beneath us surrounding us with a sickly sweet, decomposing perfume. I tried to speak a couple of times, but Nicholas cut me off, told me to be quiet, he was thinking. So we sat there silently.

I thought about a lot of things. What I would say if Lex came back with dinner and found us here, both bruised and bleeding. How I might get away if Nicholas were to pull out his cell phone and call the cops right now. Ren's smile and the warmth of her breath against me.

"How do you know Lex and Patrick know?" Nicholas finally asked. He sounded exhausted. Broken.

"I overheard them talking about it," I said. "Besides, you always knew I wasn't Danny deep down. Don't you think they would have too?"

"Yes," he whispered, plucking at the grass.

"Who made you believe you were wrong?"

"Lex and Patrick," he said, even quieter. "I kept going back and forth, but they'd always tell me it was really you and that I just couldn't let myself believe it. I *wanted* to believe it, but underneath I knew."

"I'm sorry," I said.

His head snapped up. "You don't get to say that to me, not after what you've done. Don't mistake the fact that I haven't killed you or called the cops yet for forgiveness. You'll never get that from me."

"Yeah," I said quickly. "Okay."

He pressed the heels of his hands hard against his eyes. "God. Danny . . ." He was quiet for a long moment, and then he said, "It was one of them, wasn't it?"

"What?" I asked. I wanted to make absolutely sure I understood what he was asking before I answered.

"One of them . . . ," he said. "They're responsible for what happened to him, aren't they? That's why they're using you to make everyone think he's still alive. It's the only reason they would have brought you here."

Nicholas really was the smart one.

"I think so," I said.

"So why the hell are you still here?" he asked. "Your cover is blown, or never existed in the first place. For all you know, they could be setting you up to take the fall."

I blinked. "What?"

"It makes sense, doesn't it?" he said. "You're the outsider. The transient with—I'm just guessing here—the criminal record. I think you're at least eighteen or nineteen, but here you are, posing as a kid, infiltrating this rich family. Maybe Danny ran away, or maybe he was kidnapped and escaped the way you said. You two became friends in some homeless shelter until you found out what kind of life he'd come from. Then you killed him so you could take his place."

"That's not what happened," I said.

"I bet a jury down here wouldn't find it so unbelievable," he said. "Especially not when Lex or Patrick plants something of Danny's on you. You're the cover *and* the patsy, if they ever need one."

Fuck. He was right, and I couldn't believe I hadn't thought of it myself. It was ludicrous, of course, but a jury would pick a grieving, upstanding family of their own kind over a nothing scam artist like me any day.

"So why are you still here?" he asked. "What are you doing with all that research on us?"

"I'm trying to figure out what really happened to Danny," I said.

"Yeah, right," he said. "What's your real plan? Blackmail?"

"No," I said. "I know you have no reason to believe me, but it's true. I just want to find out who hurt Danny."

He looked at me for a long minute, not believing me. Which was fair, since I wasn't sure I believed myself either. He turned his head away as he engaged in some kind of internal battle, and I saw the moment he made his decision in the straightening of his shoulders.

"Good," he said, "because that's your only chance to prove it wasn't you." He stood up and looked down at me, looming over me. "You're a psychotic, cruel, pathetic excuse for a human being, and there's only one thing you can do that will stop me from making sure you rot in prison for impersonating my brother."

"What?" I asked.

"Help me find out who killed him."

Then he walked back to the house.

The next morning I dragged myself from bed to the bathroom and found an impressive black eye staring back at me. Nicholas might have damn near broken his hand, but he had a decent left hook. I couldn't go downstairs looking like this.

I crept to Lex's room. Most mornings she was already making breakfast by the time I woke up, but I knocked softly on the door just in case. There was no response, so I ducked inside. As I'd hoped, the counter in her bathroom was littered with cosmetics. I riffled through them carefully, looking for what I needed without disturbing too much. Behind a bottle of men's cologne I found a goldish cream eye shadow, and there was a liquid concealer by the hot tap. I stuck them into my pocket and returned to my room. Lex had so many bottles and concoctions that I doubted she would notice, at least until I could come home from school that afternoon with some story about getting hit by a ball in gym class.

When I was presentable, I went downstairs and found Nicholas already eating scrambled eggs, a Band-Aid across his jaw. I guess I scratched him when we were fighting.

"You okay?" I asked.

"Cut myself shaving," he said.

"You want some eggs, Danny?" Lex asked from the stove. From the corner of my eye I saw Nicholas wince.

"No, thanks," I said. "I'm not hungry."

"We've got to leave for school, actually," Nicholas said. "He's doing a tutorial with Mr. Vaughn, and I have a lab to finish up."

"Oh," Lex said, looking down at her skillet full of eggs. "Okay."

Once we were in the car, I asked Nicholas what was going on. I didn't have a tutorial with Vaughn, and I doubted he had a lab.

"Don't speak," he said, not looking at me. "I don't want to get so angry that I accidentally crash the car."

I waited as he drove us silently toward school. Every few minutes his hands would tense around the steering wheel, turning his bruised knuckles white, and it was hard not to assume that he was imagining wrapping those hands around my neck.

There was only a smattering of cars in the parking lot at Calabasas High this early in the morning, but Nicholas parked in the very back corner of the lot. He kept the car running for the air conditioner but unbuckled his seat belt and turned to me. He felt uncomfortably close.

"Now," he said, "tell me everything."

I didn't tell him everything. But I told him more than I'd ever told anyone else. I explained the scam I used to run—posing as a younger, traumatized kid so that I could get a spot in a care home—and how I impersonated his brother just to buy myself some more time. How I ended up in way over my head.

He smiled bitterly and shook his head. "You expect me to believe it's just a coincidence that you chose to impersonate someone with a family as rich as us?"

"Yes," I said.

Do you believe that? Nicholas didn't.

"Bullshit. You make it sound like all of this just *happened*," he said. "Like it wasn't something you did on purpose, every single day. You could have stopped it at any time."

"You're right," I said. "I didn't want to stop it. I still don't."

He shook his head. "You're a sociopath."

I thought of that hole I'd felt in my chest for most of my life, the empty place where other people seemed to have something I lacked. It hadn't felt so empty lately, but did a couple of months negate the lifetime that came before it? "Maybe you're right," I said.

Nicholas shut his eyes and turned his head away from me, like he couldn't risk looking at me for another single second.

"I knew it," he said. "The second you stepped off that plane, I knew it. Every time you spoke to me I knew it, but I tried so hard to believe what everyone else told me."

"It's only human nature," I said. "You can't blame yourself."

"No, I blame you." His expression was smoldering with his hatred of me. I could feel the heat radiating off him. "I blame you and whoever else in my family knew about this. God, I can't wait to get away from these people."

He was stuck and couldn't wait to leave. I wanted to stay and knew he'd never let me.

"What about my mother?" he asked. "Does she know too?"

"I don't know," I said, "but it would explain why she avoids me so much."

"That's no kind of evidence," he said. "It's gotten worse since you got here, but she's been avoiding all of us for years."

I thought of the Jessica I'd seen in the family movies from before Danny went missing. She hadn't been the most nurturing parent, but she was usually *there*.

"What changed?" I asked.

"Damned if I know. She could be great when I was little. But then . . ."

"Danny disappeared?"

"No, it started before that," Nicholas said. He was staring at his steering wheel, but his eyes were far away, seeing something I couldn't. "When Lex and Patrick's dad killed himself, it hit her hard. They were still pretty close even though they'd been divorced for years. He used to come over all the time to watch us when Mom and Dad were busy with Mia's doctor appointments and stuff. After Ben died, Lex started with the pills and Patrick was always getting into trouble, and Mom just couldn't handle any of it. She and Dad were arguing all the time and the drinking had gotten bad, and then Danny disappeared and she went off the deep end. She's been like this pretty much ever since."

"Can I ask you something?" I said.

He looked at me.

"Why do you believe me?" I asked.

"About what happened to Danny?"

"Yeah."

"It's the only thing that makes sense, isn't it?" he said. "They wouldn't put on this show if they didn't have something to hide. One of them must have murdered him to justify all of this."

I felt suddenly cold.

"Murdered?" I repeated. I'd *never* said that word to him, had never even let myself think it.

He nodded. "If whatever happened to Danny had been an accident, why not just report it at the time? Why go through all of this? No, it had to have been something more serious than that."

It was the same thought process I'd gone through the night I discovered Lex and Patrick knew who I really was, but it sounded so much worse coming out of Nicholas's mouth. "You really think someone in your family is capable of that?"

He turned to me, his expression like stone. "They're not the perfect family they pretend to be, okay? You don't know them like I do, and you really don't know who they were back then."

"Did you mean what you said, that you won't turn me in if I help you?"

He took a deep breath. "If someone in my family killed Danny, they think they're safe right now, and that's how I want to keep it. If I expose you, it'll put them on their guard. Hell, for all I know, they might flee the country or something, and then I'll never find out what happened to my brother."

"I get it," I said. I think I even believed him. Besides, I could try to run, but how far would I get? With the Tates' money and resources after me, not to mention the FBI, my guess was not very far, and trying to get away would only make me look more guilty if Lex and Patrick tried to pin Danny's death on me. If I helped Nicholas, there was a chance, however small, that he'd let me leave quietly when this was all over. "So what do we do now?"

"I want to take you to see my dad," he said. "I think I'll be able to tell from his reaction to you if he knows anything about what really happened to Danny. Mom will be trickier. She'll never say a word to me, but if *you* get close to her, we might get an idea of how much she knows."

"I can try," I said. But unless I magically transformed into a bottle of bourbon, getting close to Jessica was going to be hard.

"Don't try, just do it," he snapped, his relatively civil attitude suddenly turning nasty. He started to climb out of the car.

"Hey, wait," I said.

He paused with the door halfway open, his back turned to me.

"You said you knew every time I talked to you that I wasn't Danny," I said. "How?"

He was still for a long moment. Finally, he said, "You were too nice to me."

Then he got out of the car and slammed the door behind him.

That night, armed with a plate of food, I climbed the stairs to the master suite. I knocked, and a minute later Jessica opened the door. She flinched when she saw me. Behind her I could see that the bed linens were rumpled, and the bedside table was covered with prescription pill bottles and a tumbler of something brown. Also sitting there, completely out of place, was a small crystal figurine of a dolphin. Although the most harmless item on the table, it was the one I looked at the longest, because it was the most puzzling.

"I figured you hadn't eaten yet," I said, offering her the plate. "We ordered from Mangia. I know you like their eggplant parmesan, so we got you some."

"I'm not really hungry," she said, starting to inch the door closed.

I grabbed the door. "Then maybe you want to come down and sit with us while we eat? Mia's going to show us the diorama she made for her science class, which should—"

"I have a headache," she said. "I'm just going to go to bed."

I wanted to grab her and shake her. For having a kid—kids—who loved her and throwing them away. For being so damn selfish. For having children in the first place if she wasn't going to take care of them.

But I had a job I needed to do, so I pushed my anger down.

"Okay," I said with a smile. "Love you, Mom."

She gave me a halfhearted smile in return and closed the door.

This was going to be even harder than I thought.

I was headed back for the dining room when Nicholas caught me on the stairs. He'd been locked in his room ever since we got home from school, poring over the documents and notes I'd collected. He grabbed my arm and hauled me into his bedroom.

"What the hell?" I said.

He had a stack of papers clutched in one hand. "Are these for real?"

"What are they?"

"You didn't alter them or something?"

"I don't even know what those are," I said, "but I didn't touch anything. What's going on?"

He swore under his breath and sank down onto the floor. I took the stack of papers from his hand and laid them out on the rug. Mia's medical records, a police fact sheet on Daniel, some kind of report from the hospital from the time Nicholas broke his wrist, and a medical intake form from one of Lex's trips to rehab. I looked up at Nicholas, who was staring at the ceiling, his hand over his mouth.

"What is it?" I asked.

"Look at the blood types," he said.

I frowned and searched the documents for the information. Mia and Lex were both B positive, and Nicholas and Danny were O negative.

"So?" I said. Unlike Nicholas, I wasn't an honors student taking all AP classes. Even if I *had* finished high school, I doubt I would have gotten what he was driving at.

"It's biologically impossible," he said. "I'm O negative because both of my parents are. O negative parents *always* have O negative children."

I looked down at the papers again, and what he was saying slowly dawned on me. "But Mia . . ."

"She's B positive, which means one of her parents was," he said. "Mia's not my father's child."

"Jesus," I said. "Are you sure?"

He nodded. "I think she's Ben McConnell's."

It all made sense once Nicholas explained it to me. For Mia to be B positive, one of her parents had to be. Ben McConnell, as evidenced by Lex's blood type, was. And as Nicholas had already told me, Jessica and Ben had stayed close even after their divorce, which made his death all the more devastating for her.

"They were having an affair," Nicholas said. "They must have been. That's why he was around the house all the time. He wasn't just helping my mom out by babysitting. He wanted to be close to her and to Mia."

"Do you think your dad knew?" I asked.

"I don't know. I think I should stop assuming I know *anything* about my family." He scrubbed his fingers through his hair. "I wonder if this has anything to do with Danny."

"I don't see how," I said.

"Yeah, you're probably right. The only thing is . . ."

"What?"

Nicholas sighed. "Well, Danny was a snoop. One of his favorite games was to find out something about you didn't want anyone to know and then hold it over your head. Our lives were kind of chaotic the last few years before he disappeared, and I think he liked feeling like he was in control of something, you know?"

As a matter of fact, I did.

"Or maybe I'm just making excuses for him because he was only a little kid, and he's . . . gone now," he continued. "The truth was, as much as I loved him, Danny was sort of a jerk. When I was ten, he guessed the password to my computer and found this journal I kept on it." Nicholas adjusted the way his glasses sat on his nose, a nervous habit of his. "I wrote a lot about thinking I was gay and what that would mean for me, really private stuff like that. I know it was obvious to everyone else from pretty much the moment I was born that I was gay, but I wasn't ready to tell anyone or to talk about it, so I just wrote it all down in that journal. Danny printed the whole thing out."

"Shit," I said.

Nicholas nodded. "He used it to blackmail me for months, right up until he disappeared. It was just kids' stuff, like making me do his math homework or give him my Halloween candy, but it was this constant shadow hanging over my head. And it made me *hate* him." His hands were clenched into fists, but there was no anger in his expression, only grief. "After he was gone, I hated myself for hating him. Like I had made him disappear somehow."

Watching the Tate home movies had put a little tarnish on the image of Danny the Innocent that had been created in the wake of his disappearance, but this was a little *too* real. It was probably no worse than what many siblings did to each other as children, but Danny had never gotten the opportunity to grow up and out of it. He probably would have matured into a good person, but he'd died as a brat. It made me think of how I'd be remembered—if I was at all—if I died tomorrow. Made me wonder if there was any chance I could change it.

"So if Danny had somehow found out about Mia, or about your mother's affair . . . ," I said.

"I know it sounds insane, but maybe he tried to do the same thing to Mom that he did to me," Nicholas said. "Maybe she'd been drinking and lost her temper. Or maybe he told Dad, and Dad . . ." He suddenly slammed his fist in the floor. "I hate this! I hate having to suspect everyone in my family of something so fucking horrible. I wish I didn't know any of this."

"What do you want to do?" I asked.

"Move to the other side of the world and never come back."

"Okay." That was an impulse I could empathize with. "But what do you want to do *today*?"

He sighed. "Same thing as before. Get close to my mother. Find out what she knows."

"What about your dad?" I asked.

"I'm working on that," he said. "I also want to try to find the file my dad kept on Patrick. I remember him getting into trouble a lot when I was young, but I never knew the details. It might mean something, and I'm sure all the information is in that file."

"You bet," I said.

Whatever he wanted, as long as it kept him from busting me.

But getting close to Jessica wasn't going to be easy. I needed help.

I went to Lex's room later that night. When she found me standing at her door, she smiled, and I could have sworn it was real.

"Hey, Danny," she said. "What's up?"

"Can I talk to you?"

"Of course." She opened her door wider. "Come in."

I sat on the low, silk covered sofa at the foot of her bed, and she sat beside me.

"I'm glad you're here, actually," she said, crushing the hem of her shirt between her fingers. "I've been meaning to talk to you about the other night."

"You don't have to," I said.

"Yeah, I do," she replied. "I'm so sorry for putting you and Nicky through that. You never should have had to see me that way or deal with a situation like that. I hope you can forgive me."

"Of course," I said softly.

She took my hand and squeezed it. "I feel so stupid. I'd been drinking and lost track of how many pills I took, and then I was waking up in the hospital and . . . It was just a stupid accident. It had nothing to do with you. You know that, right?"

I wondered if she really believed that. Maybe Lex was as good at lying to herself as to others.

"Yeah, I know," I said.

"Good." She pulled me forward into a hug. "I need to thank you too. You guys probably saved my life. You're the best brothers anyone could ask for."

I patted her back uncertainly. "You're the best sister."

Lex's breath hitched, and I realized she was crying again. She held me tight, burying her face against my neck, where I felt her hot tears against my skin. God, she was laying it on thick.

"I missed you, Danny," she said, and it occurred to me that maybe she wasn't faking after all. Maybe she just didn't mean it in the past tense.

The feeling of the hug changed as it lingered. At some point it became more than a sum of the body parts involved, more than just warm arms and the sweet smell of Lex's shampoo and the cold calculation I was sure was behind it all. I felt suddenly young and small and surrounded, in a nice way that made me feel safe. If it was all an act, well, maybe it didn't really matter. Because I couldn't feel the difference.

I thought suddenly of my mother, the real one. How she didn't even flinch when she heard I was dead. I wondered if she ever cried for me this way and was pretty sure I knew the answer.

Lex pulled back and laughed, swiping at her eyes and my neck. "Sorry! Sorry for blubbering all over you. I'm such a mess these days. What did you want to talk to me about?"

"Actually, I was wondering if you could help me with something," I said.

"Of course. What is it?"

"I want to do something for Mom," I said. "I was thinking dinner, just the two of us. It's almost Mother's Day."

"Oh." Lex shifted. "I don't know, Danny. You know how Mom is these days."

"Yeah, but I think it's a good idea," I said. "We haven't been able to spend any time alone together since I got back."

I could tell from her lack of response how hard Lex was working to conceal her discomfort.

"It's a nice idea," she said, "but I'm not sure—"

"She must want to spend time with me, too," I said. "She is my mother, after all, right?"

When Lex smiled, I saw, for the first time, the effort behind it. She nodded. "Okay."

"Will you help me?" I asked. "I want to make it a surprise."

"Of course," she said. "Let's surprise her."

By that weekend, everything was arranged.

One of the main problems with Jessica was getting—and keeping—her in the same room with me. It was impossible to talk to her and try to get to the bottom of what she did and didn't know when she spent all of her time out of the house or locked behind her bedroom door. But Jessica didn't like to make a scene.

When she left the house, she was always freshly made-up and impeccably dressed. If I could just get her to a restaurant, her desire to keep up appearances might keep her there.

Not that it would do any good. Jessica would never open up to me, and even if she did, that wouldn't involve her confessing that she'd killed her youngest son. I knew this. But Nicholas was insistent, and since he had the power to put me in prison, Nicholas was the boss.

On Sunday morning Mia woke Nicholas and me up around dawn and dragged us downstairs to the kitchen to help her make breakfast. Lex and Patrick drifted in later, heading straight for the coffee maker while Nicholas and I helped Mia cut fruit and flip pancakes. When everything was ready and laid out on a tray with a bud vase containing a flower Mia had plucked out of the fresh arrangement in the foyer, we headed up to the third floor as a group to surprise Jessica with breakfast in bed.

Mia was the first one through the door, and she took a flying leap onto the giant bed where Jessica was so buried under covers and pillows that she was almost invisible. Mia unearthed her, and Jessica blinked slowly, emerging from sleep like a swimmer from an undertow.

"What is it?" she slurred.

"Happy Mother's Day!" Mia said. Nicholas stepped forward with the breakfast tray.

Jessica looked shocked. She took the tray delicately, like she half expected it to crumble in her hands.

"Oh," she said. "I didn't . . ." She couldn't finish the sentence.

"Happy Mother's Day, Mom," Patrick said, leaning down to kiss her cheek. Nicholas and Lex did the same, so I did too.

Jessica began to cry.

"Oh, Mom, it's okay!" Lex said.

"Don't cry," Patrick told her.

"It's just . . ." She wiped her eyes with the napkin from the tray, leaving a smudge of old mascara behind. "This is just . . . so nice of you all."

"We love you, Mom," Nicholas said.

"All your kids," Patrick said, "back together again."

All eyes turned toward me. Even Jessica's, although her gaze dropped from mine when she started crying even harder. Mia hugged her mom fiercely, joined by Patrick and Lex, and then Nicholas and me. A family hug, the Tates reunited, and almost everyone involved knowing it was bullshit.

Lex and Mia had planned an entire day of activities. This was key to my plan. They took Jessica for mani-pedis, and then we all met in Santa Monica, where it had been Mia's idea to charter a yacht to take us looking for dolphins. Jessica, apparently, loved dolphins.

The structure of the day ensured that she never got a break and never had the chance for a drink. Hopefully, by the time I got to her, she'd be ready to crack.

Jessica looked impeccable as she approached the boat. Her armor was firmly in place, and there was something else there too. A smile. A real one. It faltered a little when I offered her a hand to help her on deck, but she replaced it so quickly, no one else would have noticed.

We saw a pod of Pacific white-sided dolphins, as Captain Ron informed us, just moments after leaving the harbor. Jessica had her arms around Mia, helping her to lean as far as she could over the rail to watch them riding the wake of the boat. The sight made something twist painfully in my chest, and when my eyes met Nicholas's, I could tell he felt it too.

But maybe it was just my impending sea sicknesses. I'd never been on a boat before. I spent the rest of the ride below the deck, curled up in a fetal position, trying to keep my insides from becoming my outsides. Lex came and sat with me, pushing the hair off my hot forehead with a damp towel.

"Poor Danny," she said. "You never did like boats."

Which was a blatant lie. I'd see more than one video of Danny clowning around on the boat Robert used to own. But at that moment I didn't give a good goddamn. I took her hand and let her soothe me and speak to me in that soft voice and closed my eyes against the unexpected stinging I felt at the back of them.

"Thank you, everyone," Jessica said after we had returned to dry land and were on our way back to the car. "That was a wonderful day."

"It's not over yet. We have a surprise for you," Lex said.

"Another one?" Jessica asked.

In the parking lot there was a town car waiting.

"That's for you," Lex said. "You have reservations at Mélisse."

"Oh! My favorite," Jessica said.

"You and Danny will go to dinner," Lex continued, "and the rest of us will meet you at home."

Jessica's flash of panic was palpable. "We're not all going?"

"No," Lex said. "This is a special trip just for you and Danny."

"We thought it would be nice for you two to have some time alone together," Nicholas added.

I actually saw Jessica swallow. Could see the calculations happening behind her eyes as she tried to think of a way out of this that wouldn't make a scene. I almost felt a little sorry for her.

But then the mask was in place again, and, knowing she had no choice, she smiled. "Great."

We all said good-bye. Lex pulled her mother into a hug, and I heard her whisper, "Be nice. He's your *son*."

Nicholas and I exchanged a look, and then Jessica and I climbed—alone—into the town car.

Mélisse was dark and refined, filled with the soft tinkle of crystal and silver, the kind of place where Jessica's façade was at home. As soon as we sat down, she asked for the sommelier and ordered a glass of wine.

"I'm so happy to get to spend this time with you," I said as Jessica downed almost half of her glass at once. "I wish we were able to do more things together."

"Mmm," was her only response.

I resisted the urge to shake her. "When was the last time you came here?"

"Oh." She sighed. "I'm not sure. Years ago."

It was going to be a long evening. Ever since we'd gotten in the car, conversation had been stilted at best. No matter what I said, Jessica answered with the shortest words and sentences possible. I'd anticipated this, but what I hadn't expected was how difficult I would find it to play the role of the loving son. For one thing, it was a role I had little experience with. And more than that, Jessica had never figured much into my thoughts about the Tate family since she was little more than a ghost that haunted the household. But now that I was in such close quarters with her, I realized how angry I was at her, for ignoring her children, maybe even *hurting* one of them. I just wanted to hurt her back.

"I don't remember this place," I said. The doting son act was exhausting and wasn't getting through to her. Maybe needling her about this charade we were both playing would. "Did you ever bring me here?"

She was reading the menu carefully. "Once or twice, I think."

"Well, I don't remember," I said. "My memories of that time are so spotty. I guess tonight will be like I'm eating here for the first time."

She didn't look up, but her jaw tightened. "I suppose it will."

She finished her glass of wine before we'd even ordered. The waiter asked her if she'd like another, and she turned him down.

Wanted to keep her head about her, probably, which was the last thing I wanted. When she excused herself to go to the restroom to freshen up, I flagged the guy down and told him she'd changed her mind and to keep them coming. If she was surprised to find the full glass waiting for her when she returned, she didn't mention it.

She picked at her food and mostly managed not to talk to me outside of the occasional comment about the meal or monosyllabic answer to one of my questions. The evening was going to be over soon, and I was going to have nothing to show for it. Nicholas would *not* be happy, and more than anything, I needed to keep Nicholas happy.

At least she was still drinking.

"So, where do you go?" I asked after a particularly lengthy pause in the conversation. Might as well just get down to it.

"I'm sorry?"

"When you're gone from the house," I said. "I just realized I don't actually know what you do when I'm at school. Where is it that you go?"

"I have commitments," she said, pressing her fork down hard into the plate beneath it, trying to spear a salad leaf. "I'm on several boards."

"You're gone awfully late sometimes," I said.

"I . . . I like to go for long drives," she said. "It relaxes me."

Yeah, "relaxed" was definitely the first word that came to mind when I thought of Jessica. "Where do you drive?"

She blinked a little too fast and I knew that whatever she said next would be a lie.

"The beach, mostly."

There's no orange dust at the beach.

I ate as slowly as I could while Jessica got drunker and drunker. I was hoping the wine would loosen her tongue, but it only made her slower and quieter. Once our entrées were finished, I insisted on ordering dessert. The waiter brought a list of cocktails along with the dessert menu. There was a notation under the tangerine soufflé that it required twenty-five minutes to bake, so I ordered that.

"And you, madam?" the waiter asked Jessica.

She hesitated.

"Go ahead," I said. "It's a special occasion. Mom."

It was all the push she needed.

"I shouldn't, but . . . ," she said, "double bourbon, neat."

When the waiter was gone, I leaned closer to her over the table.

"Don't worry," I said. "I won't tell Lex."

Her lips curled into a bitter smile. "Ah yes, she'd be very ashamed of me."

"Like she has room to talk," I said, hating myself for even saying it, but . . .

Jessica actually laughed. It was a soft and mean-spirited laugh, but it was real.

This was a tack I hadn't tried. The common enemy strategy.

"Sometimes I think Lex wishes she could just put me in a little box," I said, "so she could control everything I do."

"I know the feeling."

"If you knew how many times a day she tries to feed me," I continued. "Like she thinks I can't take care of myself, that I would starve if she wasn't there force-feeding me peanut butter sandwiches."

Jessica twisted her wine glass by the stem. "She's always been like that, ever since she was young."

"Yeah?"

She nodded. "We used to have this dog. Sweet creature but very stupid. She thought she could train it, and you should have seen her trying to—"

Jessica froze. She'd fucked up, and she knew it.

"Trying to what?" I asked.

She pushed her chair back from the table and tried to get to her feet, but she knocked a glass of ice water over with her elbow. It rolled across the table and crashed to the floor, soaking the tablecloth and carpet. Everyone in the restaurant turned to look. Our waiter rushed toward us.

"I'm sorry," Jessica stammered as he mopped at the mess with a napkin. "I-it was an accident . . ."

"It's okay, Mom," I said.

"It's nothing, madam," the waiter said.

People were still staring. Jessica swayed on her feet.

"Excuse me," she mumbled, and turned to flee the scene.

I went after her and caught her outside the restaurant.

"Mom, wait," I said, catching her by the arm.

She turned to me as she pulled her arm out of my grasp, and her unfocused eyes were swimming. She was, I realized, terrified.

"Hey, it's okay," I said. Why was I still lying? We both knew this was a farce, so why pretend? Maybe, for once, I could get what I wanted by telling the truth. "I think we should talk."

I paid the bill at Mélisse with the emergency credit card and then walked Jessica over to a Starbucks across the street. I bought her a black coffee, and we sat down at a table next to the window.

"I'm sorry this has been so hard for you," I said. "Me being here and everything."

She looked up at me uncertainly.

"I didn't mean to make things difficult for you. Really." I thought of a woman in an arm chair, flipping channels on the television, a phone ringing in the distance, and I couldn't keep the tinge of bitterness out of my voice. "I can see that Lex and Patrick put a lot of pressure on you to treat me like everything is the same, but I want you to know that I understand. You don't have to pretend with me."

Jessica's face went very still, and then I noticed tiny movements around her eyes and mouth, like something was happening inside of her that she was trying to contain.

I leaned closer to her. "Lex and Patrick aren't here. We don't have to pretend nothing's changed."

Moisture gathered in her eyes, clinging to her lower lashes. "Please don't tell them," she whispered.

"I promise," I said.

I was convinced; Jessica couldn't have been the one to kill Danny. How many times had I seen Lex or Patrick remind her to keep up the façade? They wouldn't have had to do that if she were the one with something to hide. She wouldn't seem so scared of them right now if it were her ass she was protecting. No. Setting aside how I felt about them, it was more likely that Lex or Patrick had been responsible, and Jessica was keeping the secret to avoid losing another child.

"I can't imagine what it must have been like," I said, "to have your son be missing for so long."

She looked down at the table and blinked to clear her eyes. "I . . . I wasn't always such a bad mother, but after . . . what happened . . ."

I wanted to tell her that Danny might be gone, but her other children still deserved a loving mother, but that would be taking honesty too far. She had to feel safe with me if I was ever going to get anything useful out of her.

"You know you can talk to me," I said. "I know it seems strange, but if you need someone to talk to about all of this, no one understands better than I do."

Her voice was so soft I could barely hear it. "I just want everyone to be safe."

"That's what I want too," I said, reaching out to touch her cool hand. "That's why I'm here."

She looked up at me and, very slowly, nodded.

It wasn't a confession, but it was progress. With enough time I was pretty sure I could get her to tell me what she knew.

The only question was how much time Nicholas would give me.

Nicholas was not happy.

"So she didn't tell you anything?" he asked as we sat alone together during lunch period. He'd banished Asher to his backup seat at the jock table so we could talk openly.

"What did you expect?" I said. "I did everything I could. Hopefully I'll be able to build on it, and eventually she'll confide more in me, but all I know for sure now is that she knows I'm not Danny."

He sighed. "Which means she must know what really happened to him."

I nodded. "She's covering for someone."

"We've got to go to Patrick's apartment and find those files," he said. "He never wants any of us to go over there, and that just makes me want to even more. Did you ask Mom where she goes all the time?"

"Yeah, she fed me some bullshit line about long drives to the beach," I said. "If we want to know, we're going to have to follow her."

Nicholas's phone rang. The administration had recently lifted the cell phone ban, and so far no one had dared to take my picture again. He frowned down at the display but answered it anyway.

"Hello? . . . Yeah, okay . . . Yes. Thank you." He ended the call and started gathering his things. "That was the prison. You're on the visitors' list. We can go see my dad."

"What, now?" I said as he shouldered his bag.

"Yes, now. I'm not drawing this out any longer than we have to," he said. "If we leave now, we can be back before anyone even knows we're gone."

Nicholas and I headed north to Lompoc Federal Correctional Institution, a prison with one of those minimum security, luxury resort sections for criminal CEOs and power brokers no one wanted to piss off too badly.

Nicholas radiated impatience the entire ride. I needed an escape plan. He wasn't going to last the weeks or months or *years* it might take to discover what really happened to Danny. At any moment he could get fed up and decide it was worth it to turn me in as a fake. And if we did find out who had killed Danny, my window for escape was even narrower. Nicholas and I had reached an uneasy sort of truce lately, and part of me hoped he would let me go in return for helping him find his brother's killer, but the chances were slim. Other than a packed bag hidden in Danny's closet, ready for me to grab and run, I hadn't made any preparations. I needed to start, or I'd end up in a place a lot less nice than the prison we were approaching.

"So what are we going to do?" I asked as we parked in the lot across from the prison. It was surrounded only by a low chain-link fence, and beyond that were a lush, green lawn and a modern building that could have just as easily been a nicer-than-average public school.

Nicholas shrugged, which was probably difficult considering how tense he was. "We see how he reacts to seeing you. It should give us some idea how much he knows."

"And the Mia thing?" I asked.

"I don't know about that," he said. "Just let me handle that part."

"Okay. What are you hoping for here?"

Personally, although I doubted it, I hoped like hell that Robert Tate had been the one to kill Danny. It would mean the members of the family that I knew *hadn't*. But obviously it wasn't as easy for Nicholas. Unlike everyone else in the family, he actually seemed relatively close to Robert. They talked on the phone, and I suspected some of his weekend "hikes" with Asher were actually trips to Lompoc.

He sighed. "I honestly don't know."

We checked in with the guard at the front desk and went through a metal detector and bag search, and then we were led to the visiting area.

"Does he know we're coming?" I asked, suddenly feeling

nervous. I'd spoken to Robert on the phone a half a dozen times, but coming face-to-face with the man was different.

Nicholas shook his head. "They'll have told him he has visitors from his list but not who."

We entered a room that looked a lot like the cafeteria at my old high school, which seemed appropriate. It had a similar smell, too: staleness and watered down bleach. The room was filled with tables and chairs where men in blue clothes sat with their family members as bored guards watched from the perimeter. Nicholas surveyed the room before heading toward a table in the back corner. I followed behind him.

"Nicholas!" A man stood up from his chair and hugged him.

"Hey, Dad," Nicholas said.

Robert Tate looked mostly the same as I remembered him from the home movies. Tall and handsome, with sharply defined features that Nicholas had inherited. The salt-and-pepper hair at his temples was quite a bit saltier, though, and he'd grown a beard that made him look about ten years older than he really was.

As he hugged Nicholas, Robert's eyes landed on me.

At first his expression didn't change. I don't even think he really saw me. But as I looked back at him, he realized I wasn't some other inmate's kid, and his face changed in slow motion. His brows furrowed in confusion, then his eyebrows lifted and his eyes widened. Realization, shock. Then a darkening of his expression. Doubt.

His arms dropped from around Nicholas, and he looked back and forth between us.

"Is . . . is that . . ."

Nicholas nodded. Robert still looked confused. He took a halting step toward me.

"Daniel?" he breathed.

"Hi, Dad," I said.

He stared at me, shook his head, and took another step forward. The frown lines in his face deepened. He reached out his arms and pulled me to him, crushing me in a tight hug, releasing a sound that was a combination of a laugh, a sob, and a punch to the gut. He rocked me back and forth, saying "Danny, oh my God, Danny" over and over under his breath.

If it was an act, it was a damn good one.

The hug lasted a long time, maybe longer than any I'd ever received, and Robert only let go of me by degrees. Pulling away to look at my face but keeping his arms around me. Separating his body from mine but keeping his hands on my arms. Sitting down across from me, but keeping my hands in his. All the time staring at me like I was some puzzling but miraculous creature.

"I'm so happy you're here," he said. His eyes were pink and shiny. "Your sister told me you weren't ready to come out here yet, so I was trying to be patient, but the waiting was killing me. My boy." He put his hands on my face, just staring into my eyes, and then he bowed his head and rubbed his beard. When he spoke again, his voice was rough with unshed tears. "I never gave up hope, and now—" He abruptly started to cry.

Nicholas and I looked at each other as Robert covered his eyes with one hand, the other still holding tight to mine. Robert obviously wasn't a part of the scheme to hide Danny's death. His joy and grief were palpable, so pointed and piercing that I shriveled a little inside. It was a cruel thing I had done to this family. This wasn't an act; Robert had no idea his son was dead.

I was disappointed. Nicholas looked relieved.

"It's okay, Dad," Nicholas said. "Everything's going to be fine, okay?"

Robert took a few deep breaths to compose himself. He gave us a sheepish smile and murmured an apology. Then he asked, "How's your little sister? Why didn't you tell me you were coming?"

"We ditched school," Nicholas said. "Danny wanted to come, and we didn't want to wait."

Robert reached for my face. "Just let me take another look at you."

He held my jaw in his hands and ran his eyes over every inch of my face. He stared at me, Nicolas stared at him, and I tried to hold Robert's eye and not to stare down at the table. I guess I did a decent job, because I saw the moment he started to truly see. To recognize all the things about me that weren't quite right. Weren't quite Danny.

Nicholas saw it too. "So, Dad," he said. "How's the joint treating you?"

It distracted Robert enough. He dropped his hands and turned to Nicholas.

"Not too bad, I guess," he said. He poked Nicholas in the side with his finger. "Haven't been *shivved* yet, at least."

Nicholas rolled his eyes, but there was an upward curve to his lips. Robert turned back to me, took my hand again on top of the table.

"So, you're back in school?" he asked, the faintest note of disbelief in his voice.

"Yeah, but I don't do any work," I said. "I just go and sit in on classes."

He nodded and frowned at the same time. "What about you, Nicky? Excited for next year?"

I snorted. It was always a little surprising when Nicholas managed to make it through a day at Calabasas High without setting the place on fire.

Nicholas shifted beside me. "Dad, I—"

"When do you find out where you're living?" Robert continued.

I frowned. "Huh?"

"We can talk about it later, Dad," Nicholas said. "Have I told you about the play Mia is writing?"

Robert didn't appear to notice the awkward dodge. His face turned instantly wistful at the mention of Mia. I wondered if he was always this expressive or if it was something about prison. Like he was trying to squeeze every emotion he could into these short, infrequent visits. "No. She's doing well?"

Nicholas nodded. "Yeah, great. She's been practically living in the pool lately, and she gets the brace off in a couple of weeks."

"You know, I never asked because I know I *should* know," I said, "but is Mia's condition genetic?"

Nicholas snapped his head around to look at me. I knew I was taking a risk by pissing him off, but I needed to know what Robert knew. I needed to know if he had a motive to kill Danny, and Nicholas believed in his dad too much to push him.

"No, no," Robert said. "It just happens sometimes."

"So no one on your side of the family ever had it?" I asked.

Robert's lips thinned just a little. "No. It's nothing like that."

Nicholas veered the conversation away again, and when Robert was momentarily distracted by an argument that broke out at the next table over, he shot me a hard look. I didn't care. I'd found out what I needed to.

When the visiting period was over, Robert hugged me again and told me how happy he was to see me. That he loved me. Then he asked to speak privately to Nicholas for a moment. I nodded and left the two of them alone, walking back to the lobby of the prison by myself. Nicholas followed a couple of minutes later.

"So?" I asked as we walked back to his car.

"He wants to believe it's you," he said, "but he's suspicious. He can't be in on this."

I nodded. It was what I suspected, but God, everything

would be so much easier if Robert had been the one who'd killed Danny. "I think you're right."

"Yeah. I knew it." Nicholas's obvious relief gave way to irritation. "And hey, I told you *I* would deal with the Mia thing."

"But you *weren't* going to deal with it," I said. "Did you see how angry he got? He knows he's not her real father. Maybe that has something to do with—"

"He *is* her real father," Nicholas said, "in every way that matters. You're still here so that I can find out what happened to Danny. That's it. Leave Mia out of it."

"You can't assume the two things aren't related," I said. "Two huge secrets like that."

"Everyone has secrets," he said, "and neither of my parents would *kill* their son over something like that. It doesn't make any sense."

I thought Nicholas was wrong—people were capable of darker stuff than he imagined when pushed—but I also thought Jessica and Robert were probably innocent and didn't want to risk provoking him any further, so I dropped it.

We climbed back into the car, which was sweltering after baking under the sun for an hour. Nicholas rolled down the windows and blasted the AC, and soon we were on the freeway headed south to Hidden Hills. I replayed the visit in my head as we drove, looking for any clues I might have missed. We were nearly home when I remembered an odd moment in the conversation. I turned to Nicholas, who had spent most of the drive staring silently out at the road in front of him.

"Hey, what did your dad mean about being excited for next year?" I asked.

Nicholas didn't look at me. "Nothing."

"Oh, come on," I said. "I know it was *something*."

He sighed. "Fine. But you can't tell anyone."

I gave him a look. "I can keep a secret."

"I'm going away to college," he said.

I frowned. "Yeah, but that's not until—"

"Next fall," he said. "I'm graduating early. I'll have all my credits by the end of the semester, and I already got into NYU."

"I didn't know that," I said.

"No one does. Just my dad," he said. "And I only told him so that he'd have the accountant unlock my trust early so I can pay for it."

"Why?" I asked.

"Because I'm sick of that school and my family and this place," he said, "and I didn't want to argue with anyone about it. It's my life. It's my decision."

"When are you going to tell them?" I asked.

He shrugged. "Whenever I absolutely have to."

I imagined what a bombshell it would be for everyone. The Tates were fucked up on a lot of levels, but they were also close-knit. For them to suddenly lose another person—even if it was only in a temporary way, just to the other side of the country—would rock them.

"You . . . don't think that's a little selfish?" I asked. I knew it was stupid to antagonize him when he held my life in his hands, but I didn't care.

He turned his head and stared at me.

"I mean, it's your life, do whatever you want," I said, "but I don't get why you'd want to hurt your family on purpose like that."

"I don't think you get to criticize me for hurting my family with a straight face. What the hell does it even matter to you?" he said.

"I care about them." I saw a brief flash of my mother as she was the last moment I saw her, with a phone pressed to her ear, dry-eyed and stone-faced. "You have no idea how lucky you are, to have a family like yours."

Nicholas laughed and his fingers dug into the steering wheel. "A family like mine? If you and I are right, one of them *murdered* my brother. A little boy who, yeah, was a pain in the ass but was just a little boy. More are lying to cover up for that person with no regard for how much it hurts the rest of us. How's my dad going to feel when he finds out the truth? Or Mia? They'll have to go through losing Danny all over again. This family is poisonous, and I'm just trying to get out while I still can."

"But you didn't know any of that when you decided to leave without telling them," I said.

"I didn't need to. They've done plenty of other things."

"But they *love* you," I said.

"It's not enough." He gave me a dumbfounded look. "Where

can you be from that you think some ingrained, biological imperative to 'love' me is enough to excuse what they've done?"

"It's not an imperative." Something inside of me was cracking and breaking loose, like a calving glacier. "Maybe it seems like it to you, but not everyone loves their family."

He was quiet for a moment. Then he said, "They didn't love you?"

"It was only really my mother," I said, "and no."

"I guess I knew that," he said. "Otherwise you wouldn't have ended up here, would you?"

I thought about the first time I ran away from home, how they'd put me into a temporary care home until they could locate my family. The adults fed me and patted me on the arm and talked to me in kind tones. A kid there taught me a card game and another lent me an extra pair of socks when my feet got cold. When my mother finally came to collect me, I screamed my throat raw and broke two fingers punching a wall. That was the day I learned: Don't give them your name, because then they can't call anyone to come take you away.

"I guess not," I said.

"How bad was it?" he asked.

I shifted in my seat. It was weird, talking about myself. "Pretty bad."

Nicholas cocked his head at me.

"I think that's the first time I've ever completely believed anything that's come out of your mouth," he said.

At dinner that night, over Vietnamese takeout, Lex asked us how school had been.

Nicholas shrugged. "It was okay."

"Danny?" Lex asked.

"Yeah," I said. "Fine."

"So, nothing unusual?"

Nicholas sighed and lowered his chopsticks. "They called you."

"Yes, they did," she said. "Where the hell were you two?"

"Nowhere special," Nicholas said. "We just didn't feel like school. You gonna ground us, Mom?"

"Just don't take off like that without telling anyone, okay?" Lex said. "I was worried."

"Well, we're fine," he said.

"Why can't I skip school when I don't feel like it?" Mia asked.

I vaguely registered the sound of the front door opening.

"You want to answer that one?" Lex asked Nicholas.

"Because, Mimi," he said, "*your* school isn't an exercise in pointless, torturous futility."

"Hey, guys," Patrick said as he entered the dining room.

"Hey," Lex replied with the surprise we all felt. It was Monday; Patrick never came over on Mondays.

"Lexi, can I talk to you for a sec?" he said. He sounded weird. Overly casual.

"Yeah, okay, just let me—"

"What is futility?" Mia asked.

"High school. Eat your pho." Nicholas turned to Patrick. "What's going on?"

"It's nothing," Patrick said.

Nicholas's phone started to ring.

"Do I have to eat this?" Mia asked Lex. "I just want some cereal."

"Hey, can I call you later?" Nicholas said into the phone.

"Try three bites," Lex said.

"Lexi," Patrick said. "I really need—"

"*What*?" Nicholas said. His tone was strident enough to cut through the chaos, and we all turned to him. He pushed back his chair and rushed out of the room, phone still held to his ear. Lex went after him, ignoring Patrick's attempt to grab her arm. Mia went after Lex, I went after them, and Patrick went after us all.

We found Nicholas in the den. He had turned on the television and was changing the channels until he landed on a local news broadcast.

"I'll call you back," he said into the phone, and hung up.

On the screen a reporter was standing in front of the FBI field office in L.A., a building I would recognize anywhere. Underneath her was a banner that read "New Clue in Case of Missing Boy."

"—told that hikers discovered the distinctive custom bicycle as many as three months ago, but the FBI had chosen not to make that information public at the time." The picture cut from the reporter to a still of a red mountain bike with chunky wheels and designs painted in gold on its frame. "This is the second major development in recent weeks in the six-year investigation into what happened to ten-year-old Daniel Tate, who disappeared from the affluent community of Hidden Hills while riding his bike to a friend's house. A recent *Los Angeles Magazine* article revived public interest in the case less than a month before Tate was discovered alive in Vancouver, Canada. The FBI is hopeful that the discovery of Tate's bicycle will be the break they've been looking for in the search for his abductors."

"Oh my God," Nicholas whispered.

I turned and looked at Lex. She was looking at Patrick. Neither of them looked surprised.

So *that's* why they'd brought me here.

I whipped my head around at the sound of a crash to my left. Jessica was standing on the stairs, the shattered pieces of a wine glass around her feet, staring at the bicycle on the television screen.

Jessica collapsed amongst the glass, immediately taken over by a fit of crying and shaking, and Mia burst into tears at seeing her mother upset. Lex hugged Mia to her, and Patrick and I went to help Jessica up. She was gulping for breath and bleeding from several shards of glass embedded in her skin. We each put an arm around her shoulders and helped her up the stairs back to her room.

"They f-found the bike?" she said.

"I know it's a shock, but this is good news, Mom," Patrick

said. "It'll help them find who took you, Danny, right?"

"Right," I said. Nice cover, Patrick. Very smooth.

We got Jessica into bed. I tried to follow Patrick to the bathroom when he went for the first aid supplies, but Jessica's grip on my arm was unbreakable.

"Hey, it's okay," I said softly. I didn't have the first clue how to comfort someone, especially in a situation as bizarre as this one, so I just patted her the way I thought I should. "Everything's going to be all right."

"I'm scared," she whispered.

I swallowed. "I know. But it's going to be okay. I'm here."

"Danny—"

Patrick walked back into the room and Jessica stopped. He handed her a couple of pills and a glass of water. "Take these."

"Patrick," I said. "Are you sure—"

"She's hysterical," he told me. "She needs some rest."

We removed the glass from Jessica's skin and cleaned the cuts, and by the time we were finished, she was asleep.

I collapsed onto my bed, body exhausted but mind racing. They'd found Danny's bicycle, the one that disappeared when he did, and they'd found it months ago. The discovery hadn't been made public, but somehow Patrick and Lex had known, I was sure of it. The *LA Magazine* article that got everyone thinking about the case again and this looming piece of new evidence, that was why they'd brought me here. I'd appeared at just the right time for them, when they were the most worried and desperate.

How had they known about the bike?

In my back pocket, my phone started to vibrate. I was too wiped out to even reach for it. And there was no one I wanted to talk to. But it kept vibrating, and eventually I gave in and fished it out of my pocket.

Ren, the display read.

I hesitated, battling with myself, and then answered the call.

"Hey," I said.

"Hey," she said. "I just saw the news, and I wanted to see if you're okay. Do you want to talk about it?"

"I thought this was all too much for you, and I was supposed to be talking to a professional," I said.

She sighed. "I never wanted to stop being your friend, Danny."

I rolled over until I was facing the wall and stared at it, finding a spot where the former paint color was showing through tiny gaps in the blue. Ren wanted to be my friend. Someone *wanted* me, in some way, wanted to know me. Why, again, was she the person I was trying to keep at arm's length?

"You're right," I said. "I'm sorry. I've been a jerk."

"You've been fine," she said. "I know this isn't easy for you. I just . . . miss you."

I took an unsteady breath. "I miss you, too."

I imagined her smiling at that. I imagined her sitting here beside me.

"So," she said. "Do you want to talk about it?"

"I really don't."

"In that case, did you see Isabella kiss Gage's brother on yesterday's episode?"

"No, tell me about it."

Ren caught me up on everything happening on *A Life of Love*, and I just enjoyed listening to her talk. When I was fully apprised of the goings-on of Bridgeport, we talked about our final projects for art class and sci-fi movies and looking at colleges, and it was just . . . simple. Nice.

"My uncle keeps buying me these college guides and just leaving them in my bedroom, like not actually *mentioning* them makes it subtle," she said. Her voice was low and warm and close to sleep. I checked the time; it was late. "But I don't even know if I want to go to college, you know? It seems like just a way to stall real life. There's no way in a year I'm going to know what I want to be for the rest of my life, so what's the point?"

"Maybe you're putting too much pressure on it," I said. "You don't have to know what you want to be for the rest of your life. Just for the next ten years, or five, or ten minutes. You can always change your mind."

"I guess." She yawned. "I just want to be *happy*."

My own eyes were starting to droop. "That's the trick, isn't it, figuring that out."

"Hmm," she said.

We were both silent, and I listened to the soft sounds of her breathing through the phone. Then my eyes closed and I fell asleep.

I woke up with my phone on the pillow beside me and a text from Ren waiting on it.

Good morning, sunshine! You snore! :P

I smiled and tried to save a piece of the feeling for later.

Lex offered to let us stay home from school—Nicholas raised his eyebrows at the notion that she possessed the power to offer such a thing—on account of the bicycle news, but Nicholas wanted to get back to his classes so he could graduate on time, and I wanted to see Ren, so we went.

"Goddammit," Nicholas said as we approached Calabasas High. The place was swarming with press, maybe even more reporters than there'd been when I first came back to school. "What do you want to do?"

"It'll be okay," I said with more steadiness than I felt. "They can't follow us inside."

"I'm going to call Asher and see where he is," Nicholas said.

We pulled into a space in the student parking lot, and Asher came out to meet us. Just in case.

"Hey, man," he said to me as I climbed out of Nicholas's car. "You okay?"

I nodded. "Fine."

"It's good, right, that they found it?" he said. "It'll help them catch the bad guys, right?"

"Hopefully," I said, exchanging a brief look with Nicholas.

We were halfway to the school when a reporter and cameraman stepped out from behind a pickup truck.

"Daniel Tate?" he said, pointing a digital recorder at me.

"Leave us alone," Nicholas said.

"Daniel, are you optimistic that your kidnappers will be found?" the man said, taking a step closer to me. Suddenly Asher was standing between us, his palm, the size of a serving plate, on the man's chest, pushing him back.

"No comment, asshole," he said.

A movement at the corner of my eye caught my attention. I turned and found a bank of cameras trained on me from the front of the school where the news vans were parked. This idiot reporter had attracted their attention. I immediately turned to hide my face.

"Nicholas," I said. "Look."

Nicholas took in the rows of cameras, with their telephotos lenses, and made an instant decision.

"Fuck this," he said. "We're getting out of here."

We went back to the car, and I covered my face with my hands until we were far away from the school.

We went home, and because only Jessica's car was there, we didn't even need to explain to anyone why we were back. Ren texted me to see how I was, and I gave her the gate code and invited her to come over later that night. Meanwhile, Nicholas and I locked ourselves in his room to go over everything we knew, since there was suddenly new urgency to our investigation. It didn't take long. There just wasn't that much evidence. One moment Danny was there and the next he was gone.

On the Saturday morning Danny disappeared, he had breakfast with the family, except for Robert, who'd been in Palo Alto on a business trip since the previous Thursday, and Nicholas, who had spent the night and the bulk of that day at a friend's house. Danny told Jessica he was going to ride his bike to his friend Andrew's. The nanny had the weekend off, so Jessica then took Mia to a doctor's appointment and to run several errands, which the FBI had verified. Patrick and Lex spent the day with friends, several of whom had been able to confirm their alibis. Everyone's movements were accounted for in the hours before Jessica called the police to report Danny missing that evening.

Some part of the story was obviously off, but so many years later, it was hard to tell which one.

"This is impossible," Nicholas said. "If the FBI can't figure this out, what makes us think we can?"

"Hubris?" I said.

He laughed in that way he usually did, not a real laugh but a puff of air through his nose that could just as easily be mocking as amusement. "You've been paying attention to Mr. Vaughn."

"Well, he's just so inspiring," I deadpanned, and he actually smiled for real.

Suddenly, someone downstairs started to yell. We glanced at

each other and jumped up, Nicholas shoving all the papers under his bed before we rushed from the room. We stopped on the landing of the staircase and looked over the railing into the foyer. Lex must have arrived home while we were working, because she and Jessica were down there somewhere, and they were arguing.

"—me what to do. I'm the mother here, Alexis!"

"Then act like it for once in your life!" Lex replied. "We *need* you. Think of Mia; she's only a little girl. If you keep going out there, someone's going to notice, and then what's going to happen to all of us?"

Jessica's voice dropped, not so much that we couldn't hear it anymore, but enough that the words became unintelligible. Lex's reply was likewise impossible to make out. Then Jessica was stalking through the foyer and out the front door.

"We have to follow her," Nicholas said.

"Now?" I asked. It was on our list of things to do, but we were checking off tasks a little quickly for my taste.

"Of course now," he said. "You heard what Lex just said. This could be important."

Nicholas ran back to his room to grab his keys, and then we headed downstairs. We crept to the front door so that Lex wouldn't hear us and then ran around the side of the house to the garage, where Nicholas had parked, ducking under windows when there was a chance we could be seen. As soon as we were away from the house, Nicholas gunned the engine, and by the time we'd reached the gate that shielded Hidden Hills from the rest of the world, we'd caught up to Jessica's SUV. Nicholas followed her from a discreet distance onto the freeway, where she headed east.

An hour later we were still driving, and the sun was sitting low in the rearview mirror.

Nicholas slammed his head back against the headrest in frustration. "Where the hell is she going?"

"Could she know we're following her?" I asked.

"I don't see how," he said. "We're a hundred yards behind her, and there are nine billion black BMWs in Southern California. Maybe she listened to Lex and isn't going where she isn't supposed to. Maybe she just likes to drive around, like she told you."

"On the freeway?" I said.

Nicholas's cell phone began to ring, and the display on his car's computer console read "Asher." He frowned but answered.

"Hey, I can't really—"

But Asher was already talking. "Want to come over?" he asked, his voice filling the car. "I just found the most terrible-looking movie on Netflix."

"I can't," Nicholas said.

"Hot date?"

"Danny and I are doing something."

"Again? What's going on with you two?"

Nicholas glanced over at me. "Ash—"

"A couple of weeks ago you barely even spoke, and now you're ditching school together and, like, attached at the hip. I mean, don't get me wrong, it's great, but what changed?"

Nicholas sighed. "Just making more of an effort."

"Liar! Oh my God, you're so bad at it!"

I grinned, and Nicholas shot me a glare.

"I'll call you later, okay?" Nicholas said, finger already hovering over the button that would end the call.

"Okay, liar! Love you!"

Nicholas jabbed the button, and the car went silent. He glowered, and I tried to hide my smile.

"It's not funny," Nicholas said. "I hate hiding things from him."

"Then why are you?"

"I just . . . I need to keep him separate from family stuff," he said. "He gets that."

"How long have you two been together?" I asked.

"Two and a half years."

I blinked. "Jesus."

The corner of his mouth turned up. "Yeah, that's the usual reaction."

"So you were, what, fifteen?" I asked. "And you've been together ever since then?"

He nodded. "He's seen all the worst parts of me, and it hasn't scared him off yet."

Those words hit something deep inside of me, and I knew they were going to linger. "That . . . must be nice."

"Sure makes the world seem less scary," he said.

I turned and looked out the window. How different might my life have turned out if *I'd* had that at fifteen? I'd been an outcast at school, barely spoke to anyone. More days than not, I ended up just sitting behind the building, watching leaves fall from the trees while I waited for the bell to ring. What would it have been like if I'd had someone to walk those halls with me or someplace safe to run to when my home wasn't? Maybe I wouldn't have dropped out at sixteen, wouldn't have run away and ended up here, with no name and no history of my own.

I started to see that imaginary person's face, and it was Ren's.

Nicholas hit my arm. "Hey, look."

I turned and saw him pointing forward. Jessica was exiting the freeway.

She drove down a series of smaller roads, orange dust billowing up behind her SUV, until she reached a parking lot with a couple of picnic tables and a sign designating it a SCENIC OVERLOOK. We watched from a distance as she parked her car and just sat there, staring out at the vast stretch of desert.

Despite the hot sun slanting in low through the window, I shivered. I didn't know why. My body had made sense of the scene before my mind did.

Nicholas suddenly revved the car and threw it into reverse.

It was only as we were leaving that I understood why Jessica would make a pilgrimage out to a deserted corner of the desert to sit and stare at the endless expanse of barren orange dust.

Because she knew there was something out there, somewhere, hidden in that dust.

Nicholas and I didn't speak for the entire ride home. Not even when he pulled over to the side of the road and retched. We both knew what we'd seen, and neither of us wanted to say the words aloud.

We'd just followed Jessica to Danny's grave.

Nicholas dropped me off at the house and immediately left again, headed to Asher's. I guess if I had someone who made me feel like the world was a less scary place, I'd want to be with them right then too. I walked blindly into the house, mind racing, and bumped into Lex on her way out the door.

"Oh, Danny, I was just—" She stopped and touched my cheek, drawing my eyes up to hers. "Hey, you okay?"

Her show of concern suddenly made me want to cry. Or break something.

"Yeah," I said. "Just tired."

"Well, I'm on my way out for the night," she said. "Mia's spending the night at Eleanor's house, so I thought I'd meet some girlfriends. Will you be okay on your own? I can bail if you want."

"I'm fine. Have fun."

She looked at me closely. "You sure?"

I suddenly really wanted her to stay. More than anything. We could sit in the rec room and watch soaps and eat popcorn and everything could be the way it was before. All I had to do was ask.

"No," I said. "You should go."

"Okay, call if you need anything!" She kissed me on the forehead, and then she was gone.

I spent the rest of the evening wandering the house aimlessly. I couldn't focus on anything for more than a minute or two at a time. The image of a little boy's body—probably just bones now, surrounded by scraps of fabric—kept rising in front of me. Buried in a shallow grave in the sand, maybe discovered by predators, fought over by coyotes and carrion birds. It made everything too real. This wasn't just playacting anymore, and my horror at what I'd done was dizzying. It was a real boy's life. A real boy's death. I thought of the smiling boy on the baseball card hidden in the pillowcase upstairs and imagined him still and cold, not breathing, his body thrown away like a piece of trash. By any logical assessment, it should have been him instead.

I had to get out of that house.

There was only one car at the house, Robert's beloved Jaguar. Patrick kept a key for it in a junk drawer in the kitchen. I didn't have a license, but Patrick had given me several lessons in the Jag. I was reasonably certain I could get it from here to Ren's house or LAX or the Canadian border in one piece, and if I couldn't, well, maybe that was for the best anyway.

I was in the kitchen, fumbling through the drawer for the key, when the front door opened. I should have just ignored it. Should have gone straight to the garage, gotten in the car, and left.

"Hello?" someone called. I didn't recognize the voice. "Anyone home?"

I went into the foyer and found Jessica slumped by the door in one of the fancy chairs I'd never seen anyone sit in. A middle-aged man wearing a Bluetooth earpiece and a rumpled polo was hovering in the open doorway.

"Can I help you?" I said.

"You can pay me," he said. I looked past him to see the cab idling in the driveway. "She couldn't find her wallet."

"Oh God." I took Jessica's purse out of her lap. She looked up at me blearily, reeking of alcohol. "Where did you pick her up?"

"Sherman Oaks. The parking lot of a liquor store."

I found her wallet and gave the guy one of the hundreds inside. "At least she didn't try to drive."

"She was out of gas," he said.

Of course. I thanked the driver, and he left while I turned to Jessica.

"Can you walk?" I asked her.

She struggled to her feet, and when she stumbled, I caught her around the waist.

"Come on," I said. "Let's get you to bed."

"Just leave me . . . ," she mumbled.

"I'm not going to leave you," I said. "Come on."

Slowly we moved up the stairs, pausing often. Jessica talked most of the way, but I could understand very few of the slurred words. All that was clear was the anguished tone of them. So this is what she did. Drove out to the desert to be near her son's bones and then drank herself into oblivion. I saw my mother sitting impassive in front of the television, and I swallowed and tightened my arm a little more around Jessica's waist.

We finally reached her bedroom, and I lowered her to the bed, where she buried her face in the mounds of pillows. I went to the bathroom and filled up the cup on the counter with water. I sat on the edge of the bed and handed her the glass.

"Try to drink some of this," I said.

She took the glass with a quavering hand and dissolved into tears.

"Danny . . . ," she keened.

"It's okay, don't cry," I said. I helped her take off her jacket, while she, childlike, did nothing to resist me. "You just need some sleep."

"My boy," she said. "My Danny."

I took off her shoes and tossed them along with the jacket into a nearby chair. The rest she could sleep in. She was sobbing now, and I helped her lie down and covered her with the comforter. I turned off the lamp on her bedside table, but when I started to stand, she grabbed my arm.

"Don't go," she said. "Danny, don't leave me."

"I . . . okay." Did she really think I was Danny? Had she had so much to drink that reality and the lie were starting to blur?

"I told you," she murmured. "I told you!"

"What did you tell me?"

She was saying something softly, and I had to lean to make it out.

"I'm sorry," she was whispering. "I'm so sorry,"

My heart stopped.

"For what?" I asked. "What did you do?"

She pressed the side of her face against the pillow.

"I'm so sorry," she said over and over, the words muffled and indistinct.

I grabbed her by the shoulders and shook her. "For what? What happened, Jessica?"

She just cried harder.

"Mom," I said. The word tasted like burnt orange dust on my tongue. "What happened?"

"I told you not to ride your bike in the driveway after dark," she said. "I told you so many times . . ."

My skin flushed hot.

"I didn't mean to," she said. "I'm so sorry . . ."

I sat there, silent and stunned, until Jessica passed out.

Jessica had killed Danny.

My head was hot and buzzing and I couldn't think. I went out to the backyard—vaguely noticing that my hands were shaking when I opened the French doors that led to the patio—and kicked off my shoes and jeans before jumping into the pool. The cool, silent water surrounded me, and I stayed under until my burning lungs forced me to the surface. I clumsily swam a couple of laps. I didn't know how to swim properly, but the movement felt good.

Jessica had killed Danny. He was riding his bike in the driveway. It was dark, and she didn't see him.

It was an accident. None of the Tates had hurt him on purpose. None of them was a murderer. I started to laugh. I floated on my back, looked up at the sky, and laughed at the stars.

I'd thought Danny's killer must have done it on purpose, because otherwise there was no reason not to just call the police and report the accident. But it was obvious what Jessica had wanted to hide. She must have been wasted when she hit Danny with her car. Her marriage to Robert was starting to go bad, she'd had an affair with her ex-husband that had gotten her pregnant, Mia had been born with health problems, Ben McConnell had killed himself, and she was watching Lex fall apart before her eyes. Drinking herself unconscious was the only coping mechanism Jessica had, and I knew very well that it didn't stop her from getting behind the wheel. She knew she would go to prison if anyone found out what had really happened that night and—

I sucked in a breath and got a lungful of water along with it. I stood up, sputtering and coughing.

That *night*?

That's what Jessica had said; she always warned him not to ride his bike after dark. But the family realized Danny was missing in the early evening, when it was still plenty light outside.

Either Jessica's drunken, sobbing confession was just another lie, or the official story was wrong.

I heaved myself out of the pool and returned, dripping, to the house. I grabbed a towel out of the laundry room and wrapped it around myself as I climbed the stairs back to Danny's room.

I knew the supposed timeline of that Saturday by heart now, but once I got to Danny's room, I opened my file anyway just to check. Jessica made breakfast for Patrick, Lex, Danny, and Mia at about nine in the morning. She left with Mia for the doctor's office at ten. As she pulled out of the driveway, she saw Danny retrieving his bike from the garage to ride to Andrew's house. Lex and Patrick left the house not long after and met their friends at the mall about an hour later.

But if Jessica had hit Danny with her car because it was nighttime and she hadn't been able to see him, it must have happened the night before. Nicholas and Robert had been away from the house Friday night and all of Saturday, and Mia was just a toddler, but Lex and Patrick both said that they'd seen Danny Saturday morning before he went missing. They had to have been lying. Almost an entire day passed between when Jessica killed him and when she called the police to report him missing, plenty of time for the three of them to come up with their cover stories, destroy any evidence of the accident, dump the bike and Danny's body in the desert, and establish alibis for themselves.

It was an extreme plan, but it was hard to blame Lex and

Patrick. They were practically kids themselves and probably terrified of the prospect of their mother, the only parent they had left, going to prison so soon after the death of their father. Nothing would bring Danny back, so why not do what they could to help their mother? And then they were a part of it, just as culpable as Jessica was. All three of them needed me to deflect suspicion from their crimes. When Jessica was on the brink of cracking, Lex and Patrick kept her in line. Even if they no longer felt so protective of a mother who had all but abandoned them for the bottle, they knew they would also be in trouble for the part they'd played in covering up the truth.

It made sense. Right?

I reached for my phone to call Nicholas and get him to come home so I could tell him the whole story. The mystery was solved, and it wasn't as bad as either of us had feared. None of the Tates were murderers.

Downstairs the doorbell rang.

What now? I hurriedly pulled on some dry pants and grabbed a shirt on my way out of the bedroom. I pulled it over my head as I jogged down the stairs and opened the front door.

"Hey!" Ren said. "You're all wet!"

With everything that had happened, I'd completely forgotten I'd invited her over this morning. It seemed like days ago that I'd attempted to go to school.

"Hey," I said, adjusting the shirt as it stuck to my damp skin. "You're here."

"As promised," she said, stepping past me into the house. "It was a good call skipping school, by the way. The place was a madhouse."

"Yeah?" I said. My brain was still struggling to deal with her presence here on top of everything else.

She cocked her head at me. "You okay?"

"I . . . yeah," I said. "Just a lot on my mind. You know."

"Oh," she said. "Do you want me to leave?"

She was trying to cover it up, but there was disappointment in her voice. Even after the day I'd had, it surprised me, and I couldn't turn that away.

"No," I said. "Stay."

She smiled. "All right."

We ended up on the sofa in the basement, watching a movie on the big screen. I don't even remember what it was, because I wasn't watching. I was thinking about Jessica and Danny and Nicholas.

I should call Nicholas, I knew that. But if the mystery was solved, there was no reason for him to keep me around. Although some of his rage at me seemed to have dissipated in the past day or so, there was a good chance he was only biding his time before seeing me put in jail for impersonating his brother.

But if I kept him in the dark, he would let me stay to keep helping him find out what had happened to Danny, at least for a little while longer. That would give me time to plan my next move and make sure I got away before he could turn me in. Or, maybe, if I could play things out long enough . . .

But I couldn't let myself think about that.

Ren laughed at something that happened on-screen and turned to me, and I feigned a smile. She shifted, pulling her legs up under her and ending up with her arm resting just barely against my elbow. Neither of us moved, and that stopped my brain in its tracks. For a little while.

I should call Nicholas. It was the right thing to do. He was the one person I'd been honest with, and we were slowly starting to become . . . not friends, but *something*. Something real. If I kept this from him, that was over.

The question was, what did I really want?

If I was honest with myself, I knew.

Ren turned her head and smiled at me. "Hey."

I smiled back. "Hey."

I didn't call Nicholas.

". . . want me to come stay with them for the summer, but I don't—Danny?"

"Huh?" I said.

Her expression turned soft and she leaned closer to me. "Where are you?"

"I'm sorry," I said. After the movie had ended we'd gone to sit out on the patio, and my mind kept wandering.

"It's okay," she said. "What are you thinking about? Is it the bike?"

"Sort of," I said.

"Want to talk about it?" she asked. "Or should I keep trying to distract you? Maybe I could do a little dance for you? I used to take tap."

I laughed. Somehow she managed to make me feel better without making light of things, and I didn't know how she did it. "I find that hard to imagine."

"Why?" she asked in mock outrage. "I was very good, I'll have you know! I probably could have gone pro."

"Why didn't you?"

"The demands of fifth grade were just too much," she said. "I decided to focus on my education. Oh, you've got an eyelash."

She leaned toward me and brushed my cheek with her fingers, and it felt like my heart constricted in my chest, became small and dense and hot under my skin.

God, I wanted to kiss her. Kiss her and hold her close and show her all the worst parts of me and have her tell me it was okay, she liked me anyway.

But I couldn't, because she wouldn't.

"Here," she said, holding the tip of one finger in front of my eyes so I could see the eyelash stuck there. "Make a wish."

Maybe I couldn't tell her all of my secrets, but I could kiss her. She was so close, and the look in her eyes was so warm. But then I remembered the way she had brushed me off the last time, and I knew I couldn't risk it.

"Go on," she said, and I closed my eyes and blew.

Do I even need to tell you what my wish was? Or whether it came true?

The next morning Jessica stumbled downstairs for a cup of coffee while the rest of us were eating breakfast. She kissed the top of Mia's head when Mia threw her arms around her, and when Nicholas asked how she'd slept, she said fine.

Then her eyes met mine and darted away again, and I couldn't tell if it was just because that's how she usually looked at me—in fleeting, furtive glances—or because she remembered what had happened the night before.

The media circus around the school had dispersed, so I was able to go back with no issues. I sat with Ren at lunch, and we talked about Miranda's recent bout of amnesia. I think I smiled the entire time, even though there was a sharp ache growing inside of me with each passing moment because I knew this couldn't last. One way or another, no matter what I did to delay it, I was going to have to leave this place and these people. The only question was whether I'd be leaving them to go on the run or to prison.

After the final bell rang, I met Nicholas at the student parking lot as usual. When I was opening the passenger's door of his car, he said, "We're going to Patrick's."

I stopped. "What?"

"It's time to look for those files," he said.

Finding the file on Patrick from Robert's filing cabinet was the last concrete item on Nicholas's to-do list. He was hoping to find out what kind of trouble Patrick had been in as a teenager, in case it could be connected to what happened to Danny. But I knew it wasn't, and what would Nicholas do when the last straw he had to grasp at was gone? How long would I last?

"Are you sure you want to do that today?" I asked over the roof of the car.

"I'm sure."

"Wouldn't it be better to wait until tomorrow?" I said. "Ditch school and go in the morning when it's less likely that Patrick will catch us?"

"No, I want to get this done," Nicholas said.

"But traffic—"

"Patrick always works late on Wednesdays. Even after traffic we'll have a solid hour or two to look around his apartment. That's plenty of time. I already texted Lex that we're going to the library."

I looked back at the school. "Then I should get one of my textbooks so it looks like we were studying. I left them in my locker—"

"Just get in the car," he said, 100 percent not buying my bullshit.

I had no choice. I got in the car, and Nicholas turned east out of the parking lot, away from Hidden Hills and toward Los Angeles.

Patrick's apartment was in a brand-new building downtown. Nicholas admitted as we rode up in the elevator that he'd never been there before.

"He always comes to see us," he said with a shrug. "He's weird about his privacy."

We found Patrick's apartment on the top floor, at the end of the hall. Nicholas knocked first just to make sure he wasn't home and then opened the door with the spare key he'd swiped from Lex's key ring that morning. We crept inside like criminals, although this was pretty much the least criminal thing I'd done so far.

The apartment was nice. It was open and expensively finished, with floor-to-ceiling windows that looked out over the L.A. skyline and thoughtful touches to the decor that suggested someone with an eye for nice things had helped him put the place together. But it felt neglected and cold. There were a used bowl and spoon in the sink and a pile of mail and other bits and pieces scattered around that stood as evidence that Patrick did, in fact, live here, but somehow it felt empty and devoid of life.

"Brr," Nicholas said. Whatever it was, he felt it too.

We started opening doors, looking for a likely place for Patrick to keep his files, and quickly found the home office. I looked through the drawers in the desk while Nicholas rummaged in the filing cabinet in the corner.

"There's nothing here," I said after a few minutes. "Just office supplies and work stuff."

Nicholas slid closed the door of the filing cabinet. "Same

here." He opened the doors to the closet. "Oh, bingo."

I joined him and looked down at the safe on the floor of the closet.

"Don't suppose you know how to crack a safe?" he asked.

"Can't say that's in my skill set, no."

"Well." He sat down cross-legged in front of the safe. "I'll just have to guess, then."

Nicholas started entering numbers, and I went back to the desk.

"He may have written the combination down somewhere," I said, rifling through the papers and Post-its on top of the desk. Maybe if I found the combination first, I could pocket it without Nicholas noticing.

Nicholas shook his head. "He would have picked something he could remember. Something with some kind of significance."

Nicholas continued entering different combinations with serene patience. Whenever he pulled on the lever and it didn't budge, he just moved on to a different set of numbers. Eventually, I got bored of watching and started to explore the rest of the apartment. I read the spines of the books on his shelves in the living room, mostly reference books and other lawyerly things but with a fair number of spy thrillers mixed in. There were lots of framed pictures of the family on the bookshelves as well. Mia blowing out candles on a birthday cake. Lex lying on a beach with Nicholas and Mia playing in the background. Nicholas and Jessica standing in front of what looked like a cathedral in some European city. A kind eyed man with two small children, which had to be Patrick and Lex with their father Ben McConnell. A teenage Lex with pink streaks in her hair, blowing a kiss at the camera.

No pictures of Danny.

I stuck my head back into the office. "How's it going?"

"I'm gonna get it," Nicholas said.

"It's getting late."

"We've got time."

I wandered into Patrick's bedroom. If the rest of the apartment felt neglected, this room was downright spartan. The only nod toward decoration was a couple of throw pillows that were piled in a corner where I'm betting they always stayed. The walls were a light gray. The bedspread was dark gray. There was a television on the wall, a lamp on the bedside table, and nothing else except for a silver picture frame that looked oddly out of place in such a stripped-down space. I turned the frame toward me to see what was inside.

It was a picture of Lex, lying with her cheek in the grass.

"Got it!" Nicholas cried from the other room.

Damn.

I replaced the photo and rushed into the office, where he was combing through the contents of the now open safe.

"What was it?" I asked.

"Lex's birthday." He handed me a folder. "Look familiar?"

It was a filing folder like the ones Robert had on all the kids. The handwritten label said PATRICK—LEGAL.

Damn damn damn.

There wasn't much inside. Nothing like the stacks of papers that had been in Mia's medical folder or Lex's addiction folder. There was just one collection of a few sheets stapled together, verifying that the juvenile arrest records of Patrick Calvin McConnell had been sealed and expunged, along with a list of said arrests.

"Jesus," I whispered.

"What?" Nicholas leaned over my shoulder to read.

July 11, 2007—Possession of a controlled substance

February 4, 2008—Possession of a controlled substance

January 25, 2009—Criminal vandalism

November 2, 2009—Possession of a controlled substance

November 11, 2009—Assault and battery

December 23, 2009—Assault and battery

January 14, 2010—Trafficking of narcotics

March 18, 2010—Assault and battery

"*Trafficking*?" Nicholas said.

"And three assault arrests," I said. I felt a little better. This would give Nicholas plenty of new things to investigate, all of them leading him away from the truth.

"We don't know what that means though," he said. "I mean, just touching someone is technically assault, right? Maybe there was—"

"There's *three* of them," I said, remembering the way Patrick had slapped Jessica. It had seemed so out of character at the time, but apparently it wasn't. "This is exactly the kind of thing you wanted to look for here."

Nicholas raked a hand through his hair. "I know. Shit. It's one thing to *want* to know the truth and another thing . . ."

This looked bad for Patrick. If I hadn't already known Jessica was the one responsible for Danny's death, he would have gone straight to the top of my list of suspects. It was more than I could have hoped for.

"Maybe Patrick was up to something—doing drugs, dealing—and Danny found out," I said. "Maybe he tried to blackmail him the same way he did you."

Nicholas swallowed. "He did have a bad temper when he was younger. And he was a big guy, even at eighteen, and—and Danny was so small . . . ."

I remembered the half-hysterical way Lex had insisted that Patrick wasn't violent and would never hurt any of us the night he'd slapped Jessica, and Kai had told me Patrick used to get him pot. If Jessica hadn't confessed, I'd buy this theory.

It's funny how naive a person can be when they want to believe the lie they're being fed. Even a liar like me, who should really know better.

Nicholas took pictures of all the documents in Patrick's file and locked it back in the safe, and then we headed home to

Hidden Hills. We were both quiet. We usually were, but the texture of it felt different this time. We were quiet because we were both too busy thinking, not because he didn't want to talk to me. An hour later we arrived home, and Patrick's car was in the driveway.

"Dammit," Nicholas said. "What's he doing here?"

We entered the house on tiptoe, and Nicholas immediately went for the stairs. Before he was halfway up though, Lex poked her head into the foyer.

"Hey, guys!" she said. "How was the library?"

"Fine," I said.

"Well, come in here. Patrick skipped out on work to come over," she said. "We're just about to start dinner."

Nicholas's hand tightened around the banister. "I'm not really hungry—"

"Don't be silly. We got your favorite."

Nicholas shot me a look, and I shrugged faintly. He couldn't hide forever, and trying to would only make them suspicious.

The two of us followed Lex into the dining room, where Mia, Patrick, and Jessica were already seated with containers of Thai takeout in the center of the table. The whole family.

Maybe Nicholas had had the right idea after all.

It wasn't unprecedented for Jessica to join us for a meal, but it was rare. Our eyes met, and I forced myself to give her a small smile. If I wanted her on my side, I needed her to understand that I was here to *protect* her and her children, not threaten them. She looked away.

Nicholas sat down stiffly in his usual chair, which was next to Patrick, who sat at the head of the table. I sat beside Lex, who passed me a container of green chicken curry, and dinner began. I was more acutely aware than ever of what a farce it all was. I was an impostor who didn't belong here at all, something most of the people around this table knew but pretended not to. Across from me was Nicholas, who was keeping my secret as well as his own, that he was leaving in just a few shorts months with no intention of coming back. Then there was Lex, the consummate actress and drug addict, and Patrick, the apparently upstanding lawyer with the history of violence. And of course Jessica, the alcoholic and the drunken driver who'd killed her own child. Even Mia, through no fault of her own, was the child of secrets and lies.

But on the outside we looked so perfect. When Mia told a story, our smiles all seemed genuine. When Lex shot me an affectionate wink as she passed me the rice, the warmth in my chest felt real. How could it feel so true when it was all built on bullshit?

I watched Jessica closely. Out of nowhere a thought occured to me. She was drinking a sparkling water instead of her usual glass of wine. Why had I believed her when she told me she'd killed Danny? It was the first time I'd asked myself the question, and I could hardly believe it. Jessica had done nothing but lie since I stepped foot in this house, but on this point I believed her unquestioningly? How I could I be so stupid? Maybe she was still trying to protect Danny's real killer, another son she *could* save, one with a criminal past and a promising future. That's what she'd been doing ever since I'd gotten here, wasn't it? Protecting Danny's killer by pretending to believe my act? Maybe her confession was just one more façade.

"You okay?" Lex asked me softly while Patrick told the table about something that had happened at work that day.

I nodded.

She smiled and reached for my hand under the table, giving it an affectionate squeeze. My stomach turned over at the touch. Because it was fake and because I was so, so scared of the moment when I would lose it.

As soon as dinner was over, I ran up to Danny's room, hands trembling as I locked the door behind me. I wanted it to be real. This stupid sham of a family. I wanted it to be real and to be a part of it more than I'd ever wanted anything, and it was killing me.

I saw Jessica smiling at me from across the table at Mélisse, and then I blinked and saw her crumpled car smoking from its collision with the planter in the driveway, its collision with a red and gold bicycle, its collision with the body of a little boy. I pressed the heels of my hands against my eyes. Saw Patrick's hand fisted around the gearshift of the Jag as he took us for a joyride down the Pacific Coast Highway and saw his fist slamming into someone's face. Danny's face, maybe. Just a little boy who could never deserve something like that. A little boy who'd been hit before, so many times that he flinched whenever he heard a loud noise. A little boy hidden in the back of a closet, biting his lip to try to stop himself from crying, because he knew crying would only make it worse . . .

I was shaking all over. My arms prickled with gooseflesh. It was always so fucking cold in this house with this goddamn air-conditioning. I'd grown up in the snow, and my blood and bones were cold enough without it. I couldn't remember ever having been warm.

There was a knock at my door.

"It's me," Nicholas said. "Open the door."

"Go away," I said.

"Open the door!"

I opened the door.

"You okay?" Nicholas asked. "You rushed off pretty suddenly."

"I'm fine."

"Well then let me in," he said, pushing his way into the room, "because I'm freaking out a little here, and you're the only one I can talk to about it."

He must have been freaking out more than a little if he wanted to talk to me. He went to the window and then the desk and then the bed, like he was looking for something but couldn't remember what it was.

"That dinner was extra weird, right?" he said. "I'm sitting there and everyone's being nice and getting along for once, and all I can think about is how they're all liars and one of them killed my brother. I'm, like, mesmerized watching Patrick cut his chicken, and for some reason I keep thinking about the time Dad took us boys camping and Danny and Patrick spent hours building a raft to send down the river and wanting so bad to join them but being afraid to let them see it." He sat down on Danny's bed and buried his hands in his hair. "Maybe you were right before. Maybe I don't want to know what really happened."

I sat cross-legged on the floor, facing him. This was an opportunity. Nicholas was usually so calm, so certain, nothing like the half-wild boy on the bed. With his walls in ruins at his feet, I could convince him to give up on his search for the truth of Danny's fate or to search twice as hard. Whichever would keep me here longer, if I only knew which one that was.

But I was just . . . too tired. Too weary of games and of having nothing real to hold on to. Of bracing myself to lose everything when the truth was I didn't really have any of it in the first place.

"It's up to you," I said, "but I think you know what you want."

He sighed heavily. "I need to find the truth. For Danny."

"You're a good brother," I said. If I'd had a brother, would he be trying to find out what had happened to me? Would he have kept watching TV when he heard I'd died?

Nicholas's smile was bitter. "Try to convince Patrick of that."

"You're only doing what you have to."

"I guess," he said. "It's nice of you to say, at least."

"I'm never nice," I said.

"You're not that bad," he said. "Not always."

"Why are you being so nice to *me*?" I asked. "You've been totally civil to me lately, and I've done nothing to deserve it."

He lay back on the bed. "I guess I just don't have the energy to hate you right now, not when I need your help. I mean, don't get me wrong. What you did was fucked up and I can never forgive it, but . . . it just pales in comparison to what they did."

I looked down at the rug.

"Plus . . ." He continued, propping himself up on one hand and looking down at me. "I think, deep down, you're probably not a completely terrible person. I might have even liked you if we'd met a different way."

There was a brutal burning in that spot in my chest that used to be a wonderfully numb hole that never pained me.

Maybe if I wanted this to be real—for *anything* in my life to be real—I had to do something about it.

"Nicholas," I said.

"Yeah?"

"I want to be honest with you," I said.

That laugh again, the humorless little huff of air. "Really?"

"I'm serious," I said. "There's something I need to tell you."

He looked at my face and then sat up. "Shit. What is it?"

"Your mom told me something," I said. "She was wasted and she thought I was Danny and she . . . *apologized*."

His face was like something breaking in slow motion. "For what?"

I took a breath. "For hitting me with her car."

Nicholas slowly curled in on himself, resting his forehead on his knees until his face was hidden from me. I told him every word Jessica had said to me about how she'd warned Danny not to ride his bike in the driveway after dark, and for a minute the room was still and silent except for his harsh breathing. Then he looked up, something fierce and fragile in his expression.

"So it was an accident," he said. "No one murdered Danny. It was just a terrible accident."

I could have just nodded. Could have let him have that moment of terrible relief of finding out that none of the people he loved was a murderer. Maybe he would have been so grateful that he would have let me go.

But he wanted to know the truth, and for once in my life I wanted to be honest with someone.

"Maybe," I said. "I'm not sure."

"What do you mean?" he said. "Why would my mother confess to accidentally killing Danny if she hadn't?"

"She could be trying to protect Patrick," I said. "Or maybe Patrick made her believe she was responsible somehow. After seeing all those arrest records . . ."

"That doesn't necessarily mean anything," he said. "So he got into some fights in high school. It doesn't mean he murdered his own brother. No. Patrick's innocent. It was just my mom, and it was an accident. You *want* me to think there's more to find so you can stay here longer."

He wasn't entirely wrong about that last part, and we each knew it. This bit of honesty worked both ways.

"Just your mom?" I repeated. "Think about it. Why didn't she just call the police if it was such an innocent accident? Knowing Jessica . . ."

Nicholas's face darkened. "She was drunk."

"Yeah," I said. "And Patrick and Lex helped her cover it up. They had to have."

He shook his head. "No. You don't know that."

"Jessica said she didn't see Danny because it was dark," I said, "but Danny supposedly went missing when it was still light out on Saturday. If Jessica was the one who killed him, she had to have done it the night before."

"And Patrick and Lex both said they saw Danny the next day. Dammit." He stood and walked over to the window, bracing his hands on the sill and taking deep breaths. "They were already lying for her."

"Plus . . ."

"What?"

"Can you imagine your mom driving out to the desert to dump the bike and . . . bury the body?"

"No," he said quietly. "It could only have been Patrick. So this is it? Either my brother killed Danny in a violent rage because he was being blackmailed, or, best-case scenario, my mother killed him accidentally and made it look like he went missing so me and my dad and Mia could spend the rest of our lives worrying about him and hoping he'd come home someday?"

"I think so," I said.

"How long have you known this?"

"Since last night."

"And you're just now telling me?"

"Yes. I'm sorry."

"I take back what I said before," he said, turning on me. His eyes were on fire. "Turns out I *do* have the energy to hate you. I'm turning this all over to the FBI. Let them sort out what really happened."

He went for the door, but I stepped into his path. I felt like a rubber band pulled dangerously tight, and my hands were fisted at my sides to stop them shaking. Nicholas took a step back from me. I think he thought I was going to hit him, when all I was trying to do was hold myself together. I lifted my hands up in surrender.

"Are you sure you want to do that?" I said. "It won't bring Danny back, but it could send half of your family to prison."

"You're just trying to save your own ass," he said. "If I expose them, I expose you."

"That's true," I said, "but it's more than that. I know what it's like to have no family; you don't. Even if they're not perfect, even if they did something terrible, they love you. They treat you well and give a damn what happens to you. What would you do without them? What would Mia do without them?"

"Don't."

He tried to brush past me, but I caught his arms. I didn't want him to turn me in, but even more than that I wanted him to *understand*. "Imagine what this will do to her, to learn these things about the people she loves. Who will take care of her with both of your parents and Lex and Patrick in prison? You certainly won't be going off to college next year, not unless you're willing to abandon her when she needs you the most. Think of what her life will be like. They'll put her in care. She'll be alone, she'll be scared—"

"Stop it!" he said, trying to pull himself out of my grasp.

I couldn't control the words now. "You're so selfish. All you want is to get away, to wash your hands of this place and these people, and you have no idea how lucky you are. They love you."

"They're liars!" he said in a furious whisper. "*Killers* and liars!"

"Who love you!" I said. "You don't think it could be worse?"

Suddenly, all of the fight rushed out of Nicholas. Like a plug had been pulled and all that righteous fury that was fueling him went swirling down the drain. He sank onto the floor, burying his head in his hands, and his shoulders started to shake with silent sobs.

"I don't know what to do," he said softly. He sounded so young all of a sudden, and I remembered with some surprise that I was the older of the two of us.

I slowly sat beside him. I didn't know what to say.

"What do I do?" he asked, raising his head. "What does any

of it even matter? Danny's dead. His bones are out there in that desert somewhere. That's all that's left of him, and nothing I do can change that."

Slowly, I put an arm around his shoulder, and he let me. I felt a tremendous lightness taking shape inside of me. I had no secrets from Nicholas anymore.

"We'll find out what really happened," I said. "Then you'll know what to do."

"I hate you," he said.

"I know," I said.

But he didn't move.

I told the truth and the world didn't crash at my feet. I thought my lies and pretending were getting me closer to what I wanted, but I'd never felt so close to finally filling that hole inside of me for good as I did after I was honest with Nicholas. I wasn't sure who the real me was anymore, but for the first time I wanted to try being that person. Secrets were the bricks in my walls, and I wanted to finally take them down.

I woke up the next morning knowing which brick to remove next.

Lex and I were the only ones at home, and I found her reading a magazine by the pool.

"Hey," I said, sitting down on the lounge chair beside hers. "Can you drive me somewhere?"

"Sure. Where you going?"

"My friend Ren's house," I said. "She just lives over in Calabasas."

Lex checked her phone. "I was going to leave in about a half an hour anyway to meet a friend for lunch. Can you wait until then?"

"Yeah, sure."

Lex cocked her head at me and put a hand on my leg. "How you doing? It feels like I've barely seen you lately."

"I'm good," I said.

"School's going okay?"

I nodded.

She smiled and brushed my cheek with the side of her thumb. "It's like it was always meant to be now. You here with us."

My throat got tight, because for some reason I was sure she was talking to *me*.

I nodded. "Yeah."

She stood up, dropping a kiss on my forehead as she did. "I'm going to go change, and then we can go."

Ren answered the door.

"Hey," she said with obvious surprise. "What are you—"

"I don't want to be your friend," I said, because I knew if I waited even a second I would lose my nerve. "I want more than that. I get it if you don't, but I do and I'm ready for it."

Her mouth opened and closed but no words came out.

"Here's the thing," I said. "Someone told me once that being with the right person makes the world seem like a less scary place, and the world seems less scary when I'm with you. And I like myself *better* when I'm with you. And I think that's a good thing and something I'm finally ready to deal with, so . . . I want us to be together."

She didn't say anything, just reached out and took my hand and pulled me inside the house. She pulled me up the stairs and into her bedroom, where she locked the door behind us. Then she pulled me toward her, so close I could feel the pattern of her sweater and the button of her jeans pressing against my body, and then she kissed me.

Later Ren and I were curled up on her bed, watching a movie on her laptop. Well, she was watching the movie. I was mostly watching her.

It was a perfect moment. Deep in the marrow of my bones, I was warm.

"My throat's so dry," she said, sighing and burrowing closer into my side. "It's too bad I'm so comfortable here."

I raised an eyebrow at her.

"I guess I'll have to get up," she continued, "and then I'll have to get comfortable all over again, which can be tough. You've got to find the right configuration of pillows and make sure—"

I groaned and rolled out of the bed. "What do you want?"

"Diet Coke, please!" she said. "Good job picking up on my very subtle clues."

Downstairs I found Kai already standing in front of the open refrigerator. It was basically where he lived.

"Hey, man," he said when he noticed me. He took in my slightly rumpled appearance and grinned. "Whatcha been doing?"

"Nothing," I said.

"Right." He offered me his fist to bump and then started gathering ingredients for a sandwich. "Be good to her though, seriously. She's a good kid."

"I'll try," I said.

"Dude, this sandwich is going to be *epic*. Hey, you need to give me your sister's number. I want to catch up with her. Sexy Lexi! I never hit that in high school, and it's a damn shame. Came close a couple of times, but she and your brother were, like, attached at the hip, and he would have killed me."

I tried to smile to humor him. Even though Lex wasn't actually my sister, I didn't want to hear about the possibility of him "hitting" her.

But then I realized this was an opportunity.

"I forgot you knew Lex and Patrick in high school," I said. "Patrick was pretty tough back then, huh?"

"Shit yeah. He could be a scary dude when he got worked up, and he was crazy protective of Lex." Kai looked down at his sandwich as he squirted mustard haphazardly across two slices of bread. "They were close, you know. Like *really* close. No one ever messed with her because they knew they'd get cut off or worse."

"What do you mean?" I said. I pulled my phone out of my pocket and pretended to check my texts. What I was actually doing was starting an audio recording. I wasn't sold on Jessica's confession, and Kai, who obviously knew about Patrick's checkered past, might say something interesting I'd want Nicholas to hear.

"I mean he'd beat the shit out of them, man. Damn, where did I put the cheese? I just had it." Kai searched through the ingredients on the countertop. I reached for the bag of deli cheese slices that was about four inches from his hand and gave it to him, and he dissolved into giggles. That's when I realized just how high he was.

"No," I said. "What did you mean by 'cut off'?"

"Well, before he was Mister Big Important Lawyer Guy, Patty was the biggest dealer at Calabasas High," Kai said. "If you pissed him off, *no one* would sell to you."

"Yeah?"

"Hell yeah. He was a badass, and no one touched his little sister." He took a giant bite from his sandwich and started to laugh. When he spoke, it was around a mouthful of food. "This one time a guy grabbed Lex's ass in the hall, and after school Patrick just started whaling on the dude's car with a baseball bat. It was awesome. They got into this big fight. Pretty sure Patty put the guy in the hospital."

I could see it all in my head. Danny poking around Patrick's room, looking for money to spend at the arcade with his friends or just looking for dirt on him. What he stumbled on instead was Patrick's stash. So much pot and pills and powder that even Robert Tate wouldn't be able to pull enough strings to keep Patrick out of serious trouble. Danny told Patrick he'd need a hundred bucks to keep quiet. When Patrick refused, Danny yelled for their mom, just to scare him. But Patrick lost his temper. He hit Danny, harder than he'd meant to, and Danny never got up again.

"No one messed with Lex after that," Kai continued, "even though she was pretty much the hottest girl in school. Such a fucking waste of a perfect rack, but no one would risk asking her out."

"Not even you?" I asked.

He laughed. "Not even me. I wasn't suicidal. But maybe now that Patrick's all upstanding and shit, he wouldn't mind me getting back into touch with his little sister, you know?"

"Why did you two stop being friends?" I asked.

He shrugged. "You disappeared, and they hauled his ass to jail because they thought he'd killed you or something. He went straight after that, got totally boring. He wouldn't even talk to me anymore." He sounded actually hurt about that last part. "The last day I talked to him was actually the day before you got snatched."

"Yeah?" I said. When Kai stuck his head back in the refrigerator to fish out a beer, I glanced down at my phone to make sure it was still recording.

He nodded. "He called me and asked me to go to the movies and buy him a ticket."

"Huh?"

"It was this thing we'd do for each other sometimes," Kai said, "if we were doing something we shouldn't be. I had this girlfriend, right, that my parents hated. Forbid me to see her, like some *Romeo and Juliet* shit. She lived up in Ventura, so when I'd go see her, Patrick would go to the movies and buy two tickets. He'd give me one of the stubs, and when my parents asked where I was, I could show it to them. Couldn't have been up in Ventura, I was at the movies! I'd do it for him sometimes too."

My heart was thumping. "And he asked you to do that for him the night before I disappeared?"

"That afternoon, yeah," he said. He started rooting around in the freezer. "I never even got to give him the stub. It was a zoo around your house, and he wouldn't take my calls. Damn, I could have sworn there were ice cream sandwiches in here!"

"Did you tell the police?" I asked.

"Why would I?"

"Because . . ." Then I realized. The police would never ask about what Patrick was doing the day *before* Danny was reported missing.

"Just, like, *one* ice cream sandwich . . ."

As far as they knew, Danny was alive and well that Friday, so it didn't matter if Patrick was building a false alibi for himself the day before he disappeared.

The day before he disappeared.

The *day* before he disappeared.

"Wait, Patrick called you that *day*?" I asked.

Kai raised an eyebrow at me. "Yeeeah. I remember it was practically right after school, 'cause he'd ditched that afternoon or else he would have just asked me in person."

Patrick was building himself an alibi for that Friday *afternoon*, hours before the time Jessica claimed she hit Danny with her car.

Danny found Patrick's stash, Patrick hit him, and Danny wasn't breathing. Patrick panicked and called Kai, asking him to go to the movies so he could show he wasn't at the house when Danny died. But he quickly started seeing all the holes in that alibi. His cell phone was pinging off a tower near his home at that moment, not the movie theater Kai would go to. The theater would probably have some kind of video surveillance that would prove Patrick wasn't with Kai. The cops wouldn't buy that this was an accident, not with his record. He'd go to jail unless he could come up with a better cover story, something that protected him completely.

So he called Lex, his devoted sister. She loved Danny, but she loved him more. She took Jessica to dinner, kept her out until it was dark, slid another cocktail toward her, maybe one laced with one of the pills Patrick was pushing and Lex was taking. When they came home, Jessica blurry behind the wheel, Patrick was waiting. He hid behind the bushes around the driveway, hit the back of Jessica's car with a baseball bat and left Danny's body there by the wheel. Waited for the screams and wails of the women discovering the body to come rushing to the scene.

Then together Lex and Patrick convinced a not-right-in-her-mind Jessica to let them bury the body in the desert where no one would find it and fake the kidnapping. By the time Jessica would regret the lie, it was too late. Telling the truth would send two of her children to prison for her crime.

It all made total, terrible sense.

I knew the truth now. The details might have been wrong, but the overall picture was right, I was sure of it. I knew what had happened, but I didn't know what to do.

Part of me wanted to just run. This was all too much for me, and running was my strong suit. If Patrick had killed his actual brother and made his mother think she was responsible to protect his own ass, he was definitely capable of killing me. His need to keep me around to maintain the fiction of Danny still being alive had protected me this long, but he might risk getting rid of me now that I knew what I did.

Except . . . I had protected his secrets until now, hadn't I? Maybe if Patrick knew just how much I'd discovered and that I was willing to play ball, he would make sure I could stay. Maybe I could use this information to get what I really wanted.

Only *that* would mean lying to Nicholas, the only person I'd ever been completely honest with, and who maybe, someday, would care about me anyway.

I guess the real question was, what was the most important thing to me? To be comfortable and happy and surrounded by lies? Or to risk it all for the chance of something better and purer?

Which person did I want to be?

I didn't know yet. I asked Ren to drive me home.

"You okay?" she asked.

I nodded.

"There's something you're not telling me," she said.

"You're right." I pressed my forehead, and then my lips, to hers. "But I want to. And I will soon. Everything. I promise."

It didn't *feel* like a lie.

After Ren dropped me at home, I raced upstairs to transfer the audio file of Kai's admission from my phone to the password protected folder on my laptop and then deleted it. It would be safe on my laptop until I knew what, if anything, I wanted to do with it.

When that was done, I went to a window and looked out over the backyard, the pool glittering in the sun, the hazy red mountains in the distance. The longer I stood there, the more my vision seemed to darken around the edges, like the walls were closing in, the doors starting to swing shut, and there was nothing I could do to stop it.

Lex took me to school the next morning. Nicholas had gone in early on some flimsy pretext, because he didn't want to see me. Maybe he was angrier than I thought. I waved good-bye to Lex and walked toward the front doors of the building. There was a black car parked at the curb, and as I got close, the driver's door opened and Agent Morales got out.

My stomach plummeted. Nicholas had turned me in.

"Hi, Danny," she said, like it was the most natural thing in the world for her to be there. "Can I have a word?"

"I'm sorry, Agent," I said, unable to believe how calm I sounded, "but I think school is about to start."

She took a couple of steps toward me, until we were face-to-face. "Here's the thing, Mr. Tate. I've got some questions, and you've got the answers. You can either come with me now, or we can wait here together while I call your brother-lawyer and get him to join us. Either way, you're talking to me today, and something tells me you might rather do it without a chaperone."

She was smiling, and the expression chilled me to the core. I tried to think of a way out of this, a way to run, because I was sure that once I left with her, I was never coming back. But my mind was numb. There was nothing I could do. I nodded mutely and climbed into the back seat of the car.

Morales took me to the L.A. field office, where Agent Lynch met us in a familiar interrogation room. Morales offered me a glass of water.

"No, thanks," I said.

Morales smiled and opened the file folder in front of her. "Here's the thing—"

"Is it legal for you to be questioning me without my guardian present?" I asked.

"It's perfectly legal since you're not under arrest," Morales said, "plus, those rules only apply to minors."

"I'm sixteen," I said.

"Sure you are," she said, and the hollow ball of fear inside of me grew. "Here's the deal, kid. I know you're not Danny Tate. Lynch there knows it. I'll wager most of the people you've come into contact with since you got here know it."

She hadn't said Nicholas knew it. If he'd talked, it would have been the first thing she'd have flung in my face, that my supposed brother had ratted me out. Nicholas hadn't turned me in, and even in this moment, that fact gave me back a little bit of strength.

"You're wrong," I said.

"What was your third-grade teacher's name?" she asked. "Who was the first girl you kissed?"

"I have incomplete memories of the years before my abduction. The trauma—"

"What was your favorite book? What color are the walls in your grandparents' living room? Where did you have your ninth birthday party?" Morales continued. "You can't answer any of these questions because you're not Daniel Tate. I bet you didn't have a clue who Daniel Tate was until you decided to start impersonating him, or you would have done a better job of it."

"That's not—"

"Want to see something?" she said. She pulled a sheet of paper from her folder and placed it in front of me. There was the name of a laboratory at the top and a long string of numbers I couldn't make sense of. Morales pointed to a section at the bottom.

Probability of relation: <.0067%

"This is a DNA test we ran on samples from you and Nicholas Tate," she said.

The ball in my stomach contracted painfully, becoming tighter and hotter, and a bitter taste flooded my mouth.

"We didn't give you any samples," I said.

"No, but you did both have bottles of water with your lunch the day I came to see you at school," she said with that calm, terrible smile. She was enjoying this.

"You can't do that—"

"You abandoned the DNA," she said. "It's perfectly legal."

"You must have gotten the wrong bottles from the trash."

"It's possible," she conceded. "This could all be some horrible mistake. Lynch and I could be dead wrong about you, and you could be exactly the miracle you seem to be. We don't really have any solid evidence."

"That's right," I said. "So I think I'll be leaving."

"Okay," she said.

"Okay?"

"Sure, just as soon as you tell me"—she reached again for a sheet in her folder—"who this is?"

She slid a photocopy across the table to me. The image was

small, taking up just a corner of the sheet. On it was a boy with a gap-toothed smile holding a T-ball bat, his name printed in block letters at the bottom.

It was over.

Morales, unaware that the world had just ended, was still talking.

"This was found in your locker when the school coincidentally conducted a random drug spot search on the day we happened to be visiting," she said. Just hours before I'd taken the picture home, because her presence at the school had spooked me and I was worried the picture wasn't safe there anymore. "Now, this is a pretty common name, and it'll take me a while to track down every boy in Canada who has it, but what do you want to bet that I'll do it and that eventually I'll find him?"

I could barely keep my head up, and my voice was faint even in my own ears when I spoke.

"What do you want?" I asked.

She smiled. "To put you in prison."

"You've got nothing," I said. "Some picture and a water bottle you can't even prove was mine."

"That's true," she said. "I don't have anything now. But in about ten minutes I'll have a court order for an official DNA test."

She could be bluffing, but I doubted it. As soon as they got my DNA, the game was over.

I had only one chip left to play. If I could do it.

Morales didn't want me, some two-bit con artist. She wanted a win in this case, the one that had been hanging over her head for six years. She'd let me go if I offered her the bigger fish she was really after wanted: Danny's murderer. Patrick. I couldn't give her bulletproof evidence that Patrick had killed Danny, but I could set her on the right path. The only reason she hadn't cracked this case already was that she'd been looking into the events of the wrong day all of these years. As soon as she knew that Danny had died on Friday afternoon and not Saturday evening, she'd find some evidence—cell phone logs, surveillance at the Hidden Hills gates, something—that would show what had truly happened.

All I had to do was tell her the truth.

I tried to tell myself it was the right thing to do. That Danny deserved to have his fate known and his killer brought to justice.

But I knew, if I did it, it wasn't because I gave a damn about Daniel Tate. It was because I wanted to save my own skin. If I told Morales, I was no better than I'd ever been taught to believe.

"You don't want to expose me," I said, hating myself with every word. "You want to know what I know."

Morales cocked her head at me. "And what is that?"

"You give me unqualified immunity and let me leave," I said, "and I'll give you Danny's killer."

"How?" she said. "Have you got proof?"

"Ironclad, no," I said. "But I know things. Where you should look, who you should talk to. You'll finally be able to nail Patrick."

"You're going to have to be more specific than that," she said.

I clenched my jaw shut hard, until it hurt. But it didn't stop me speaking. "I have an audio recording. Someone explaining how Patrick had them create him a false alibi for the time Danny went missing. It's on my computer at home."

"You bring me that," she said, "and *then* you'll get your immunity."

Lynch drove me home to collect the evidence, while Morales stayed behind to get started on the paperwork. He stopped his car down the street from the Tate house, close enough that he could see the front gate at the end of the driveway, but not so close that anyone could see him. He didn't want to accidentally tip Patrick off that the net was closing in around him.

"You've got ten minutes," he told me.

"It might take longer than that," I said, "especially if my mother or sister is home."

Lynch's lip curled in disgust, and it took me a moment to realize why. I'd called them my mother and sister, and I hadn't thought twice about it.

"Just don't fuck around," he said. "I'll be here watching, so you've got nowhere to go."

"Believe me," I said. "I just want to get my immunity and get the hell out of here. I'm not going to do anything to screw that up."

He checked his mirrors to make sure no one was coming and then motioned for me to get out of the car. I walked back to the house slowly, casually, my head down and my hands in my pockets. I reached the gate and entered the code that would open it. As soon as the gate was closed behind me and I was out of the sight of Lynch's car, I began to run.

"Hey, lover," Ren said when she picked up the phone. "Where are you?"

"Can I ask you something?"

"Are you running?" she asked. "Your breathing is weird."

"Yeah," I said. "Will you run away with me?"

"What?"

"Ren, listen to me." I tried to keep my voice calm. "I have to leave Hidden Hills, the States, everything. Today. *Now*. But I don't want to leave you. For the first time in my life there's something I don't want to lose and it's you, so I'm asking you to come with me."

"What's going on, Danny?" She sounded alarmed.

"Just say you'll come with me," I said. "Even if it's only for a little while. I'll tell you everything."

She was silent a moment and then whispered, "Okay."

I stopped. "What?"

"Okay, I'll go," she said. "The school year's practically over, and I was supposed to go to Dubai to visit my parents, but they asked me to delay my trip, so why not? I'll go with you."

"Really?"

"When can we leave?"

I laughed, out of breath. "Can you meet me at the movies where we met? I'll be there in thirty minutes."

"I'm on my way," she said.

"You're the best."

"Damn right I am."

I wouldn't turn anyone in. Maybe it was wrong, but I couldn't do it to Patrick and Lex and Jessica. I would just run away, like I always did. But this time I wouldn't be running alone, and that made all the difference.

The house was empty, and I was glad. I didn't want to have to look any of them in the face, knowing it was the last time I would see them, and lie. I dug out the packed bag I had shoved in the back of Danny's closet so many weeks ago and slung it over my shoulders. I grabbed my laptop and found the baseball card with the smiling boy. It was in the dictionary on the bookshelf where I'd hidden it after I'd decided—too late, it turned out—that my school locker wasn't safe.

I took one last look around the navy blue bedroom. It had never been mine, but I would miss it all the same.

"Bye, Danny," I said, and closed the door. I hoped he would forgive me.

I went to Nicholas's room and placed my laptop on his desk. The audio recording of Kai was on there for him to find. Nicholas was smart; he'd put the pieces together the same way I had. I couldn't turn in the Tates, but if he wanted to, it was his right.

I grabbed a piece of paper from his printer and wrote a short note at the bottom. *I'm sorry. Thank you.* It was screamingly inadequate, but I didn't have the words for what I wanted to say. I folded the paper and placed it under the laptop.

I passed Mia's bedroom without looking at it. I couldn't think about her, couldn't try to leave her some kind of good-bye. It was too hard.

Instead, I went to Lex's bedroom. Lex had lied to me, used me, but I didn't care. I'd done the same thing to her, and, underneath it all, I think she really cared about me. Probably better than anyone else in my life ever had. For better or worse, Lex was my family, and I wanted her to know who I was. I took one last look at my baseball card—that little piece of my soul, the only proof that I'd ever actually been happy—and I placed it on her pillow, in the dent where her head had been when she last slept. I hoped she would understand what I meant by it.

I went downstairs, backpack on my shoulders, and checked my watch. Ren was going to meet me in twenty minutes. All I needed to do was get out of Hidden Hills. I went into the backyard, dragged a lounge chair to the high wall that separated us from the neighbors, and climbed over.

After hopping a couple more fences, I emerged onto the street. I was well behind Lynch's car now. As long as he kept watching the gate, he'd never see me. I turned and started to run.

Twenty-five minutes later and pouring with sweat, I collapsed into Ren's car, my chest heaving. She laughed and kissed me, and I held her close, breathing her in, trying to make sure this memory would burn brighter than any of the false ones I'd created inside of myself.

"What now?" she said when we were on the highway, headed toward the mountains I'd looked at through windows for the last few months, the air getting sharper and crisper with each mile, my chest feeling lighter with each layer of deceit that dropped away as we fled Hidden Hills.

"Now," I said, "I tell you who I am."

She smiled and took my hand, and together we headed toward a new life and a new truth all our own.

Yeah.

Or maybe not. But it makes a nice ending to the story, doesn't it? I think it does.

But maybe instead of calling Ren and asking her to run away with me, I only imagined doing it and wished I were the kind of person who could make that call. Wished I were the kind of person she could have said yes to.

The house was empty when I got home, and I was relieved. Good-byes had never been my thing, and I couldn't stand to look any of the Tates in the face and pretend everything was okay when I was about to bring their whole world down around them.

I'd turn over my evidence against Patrick to save my own ass, because *that's* the kind of person I was. The kind I'd always been and always would be, no matter how much I hated myself for it.

I went to Danny's room, grabbed my laptop, and stuck it into my backpack along with a change of clothes and my stash of cash. I found the baseball card in the dictionary and spent a long moment staring at that boy's face.

He'd already gotten a raw deal from life, but he was still hopeful. Could still smile and get excited about T-ball practice and appreciate the perfect blue of a cloudless sky over his head.

Maybe I could learn to be that boy again. Beaten down, maybe, but not beaten. I'd had moments of that here, glimpses of what a happy, honest life could be like. Playing Marco Polo with Mia, helping Lex chop vegetables for dinner, laughing with Patrick as I took a turn too sharply in an abandoned parking lot during a driving lesson. Talking to Ren. Almost any moment with Ren, really.

Maybe it was time to try being myself for once.

I said good-bye to Danny's bedroom and Danny's ghost as I closed the door, and then I laid my hand on the doors of Nicholas's and Mia's bedrooms as I passed them, saying good-bye to them, too. I went into Lex's bedroom and left her the baseball card. No matter what else might have happened, I loved Lex, and I think part of her loved me, too. I trusted her to take care of that little boy with the gap-toothed smile.

I walked downstairs slowly. I wanted to take the time to remember all of this. This life I had led, this house, this family, the best and the worst of my life. I couldn't think ahead—the world after this was over was nothing but a big, black blank looming in front of me—so I thought about the past. This house and the people in it were already the past to me.

I went and stood in the kitchen, where the family always congregated. It felt cold now. I'd almost forgotten how cold this entire house felt to me when I first came here. Somewhere along the way I'd gotten comfortable, but now I spread my hands against the marble countertop and felt the cold seep back into my veins and my blood.

It was time. I'd get in the car with Lynch, hand over my evidence to Morales, and then I'd disappear, leaving this house and this family for good.

Behind me, I heard the front door open and footsteps in the foyer.

"Danny?" Patrick called.

I froze.

"Danny?" Patrick said again. His fancy leather shoes against the marble made it easy to hear him walking through the foyer toward the stairs, and his voice moved up toward the second floor. "Are you here?"

It was now or never. I moved as quickly and quietly as I could toward the front door, hoping to get out of the house before Patrick realized I wasn't in my room.

I had a hand on the front door handle when Patrick appeared at the top of the stairs.

"Danny," he said. "There you are. Didn't you hear me calling for you?"

I turned to face him and managed a little shrug. "No. Sorry. What's up?"

"Where are you going?" he asked.

"Back to school. I forgot my homework." It was a terrible, utterly transparent lie. I didn't do homework. Even if I did, how was I going to get back to school? There was no one waiting in a car in the driveway to take me there. Patrick's eyes landed on my backpack, the dirty and battered Jansport I'd carried with me from city to city for years as I ran my petty scams, not the new leather messenger bag I took to school as Danny.

"That's strange, since I heard Morales brought you in earlier," he said, and his voice was suddenly different. Harder. He wasn't talking to his kid brother anymore; he was talking to *me*. "I have a friend in the field office who keeps me in the loop about these things. Where are you really going?"

"Where I've got to," I said.

"The FBI?" he said. "You think you know something?"

"The FBI already knows everything I do," I said. It was a better lie than my last one, and the flash of panic in his eyes proved it. "I'm just getting out of here. Let me go, Patrick."

He shook his head and took another step toward me. I

backed away until the knob of the front door was digging into my spine. "I can't do that," he said.

"You can't stop me," I said, my voice calmer than I felt. "The damage is done, so you might as well let me go. Don't make it worse."

"I don't know what you think you know—"

"That you murdered your little brother?" I said. The words just burst out of me. I couldn't stop thinking of the boy on the baseball card, of how Danny was only a little older than that boy. "Dumped his body in the desert somewhere?"

Patrick stepped back as though I'd shoved him. "I could *never* hurt Danny."

A liar knows his own kind. I should have been able to see the falsehood, but Patrick looked sincere. I guess he was a better liar than I thought. Better than me.

"He was just a little boy, Patrick," I said. "Maybe he wasn't perfect, but he deserved a family who loved him. Not one that would kill him and cover it up."

"I didn't do that!" he said, and he lunged toward me, not like he wanted to hurt me but like he wanted to bring me close, to make me understand. "He was my brother, and I loved him. I would have never touched him."

"But you'd make your mother think she killed him," I said, wheeling away from Patrick's grasp, "and you'd blackmail her into covering it up. Make her live with that guilt and watch it destroy her a little more every day. What about that? What about

Mia and Nicholas, having to live with the hope that Danny's alive and will come home some day, when you know he's dead? When you know because you killed him?"

Suddenly, the front door opened and Lex, loaded with grocery bags, came in.

"Hey, what are you two doing—"

"Lex, get out of here," Patrick snapped.

"Does she know?" I said. "She must. You made her lie for you and say she'd seen Danny the morning he went missing."

Lex's face went lifeless and white, and the bags dropped from her fingers.

"Lex," Patrick said softly. "Please. Go."

But I was on fire. With the unfairness of what happened to Danny, with the unfairness of what happened to the boy on the baseball card. With what Patrick had done to Nicholas and Mia and Lex. Of how he took this wonderful family and twisted it until it broke.

"What else did you make her do?" I said. "How did you tell her you'd killed him?"

Lex covered her mouth with her hands. "Oh God," she said.

Patrick rushed to her, putting his arms around her. She was crying, and she mumbled something into his chest I couldn't make out.

"Please," he said to her. "Please leave."

"He killed Danny, Lex!" I said. "How can you be okay with that? He's a monster!"

"No!" Lex cried. She held harder on to Patrick. "I'm sorry. I'm so sorry."

Patrick shook her. "Don't say another word."

I stared at them. Lex was sobbing, and they weren't tears of grief or anger. They came from somewhere deeper and darker than that. And the way she held on to Patrick, desperate for his comfort and his . . .

His *forgiveness.*

The realization came to me slowly and in waves. Each time I tried to push it back, it came in stronger, a high tide that couldn't be held back.

I looked at Patrick, whose expression was stricken and pale. "You didn't kill him," I said. I turned to Lex. "*You* did."

Patrick let go of Lex. My head was swimming. Of course it was Lex. While Jessica had avoided me, and Patrick had put in just as much time with me as he needed to maintain the illusion, Lex had always been around. Either to keep an eye on me, because she had the most to lose, or to, in some sick way, assuage her guilty conscience by caring for me the way she hadn't cared for her real brother. Patrick had helped protect her, because that's what Patrick did; he was devoted to her above all people. She was the only one he'd create such an elaborate fiction for. He helped her convince Jessica that she'd been the one to kill Danny to protect Lex, he'd probably buried the body himself to protect Lex, and he'd taken the heat from the FBI to protect Lex.

"Why did you do it?" I whispered.

"It was an accident," Patrick said.

"Bullshit." I backed away from them. "You wouldn't have gone to so much trouble to cover up an accident. Why are you protecting her?"

Patrick jumped at me, but Lex stopped him by grabbing him around the arm. "Stop it!" she said. "Stop!"

Then she put her hand on his cheek and turned his face to hers.

It was a simple movement, but there was something about it. The way her fingers lingered on his skin. The way the touch stopped him in his tracks and the way he leaned into it. It was . . . intimate.

It was not the way a sister touched a brother, and with a shiver, I heard Kai's voice in my ears.

That's some seriously ironic shit.

They were close. Like, really close.

Patrick beat up any guy who came near Lex until none did. He was in Lex's bedroom in the early hours the night I'd discovered they knew I wasn't Danny. His safe combination was her birthday, and he had a picture of her on his bedside table. One where she was lying on her side with her cheek in the grass, and if he was lying down in bed looking at it, it would be almost like . . .

"What did Danny see?" I asked softly. "Did he walk in on you two together? Is that why he had to die?"

I could see it all in their faces as they stared at me. I was right. They had ditched school; no one was supposed to be home for a while. But Danny had left baseball practice early. He went looking for Lex because he wanted her to make him something to eat, and he'd found her in bed with Patrick. Naked. Maybe the grief of their father's death had brought them together or maybe it had been going on longer than that, but it was the one secret no one else could ever, ever know.

The scene played in my head like a movie, the same way my lies did, and I watched it superimposed over the present.

Danny ran, and Lex caught him at the top of the stairs.

"I'm telling Mom!" he screamed.

"You're not telling anyone!" she said, shaking him.

"Let go of me! You're disgusting!"

She slapped him. "Don't you say that!"

"I'm telling everyone!"

Danny tried to run. Lex knew she couldn't let him go. She shoved him hard in the back. A spontaneous response. He went tumbling down the stairs, his head hitting the marble floor at the bottom with a crack, and then he was still.

I stared at the floor at the base of the stairs, just feet away from me. I saw the blood like it was still there.

Patrick lunged at me and wrapped his hands around my throat.

I fell to the ground, into the pool of blood I still saw in my mind. Patrick had his full weight on top of me, his knees digging into me as he pinned me to the ground. Lex tried to pull him off, but he shoved her away again and again. My vision started to go dark, like the closet door was closing and shutting out the light. I was the only one who knew the secret, so I had to die. He had to protect Lex.

I flailed with my arms, trying to find some way to hurt Patrick enough to get him off me. My lungs were burning for air, and I was wild. I scratched him across the face and dug my fingernails in. With one last surge of dying adrenaline, I reached Patrick's eye with one of my hands and gouged. He yelled and reeled back, clutching at his face. In my darkened peripheral vision, I saw Lex run from the room, up the stairs. I gulped in fresh air through my burning throat and threw myself on top of Patrick. He was heavier, but I *really* didn't want to die. I got my hands around his throat. Not so nice, was it? He struggled, and I slammed his head against the marble. I'd never thought I had it in me to kill a person before, but if it was him or me, maybe I could do it.

As I slowly squeezed the life out of Patrick, I realized the drops appearing on his face came not from him, but from me. I was crying, my tears falling down onto him. I never wanted this.

All I wanted was a family. All I wanted was to be loved.

But I guess we don't always get what we want.

There was a sudden bang, a noise so loud it felt more like a sensation than a sound. I didn't feel anything, but suddenly I was falling forward. Patrick rolled me onto my back as he scrambled out from under me, and there was Lex standing over me, Robert's pistol smoking in her shaking hand. I touched my chest and felt wetness there. I lifted my hand and saw that it was red. Blood. My blood.

I felt my body turning cold as the blood drained out of me, pooling on the white marble of the foyer, but there was no pain. Above me, Lex was crying and Patrick was taking the gun from her hand. I knew what would happen now. I would "disappear" too, only this time there would be no one to worry or mourn for me. I would rot in a shallow desert grave, turning to bones and then dust, while the world wondered what happened to Danny Tate and never again thought of me. Just what I'd wanted for so long.

Lex collapsed at my side, crying ugly tears that contorted her pretty face. She reached out to me, but if her fingers touched me, I couldn't feel it.

"I'm sorry," she said. "I'm so sorry."

I tried to speak but found I couldn't. Blood gurgled in the back of my throat. I don't know what I would have said to her anyway. *Go to hell*, maybe. Or *I forgive you*.

Somewhere there was a sound I recognized, but the world was slipping away and I couldn't name it. But then I saw. Familiar beams of red and blue painting the white marble. I couldn't remember what those meant anymore either, but I knew it was good. I smiled.

And then I died.

It was the FBI. Lynch had heard the gunshot and recognized it for what it was. He got Hidden Hills security to override the gate and call for backup. He'd arrived outside the front door, his siren blaring, just moments before I exhaled my last breath. After a brief standoff during which Patrick and Lex destroyed my laptop and Lynch waited for the cops to arrive, Patrick marched out of the house with his hands raised, the pistol clutched in one of them, protecting Lex one last time. They took him to jail, where he confessed to the murder of Daniel Tate. When they asked him why he'd done it, he wouldn't say.

Nicholas went to see Agent Morales. He wanted to know why she was pretending the body they'd found on the floor of the foyer was his brother's when he was sure she knew it wasn't.

"What do you want me to say, kid?" Morales said. "His government issued passport identified him as Daniel Tate. His family—including you—told me he was Daniel Tate. Now you want to tell me he wasn't?"

"He wasn't," Nicholas said. "You know he wasn't."

Morales shrugged. "Prove it."

"Do a DNA test—"

"The body's already been cremated," Morales said, "at the request of your mother."

Nicholas went still, his every muscle wound tight. "This isn't right. You know it isn't. You just want to be able to close your case."

Morales leaned forward. "You want some advice, kid?"

"No."

"Well, you're going to get it," she said. "Move on with your life. Your brother *is* dead, and the person who killed him will spend the rest of his life in jail. All that's left for you to do is put up a nice headstone somewhere and let your parents and sister have some closure. What happened here . . . it could be a lot worse."

Nicholas remembered something I'd said once, about how Mia would be left with no one if the truth about what had happened to Danny all those years ago was exposed.

"Thanks for your help," he said, and left.

In her bedroom Lex stared at the baseball card. My picture, with my real name printed underneath, stared back up at her, smiling. Deliberately, moving slowly so that she wouldn't burn her shaking hand, she held the baseball card over a candle until it caught, curled, and blackened.

A few weeks later that headstone Agent Morales had suggested was up, and Nicholas and Ren jumped the fence at the cemetery to meet there late one night.

Daniel Arthur Tate, the headstone read. *Beloved Son, Brother, and Friend.*

It was not exactly what I had imagined, but it was home.

Nicholas and Ren sat in the grass beside my grave and took turns drinking from a flask.

"I think he was going to tell me, you know," Ren said. The day after my funeral, Nicholas decided he wasn't keeping secrets he didn't have to anymore. He brought Asher home to meet his family. He told them all about NYU. And when Ren cornered him one day at school and told him she wanted the truth, all of it, he gave it to her. "The last time I saw him, he promised he'd tell me everything."

"What would you have done?" Nicholas asked.

She sighed. "I don't know."

"Did you love him?"

She took a long sip of the alcohol and shook her head. "I didn't really know him." She sighed. "But maybe I could have loved the real person he was. Someday."

"I know what you mean," Nicholas said.

"When are you leaving?" she asked.

"Next week," he said. "Asher and I moved up our trip. I just . . . have to get out of here. I heard you're moving?"

She nodded. "Joining my parents in Dubai."

They sat in silence for a long time after that, passing the flask back and forth. I wished I could talk to them. Tell them I was sorry, tell them the truth, make it all right.

But you only get one life to do those things, and mine was done.

"I'd better go," Nicholas finally said, standing.

"Yeah, me too." Ren pressed her hands to the grass, and I recognized the unspoken good-bye in the gesture. "You know, I never even knew his real name."

Nicholas looked down at the headstone, where the name of his brother was engraved.

"Me neither," he said.

And then they left.

I've imagined a hundred lies I could tell you about what happened to me. Maybe Ren and I really did run off together. Maybe I was arrested right alongside Lex and Patrick and I'm composing this from my prison cell. Maybe I'm actually a grown Nicholas sitting at a laptop in my apartment in New York City, trying to use words to sort through that terrible period of my life.

But, strangely enough, I think the truth is the best version this time. My little burial plot isn't much, but it's a place to belong. A place where people I love, who love me, too, come to see me. Jessica visits often with Mia, who always has a handpicked bouquet for me and kisses my headstone before she leaves. Robert and Nicholas come whenever they're in town. And every once in a while Lex comes to stand at a distance, silent and pale faced. It's not a lot, but it's enough for me. I'm Daniel Tate, and, weirdly, I'm finally at peace.

Do you believe me?

ACKNOWLEDGMENTS

I'd like to thank my editor, Zareen Jaffery, Mekisha Telfer, Chloë Foglia, Justin Chanda, and everyone else at Simon & Schuster for their hard work and backing of this book.

Much appreciation also goes to those who read *Here Lies Daniel Tate* in its early stages and offered their suggestions and encouragement: the Moor women (Lynn, Annie, Ava and Amrita), Diana Fox, Shae McDaniel, and Eden Grey.

Lastly I'd like to thank my friends and family for their unceasing support and my readers for their patience and continued enthusiasm. Love you guys!